To my dearest
friend and
companion —
Dear Peggy

_____

with love,

[signature]

[heart drawing]

THE TETRALEMMA

A Buddhist Entertainment

by

Joel Ash

ISBN# 978-1-66783-901-1

eBook ISBN 978-1-66783-902-8

©

Copyright 2022

On the Cover: The mathematical logic formulation of the tetralemma, or the theorem of paraconsistency, may well denote the Buddhist concept of "emptiness" (*Sunyata* in Sanskrit).

Hapax Press – POB 1988 – Santa Fe, NM 87504

www.tetralemma.org

For Bettina, my dearest love

All the objects of the world

All the names and forms of experience

Are nothing but a complex manifestation of mind

Devoid of selfness and its belongings

Consciousness is the only reality

The trouble is you think you have time

——- Lankavatara Sutra

To begin at the beginning, when in the beginning were words,
and the words were made into thoughts.

PART ONE

Buddhism first entered the mind of a clever boy in a Chinese laundry in the Chicago suburb of Winnetka. Every other Saturday morning he was sent to pick up the family wash, pressed, folded, bundled in stiff paper and tied with a string. On a shelf at the laundry's entry a brightly colored porcelain statuette portrayed an extremely fat and bald Asian man reclining and laughing. Half-clad in a bare robe, his right hand was pointed at the sky, and his left was holding the neck of a large cloth sack. The porcelain figure personage was clearly very happy and seemed to be sharing a joke about something unknown to the viewer. The boy wondered, what on earth could it mean?

Observing the lad staring at the colorful figurine, Mrs. Huang, the proprietress spoke to him in accented English. "Touch big stomach, make wish. Buddha bring good luck". This was the very first time the boy had heard the sound "booduh." And as a result, on his errand every other Saturday, he touched the belly, made a wish, and couldn't help but remember the word. After some time, learning the correct spelling, the curious boy looked up "Buddha" in his family's encyclopedia and found it quite interesting. But the obscure quizzicality of the jolly laughter of the fat man's spirit stayed in his memory.

Causality, we are told, is an abstraction, a causal calculus, a subtle metaphysical notion, where a cause is in part responsible for its effect, and the effect

1

is partly dependent on the cause. It is said that the conditional probability of the intersection of events filters our understanding of outcomes by means of an intuition, which in Buddhism is called "interdependent co-arising" where everything is connected. Where everything arises in dependence upon myriad causes and conditions. Where nothing exists independently, and the relationship between one thing and another is simply a strange movement through a porous medium called time. In this way, the clever boy in the Chinese laundry was to find himself connected to the figure of an ancient mastermind named Siddhartha Gautama, and eventually to begin his own philosophical quest to understand the meaning of meaning. Is this not seriously funny?

And actually, Mrs. Huang didn't have it quite right. First of all, the Buddha doesn't laugh or grant wishes. The fat figure was only of a semi-historical vagabond from the 10th century known as "the hemp sack monk", who is considered the protector of children and of common people in the mortal world. In legend, celebrated as a Buddha of the future, he is always and everywhere considered the God of good luck.

A life story: Reuel Hersh Antenor, "Roo" to his friends, lived to be nearly one hundred years old and pensively recalled this odd seminal event until the end of his life. He was born in Winnetka, a Chicago suburb, and his parents were middle-aged and middle-class Italian Jews, who had arrived to the United States in the mid 1930s, on fleeing the fascism of Benito Mussolini's blackshirts. Reuel's mother, was born Eliana del Vecchio, a name suggesting it was "of the ancient ones". Some students of ancestral surnames supposed the reference was to Jews who resided in Italy before Sephardic exiles arrived from Iberia in the 15th century. Eliana corrected them. It was a point of pride. The del Vecchios, she insisted, were actually descended from Jews living in Rome before Titus Vespasian brought 100,000 Judean captives there in 71 Anno Domini as the Christians had it, or in the year 3831 by the Hebraic calendar. Reuel's father, David Antenor, rather more like his less renown ancestors, was born simply in the Ghetto di Roma. Ambitious to earn a living, modern and politically liberal, he held an engineering degree from the University of Padua and had a promising technical career in sight until the arrival of national fascism.

At their first opportunity Reuel's parents acquired American citizenship. While speaking Italian between themselves, they were fluent in both accented English and French. Reuel's father had gained professional employment at the well-regarded diesel mechanical-engineering department of the International Harvester Company, headquartered in Chicago. And though Reuel's piano-playing mother was described as a "homemaker", she provided translation services on numerous occasions for the library of Northwestern University in adjacent Evanston. As a new immigrant family, they had no relations in America, and Reuel, their only child, was a late arrival to their new lives.

It is a commonplace that a person's character begins to emerge and crystalize in their pre-adolescent years. Reuel's case involved at least three notable influences: chess, science-fiction, and a first taste of metaphysics. The rules of the ancient board game were learned from his father, and within a year Reuel routinely defeated him. A gifted young player, he was welcomed to a chess club at the local YMCA on weekends, and before long was coached by a university professor of mathematics who took a liking to him. Nevertheless, though talented, Reuel was not particularly competitive. What interested him mostly were the abstract formal structural relationships between pieces and positions and before long his diminishing interest in aggressive match-play gave way to the laborious idea of inventing three-dimensional chess games. His coach, a Professor Hertz, encouraged him and went along with this detour. In short order Reuel realized that the main intellectual challenge was to invent new rules, and even pieces, which could apply to different levels and to boards of different sizes. Ultimately, he abandoned the whole idea of competitive chess but grew continuously fascinated by Hertz's cheerful introduction to an attractive branch of chess-related mathematics dealing with combinations of objects belonging to a finite set, in accordance with various constraints, as in the theory of graphing. And it was Professor Hertz who, in a boastful moment, introduced Reuel to the mathematical idea that vibrations had periodic frequencies called 'hertz' as discovered by his great-uncle Heinrich. When Reuel told his mother that middle-C on her piano was a sound wave vibrating at 256 times per second she touched him on his forehead and said he would be a mathematician. Reuel's father, hearing of this anecdote at dinner, used it to introduce Reuel to quantitative exponents, by showing him the power of 2. To his immense surprise Reuel instantly grasped the phenomenon of octaves, which was why middle-C was a power of two on the piano. So began Reuel's wedge into mathematics.

And at about the same time, fantastic technological story-telling provided Reuel with a different kind of imaginative pleasure which began when he encountered a pulp magazine called Astounding Science Fiction. Scattered between tales of genuine literary quality down to dime-store prose were ingenious futuristic concepts such as time-travel, paranormal beings, extra-planetary environments, star-ships, the subterranean earth, advanced weaponries, teleportation, extraterrestrial aliens, parallel universes, mind-control, and hyper-galactic journeys. And holding at the gravitational center of Reuel's narrative interest were the stories of intelligent humanoid robots, lacking instincts or understanding. Mere automata which had escaped control, capable of outwitting their masters, and without feelings or ethics, beating them at chess.

As for an interest in metaphysics, it came about in the following way. Reuel had a very close friend from his earliest childhood. It was a boy named Luca Baca, whose family lived in the house next to his own. The two families, Jewish and Catholic, became friendly and somewhat playful, and Luca's father, a Professor of Romance Languages at Northwestern University, frequently engaged the boys in Italian. One Sunday afternoon while watching them playing a finger game called 'rock, paper, scissors' he asked them a question.

"*Ragazzi, siete liberi di fare delle scelte o è già tutto deciso nel vostro cervello prima che ve ne accorgiate?*" [Guys, are you free to make choices or is everything already decided in your brain before you know it?]

"*Certo, che faccio delle scelte*" said Luca. [Of course I make choices]

"*Ci devo pensare prima*" added Reuel. [I have to think about it first]

"*Bravo, chiedi a tuo padre*" [Bravo, ask your father]

Reuel asked his father. "Papa, Luca's dad asked me like if my choice of a chess move was already fixed in my brain before I knew I would make it. What do you think?"

"I think that is what is *una distinzione senza differenza*, a distinction without a difference. He is mostly playing with words, mixing categories. If he's so smart, next time you see him ask him to tell you the difference between a discovery and an invention. Words are not like mathematics. The meanings are not specific. *Capisce?*"

This fresh insight gave Reuel a strange kind of pleasure and began a life-long curiosity about how the vocalized sounds called 'words' were understood. It had something to do with the brain. A sound would come in through the ear, but the brain would hear it. How could the brain hear? This question remained in the back of his mind for many years. However, starting with an initial base of 'pig-latin' that summer, he and Luca improvised new word formations in a conversational vocabulary incomprehensible to their parents, or anyone else. This adolescent practice had its benefit in the future as Reuel mastered German and Luca perfected Roman Latin.

There was one additional activity of those early years which also had life-long consequences for Reuel. He and Luca had a childhood friend, later lost to memory, who was a mischievous boy named Mikey Thalweg. He lived a block away on the top floor of a six-story apartment building. The boys were freely welcome to the Thalweg apartment and admired Mikey for his boldness, his capacity for tricks and jokes, and especially because his father owned a small sailboat on Lake Michigan. Mr. Thalweg had been a naval officer in the Atlantic during the First World War with duties as a navigator. He showed the boys the use of short-wave radios, and at times he took the them up to the roof from where Lake Michigan could be seen, and showed them how to use a sextant. When extracted from its fitted leather case they learned to measure the angle between an astronomical object and the horizon to rehearse the technique of celestial navigation. Using a dark filter, they "shot" the sun at noon, and used the star Polaris at dusk. And Reuel grew keen on technology and science, which affected so much of his life.

Mr. Thalweg's 16-foot sloop was berthed at the Wilmette harbor, a short bicycle ride from where they lived. It was called *Ishmael*, and occasionally on warm weekends when the weather was good Mr. Thalweg took them sailing on the lake. After four years of this, one summer when they were to enter the seventh grade, they were allowed to sail out on the water by themselves. In the following year, they were permitted to go out beyond sight of land and several times crossed Eastward to the sight of the Michigan shore. It was the boldest and most physically exciting thing Reuel had ever done and was likely a foundation reason for becoming a yachtsman in his adult years.

Like many young boys, he played with toys, mechanical and electrical, from gyroscopes to magnets. As he grew older, he developed a habit of perusing through his father's engineering journals, in reading issues of Popular Science magazine, and the near endless depth of the family's second-hand copy of the Encyclopedia Britannica. It was obvious he had the makings of an autodidact. From his earliest days, the great speed with which Reuel completed his school homework merely convinced his parents that the boy was clever. But the swiftness with which he absorbed his father's tutorials on physical forces and illustrative problem-sets deepened their view. Perhaps the boy was not quite a prodigy, but without doubt they could see he was unusually gifted as well as intellectually ambitious. His precocity in mathematics at grammar school led to an inquiry by educational authorities. Would Reuel's parents permit him to attend New Trier High School, starting in the 8th grade, even though he would be several years younger than his classmates? Flattered, they agreed without hesitation. And Reuel's only regret was separating from his friend Luca, who was to go on to Cardinal Hayes High School for boys. Still, they would manage a life-long friendship.

Six years of his growing up took place during the great conflict of the Second World War. Reuel's consciousness of that period was shaped largely by Hollywood films, scrap metal drives, the existence of ration coupons, and the inescapable evenings of serious listening to radio news of the war by his parents. After D-day, and the overthrow of Mussolini and Hitler were duly celebrated, the following year was occasioned by the extraordinary event of an atomic bomb dropped on Japan. As a result of his strong curiosity about this world-shaking scientific event, Reuel began receiving additional short evening doses of techno-scientific tutelage on physics from his engineer father. Much of it was to illustrate that the fundamental mechanical forces of the cosmos could be logically understood by mathematics, which was in fact the very language of nature. *"La linguaggio della natura"*. And far from being narratives of high abstraction, his father's stories were enlivened by the lives of great Italian scientists. From da Vinci to Fibonacci to Galileo to Avogadro to Schiaparelli to Volta and Marconi and finally to nuclear physics and to their old friend Enrico Fermi and his family. That great scientist and Nobel Laureate had recently returned to his professorship at the University of Chicago after having worked on the Manhattan Project at Los Alamos, New Mexico.

Reuel was deeply impressed by the awe and respect displayed by his father toward Fermi, "Enrico", on those occasions when they attended social gatherings at his family household on Woodlawn Avenue, virtually on the university campus. Though they were of roughly the same age, Reuel's father had only received an unpretentious mechanical engineering degree from Padua at the same time that Fermi had been awarded a full professorship in the physics department at the University of Rome, "La Sapienza". It was through their wives that the two families were ultimately connected in Chicago.

They were two Jewish girls, Eliana, Reuel's mother, and Laura Capon, who had been her classmate and close friend at the Roman university. They shared a social life, appeared at synagogue together, and had attended one another's weddings in Rome in the same year, one rabbinical, and the other civil, as Enrico was born a Catholic. Their escape from the dark tide of anti-Semitic pre-war fascism was the reason that both families fled to safety in America. Then, the post-war peace brought the two Chicago based families into frequent contact, since the Fermis hosted frequent social events involving faculty members. Reuel was always happy to be invited along with his parents as he enjoyed seeing the

Fermi's son Giulio each time, who was of his same age. On several occasions they went together on their own to the nearby Museum of Science and Industry on Lake Shore Drive.

When Reuel arrived at New Trier High School he was immediately immersed in a student population of boys who were transitioning into sexual maturity, with their facial and genital hair, their cracked voices and coarse humor. Reuel was ignored at first as a freakish pre-pubescent child, but as he was gawky tall with an outgoing self-confidence and cheerful boldness, it led to his total acceptance. Within a month of his arrival, he was mirthfully elected assistant manager of the basketball team and could be found at lunch time in the cafeteria helping friends on math problems which added to his uncompetitive popularity. Algebraic notation and his approach to the calculus were facile undertakings. Verbally bold, at times he appeared smarter than a teacher.

There was an entirely different social dynamic when it came to his girl classmates at New Trier. As is well-known, adolescent girls of the same age as boys, were substantially more advanced when it came physiological and mental maturity. Reuel, not in the least shy, became a kind of friendly puppy for a cohort of young ladies a couple of years older. In the many ages of life which followed, this novice heterosexual social experience stood him in good stead, as he never felt nervous or awkward or tongue-tied when meeting a new girl. And indeed, he would truly feel indebted to more than a few women in future years, who would usefully educate him on a universe of matters and manners having nothing to do with mathematics.

Then, once in the autumn of the following academic year, Reuel accompanied his father to a Medallion lecture at the University of Chicago by Fermi on 'The Atomic Age'. It was scheduled for delivery at the auditorium of Mandel Hall, to be followed by a reception at Fermi's house. Reuel's mother was already there with Laura Fermi and he looked forward to seeing his friend Giulio again. Before the talk began, he and his father waited for the speaker's arrival as they sat near the middle of row F in the auditorium. Sitting at Reuel's right was a lanky young man with a shaggy haircut and a wispy moustache. His name was

Daniel Melinsky and he was a graduate student completing a Ph.D in the mathematics department of the university.

Melinsky turned to his young seatmate and asked in a friendly and inviting way "Are you interested in physics?"

"As opposed to pure math?"

"Ah, ha! You understand the difference?"

"Of course."

"Tell me what you're interested in. Girls?"

"No. They're nice, but I'm interested in numbers."

"Like what?"

"Like what is a number?"

"Oooh."

"Do you know what a number is?"

"Ouch. Why don't you tell me?"

"It's a piece of information."

"Who are you, anyway?"

"I'm Reuel. Who are you?

"I'm Daniel. Pleased to meet you. What are you studying right now?"

"It's related to musical sound vibrations called time series. Periodic functions."

"Do know Fourier transforms?"

"Not yet, I....."

The audience broke into loud applause as Chancellor Hutchins and Professor Fermi entered beneath the proscenium and the audience's attention rapidly became fixed attentively upon the stage.

Fermi's speech was geared to the non-scientist. Largely anecdotal, and filled with references to Einstein, Szilard, Oppenheimer, Teller, Bethe, Lawrence, Feynman, Ulam, and others. And incidentally, policy issues like peaceful uses of nuclear energy, hazards and uses of radiation, implications for ending military conflicts, and so forth. Fermi ended on the importance of optimism. Afterwards, some thirty-odd guests, mostly university faculty, were invited in walking distance to the Fermi household for wine-tasting and home-baked panettone.

"*Bel ragazzo*" said Laura Fermi to Reuel's mother of Reuel.

"*E cresciuto*" said Enrico, gesturing upwards with his chin.

Courtesies accomplished, Giulio and Reuel adjourned to the back porch and sat on the steps with glasses of orange flavored San Pellegrino water. They were comparing their schools.

"Why do they call it the Lab school?" asked Reuel.

"There was this guy at the university called John Dewey. He wanted to test his ideas about education, so they called it the Laboratory School."

"Lot of science?"

"Yeah. And half the students have a parent on the university faculty."

"You doing physics?"

"Never."

"How come?"

"Father says to do something else. I'd always be overshadowed by his Nobel prize. Mom says I should go into medicine. What about you?"

"I'm sticking with math so far. But I don't know. I'd like to do something applied. My dad says electrical engineering is going to be big."

"Biology's going to be bigger. I've started working on blood."

"Blood? Yuk!"

"Yeah, I got a microscope. I'm studying red blood cells."

"How do you study blood cells?"

"You got to learn chemistry. Biological chemistry. I'm concentrating on Oxygen. No oxygen and you die. No mathematics without oxygen. It's the food of the brain."

"Can it make you smarter?"

"Mmmm, that's an interesting question."

"How do you measure something like that?"

"I don't know. You ought to come to our science club meetings on Saturdays. We always get profs from the college. Lots of math stuff."

Later, inside, while they were eating panettone with glasses of milk, Daniel Melinsky came over to join them. It turned out he was a regular at the science club of the Lab School and seconded Giulio's invitation to Reuel. In fact, he would be at the club in two weeks to talk about a new book called "Cybernetics". It had just arrived in the bookstores.

In the following month Reuel found that he was welcome to take a train south to sit in on informal tea-time colloquia at Chicago's math department in Schermerhorn Hall where he managed to shake hands with a few academics.

Emboldened by his new circles of acquaintance, and without any fear or the permission of others, Reuel impulsively decided to use the family typewriter and mail a letter to the author of a book he had just finished.

Dear Professor Wiener,

I am a sophomore at New Trier High School in Winnetka, Illinois, just North of Chicago. I am interested in the relation of mathematics to biology, especially in the relation of information to the brain, and in combinatorics. Also electrical mechanics. I know your view that information is something other than either matter or energy, which is really very interesting. I've learned of your work on time series and I have just read your book "Cybernetics". I also know that Harvard University awarded you a Ph.D when you were 19 years old. The reason I am writing to you is to inquire if Harvard University or MIT might admit me before I graduate from high school.

I know Daniel Melinsky of the mathematics department at the University of Chicago. He introduced me to other members of the faculty and I was given the opportunity to come down from Winnetka to the South side of Chicago a few times in order to audit some of their talks. Professors Carnap, Rashevsky, and Rapoport all know me slightly and made me bold enough to write to you. They could provide references. I also know Professor Fermi through my family.

I've learned a little bit about the work of Warren McCulloch and Walter Pitts if
that helps.
Yours truly,
Reuel Hersh Antenor

Norbert Wiener replied.

Dear Reuel,
Thank you for writing to me. I am acquainted with the mathematics faculty at
Chicago. Why not apply there? However, if you wish to leave the Midwest your
friend Daniel Melinksy might agree with me that young Reuel Hersh Antenor
could do better seeking admission to Columbia University in New York rather
than the genteel restricted quota environment in Cambridge. You might write
to Professor Moses Cohen at my reference.
Best wishes to you, young scholar,
Norbert Wiener
Cambridge, Massachusetts.

And so, having a slightly charmed life, Reuel applied to Columbia
University and was admitted to matriculate in his mid-adolescence. Utterly surprised, his parents were extremely proud, and happily paid the tuition, room
and board, and stipends for his allowance. Somewhat sadly, from that event
onward they gradually lost physical and emotional contact with their only
child. Accepting this as a doleful but not uncommon bitter fact of life, they
saw him off from Union Station in Chicago. They kept a long-lasting memory
of a boy, soon to be six feet tall and bearing an unconventionally handsome
face while betraying a fleeting trace of masculine ugliness which yet, strangely,
became attractive to certain women.

Reuel's three condensed university years in New York City leading to his
undergraduate degree were divided in two spheres. On the one side, there was
an academic life, with cerebral studies in his major concentrations, philosophy

and mathematics, plus a year of German. On the other, a free-spirited and nonconforming student lifestyle, which in those days of the late 1940s was described as "bohemian", a fanciful tribe, perforce more impressed by philosophy than mathematics.

The key to the transformation, or deformation of Reuel's personality, lay in his discovery of the existence of a part of the city known as "Greenwich Village", which was filled with artists, writers, musicians and poets, as well as alcohol and marijuana. It was easily accessed from the university merely by riding the subway downtown, from 116th Street to Sheridan Square, for merely twenty minutes. His few early days of street wandering there located two magnetic foci. The first, a tavern called the San Remo Bar & Grill, the second, a large shop called Sammler's Bookstore. Both lay within walking distance of the subway station, and Reuel, encountering habitués and making friends easily, was to be found at one or both of these places which he haunted on many weekends during his first college year.

Uptown at Columbia he developed a reputation as a brilliant oddball philosophy and math major. Unlike typical students in those days, mostly male, in jackets and neckties, Reuel allowed his hair to grow long and unkempt, shaved and bathed infrequently, was usually in a black turtleneck sweater, and began smoking cigarettes. Toward the end of his freshman year, he was considered a "character" who somehow qualified for graduate courses, and was affectionately indulged by his faculty. This began his major academic and intellectual interest for much of his life concerning the very idea of knowledge, of knowing. Epistemology. He had a passage from Plato tacked above his desk:

> Socrates: Let us begin again and ask, in the first place, whether it is or is not possible for a person to know that he knows what he knows and that he does not know what he does not know, and in the second place whether, if perfectly possible, such knowledge is of any use.

ॐ

Following the end of his freshman term, Reuel enrolled in a summer philosophy course entitled "Existentialism 101". Therein, Barbara Wulf, a young instructor on the faculty, mischievously deconstructed the intellectual value of the word 'meaning' to her callow undergraduates. Reuel had never actually thought about the question of 'meaning' before this, and so the diabolically seductive idea floated about concerning life's meaningless absurdity caught him unarmed. The idea was that there was no meaning in the world beyond what meaning we give it, which could only result in a blind search for meaning in a meaningless universe. There was no such thing, for example, as a good person or a bad person, only just that whatever happens merely happens. Nothing meant anything. Nothingness. What a disturbing absurd truth!

According to their instructor, Ms. Wulf, the task of existentialist philosophy was to alleviate the confusion or anxiety of an individual's experience of thinking, feeling, and acting in the face of such an apparently meaningless or absurd world. That task constituted the path whereby one could acquire freedom.

And this, she pointed out, involved understanding the famous claim of Monsieur Jean-Paul Sartre that what all existentialists had in common was the fundamental doctrine that "existence precedes essence". This reversed an old philosophical view that the essence, or the nature of a thing, was more fundamental than its existence, or the mere fact of its being. However, existentialists, she explained, claimed the opposite, that existence precedes essence. And therefore, that there was no such predetermined essence to be found in human beings. An individual's essence was only defined and created by the individual through how that individual lived her or his life. In this way, she declared, the Existentialists committed philosophy to a radical conception of freedom.

As he had never thought of it before, the idea of a universe without either values or meaning was new to Reuel. Indeed, his full freshman year of an academic introduction to philosophy, from Plato to Kant, was dedicated to comprehending the metaphysical idea of the 'good'. To have this taken away from his higher thoughts was slightly unsettling. Perhaps the universe was empty of meaning, but was life also that way? Was his whole life merely a chunk of existence without any real essence to date? Who was he actually? His self was simply the undefined object of his own reflective consciousness and was necessarily subjective. But was he free? He certainly felt free, but perhaps it was an illusion? Not to worry. At length, he found these ideas interesting, but more amusing than disturbing, received a grade of B+, and learned a telling French expression, *"cherchez la femme"*.

During that first summer in the city, with his sojourns downtown, he became a familiar regular at his favorite hangouts, Sammler's bookstore and the one or two taverns where he made new acquaintances and learned to drink beer. Also, to Reuel's delight, he received a letter from his boyhood chum, Luca Baca, that he had been accepted at Fordham University, up in the Bronx, and mentioning, incidentally, that he was intending to become a candidate for the priesthood.

During the ensuing year in New York two important experiences had a profound effect on the rest of his life. The first of these involved his relation with a girl named Astrid Galen. The second concerned his introduction to Buddhist thoughts.

Astrid was an artist who lived and worked on abstract oil paintings from a small loft on East Bleecker Street. Several years older than he, Reuel met her one night at the San Remo tavern at a table shared by some friends called "writers". The two shared a surfeit of eye-contact. Before very long they went to the movies, once to a jazz club, and then, something familiar to Astrid, they became lovers, as she delivered the loss of virginity to her new friend. However, somewhat more than a month later Astrid informed Reuel, as well as several of their promiscuous writer friends, that she was pregnant. No one could be sure who was responsible for the paternity. Astrid was determined to obtain an abortion, which was in those days frightening, dangerous, and difficult to procure, as well as being illegal.

The males, mere boys in fact, had no idea what to do. One lad said he was certain it wasn't him. Another made himself scarce. A third said he would ask around. Reuel inquired if he could help to contribute financial assistance.

However, on her own, Astrid had located someone who could furnish this terrifying procedure if she went to a certain small town in Eastern Pennsylvania.

No one learned exactly what happened. Astrid had gone to Pennsylvania and there was an ominous quiet about her ensuing lack of presence. Some weeks later an older sister of Astrid came to collect her belongings from the loft, found an address book, and called one of the writers asking him to inform Astrid's friends. While the abortion had succeeded, the procedure caused Astrid to suffer a low-grade hemorrhage accompanied by a virulent and deadly staphylococcus infection. In panic, she rushed to her family home upstate to Schenectady where she died abruptly and unexpectedly from septic shock due to a violent and fatal fever before she could be hospitalized. This was young Reuel Antenor's first painful confrontation with death, no longer merely an abstraction. He could not help but wonder if it was not his own spermatozoon which had caused the tragedy.

It was just about that time that Reuel had encountered a philosophical point-of-view which improved his understanding of life and death. It was at Sammler's Bookstore, where he was a familiar browser but a penny-pinching buyer of new and used books. In fact, bookstore browsing became a persistent feature of his life. An avowed and philosophical atheist, like his parents, he was engaged in examining the non-fiction stacks at Sammler's, with his head tilted to the right to improve the reading of titles. A book on Charles Darwin caught his eye as did a new book by a French anthropologist. And nearby was a large series called *"Sacred Books of the East"*, exposing him to unearthly and untranslatable Sanskrit words that fascinated him, like *"dharma"* which he found philosophically deep and mysterious, and in a vocabulary which he would study for many hours. One day, for a moment, his gaze strayed over to an adjacent stack of shelves where a title called *"Buddhism & Death"* published in English by the hitherto unknown Pali Text Society caught his eye.

Reuel was still an adolescent who, but for Astrid Galen, rarely ever thought of death and who still lacked any familiarity with Asian Buddhism. Back in Winnetka he had once skimmed the entries in the family encyclopedia, and had only studied European philosophy to date. Death? So, he pulled the book and continued to sit on the bench to have a browse. A convinced atheist, he stood against religions, conceding he really only knew of the deistic Abrahamic ones. As a result, he spent nearly an hour page-turning which then convinced him to buy the title. He apprised that Buddhism was not a religion like the ones he knew. It seemed more like an appealing philosophical and psychological doctrine.

He studied it continuously that night in his dormitory room. So different from Western philosophy it was not remotely theological. There wasn't a single word about God. However, there was one intellectually enticing Sanskrit word, *"tathata"*, for a type of experience which was being translated as "thusness" or "suchness". *Tathata*, he said it aloud a number of times, as it became one of his first magnetic words of Sanskrit. What could it possibly mean?

While it took hours of close reading to convince himself that Buddhist philosophy was relatively simple and accurate, he thought one or two points about the "self" required further consideration. Otherwise, the doctrinal narrative merely consisted of mastering four evident truths, an octagonal path of practice, and three alleged marks of existence.

Young Reuel considered the package of ideas and tried to rephrase them in his own words. As for the so-called four truths, the first was the omnipresence of human unhappiness; the second, that the cause of that unhappiness was unsatisfied desire; third, that the way to end the unhappiness was to get rid of the desire; and fourth, that the way to get rid of unrequited desires lay in eight practices.

They consisted in (1) meritorious views, (2) meritorious intentions, (3) meritorious speech, (4) meritorious conduct, (5) meritorious livelihood, (6) meritorious efforts, (7) meritorious thoughts, (8) and meritorious mental concentration.

It was said that fulfillment of these practices depended on recognizing three marks of existence: (a) impermanence, (b) unhappiness, and (c) non-selfhood.

Almost all of it seemed understandable to an average person. However, though it seemed reasonable and wise, even virtuous, he had to give some attention to the idea of "non-self", or "no soul". Those being the English translations of the Buddhist linguistic terms *"anatta"* in Pali or *"anatman"* in Sanskrit. This disquieting concept seemed strangely familiar. Like something he had recently studied under Barbara Wulf.

He recalled his earlier readings from the 18th century Scottish philosopher David Hume, in his "Treatise on Human Nature", written when the man was merely in his twenties. Like the existentialists and Buddhists, Hume submitted that the "self" was nothing more than a transitory and causally-connected bundle of sensations and perceptions. That our feeling of self-hood resulted from our habit of attributing unified existence which we call the "self" to a momentary collection of associated parts. And while this self-hood did appear to be natural there was no logical support for it. Only custom and irrational mental habit which became its essence. We couldn't actually perceive how one event caused another, but only experienced Hume's "constant conjunction" of a chain of causality. Was David Hume then a Buddhist?

One of those days he decided to phone Luca Baca, who was now studying theology at Fordham, a Jesuit university.

"Luke, do I have a soul?"

"Of course, you do."

"No. I don't."

"You poor fellow."

"I think we should meet."

They agreed on the Bronx Zoo, within walking distance of Fordham, on the following weekend to meet at the great ape's exhibit.

"So, we can see our ancestors" said a grinning Reuel on his arrival.

Luca smiled to his old chess opponent: "Only our cousins Roo, if you please, merely our collaterals, definitely not ancestors. Our lineage is unique and angelic, created by God and blessed with a Savior."

"Soteriological bunkum" went Reuel's riposte.

They went on in this vein a bit and ran out of material as they strolled. Finally choosing a bench facing the wolves and foxes pen, they sat with bags of salted peanuts, catching up on life.

Luca related that he was practicing with foils and had joined the fencing team as he wasn't big enough for body contact sports; that Mikey Thalweg had joined the Navy; that Fordham had a decent chess club; that he was studying Latin and would be going to Mexico over the summer to brush up on his Spanish; and that he wasn't planning a return to Winnetka in the foreseeable future. As for having a soul, nothing could be clearer. He had a soul and it was immortal. And what about you?

Reuel delivered. He missed sailing, gave up time-stealing chess, tried writing poetry, was getting more interested in information coding than pure math, especially how language coded information in the brain, had had a girlfriend who had died of a fever, had a cigarette habit, and was getting interested in Buddhist philosophy. And decided that he had a body, and a brain within it, but didn't have a soul. And even if he did have a soul it would die with him since souls were impermanent like everything else.

They went back and forth on this question of self and soul for a while, using conventional supporting arguments. Reuel always enjoyed philosophizing. Yet the exercise of thinking sharpened and deepened their minds as well as the language they used. It took nearly an hour until they grew exhausted, and yet strengthened themselves for distant encounters. Both sensed they would be revisiting the subject again in the future, with greater clarity and vigor. They agreed to stay in touch.

ॐ

The psychological process leading an undergraduate student to choose his academic concentration, his major, is reasonably unforeseeable, but nevertheless in other circumstances reveals an unmistakable logic. For Reuel, growing hungry for big answers to big questions, it was a predictable evolutionary course leading from the narrower problem sets of mathematics towards the gigantic set pieces of philosophy. And so, in the middle of his sophomore year he had changed the bulk of his major from mathematics and began returning again to the querying wit of Socrates, the idealism of Plato, and the formalisms of Aristotle.

Yet two items he first encountered through the Pali Text Society stayed persistently in his mind. Impermanence and the omnipresence of unhappiness. Though Reuel was conscious that he had led a relatively pleasant and privileged life, in his imagination he could easily see the main point. Whether in cancer, depression, heartbreak and mortal grief, or even down to minor irritations of his own, such as boredom, a headache, and girls who rejected him, unsatisfactoriness was everywhere. Simply everywhere. No one was exempt.

In the middle of that year of Professor Schmidlapp's intensive course for philosophy majors, after having plunged into readings on the metaphysics of Immanuel Kant, and by pointed reference in the manic persuasions of Friedrich Nietzsche, he was led to the writings of Arthur Schopenhauer. And to his surprise here he found a Western philosopher who first and foremost was interested in the central problem of human suffering, exactly like the Buddha. There was his ghost once again. The most remarkable thing of all was that Schopenhauer even called himself a "buddhaist".

The obvious fact that translations of the religious and philosophical literature of Asia only began to appear in Europe at the outset of the 19th century had never occurred to Reuel. The fact that Schopenhauer had a 45-year love affair with Buddhist thought momentarily revived his own embryonic interest. According to Schopenhauer the fact that Buddhism's radical message of atheism could be received and adapted to Western culture seemed a piece of intellectual boldness. The simple fact that an endlessly blind foundational "will to live" was found in all creatures was as obvious as the shape of his hand. Consequently, the fact that suffering, sickness, old-age, and death was a universal experience of life was undeniable. The fact that compassion could be the basis of ethics was easily compatible with his own mental view. Still, the fact that anguish was educational and that beauty was a promise of happiness guided and inspired him to go further. It dawned upon him that the origin of human philosophy itself was the awareness of a gap, an uncertainty, in our knowledge of the world. The fact that everything was illusion and empty actually simplified his explanation for the experience of intellectual fulfillment.

Reuel entitled his typed 12-page mid-year term paper "Schopenhauer, the Buddhist Philosopher". Professor Schmidlapp, who never once in thirty years of teaching had ever given an A level grade, awarded the essay a B+, his highest accolade, and used the margins and end-space for handwritten comments in green ink.

> "But there is considerable happiness and pleasure in life, even if it is an illusion. Why not discuss this?"
>
> "Isn't Schop's pessimistic weltschmerz merely the bourgeois affectation of a pampered soul? You have too much admiration and too little critical perspective."
>
> "Compare the opening words of Schop's magnum opus: 'The world is representation.' - What modern philosopher begins great analytic writing with almost exactly the same phrase?"
>
> "Isn't Schop. merely playing a verbose language game, gliding and linking from thought to thought instead of giving us arguments that are clearly expressed? Of course, a great writer's texts are written in such a way that they persuade, regardless of the quality of the arguments. Schop. tells us of his views but where is there sign of any rigorous logic? The world is not a fiction, is it?"

By the end of that academic year Reuel went past flirting with Buddhist pessimism and finished the course by studying the logical theory of linguistic sign-action, "semiotics", by the American philosopher Charles Peirce. Thus reviving his interest in language, and indirectly preparing him for the logic of neuroscience. The historical vectors of philosophy had by then reached the 20th century. And thereafter, in the last days of the course, led to Reuel's clarifying reading of the *Tractatus Logico-Philosophicus* by the deeply unhappy and long-suffering Austrian philosopher at Cambridge University, Ludwig

Wittgenstein. There lay the similar opening words of this other philosopher's analytic masterpiece, to whom Professor Schmidlapp's note had referred. "The world is everything that is the case."

And here, predictably, the labile psychological process leading to Reuel's choice of an academic concentration, changed once again. Having arrived at a conclusion that there was nothing ennobling in the philosophical study of suffering, he thought it more worthwhile to investigate the achievement of pleasure in happiness, in eudaemonia. As in, for a good instance, the sexual act, which itself seemed an oblique counter-reference to Schopenhauer's 'will to live.'

Thanks to Professor Schmidlapp's guidance Reuel's hunger for bigger answers to bigger questions led him back to accept the importance of science, the undoubted child of philosophy. And there, specifically, to his curiosity about how language was processed within an organ of soft nervous tissue contained in the skull of vertebrates. Giulio Fermi was right, biology was where it's at, and where it's going. Therefore, it became the reason he ended up considering medical school. And the following year led him to absorb the unique symbolic language of organic chemistry and to an exploratory framing of the concept of neurolinguistics in the complex body organ called the brain. Enticed by the idea that thoughts consisted of unspoken English words which were merely imaginary sounds in his head, he plunged on to a potential research vocation.

That summer between his second and third years at Columbia University, was transformative. He was no longer a cub and had moved out of the college dormitory by finding himself a pleasant furnished room on West 4th Street in Greenwich Village. Only a twenty-minute subway ride up to the university. Plus, a coming- of-age summer-job with the Funk & Wagnall's company. They were publishers of the immense unabridged American Dictionary of the English Language, which was called the "library edition". Several years earlier the publishers had decided to publish an abridged "college edition" and hired undergraduate students to assist in editorial work. Progress from prior years had preceded that summer so far as the letter P.

The task of a summer copy-editor and apprentice lexicographer was two-fold. First to make a red checkmark for each entry proposed for deletion to a senior committee, and second, to take an entry from the unabridged version and prune its length while maintaining its utility for a college student. The plan was to reach the letter S by the end of the summer. Reuel loved the work and put in extra unpaid hours. Best of all was his working exposure dealing with word etymologies. Particularly from the Indo-European branch which had created Sanskrit. By mid-summer he was near expert on guessing an English word's origins. A bonus skill was the speed with which he could do challenging cross-word puzzles.

There were several other educational features to his employment. To begin with, two senior editors, elderly scholarly homosexual New Englanders, introduced him to English literature. From essays, to plays, to novels, to poems. From Chaucer to Shakespeare to Coleridge to T.S. Eliot. They had no interest in him as a "toy boy" but lavished serious attention to any curiosity he displayed about language. He was treated as a young scholar and with affectionate respect which was reciprocated. It was Reuel's first sustained experience in being regarded as a near equal in the company of adults.

The second educational benefit of his adolescent summer employment was his introduction to mainframe office computing. Funk & Wagnall's was transitioning from "punch card" information storage to large spools of magnetic tape. The main challenge in those months was to permit the integration of commercial business accounting and the management of editorial content on the same piece of office equipment. A sales engineer from the IBM Corporation, named Lars Soderberg, worked in their midst all summer and he became Reuel's tutor and mentor on the subject of computing platforms, system architecture, process control and programming assembler languages. It was an intellectual feast and would have long standing consequences. To his regret, his friendship with Lars was severed after Labor Day when the man was promoted and moved overseas to spearhead IBM's expansion in Sweden.

Aside from being Reuel's first paid employment, several other life-forming events took place in the summer months of that year. Their most significant social venues were universally referred to as "parties". Though previously confined to the bar & grill scene, Reuel's network of acquaintances was now yielding invitations to a different class of companionable events taking place in a variety of residential apartments and brownstone houses. It created an ambitious young man's social perception of sophisticated lives in Manhattan.

Reuel discovered he was an easy conversationalist, witty, and intelligent. Moreover, he had cleaned up his physical appearance and paid attention to his clothes. He learned to be seductive and to modulate his baritone voice and to use his eyes expressively. His social network thus expanded. Still younger than most he found himself quite comfortable among male and female fledgling copy-writers from advertising agencies, unworldly musicians and songsters, green lawyers, youthful book editors, young jazz saxophonists, untrained film editors, fashion models, experimental painters, unseasoned journalists, immature real-estate brokers, juvenile investment bankers, inexpert assistant-vice-presidents, callow photographers, backgammon gamers, amateur novelists, unskilled poker players, ill-equipped playboys and rich girls, unqualified art-critics, and similar varieties of puerile smooth-talkers.

He had developed a signature taste of what it was like to 'shock the bourgeoisie'. Whenever asked about his religion, not unusual in those days, he would coyly say he was a 'Buddhist' and use his interlocuter's response as a sort of filter to judge their personality. Curiously, this particular back-and- forth paid dividends with members of the opposite sex. Indeed, several productive sexual flirtations from that source led him to bedrooms on more than a few occasions. He profited in these gratifying adventures from his attractive face and his reassuring athletic anatomy, as well as his philosophical and intellectual self-confidence among so many non-academics. To the changeable fortunes of many young people in America in those days, a "sexual revolution" was also underway. It had several interesting components.

First there was the literary expression in several popular books that female sexual pleasure was not only a commonplace, but that it was to be sought and valued. Next was the transformation in women's costume, particularly in undergarments. Gone was the presence of stockings, and the associated use of garter belts. This, of course, favored and accelerated acts of intimacy. And then, of the greatest significance, was the technological evolution to the word "contraception". This recognized the recent invention and availability of a birth-control steroid hormone known as the "pill", which eliminated the clumsy practice of unrolling a condom or of inserting a flexible rubber membrane, known as a diaphragm, into a female body to cover the cervix.

It was notable, and goes without saying, that these carnal restructurings also enormously benefited the male partners to venereal activity. Accordingly, Reuel was an early beneficiary of this cultural metamorphosis, and took it completely for granted. Before long, after a few brief liaisons, he had made his first steady girlfriend. Her name was Rosie Santini, black haired, dark eyed, assertive, an attractive native New Yorker, Barnard graduate, and a script-editor and production assistant on live network television dramas. She had a small apartment on East 9th Street and following the autumn of his third academic year he had moved in with her. At social gatherings, they were treated as a "couple".

There were other noticeable couples. There was one that fascinated him. An older fellow named Willard Baldwin, usually at a backgammon board, and frequently accompanied by one of the most beautiful girls Reuel had ever seen. A Swedish fashion model whose name was Ulla Bergström. He wanted to rush towards her but found himself tongue-tied. Even worse, he was now uncomfortably tethered to Rosie.

Rosie had three older unmarried brothers who were in the freight business and a widowed mother who lived in a large apartment in the neighborhood called "little Italy". Sunday family dinners were traditional and near the onset of winter Reuel's presence was mandatory. The brothers frequently teased him in the accented Italian of Naples. Aldo, the oldest now asking if he would marry her. *"Eh fratellino, contadino, hai intenzione di sposarla?"*

No, he was too young. *"No, sono troppo giovane."*

"Troppo giovane per scoparla, stronzo Romano?" Too young to marry her, you stupid Roman asshole.

Mama Santini tut-tutted. Rosie blushed. Reuel was unexpectedly frightened. Was he getting in over his head? What about his fantasies of Ulla Bergström?

He saw the Swedish girl again at a Christmas party at a loft near the Bowery. He was smitten. Their eyes met across the room. She smiled at him. Willard seemed absorbed at a game board. Rosie was in a conversation somewhere. Reuel moved towards his target, waiting for an opportunity. Ulla saw him and gave a slow nod. An acquaintance detained him for a moment. He moved near to approach her when Willard stepped-in to take her arm decisively, giving Reuel a cold look, and said something to her about another party. It seemed hopeless. Willard's proprietary physical gesture felt like a kick in the groin. As they went out the door, she glanced at Reuel, smiled softly, and gave the faintest shrug. A nearby older man looked at him and gestured to the door with his chin, and said "arm candy". Her face remained in his restless night-thoughts.

And then, once again, days later. A different party, at a brownstone on West Christopher Street. Crowded. It was New Year's Eve. Willard and Ulla and Reuel and Rosie. It was thick with people and Reuel maneuvered close to her, joining three other young men attending. She offered an indistinct nod. He waited for a moment to say something introductory, something brilliant and enticing, but could not find words or a conversational opening. Fortunately, another beautiful Swedish looking girl joined their little group. There were introductions.

"This is my friend Greta" said Ulla, introducing her to the lads. It diverted attention for an instant and Reuel seized the opportunity. With the barest of nods to Greta he proffered his hand to Ulla, which she took and shook, quite firmly. "I'm Reuel" he said. "And you are Ulla, am I right?"

"Rule? That's a strange name." Said with a slight Scandinavian accent.

"No. It's Roo-El. From the bible."

"It means what?"

"God's wind."

"Very nice. Are you a photographer?"

"No. Something else. Can you guess?"

She looked him up and down. "You are a student!"

He felt crushed for an instant. It was as if she was telling him he was in kindergarten. Just then Rosie arrived, and another round of introductions transpired. A trivial remark was made by one of them about an impending snow-storm. Another comment about the weather. Rosie took his arm in a proprietary manner mentioning she wanted to introduce him to a friend she worked with. As Reuel turned he saw Ulla was shaking hands with a new arrival.

Later he and Rosie were walking back to the apartment. He felt their relation was at an end. A cutting icy wind brought a few snowflakes. For no reason he could think of, the recollection of the first Buddhist truth was borne to mind: Unsatisfactoriness was everywhere. He thought about this for a bit and consoled himself with a second Buddhist thought: that all things were impermanent. A wise and generous philosophy he reassured himself, filled with compassion and solace. Its magnetic core, he felt, was to be studied at greater length at another time. Then, after several months had passed, he no longer lived with Rosie and was back at a furnished room uptown near Columbia.

He had fulfilled the academic course requirements with distinction, and would graduate with honors that Spring. Deciding somehow, for want of something more attractive, with the belief that his interest in what he called "the semantic brain" would benefit from a study of neuroscience, Reuel applied to and was accepted at the Medical School of Johns Hopkins University in Baltimore, Maryland. The relation of language to mathematics and the human nervous system became a mental focal point. It was simply about what took place in the brain and nothing more.

He was no longer interested in being a philosophy or mathematics major. His interest in the mental properties of human thought had been bringing him over to theories of language, alongside a newly emergent field of "information theory" and his own ideas for an artificial brain. He persisted in revisiting and rewording a famous theoretical question:

Originally, "what is a number, that a man may know it, and a man, that he may know a number?" But in time he revised this query to "what is a thought, that a human may know it, and a human, that it may know a thought?" And then once again to a third formulation "what is a word, that a person may know it, and a person, that it may know a word?" Before long this fascination with "words" became an inflection point to his intellectual interests and which led to a fresh emerging focus on linguistics and the existence of thought in the human brain.

Around that time, he saw notice of a lecture on "network theory" to be given at NYU's Courant Institute of Mathematical Sciences, just across from Washington Square Park, and decided to attend. It was a bright cold sunny afternoon in late-February and he crossed the park diagonally from its Northwest corner. As he passed the empty fountain in the center he saw her. She was coming from the other direction, carrying a violin case.

"Ulla?"

"Oh, hello."

"I'm Reuel."

"I remember. God's wind."

"You play the violin?"

"No. This is a harmonica" said as she held the case aloft.

"Would you have time for a coffee?"

"Good idea. Where shall we go?"

"That place on 8th Street and University?"

And so, it was, with mathematical network theory and philosophy consigned to oblivion, that fate in its usual form of random collisions, intervened, and once again changed the course of his life. Indeed, their lives.

Sitting down, face-to-face, at a small table aside a sun-filled window they took in a few silent and cool moments of eye contact, examining one another.

"You're very beautiful."

"In Sweden, I'm average. No one notices me."

"Is Willard Baldwin your boyfriend?"

"That's funny. Get right to the point I see. No. He has a lot of money and he invested in my friend Greta's modeling agency. She introduced us. He took me out some times. He's very sad. Too much inherited money and never had a job. And I slept with him once to make him feel better, if that interests you. But I no longer see him."

"That was very kind of you."

"I'm a kind person I think."

"Will you be kind to me?"

"Of course. I would like to be kind to everyone."

"But you don't sleep with everyone."

"Don't be silly. You have sex on your mind."

"It's human, isn't it?"

"There are more important things. Tell me about yourself. You are a student?"

"Yes."

"What are you studying?"

"Neurolinguistics."

"Wow."

"I start medical school in September."

"You're very young. You want to be a doctor?"

"No. I want to do research on the brain and language. What about you?"

"I'm an exchange student. Violin."

"At NYU?"

"No. Manhattan School of Music."

"On Claremont Avenue?"

"You know it?"

"I live two blocks away, on Amsterdam, near the corner of Thiemann. I'm just finishing up my degree at Columbia."

"My goodness, then we're neighbors!"

They sat talking in this way for nearly two hours and then took a taxi uptown together, agreeing to meet for dinner at a Chinese restaurant the following day. What had Reuel learned? That she was two years older than he. That she was the youngest in her immediate family having three older sisters and a much older brother. That her mother came from a large family as did her father. Her father now lived with one of her mother's sisters, Ulla's aunt. That she had nieces and nephews from her sisters and step-siblings, and more cousins than she could count. That family was the most important thing in her life and she wanted many children. That she started the violin when she was 10. That she rarely played in chamber music and never with an orchestra.

That she mostly played for herself and mostly practiced Bach's sonatas and partitas for solo violin, "the Himalayas of violinists". That these pieces deliberately formed the only music in her self-limiting repertoire. That playing them gave her a mental trance, a reverie. That she had graduated from The Royal College of Music in Stockholm, the *Kungliga Musikhögskolan*, and was returning to Sweden in September. That her father was a naval architect who designed yachts and lived in Sundsvall on the Gulf of Bothnia. That she had sailed over much of the Baltic Sea with family members since she was a child. That she had crewed on tourist yachts in the Mediterranean. That she had traveled throughout Europe with friends in her teen-age years. That almost everyone in Sweden spoke English. And that if Reuel was going to medical school only to do research he ought to look into the Karolinska Institute in Stockholm which was world famous.

They began a relationship. For quite some time before sexual intimacy occurred, they simply spoke to one another with an unusual degree of frankness, even a confessional nakedness, about their thoughts, their views, their ambitions, their weaknesses, their values, and their hopes. As if they had nothing to lose, knowing their lives would have to be cast apart at distant summer's end. As the poet wrote, "the conjunction of the minds, the opposition of the stars." Only seize the day!

Over several weeks they walked lengths of Riverside park, up and down. They tasted the restaurants of Harlem. They went to movies and held hands. Browsed bookstores. Attended poetry readings. Introduced Ulla at the San Remo Bar & Grill. Introduced her to Luca Baca. Introduced him to Greta's friends who owned a modern art gallery. They went to parties together, Willard Baldwin winked at him. Toured the Metropolitan Museum and The Cloisters. Went to jazz concerts at Roseland and at Madison Square Garden. Went ice-skating at Rockefeller Center. Heard Beethoven Quartets at her Manhattan School of Music. Listened to a visiting university professor's lecture on the physiological phenomena of sleep. All of this happening before the first day of Spring. All of this before they became lovers. All of this knowing, and in shared delighting, that they were deliberately holding back. Until the day arrived.

Ulla lived in a four-person shared apartment with her Swedish friend Greta, a long-legged Brazilian model named Luisa, a freckled model from Kansas named Holly, two cats, a messy kitchen, and occasional boyfriends overnighting with the roommates. Nothing was to the taste of Ulla and Reuel who aspired to a venue more elevated, even magical, for their patient and expected rendezvous with sexual destiny.

To his own discomfort, Reuel lived in an 8x12 furnished room on the fifth floor of the Yorkshire Arms, an apartment building for impecunious students on Amsterdam Avenue. Its bath and toilet area were down a hall and his floor was accessed by a creaking and slow elevator. His narrow single bed, with a pronounced concavity, was just as unappealing as the warned description he provided her. With scattered academic papers, text books, strewn clothes, a hot plate, typewriter, and a filthy rug adding to the prospect.

Their opportunity arrived during Spring break. A new Papal Legate, a Cardinal, was to be installed in Washington, D.C. and would be celebrating Good Friday and Easter Sunday at The Basilica of the National Shrine of the Immaculate Conception. Many Catholic students of Fordham University were planning to attend and Luca's attractive top floor apartment in a brownstone building on Southern Boulevard was available for five days. It had a kitchenette, a small parlor with an unobstructed view facing East over the Bronx Zoo, and a separate bedroom with a double bed. And all of it exceptionally neat and tidy. Luca even left them fresh tulips in a pottery vase.

The intimacy of their romance on this occasion can be left to the imagination, but it placed a seal upon them. Thereafter, the particular mundane venues of their love-making, his and hers, became a matter of comic indifference. By the beginning of Summer, they were never apart for as much as a single day. They never spoke of the melancholy foreknowledge of their impending September separation.

Reuel's baccalaureate graduation at the end of May was attended by his frail and aged parents. They were pleased to meet Ulla and took the two youngsters out to a celebratory dinner and to a concert by the New York Philharmonic at Carnegie Hall. In diminished health, as things turned out, it was the last time Reuel would ever see them.

Luca had also graduated. He would be going to Rome in September, enrolled at the Pontifical Gregorian University, the "Greg", to matriculate for a Doctorate in Church history. For his last two months in America, he and three camp classmates were renting a house on Fire Island at a tiny "gay" community called The Pines. Reuel and Ulla were very welcome to visit and crash in a spare room.

With this in mind, while free of academic obligations and footloose, Reuel bought a used Volkswagen bug which was just barely able to hold their combined possessions. They drove it to attend a music festival at Tanglewood, Massachusetts, proceeded onward to tour Boston and Cambridge, and then to the Shakespeare Festival in Stratford, Connecticut. Next, the lingering attractive idea of visiting Luca was discussed. There was a car-ferry they could take from nearby Bridgeport to cross Long Island sound over to the town of Port Jefferson. And from there it was a short drive across the island to Sayville's town dock, where beach lovers could take another smaller ferry across the Great South Bay to Fire Island, a barrier formation 30 miles long and merely some hundreds of yards wide, where cars were unknown and the beach fronted the Atlantic Ocean. This was exactly what they did. Luca and his friends were delighted to have guests.

The summer houses, the beach and the ocean were enthralling. They made inquiries. There was a tiny dwelling without electricity, scarcely more than a shack, at the Eastern end of the little community. They rented it for the remainder of June and all of July. Free of any duties, pressures or obligations they swam in the surf, wandered the uncrowded Eastward beach, and learned they could rent a sailboat from a yard in Sayville where they had parked the Volkswagen. It was an old 15-foot sloop-rigged model called a "Chesapeake Sharpie" with a retractable centerboard for a keel. They relished it and tacked and ran up and down and across the great interior bay, 25 miles long and five miles wide. They did it after dark, on rough windy afternoons, with failed attempts in sad calms. They lived happily together, Reuel with books and Ulla with violin, such that never again in their lives would they enjoy such a free and light-hearted summer.

One night well after dusk, toward the end of July, there was a promising full moon ascending from the Eastern horizon. They took a blanket, a box of crackers, a Camembert cheese, a bottle of red wine, and a violin with them as they walked bare-footed for half a mile to where they had the beach entirely to themselves on a clear unclouded night.

With the moon some twenty degrees above the horizon Ulla took up her violin, stood so the lunar light behind her cast a shadow where he lay, tuned her instrument to the night air, and spoke softly to him.

"Roo, my love, tonight is very special. Very special. I will tell you something of supreme importance. You will never forget this, I promise you. But to help prepare your mind I am going to play for you Bach's entire second Partita, parts of which you've heard me practice so many times. I always work on having the whole thing right. You will forgive my mistakes. Life is full of mistakes."

So, against the soft background murmur of a quiet ocean surf Ulla stood with her back to the moon and performed an uninterrupted half an hour of intellectual beauty, Bach's five connected suites of the partita: allemande, courante, sarabande, gigue, and chaconne.

She was correct. He would never forget it. A shadowy wraith with a fiddle silhouetted against a bright moon conveyed him into a state of primordial awareness beyond anything comprehensible, simultaneously empty and full, beyond thought. When she finished, she put down the violin, knelt and kissed his brow.

"Roo, I'm pregnant."

A whirlwind went through his mind. Dead infected Astrid. Becoming a parent with great responsibilities of maintenance. For still a boy without profession or income.

"We're so young" he says in a beseeching inflection.

"I'm so happy. I want this. To have you in me. To make a family." She is determined.

They spend hours in examination of the situation, contemplating. Live pitifully in Baltimore while he's at Hopkins memorizing somatic anatomies. American citizenship. Or Ulla bereft of him in Sweden. Flights across the Atlantic on holidays. Leaving offspring with siblings and aunts and rejoining him in Maryland. Student housing. Study medicine in Stockholm. Why be a doctor anyway? A regular income. Yes, research science is indeed more interesting. Fellowships. The Karolinska Institute? Great prestige. Sister Marta is the Institute's Vice Registrar. Call her. A family house in Uppsala. A house rental in Stockholm. Family support. Sailing on the Gulf of Bosnia on one of father's boats. Research on language and the brain. Not medicine. Everyone speaking English. Arctic summers. Music. Music.

त

Three weeks before term starts at Johns Hopkins. Ulla phones her sister of the new plan. They agree to sell Reuel's Volkswagen and fly economy on SAS to Stockholm in August to explore possibilities. Appointments made at the Karolinska. Excitement in the air. A promise of eating *Tunnbrödsrulle* and *Inkokt Lax*.

They arrive at Arlanda airport at 7 a.m. Three sisters are waiting. Ulla is pregnant! A huge house in the city. Ulla is pregnant! Scores of an extended family congratulate Reuel. What a catch! Handsome. Brilliant! Splendid family name. Marta has arranged appointments at the Institute. Neurolinguistics is hot. Interviews with two professors. Undergraduate record sent. A junior research fellowship at the medical school is available. A modest stipend. Can rotate into a physician track if desired. Science! Music! Loving family! Children! Reuel informs Hopkins. He forfeits his tuition deposit.

The next year was filled with disappointments, yet not exactly unhappiness, nor depression. More like an "unsatisfactoriness", which he has come to believe is the most apt English translation of Buddhist Pali-Sanskrit *"dukkha"*. To begin with there was a puzzling family situation. Ulla has told him on several occasions that there is no need of formal marriage, unless he insists on it, which he doesn't. He is told that marriage in Sweden is generally for church goers. He senses a distancing. Then, he feels mostly surrounded by women, Ulla's omnipresent mother, her three sisters, several aunts, nieces, and female cousins. Reuel feels starved for male companionship. This matter is augmented when it was discovered that Ulla's pregnancy consists in carrying twins, who are revealed at birth as girls, Kristina and Karen. A post-partum ostracizing.

Reuel spends most of his hours at the Institute laboratories and discovers, to his scientific regret, that he is fundamentally disinterested in applied biology.

The series of brain imaging projects at the Karolinska were superficial and uninteresting. And his original hope to study the neural mechanisms in the human brain that control the comprehension, production, and acquisition of language now seemed sophomoric. The immensity of the central nervous system, the galactic universe of its brain structure and colossal neuronal network, will not yield to his mathematically inclined imagination. A bridge too far. Computers seemed to be of no help. It appeared clear that the seductive and imaginative concept of neurolinguistics defied computation. What is a "thought", leave alone a number, that a scientist may know it? Even the great phenomenologist, Edmund Husserl, could not reduce a psychological process needed to obtain the simple concept of a number. Searching for an algorithm, any algorithm at all, to divine the hundreds of thousand miles of billions of neuronal threads that lay between his ears to create thoughts, seemed fruitless. His only saving grace was to realize that Johns Hopkins Medical School would not have provided a better outcome. He feels somewhat lost in the space between zero and infinity.

Moreover, the constant cloudy sub-arctic darkness of short daylights produced an unfamiliar melancholia. His male colleagues took refuge in alcohol which did not agree with him and the Swedish language did not come easily enough to enable or understand any casual bantering. He felt lonely. Ulla, now preoccupied with motherhood, had gained seven kilos and barely paid attention to him. By the first day of Spring in March he felt a fatigue of the soul. He looked forward with waxen hope to long days of summer.

There were, of course, interesting moments of comparative relief. While shopping downtown one day for a rain-jacket he stopped for lunch at an unpretentious Thai restaurant to choose a satay noodle curry. While waiting, his gaze alighted on an evocative framed poster reproduction of a painting picturing the Buddha preaching to an elephant. He tries asking the Asian waitress if there are Buddhists in Stockholm. She calls her father from the kitchen.

Yes, Reuel is told, there are several thousand Buddhists in Stockholm. The proprietor goes to the cash register, opens a drawer, and finds a slightly soiled business card which he is given. It bears Thai letters on one side, and on the obverse, the name *Phra Luang Ayutthaya, President — Sveriges Buddhistiska samarbetsråd*, with a Stockholm address. It is only three blocks away he is told, upstairs.

Wandering over, Reuel finds the building with a plaque attached showing its name in three languages. The one in English reading "Swedish Buddhist Cooperation Council." Upstairs there is a reception area with an English-speaking ash-blond Swedish lady at a desk. She is happy to be of help. A small mutual aid congregation uses the space for ceremonies such as marriage and funerals, for assistance with a variety of matters pertaining to government administration, as well as travel arrangements, import and export facilitation, and congregational meditations, especially on Thai holidays. President Luang Ayutthaya would be happy to meet Reuel.

She arranges an appointment for the following day at tea time and is forthcoming. The President, she explains, is usually referred to as "Phra Luang", indicating that he is, or was, actually an ordained monk, though he dresses as a businessman, which he is. In fact, he is also the President of the sewing machine factory which produces a popular domestic model trade-named "TakTak" after the slight sound it makes.

Phra Luang was waiting for Reuel at the appointed hour. A thermos of tea and a plate of cookies were set on a table between them. Phra Luang introduces himself. He is a cheerful little man in his sixties. A round face with a broad smile revealing yellowed teeth, a shining bald head, and wire spectacles atop his somewhat squashed nose. He speaks English with a Thai accent, expressing his honor at meeting a young scientist from the Karolinska. He explains that he was once a senior monk at one of Thailand's forest monasteries but returned his robes on returning to secular life. Not an uncommon practice in his native country. He is very happy that he can serve as spiritual advisor to the local congregation.

They are not only Thai, he explains, but also Sri Lankan. Buddhism actually came to old Siam from old Ceylon and the two communities share the Theravada school of *Vipassana* practice. It was regrettable that practitioners in other countries referred to "the way of the ancients" as *Hinayana*, as if it was a lesser vehicle in comparison to the so-called *Mahayana*. The way of the Theras, he insisted was unmistakably authentic. Unlike the Japanese, for example, who were militarists who claimed to be Buddhists, and had not only made war on Buddhist Thailand when he was a child, but had a style of practice which seemed far from authentic, in his opinion. Similarly, Indians, Tibetans and Nepalese had no right to look down at South Asians such as those living in Sweden.

Reuel attempted to describe his research on the brain and the phenomenon of human language. Phra Luang nodded as he listened. Science was very interesting and valuable he agreed. But it was not the only path of knowledge. Human language is what produces thoughts, he explained as if to an innocent, but thought was different than awareness. And it was awareness that led to realization, to a durable enlightenment. Reuel asked if he would explain this in greater detail.

Phra Luang stared directly at him in a lengthy silence then drew himself upright at the edge of his seat. It was as if he was transformed from a businessman and returning back into being a monk.

"I explain to you. You know most people in Thailand are Buddhist. Many children, young people, take novice ordination. Shave head, eyebrows. Wear yellow robe. Some leave one week. Most usually a few weeks. Most returning to secular life after getting first lessons in Buddha Dharma. Very very few really want to become monks. Everyone taught not to steal, not to lie, not to drink whiskey, to be ethical. Only little teaching on mind. How to explain Right Concentration to children, to novices. Difficult. I explain to you same way. Okay?"

"Of course. I would like to know. And also, I am still young too."

"Okay. There is a rat. You know what is a rat. A big fat rat. And there is a young and little kitten. Imagine the rat is thought and the kitten is awareness. When thought arises, our original mind is grabbed and dragged away. So, imagine kitten trying to catch a big rat. Rat of thought is bigger and stronger than kitten of awareness. For novices, when rat appears, kitten feels it's real nature, and tries to catch rat. Rat instinctively wants to run away, and kitten tries holding on. Then the kitten, only novice cat, becomes tired and lets rat run away to someplace else. And like, similar to rats, thoughts arise, and stop, and change by themselves. But we get older, learn to cultivate our own self-awareness more and more. Meditation practice is just like we are feeding the kitten till it becomes a big strong cat of awareness. Then, when thoughts arise, and our original mind cannot be dragged along, so thought stream will stop easily. Do you understand? Main thing for novice to learn. Thought is different than awareness."

"Interesting," said Reuel. "Brain science might call this a shift in plasticity."

"Plastics?"

"No. Plasticity is something else. Like wet clay has plasticity. After an empty infant's mind, thought becomes natural to people. But learning to increase what you call awareness is something new in the West. Almost like how one part of the brain can look at another part of the brain. What we call "neuroplasticity" could increase the awareness skill by practicing. Like feeding the kitten."

"Ah yes. I see. Of course, many kinds of thought are important in other spheres of human life. Like you doing science. Like me making sewing machines. That is normal. Meditation a different sphere. Usually, we see world and everything around us through filter of concepts, thoughts are how we think, through mental images, ideas and patterns we collect since childhood. While thoughts can of course be source of human benefit, their same existence in our mind can also be source of human suffering. Thought is also the source of wanting things, cravings, egoism, greed, anger and delusion. The Buddha's purpose of meditation was to develop the art of seeing things as they really are, with awareness and wisdom and yet without thought."

"How do you teach meditation?" Reuel asked.

"Not so easy. Small steps. Especially for novices. You come again. Next time we talk more. I am here every Wednesday afternoon."

Reuel took a long walk home rather than using the bus. He tried getting his mind around the difference between thought and awareness. And his mind only jumped to another thought. Tonight, was a Wednesday ritual when Ulla's three sisters, and their mother Hedda, would all be visiting. He glimpsed that he was having rat-like thoughts about what it was going to be like, submerged alone among incomprehensible Swedes. And then aware that he was a kitten, irritated at thinking about them. Was this his demonstration of neurological recursion, of what Phra Luang was describing? Or was it about the possibility of an empty mind being wide awake? And what was the use of that?

He was still pondering this when he arrived home. The coven was oohing and ahhing over the twins. He received a series of perfunctory kisses. An ocean of Swedish was in full maelstrom. Alone with his thoughts in English. Thoughts requiring silent words in one's mind, and that, he thought, was actually interesting. Language inside your head. Communicating with yourself. Inquiry.

"What are you thinking about?" asked Marta, the oldest and bossiest of the sisters, in English.

"I met somebody who used to be a Buddhist monk. It was quite interesting."

"An Asian?" asked mother Hedda. "They are celibates, just imagine. No sex."

Linnea, the next youngest winked at him. Alice, who ranked below her, volunteered that Buddhism was known in Sweden more than a thousand years earlier.

"That's preposterous" said Reuel.

"Want to bet?"

He sensed a trap, but was committed. "Certainly."

"How much?"

"A hundred Krona."

"I accept."

Ulla turned to him. "It is unwise to bet against Alice about anything."

"Tack sa mycket", she said, which is 'thanks–a–lot', and went to the bookcase to fetch the Swedish *Nationalencyklopedin* found in every household.

She flipped pages, found what she was looking for, and read her smooth English translation aloud.

"This is from the entry on Helgo, a little island just west of Stockholm where a Buddhist statue was found. Are you ready? Here it is. Trust my translation. Quote: 'Undoubtedly the most extraordinary find discovered during the excavations at Helgo was a small, bronze Buddha. This sculpture dates from about the 6th century and was probably made in Kashmir. The Buddha has a silver knob on his forehead, symbolizing a third eye, while his ears have long lobes, the sign of royalty. He sits in a meditative pose on a doubled lotus throne. The Buddha statue probably arrived in Helgo from Swedish merchants of the Viking era whose eastern trade routes reached as far as India. This beautiful sacred item is on display at the History Museum in Stockholm.' So Reuel, One hundred Krona if you please."

"I told you so" said Ulla.

"How come you knew that?" he asked Alice.

"It was on a one Krona postage stamp a few years ago. Now pay up."

That weekend there was a lecture at the British Council auditorium on the Riddargatan by a visiting Scot professor. Its title was "Algorithms in a Mechanical Computation Engine" and was supported by the IBM Corporation. Reuel and several of his colleagues from the Karolinska attended. They all agreed it was intellectually stimulating. As they collected their things from the cloak-room Reuel felt a hand on his shoulder.

"Hello young fellow."

Reuel turned to behold Lars Soderberg his old tutor on the subject of computing platforms at Funk & Wagnall's summer dictionary project. Where he learned the concepts of system architecture, process control and programming assembler languages. Lars was now IBM's man in Sweden. They went for coffee.

"What are you doing here? What are you up to?"

Reuel took half an hour explaining how he had come to the Karolinska, his interest in researching language and the brain, and his disappointment at having underestimated the scale of the challenge. The academic attempt to construct a mathematical activity model of the brain failed to increase any understanding of how hierarchical networks of billions of neurons interacted. His goal of understanding the relationship between cognitive phenomena and the underlying physical substrate of the brain remained a mystery. He could see that high-level functions of linguistic memory related to neural substructures but the issue of deep memory was another story. And the newly invented imaging technologies were merely very crude tools and of little theoretical interest. Of course, he had learned Unix and C+, and the use of computers for data management and analysis in the lab, but that seemed trivial against the challenge of deep understanding. He felt impatient, at a dead end, and unsure of what he was doing.

Soderberg listened attentively, reflected aloud on the differences between "wetware" and hardware, and speculated that there might be interesting overlapping areas such as syntax, for example, in the emerging technologies of computational software, specifically in the emergence of novel programming languages for the growing computer industry. Languages without emotions, he added.

As their coffee was now cold, Soderberg suggested that they could continue discussions the following Monday at his office in Kistagangen. Reuel might find IBM's activities to be of interest. He could take the underground Blue Line to the Kista Galleria stop and find IBM's offices a five-minute walk from there.

Reuel said nothing of this invitation to Ulla. It was too soon and he was unsettled. She was preoccupied with the twins and little Karen had been coughing. On Monday Reuel arrived to IBM at 10:00 o'clock. Soderberg asked about the size of his junior fellowship. Kr30,000 he was told, about $2500 US. Although Reuel had a modest family inheritance, he had been living food and rent-free on the generosity of the relatively affluent Bergstroms. He still thought of himself as a student.

Soderberg provided him with a tour of the commercial horizon. IBM had recently introduced the innovative system/360 family of general-purpose computers which used interchangeable software and peripherals. It was promising to be the dominant mainframe computer design in the marketplace and its architecture was likely to become an industry standard. Furthermore, the company was starting to unbundle its marketing efforts and would shortly start selling software and services independently from hardware. Of course, this might be an opening in the market for independent computing software services companies to develop their own programming languages. A risk worth taking.

Reuel's background in mathematics and his focus on languages was of personnel interest to IBM. The company's current programming languages employed detailed forms of mathematical notation which could be used in scientific and financial applications. For instance, he described to Reuel its use in business accounting, which consisted in nothing more than basic calculations and accumulations of numbers. Using accounting merely as an illustrative example, the general ledger, the accounts payable, expense categories, the accounts receivable, the payroll, the inventory, job cost estimating, fixed assets, sales orders, budgeting, human resources data, loan interest computation and payment amounts, taxes due, cash flow, depreciation schedules, pension obligations, and so on and so forth, on and on. A transactional universe reduced to numbers. And standard language codes for information interchange between machines of different manufacturers was now becoming routine. Machine language was the key to the future of information computation, he said. Government procurements were driving the industry. Object-oriented languages using grouped data and instruction sets were evolving rapidly and facilitating the use of simulations in new social environments. Of course, it might sound dull for some people but it was highly profitable. Soderberg studied Reuel's face as he spoke.

The future he sketched out resembled Columbus landing on a new continent. Consider how the transistor and random-access memory increased the reliability and lowered the cost of obsoleting vacuum tubes. And then integrated circuits on a microchip would soon arrive like another catalyst and lead to 4-bit micro-processer designs, which were promising to double and redouble their processing capability every few years. Solid-state computers in the future were going to be like "crude oil". Everything was getting smaller and faster and requiring less power. One day there would probably be computers the size of valise or a standard typewriter. It was changing the world. Color television was arriving in the marketplace. Communication satellites were going up. There was going to be a human moon landing in the near future. And it was just yesterday when they had been using punch cards and spools of magnetic tape at Funk & Wagnall's. Consider IBM's motto: "THINK". It was worth a thought.

He offered Reuel a job as a research associate in computer language design at Kr200,000 annually. If he developed something promising he could move up to a project director, at Kr300,000. How did that sound?

Reuel made a face of near surrender. "It would put an end to my future in biological research on neurolinguistics. But the machine language game sounds equally fascinating. Computers will change the world. Economically it's a no-brainer. It's really a major career choice for me. I'd still be left with my interest in the philosophy of mind, but that's purely academic, and there's not a single penny from it. When do I need to tell you?"

"Take all the time you need. Use your wet brain. Hardware can't help."

"What kind of commitment would I be making?"

"Let's say a year, renewable."

"What's my job description?"

"Scouting next generation operating system programming languages for starters. Work on application interfaces. Syntax formalization. Network issues. Security. Intellectual property. Development responsibility if you find a suitable project. You've got the math."

"Expenses? Travel?"

"Anything within reason. A workstation of your own, the usual benefits."

"Support staff?"

"Routine secretarial and administrative. New hires by you need my approval."

"Give me a week."

"No rush. This is new for us too. I'd be taking a chance on you."

"Starting when?"

"You say. September would work."

They shook hands.

"One more thing" said Soderberg.

"Oh?"

"Coat and tie, all the time."

Reuel took the underground home, his head swimming so much he overshot his station. Ulla and the entire Bergstrom family would be pleased. Still, he needed to think through the offer very carefully. "This was a life choice."

ॐ

Then it was midweek. The Thai monk, Phra Luang, had extended an open enticement to come by the Buddhist Cooperation Council on Wednesday afternoons. Reuel planned on a trial visit. It promised a bump, a novel change in his mental texture.

Phra Luang was pleased to see him, and once again arranged a thermos of tea and a plate of cookies. "Where were we?" he inquired.

"I asked how you taught meditation."

"Ah, yes. For novices. Beginners. Rats and cats."

"I try to watch my mind constantly."

"Do you? Perhaps you can learn to use it in order to watch the mind that is doing the watching. So, let me begin by saying that there are many different forms of meditation. Some teachers use mind-watching. Some use breath-counting and breath-concentration. Others teach concentration on a mantra or a paradoxical riddle. Some just look at a wall and expect nothing. Some tell students to visualize a religious image or a form of light or color. All of these methods share the same central theme - learning focused concentration by the mind. Mind finds it hard to gain focus, easy to lose focus, you may have noticed."

"I have."

"A common meditation, well-known to us in Thailand, uses movement of the body to generate what we call a "choiceless awareness", which becomes a powerful tool for realizing your own nature. While the body's motion is natural, sitting still is difficult for novices. There is actually no need to sit still for a long time, which might even cause needless pains and aches. Especially for Westerners who are not used to sitting on the ground with legs crossed. There is a proper place for sitting - along with standing, walking and lying - but to imagine that sitting itself contains some special virtue is attachment to form. We teach a simple method of meditation suitable for anyone, regardless of their religion or nationality. In our uncomplicated kind of meditation, you can move rhythmically, observing your awareness of movements by a unified body and mind. These elementary movements may be simple and repetitious, but they form a powerful basic method for beginners in order to achieve self-understanding."

"Even while walking?"

"Why not, if you develop your skill. You can practice mind awareness, without thoughts, by using different parts of your body, and for beginners by doing all your movements very slowly. Slow movement are revealing. You can start by sitting and practice slow hand movements. You can even do slow hand movements while lying or standing and concentrate only on being aware of the body's feeling as you make the movement. You can try slow walking and feel each footstep. You can even observe and be aware of your diaphragm moving up and down when you practice slow breathing. These are just elementary practices. You can easily use them to gain a focused awareness of your body's movement. By practicing these movement methods as much as possible you will cultivate the skill of self-awareness without having a stream of thoughts. These practices are easily taught to children. Cultivating mindful awareness while sitting completely still is for much more advanced practitioners."

"Why does slowness work?"

"It is just for beginners. Slowness is valuable. It automatically illustrates and brings to awareness the body-mind connection of habits. You can practice these slow movements even when in a car or on a bus or on an airplane. For example, by laying your hand on your thigh and slowly turn the palm up and down, or slowly run your thumb against a fingertip. Or make a fist and open it slowly and repeatedly. The key is to do every movement slowly and focus your awareness on the movement. This is a natural beginner's way of cultivating self-awareness. Once you have this kind of starting point you are ready for higher things. You can do this simple practice anywhere. It grows to be familiar. And then in time you become more easily aware of movements of the mind and so developing a higher consciousness. Basically, the practice of awareness is the foundation for the elevation of your character."

"What's so good about awareness once we achieve it?"

"Ah, yes. Because it allows us to go to the root of unhappiness. Otherwise, we cannot just suppress our desires, our anger, and our delusions using the excuse of good intentions. Obviously, right conduct cannot be achieved by unconscious ignorance. Conscious awareness, when one sees oneself, when mind changes its qualities completely, permits us to see through and break through suffering and see things just as they are. Just as they are. Just as they are, I say. At the exercise of awareness, the mind immediately becomes active, clear, pure, and we become mentally strong and completely honest."

"What about this moment, here and now?"

Phra Luang seized the moment. His eyes widened as he stared at Reuel and leaned slightly forward. Very slowly he raised a finger. For several minutes, they both sat in utter silence.

Reuel walked home aware of feeling fortified, self-confident. Aware that his feelings were impermanent. Understanding clearly the message at the heart of Phra Luang's guidance on practicing awareness. Use it or lose it. Brain plasticity at work, as he reduced it. Something novel and valuable in the instruction. How to put it into a lifetime's practice was the challenge. The first thing was to keep the utility in his working memory. Aware momentarily of his life-long sense of impatience. Why the rush?

Reuel decided to accept the employment offer from IBM, coat and tie and all, commencing on the first of September. He informed the research department of his decision and, since the academic term at the Karolinska ended on May 31, he had a three-month Summer holiday before him. He had decided on two attractive opportunities. The first was to work with Ulla's father at his boatyard in Sundvall. The second was to take a ten-day holiday in Italy, mostly in Rome, with Luca Baca.

Ulla's father, Erik Anderson, had written to him several months earlier, apologizing for the fact that he had not yet met the young progenitor of his granddaughters. The letter inquired if Reuel would be interested in spending summer time in Sundvall, as he understood Reuel had some sailing experience. Anderson had been crafting a 19-meter sloop-rigged yacht of his own design over the last year and the unnamed craft was expected to be ready for sea trials on the Gulf by mid-summer. Before then they would be installing the mast and working on the choice of a propeller, using computer assisted design, CAD.

Reuel accepted this proposition with considerable pleasure. He had longed to meet the man and the idea of working on, and trialing, a sailing yacht on the Gulf of Bothnia was a dream. Obtaining a taste of computer design on top of this was dream within a dream. He proposed to arrive in Sundvall just after Sweden's Midsommardagen holiday and could stay until the end of August. It was arranged that he and Anderson would live together in the family house.

As for visiting Luca, the opportune window was in early June, in the gap before Midsommar. He made travel arrangements accordingly. Ulla was cheerfully indifferent. Men and women were free to make their independent arrangements, it went without saying in Sweden. Reuel had become used to this aspect of Scandinavian culture and it had suited him so well that it seemed natural. America even seemed backward in its conventions between sexes.

Luca was waiting at the arrival hall at Fiumicino airport. An aspirant for the priesthood, he was wearing a short-sleeved non-liturgical black shirt with a tabbed removable clerical collar. He had a second-hand Primavera model Vespa scooter in the parking lot and they took it to Luca's small apartment on the third floor of an older building in Trastevere. Reuel would sleep on the sofa.

Except for sexual intimacy they were like an old married couple who had no secrets. Lucas's same-sex preferences had been understood for years and were scarcely worthy of discussion. At present, he explained that he had taken a vow of a non-carnal Platonic love, free of desire. It suited him. He was not only an aspirant for the priesthood he was also a candidate for a doctorate in the Church's missionary history at the "Greg", Rome's Pontifical University. He was at ease with his life, which was more than Reuel could say. During their shared days together, Luca acted as tour guide to Rome and described its history at length as they walked the city and sampled the cafes.

While surveying the current status of their personal lives with its illustrative stories they enjoyed discussing world history, the history of science, Galileo and the church, Swedish culture, their interests in contemporary politics, literature, music, technology, philosophy and religion. Reuel recounted his meetings with Phra Luang and described the Helgo Buddha statuette which he had seen in Stockholm's history museum. Buddhist philosophy was enticing.

Luca was not surprised and related the story of the Jesuit missionary to Tibet, Ippolitos Desideri, who was considered the first European to study and understand Tibetan language and culture. Reuel was fascinated. He frequently dreamed of seeing a Tibet which had been closed to Westerners for years, as if it was on another planet. Luca recounted that ever since Marco Polo there had been numerous engagements between Europeans, most notably Jesuit and Capuchin missionaries, to various parts of Asia, reaching even as far as Japan. Desideri of course was unique to Tibet. At age 28 he left Rome, in 1712, and took nearly four years of dangerous journeys to reach Lhasa.

"That must have been a pretty wild encounter. How much do we know about it?"

"We know a great deal. Desideri wrote quite a bit about his experiences. He rented a house in Lhasa and lived there for five years. The Lamas were extremely tolerant and kind to him. They encouraged him to learn the language, which he mastered, and to study Buddhist philosophical and religious literature. Most of which had come from Nalanda University in India centuries earlier. Just imagine, this guy arrives from Rome after years of traveling and ends up studying intensively at the cloistered university of Sera Monastery, famous for its practice of debating. There he learns Buddhist techniques of scholastic argument. He writes five books in Tibetan no less, trying to teach Christian doctrine. The Christ is treated as just another God with analogues in the Tibetan pantheon. He has no problem with Buddhist moral philosophy, but struggles to refute two central Tibetan religious, or philosophical concepts. He can't accept the idea of literal rebirth, of reincarnation, which he calls "metempsychosis". And even more difficult and troubling to him is the Buddhist concept of emptiness, the insubstantiality of all phenomenal things, including the self."

"He's not the only one."

"How about you, so philosophically talkative?"

"I'm trying it out."

"Beware of a dark abyss!"

"But Luke, do things really have an intrinsic nature? Like Kant's *ding an sich?*"

"The glory of God."

"Which is produced without a cause?"

"Let us stop right here."

ॐ

Reuel returned to Stockholm in time for a festive and pagan Midsommar. He circled phallic maypoles with the Bergstrom sisters, learned to frog-dance, ate herrings, prayed for sunshine, wore a flower wreath crown, swallowed tiny strawberries whole, and learned a drinking song whose English translation was "hup-de-la-la-la-loo-lah-lay."

At month's end, he took a luxurious bus to Sundsvall and was met by Ulla's father, Erik Anderson. It was the first time they had ever seen one another. Anderson was a bearded man of medium height with a mop of unruly hair. He looked like a rugby center fielder. His hand-shake was nearly bone crushing. He drove Reuel to his commodious house, helped him to an upstairs room, and instructed him to meet in the kitchen when he had unpacked.

When Reuel descended Anderson was reading a book at a long oak table separating two unpadded benches. He was gestured to sit opposite his host who poured each of them a small glass of throat-burning aquavit with a strong caraway flavor.

"Skol. Welcome to Sundvall. Father of my granddaughters."

"Thank you. I've been looking forwards to it. How is it you are named Anderson and the girls are Bergstroms?"

"Ach. Swedish women. I can't live with them so they use their matronymic. It suits them. It's not unusual. You know the Yin Yang concepts? They are too much Yin. I am too much Yang maybe. Anyway, they say you are mathematician. That you know computers."

"Somewhat."

"Good, you can help me with some physics. We are building a 19-meter sloop in my boatyard, down by the shore. She is still "namloss", no name yet, but should be ready for her first sea trial on the gulf in a few weeks. Ulla says you can sail."

"More like dinghies. Nothing motored. But my father was a diesel tractor engineer."

"That's very good. Marine diesels, same design. But you can help me choose and fit the right screw propeller. That is the challenge. We have to model the thrust. There are plenty of variables to work with. Geometry of the hull and keel, overall weight, maneuverability and variation of speed, torque and resistance. So, you surely see, propulsion is a universe of issues. So far, we have dimensions of the shaft and boss. But it's the rake and skew of the blade shape which I need for the foundry. You follow?"

"I think so. You need computer assisted design. CAD."

"Exactly. We have an Ericsson and monitor down at the shop, using IBM's 360 software. You follow?"

"I actually do."

"Good. We can start on it tomorrow. Otherwise, she's almost ready. We should step the mast in next week, another week for sails and rigging and we are about ready to put her in the water. Linnea will be coming up to help us furnish out with the cockpit and main cabin gear, galley stuff, upholstery, blinds, you know."

They liked one another and over the following weeks enjoyed working together. Reuel was as eager as Anderson to put the sloop afloat which had been designed to permit one-handed sailing from a cockpit. The new computer designed propeller finally arrived from the foundry, and attached; the ultra-modern mast was stepped in, the rigging and sails suited up, the installed hardware tested, winches, furlers, tracks and travelers, rope clutches, cam cleats, shackles, shrouds, stays, lifeline hardware, wind indicator, compass and binnacle, clinometer, sail lines, and the recent experimental idea of a self-steering wind-vane on the mast-head geared to an auxiliary servo-rudder. And finally, double checking, the navigational electronics, depth finder and the VHF radio.

Linnea arrived for the launch formalities and the add-ons. That evening at dinner, as Reuel watched, she and Anderson went back and forth on deciding the sloop's name. They agreed not to leave the appellation to an ultimate buyer of the boat. That pleasure was pre-emptively reserved to the architect and his daughter. Anderson insisted the name had to be Norse, female, brief enough to paint in large characters on the transom, and must be easily understood spoken aloud during a VHF radio broadcast. Reuel remained a silent spectator. It took close to an hour lubricated by Aquavit until they finally agreed to name her "Saga", a Scandinavian goddess of storytelling whose symbol was a fish and who emerged up to the world from beneath the waves.

The following day Linnea poured a liter of Swedish birch sap wine on the bowsprit before the launching. Finally, they carefully took away the retaining chocks, and let a winch ease the sloop to slide slowly down the tilted bar rails to the water where she rested rocking softly, at home in the sea at last.

The next day they took the Saga out for a taste of the Gulf. There was still a job remaining to complete outfitting of the main cabin but they couldn't wait. The sloop's construction foreman, the chief carpenter, the master machinist, plus Anderson, Linnea, and Reuel crowded aboard. They motored out to the open water, raised the mainsail and jib, and with Anderson at the helm, let her fly a kilometer with an easy breeze abeam, holding a starboard tack.

That night Anderson hosted a large dinner party with musicians for the entire construction crew and their mates at Sundvall's best eatery, the "Gastrologik". Alcohol fueled, it was exceedingly merry and loud. Linnea sat bodily pressed next to Reuel and translated the joking and the shouting, explaining Swedish morés, tousled his hair, and made him dance with her between courses. She was not exactly unattractive.

Over the next week Linnea worked to dress up and complete the furnishing of the main cabin. Reuel learned more about her than he had from Ulla. Her name was botanical, from a lime tree. She was the only Bergstrom sister without children. She was a clothing designer with a high-end boutique in the chic venue of Kungsholm. She had measured, designed and produced the maritime motifs of the upholstery and linens. The galley was completed with George Jensen cook-ware and utensils, and all the woodwork came from Ikea. It was near summer's end and she was very pleased that Reuel, liberated of work, was free to watch and chat with her. They shared a subtle vibration which was becoming palpable.

A few days passed. Evening. The boat's cabin was finally outfitted. Anderson was off to sleep. Reuel and Linnea playing chess. He won the first game, spotting her a rook and a bishop. Now the second, Reuel playing black without a queen. Seven or eight moves in, she spoke.

"I'm tired of this. Let's go see what Saga's cabin feels like at night." What followed had a slight sensation of inevitability. There was a low and waning half-moon to light the stroll to the pier where the Saga was tied. They took off their shoes and went aboard and descended through the cockpit to the main cabin aft of the galley and two stacked berths. Linnea tried the boat's lamps, wired from the batteries, but the light was overly bright and harsh which made them wince and was quickly doused. A squat new candle in a red glass was found and lit. The hard and narrow bench and table, both fixed to the floor were uninviting. They fussed around and found the Aquavit, toasted and swallowed some, and examined the bunk arrangement. A one meter wide navy-blue canvas-covered foam mattress and a few yellow throw cushions. They sat down and immediately embraced and slowly began kissing, tongues exploring.

Some moments later he said "I don't think this is a good idea."

"I think you are right."

"Let's go and sit out in the cockpit."

She blew out the candle and they moved outside to the helm, where they sat on cushioned lockers facing one another, five feet apart, the turned-up tiller between them. The moon was down and the sky shown a beautiful night, filled with an immensity of stars with scarcely a breeze. There was a long silence which she finally broke.

"I'm six years older than you. Ulla says you are very smart. You know many things."

"What can I tell you?"

"What's it all about?"

"What?"

"How did we come here? As people like us who kiss. What does it all mean? How come we exist? What is sex? You are handsome. Would I feel this way if you were old and ugly? Would you have kissed me if I was ugly, fat and short with pimples? Where comes this sexual arousal, this excitement which makes us lose our minds? *Knulla.* You know the Swedish word? To fuck. *Knulla.*

I like to do it. I don't want children. I'm the only one of my sisters. Children are a pain, a torment, little parasites. Already too many people on the planet. We don't need them. I don't want to reproduce. How come we enjoy that feeling of *Knulla* so much if we don't want children? Why does that exist? Tell me."

"Well, there are hormones and...."

"No, no, no. Tell me from the beginning of time, in the universe. Tell me how humans came to fuck. My parents fucked and I came to be. Same as you. The parents of our parents fucked, and their parents did too, all the way back. Even at this exact moment, all over this world, I guarantee you that millions of people are fucking right now, most of them enjoying it. Maybe a few on one side or another not enjoying it, but they are all still doing it. What does it mean? That's what I'm asking you if you are so smart."

"Are you asking about love?"

"No, I'm asking about sex. People say they 'make love'. People say they 'sleep together'. They use different ways to speak of *Knulla*. Where does it all come from? What is the purpose of it? Do they do it on other planets? How do you even explain something as simple and as fundamental as being called sexually attractive?"

"Well, actually, *Knulla* might not have a purpose. Just a frozen accident of evolution."

"So, it exists without a purpose? Is *Knulla* just Mr. Darwin's 'adaptation'? Please. adaptation to what? Are you going to tell me about a God in heaven?"

"Look, let me tell you what I think. All those questions you ask are not really so important. Maybe what people do with their genitals has no meaning at all in terms of absolute reality. But we don't live in absolute reality. We live in ignorant relativity. The universe is billions of years old. There are billions of galaxies, each with billions of stars, and there are billions of planets around those stars, and some of them have a narrow band of temperature and some water, and some of those have organic molecules, and some of those, billions of more years ago, have single-celled life-forms like bacteria, and some of those evolve into multi-celled forms like algae and fungi and sea life, and some of those become worms and fish and bugs, and even some with backbones, and some become lizards and some grow to dinosaurs, and some are smashed by an asteroid, millions and millions of years ago, and most things die away, probably even humans will die away some day, and some things survive, more millions of years ago and some of them become warm-blooded, and become like cats, and bears, and giraffes, and monkeys, and they all begin to have sensations and feelings, and some of the monkeys become apes millions of years ago, and some of the apes not only have feelings but slowly, generation after generation, become smart and learn to manage fires, and break stones and to make sounds that have a little bit of meaning and they make tools, and learn to predict simple things, and they start wandering all over the planet, and hundreds of thousands of years pass, and they live in caves and hunt and paint on walls and make jewelry, and bury their dead, and plant seeds in the ground and tame dogs, and live in little towns, and invent gods to explain things, and tell stories which invent crazy meanings to the mystery of their existence, and invent writing to make records, and they start to ask themselves the exact same question just like you everyplace they live: What's it all about? Do you follow?"

"No. Fantastic!"

"Linnea, there is no answer. There is no real meaning. We are a rare lifeform which emerged on a rock moving around a small star in a small galaxy in the universe. Our life in cosmic time lasts but a fragment of a second and is frequently painful. We have no meaning other than ones we invent with our imagination to keep our minds fixed on avoiding suffering and unhappiness. That's all."

"That explains sex?"

"Yes. Because sex is so incredibly enjoyable, don't you see? The fact that it frequently makes babies is something we have turned into something useful for us, which we call tribes, societies, laborers, cultures. None of that would exist if animals didn't like fucking so much. *Knulla*. It would all come to an end without fucking."

"You are ridiculous. Ulla likes the twins much more than she likes fucking."

"That's called middle-class culture. Before she liked the twins, she liked fucking."

"You're impossible. You talk so much, full of words. Just tell me why did you stop just before?"

"Maybe I'm becoming a Buddhist."

"What?"

"Never mind. I think we should change the subject. Do you notice it's barely four o'clock and getting light already?"

The following day, as scheduled, Linnea took the bus back to Stockholm. They briefly embraced like in-laws at the station and kissed cheeks. Reuel had two weeks of holiday left in August.

Anderson decided they should take the Saga out on the Gulf every long day, trial her through a variety of conditions, test the self-steering mechanical autopilot, and keep a detailed log noting every nuance. Then, after a week of this, at an early breakfast on the 26th of August, a promising clear day of good weather, Anderson suggested Reuel take the boat out by himself. After all, she was designed for single-handed sailing and control. "Just bring her back before dark. You have plenty of summer daylight. Take a lunch and enjoy yourself."

Reuel was thrilled at the opportunity. He packed a hasty sandwich of cheese and sausage, a chocolate bar, a liter of lemon-water, took a wind jacket, sunglasses, hat, light gloves, and calculated there were nearly 14 hours of daylight available. He thought of jogging to the pier but confined himself to a fast walk. There was a fresh and variable Northeasterly breeze promising a degree of constancy. He thought to sail a good-sized triangle, beating up close-hauled on the first leg, keeping the coast in sight. Then a long beam-reach due East towards Finland and the Gulf's middle for the feeling of an open sea out of land's sight, and then, depending on the breeze, a long run downwind home to Sundvall.

For the first few hours he was all nervously attentive, eyes and mind fixed on every detail of sail, of taut lines, the bounce of the helm, the wind vane and the compass, until it grew familiar, joyful and then at ease. What luck, he thought, what a wonderful thing it was to be alive and doing this.

Midday, and he made the turn Eastward towards Finland, eighty nautical miles across the Gulf, and decided to test the wind-vane self-steering autopilot. Cautiously he set and engaged it while removing his hand from the tiller. The technology delivered. It worked. Holding a halyard, he stood on the leeward gunwale for a pee, went quickly down to the cabin to grab the sandwich and his hat, and returned to the helm greatly impressed at the possibility of solitary hands-free sailing, while always remaining attentive.

For the next few hours in the cockpit, at one with the boat, Reuel was alone with his thoughts. The experience was radically different than riding in a bus, or being a passenger in a plane. The solitary nature of his presence within the vastness of the watery space around him unified and accented the passage of space and time, and produced an unprecedented mental plane of self-awareness. He could not sense what he was, and rather than feeling lost it was as if he had momentarily disappeared. As if he was non-existent. As if he was in contact with the calm emptiness of the universe. Yet as soon as he tried to hold on to the feeling it escaped. What remained was only a watery hiss and light slap of wavelets against the hull.

He considered his life. Ulla's displeasure at his frequent irritability and bouts of impatience accompanied by bursts of anger. The scorn he felt towards his laboratory colleagues at their superficial hackwork of research attempts to connect brain and instruments with mind. And the futility of computer intelligence to explain the mind. The mysterious futility of talking about language itself, the mind's method of manufacturing thoughts, echoing Wittgenstein's conclusion: "Whereof one cannot speak, thereof one must be silent." Was this a stark message rendering much of human life to be unspeakable? Was that so pessimistic? Was Phra Luang's silent meditative awareness more beneficent than this?

Why did he stop kissing Linnea? What did he mean when he told her he was becoming a Buddhist? Was it conscience? The fabrication of a raft called super-ego by an intuition of emptiness? The brain's hard-wiring for survival? Or just his way to avoid getting into trouble with Ulla? So many words chaining themselves into questions which rattled in his brain. He had never experienced the intensity of so much solitary introspection. He had always coasted along with the flow, somewhat uninterested in self-examination. What was there to examine? Something called a self which was a non-self? It was fatiguing. What was clear to him was that he was approaching a turning point in his life. All till now had been youthful folly.

Near mid-afternoon he was ready to make the turn homeward, but decided to stop and enjoy a breather. He pointed the bow up into the breeze, lowered the luffing mainsail and jib, and let the Saga float, "in irons", on the gentle swells, hands free. This was a chance to examine the vessel below deck, stern to stem. The master's cabin was directly below the tiller and had a duplicate compass fastened to the low ceiling. The adjacent companionway had a hatch down to the engine compartment. Forward of that was the main cabin with a passageway between an ample galley on one side and a pair of bunks on the other, with a tiny toilet on the far side. A hatch led below to a storage compartment of fluids and victuals. Then a watertight bulkhead, open to an inventory of marine equipment, then another with two bunks and the last space, at the stem, holding the boat's hawsers and anchors. A ceiling hatch opened to the main deck, up through which Reuel crawled and from there to stretch out on the bowsprit extended forward over a sturdy safety net. Oh, how to own a craft like this, he thought. He rolled over to lay on his back and examined the clear blue sky.

Offered this voluntary absence of activity on a quiet sea, Reuel tried the reputed mind-calming practice of observing his breath, and allowing the sloop to have a meditation of its own, resting on the slow undulations of the Gulf's breathing. And like himself, soon ready to return to the world of human activity, which, as he recollected, the Buddhists called "*samsara*".

After some time, he started the diesel for a minute to put some way on, raised the jib to turn her, hauled up the mainsail, cut the engine, studied the compass and let Saga fly, dead-run, wing on wing, homeward bound to the next chapter of his life.

Months passed. Reuel was living alone in an attractive rented apartment near IBM's Swedish headquarters, had purchased a used Volvo, and fed himself at a handful of eating establishments where he had become a familiar client. He enjoyed an almond roll and coffee and the International Herald Tribune at daybreak; grazed in the IBM cafeteria at midday; and considered his frequent dining alternatives for the evenings. A choice basically between carrying a take-out sandwich, beer and a pastry to the apartment; or eating out with a book for seafood, meat, or Asian; or, when in pursuit of female companionship, selecting a high-tone establishment with a dress code. Creating cooked food eluded him, although he knew to immerse plastic envelopes of frozen meals in boiling water. He had heard talk that the Svedatek company had invented a countertop device employing microwave frequency radiation to warm or heat packaged meals at room or refrigerated temperatures but had not seen one. Swedish television news remained incomprehensible. On the whole, given the domestic arrangements alongside his intellectual interests, Reuel was not at all uncomfortable with solitude, but was lonely for America.

Following quarrels with Ulla of increasing frequency he had moved out. They stayed friends but had shifted gears. Everyone understood they were not married and this type of situation was not uncommon in Sweden. The twins were still too young to comprehend such social dynamics. Moreover, a violinist named Lennart Bjork from the Stockholm Symphony had become a daily practice partner with Ulla, and frequently stayed for dinner.

The emotional reverberations of this situation were mitigated by Reuel's absorption in his new job at IBM. Lars allowed him a free-ranging research scope to determine if he could find a future area of interest to the company. It took several months for Reuel to become current with the state-of-the-art of the rapidly growing computer industry. Learning how to parse on-line calculations in algebraic language and to define terms of commands in symbolic instruction codes for the general syntax of time-sharing machine language became a pleasing self-instructional assignment which he enjoyed. IBM was becoming his graduate university.

Before long he started concentrating on the development of a heuristic computer algorithm which could search large scale encoded "knowledges" or data-bases. His trial algorithms could not guarantee a precise search but could reduce the number of possible searches by discarding unlikely and irrelevant solutions. This self-instructional challenge in developing appropriate computer languages led Reuel, and many others, to confront the question of whether humanistic characteristics of intelligence could be added to machine behaviors. In short, could machines think? This question led to a scientific domain named "artificial intelligence," and was a toy simulacrum for Reuel's ongoing curiosity about thought, language and the human brain.

During this period, he had engaged in several romantic liaisons. On two occasions with IBM co-workers which had devolved into friendships with sporadic sexual privileges. And once with Linnea. He had been window shopping on a Saturday in the city's old town, Gamlastan, when he passed Linnea's boutique, saw her within, waggled his fingers, and was beckoned. This led to dinner and then to her bedroom. Then, after having fulfilled their allotted functions, normalized their breathing, and had just now become intimates, Linnea inquired of him.

"Do you remember that night on the Saga when I asked why you had stopped kissing me? You said you were becoming a Buddhist. What did that mean?"

"I thought you were asking about the meaning of sex. I think I was saying that sex was empty of absolute meaning. Even to having children. I believe that's a Buddhist point of view."

"You talk and talk, but what about pleasure?"

"That's in the relative sphere of desire, lust, craving, and attraction, all of which lead to unhappiness."

"But we just enjoyed ourselves!"

"It will pass and then you will want more and won't be able to get it."

"And love?"

"Leads to heartbreak."

"Then why on Earth would anyone want to be a Buddhist?"

"That's a very good question."

"You are a sly one."

They parried and riposted in this way for a while and finally fell asleep together. The next day, after Linnea made them breakfast, she casually informed him that Ulla was sleeping with Lennart Bjork.

"Oh, my" he said with a painful sigh.

"Heartbreak?"

"A little, it is just as I said."

She took on the role of an older sister and insisted they go out to walk in the wintry air and heal themselves. Had he been to the Ethnographic Museum? No? She insisted. Father was a distant cousin of the Hedin family, and the museum was full of Buddhist artifacts collected by the famous Tibetan explorer, Sven Hedin. A bit of a Nazi, unfortunately. Following several hours in the museum Reuel was relieved that it surprisingly took his mind off Ulla and ignited within him a curiosity and long-lasting desire to travel to Asia, to India.

Yet on Monday, he was at his desk with feet up on the window-sill, wondering about the problem of producing the equivalent of painful feelings in a machine, the absurd challenge of artificial sentience. Feelings. Different than thought. How to write a paper on wet machines?

IBM however had other ideas for him. A team had recently arrived from the US and had been conferring with Lars Soderberg for several days when Reuel was summoned to hear the news.

"Reuel, my boy, it's one of two things. They genuinely like your theoretical work on artificial intelligence and would definitely like to support it. However, you would have to move to IBM's research center in Yorktown Heights, New York. A small raise and all expenses of moving the family. But it's a no-go here in Stockholm. If you want to stay here, they have me move you to marketing and sales engineering support. That would mean a big raise, a secretary and two new hires for you. You'd be working for clients like Ericsson, Volvo, Electrolux, SAS airlines, and the Sveriges Riksbank. That's the oldest central bank in the world, you know. For someone as young as you that could be a pretty feather in your cap. A fabulous career move. They might even make you my boss one of these days!"

"When do I have to decide?"

"Best by year's end. Late November now. I know it's short, but try to let me know before the holidays. Everything's useless after Christmas. Talk it over with your wife. It's a high-class decision either way. Good on you."

He took the rest of the day off and walked to the Ethnographic Museum again. The strange cultural exhibits were entrancing. The exciting story of the Hedin explorations to Tibet made him feel like a minor serf in an office-bound white-collar bureaucracy. Working for a big company was not at all what he had planned for himself. He had planned not to make plans. IBM would mean a loss of independence. He would be a wage-slave working in the court of an emperor. A high-class clerk. A cog in the wheel. Bureaucrats would end up controlling his thoughts. When he himself could not control his thoughts. There had been more freedom as a junior researcher at the Karolinska. He wanted to chase girls. He wanted to study Buddhism. He wanted to go sailing in the South Seas. He wanted to daydream about language and the brain. He wanted to see Mongolia. Ulla would never go to Yorktown Heights. He was tired of Sweden. The twins would never remember him. He wanted to be in bed with Linnea. His mind was racing. It felt like looking at life though a kaleidoscope. What was it all about? Chaos. Ontological nebulosity. Indecision. Time. "The world is everything that is the case."

He was suddenly only conscious of himself standing in the ethnographic museum staring through a wall mounted vitrine enclosing a fantastical Tibetan scroll painting of a wild and naked red female with three eyes, a necklace of skulls, apparently dancing on the corpse of a dwarf in the center of a field of blazing fire. His mind had unexpectedly stopped, becoming one-pointed and transfixed, effortlessly aware of a wordless space between mystery and meaning.

He decided not to decide. To do nothing and let events take their course. "Choiceless awareness" as someone remarked. He met and shared intimate pleasure with an art student from Uppsala, who then disappeared from his life. There was a big snow which embedded his Volvo. President Kennedy had been assassinated. A male co-worker invited him home for dinner. Their adolescent children practiced their English on him. The wife offered to teach him ice skating. They insisted the new American President from Texas was a warmonger. Ulla informed him he was expected for Christmas dinner. Lars Soderberg said nothing yet about Reuel's employment decision.

Christmas eve dinner at the Bergstroms was a jolly affair. Reuel was at peace and the recipient of warmth. All the women were happy and busy. The twins, more than a year old, clearly weren't sure they recognized him. Erik Anderson had come down from Sundsvall. He had sold the Saga to a French banker for a nice profit and was thinking of a new boat, a ketch. They drank lots of Aquavit, carved up a goose, and sang Swedish carols. Linnea kept a distance but winked surreptitiously and smiled privately at him once or twice. Lennart Bjork, years Reuel's senior, who was living there, came over carrying one of the twins. Reuel wasn't sure if it was Karen or Kristina. The infant's eyes were absorbed in comparing the faces of the two men. Lennart was extremely friendly and quizzed him about American politics. Ulla joined them briefly and they discussed Bach's mathematical imagination. Lennart complained that Ulla refused to join his chamber music quartet which had a vacancy and was seeking a second violin. Soloism was not open to discussion, she demurred. Reuel began to feel more like her older brother, thinking Lennart would be a good match. On the way back to his apartment he found himself wondering why he rarely thought about Buddhism despite its philosophical weightiness. Did Christians or Jews or Muslims also rarely think about their faiths? And when they all did so, what were the circumstances eliciting that awareness?

Then it was New Year's Eve. Linnea had asked him over. There were two other couples. An old boyfriend with his new lady and a pair who managed her boutique. Very nice people, friendly adult conversations which easily vanished from memory, who left separately before midnight to attend other events. Was boredom of others just a sign of rudeness, due to lack of curiosity? Such speculations, however, vanished when Linnea and Reuel hastened to bed to enjoy themselves.

Later, upon pillow talk, he spoke of IBM and the choice facing him. She sat up and lit a cigarette before speaking.

"Unlike me, you are still young and free. You don't know how fortunate you are. You don't need IBM. They need you more than you need them. And to tell you the truth, I don't think Sweden is good for you. We are an old and stiff culture. We don't change our ways easily. America is a rather new turbulent experiment. You will thrive there. You are a mentally and physically seductive boy. Intellectuals and women will find you attractive. Go home Reuel. Some day when you are older you can invite me."

"It's a deal" he said.

In January Reuel made two decisions. The first was to return to America. The second was to return to academic life. Informing Lars Soderberg and IBM of this, he fashioned his curriculum vita, added exhibits of his work, wrote a three-page application essay to the graduate faculties, and sent twin packages off to Caltech in Pasadena, California and to MIT in Cambridge, Massachusetts.

In February, Ulla informed him that she was pregnant again. Lennart was the father to be. And on this occasion, she had agreed to be married in the *Svenska Kyrkan*, the Evangelical Lutheran national church, inasmuch as Lennart and his family were rather old-fashioned. Reuel was expected to serve in the bridal party and to carry the twins in his arms down the aisle. The wedding would be in May.

In March, he received letters of acceptance from both Caltech and MIT as a pre-doctoral candidate and gave notice of this to IBM. Soderberg sent him an effusive letter of congratulations, urging him to stay in touch with the company, and signed off on a termination bonus of two-months' salary. Then, after weighing the alternatives Reuel decided for MIT. Unlike California, where he had never been, the East coast and its institutions were familiar, and closer to Europe, for whatever that might mean. He wrote a grateful note to Caltech informing them of his choice.

At leisure for some weeks to wrap up his affairs, to make farewells with all the Bergstrom sisters and his tiny daughters, to have decent lunches with Lennart, now step-father of the twins, package his possessions, sell the Volvo, book his flight from Stockholm to Boston, and make inquiries for student housing in Cambridge, he experienced a deserved feeling of freedom and a sweet experience of anticipation.

A visit with Phra Luang was one of the few remaining thoughts before departure. This was easily arranged and once again they sat face to face across cups of tea and a plate of cookies. Reuel informed the retired Thai monk of all that had happened since their last meeting. He frequently asked himself what it meant to be a Buddhist. Could one pick and choose from pieces of the faith? There was no apparent act of conversion, merely of selective adhesion. Was that not so? He left the question hanging in the air as Phra Luang took his time in a lengthy silence before answering.

"Look, many people consider themselves to be part of an organized, well-established religion but do not know much, or indeed anything, about its past, its founders and prophets, or its precepts. Millions of illiterate Hindus have never read the *Bhagavad Gita*; many Christians deny that Jesus was a Jew; many Muslims drink alcohol. Likewise, many of the ninety percent of Thais who are Buddhists actually know less about Buddhism than you or I. This does not demean them. You know, fish are not experts at hydrodynamics. Many times, adherents to a religion may not even understand its principles. In most religions, its ancient canonical texts are incomprehensible to ordinary people.

Most people belong to a religion not by individual choice but just through historical accident and social conformity."

"Well, can I call myself a Buddhist?" asked Reuel.

"Look my friend, you are an American. I can only tell you about Buddhist culture in Thailand. Everyone there knows the five vows. Don't lie, don't steal, don't commit adultery, don't kill living things, and don't get drunk. Slightly similar to the Ten Commandments which provide people with a short guide to ethical conduct. Perhaps you might say that breaking a commandment is like sinning, and that breaking a vow is more like blundering. Maybe Buddhism is more forgiving. There is only a small difference between saying "thou shalt not' as an absolute, and saying you should avoid something, like 'avoid drunkenness' for the sake of your own health and happiness, not because drinking alcohol is an a priori and absolutely immoral."

"Isn't that like saying vows are more like recommendations rather than commandments?"

"Perhaps. You know many Thais eat meat and drink whiskey. Many Thai men and women have been sexually unfaithful. And while Thais may not lie or steal so much, their ideas of truth and private property are slippery at times. What is called 'Karma' in Sanskrit is always there. While the connection between action and consequence isn't set in stone, it exists more or less. Think of it in the practical way Buddhists speak of 'accumulating merit'. Like having good health habits. As if you had a spiritual bank account. Doing harmful things are like withdrawals; creating merit is like a deposit. You try to keep your soul in the black, so to speak."

"What about worship?"

"Ah yes. I admit that is problematic. Like many other Buddhists, Thais worship the Buddha in a way he would not have favored, that is, as if he were a god. That is just culture by simple people. Even though we know he was a man who lived a life on earth like any other human. But like Jesus or Moses, their godliness remains a subject of debate. Human beings, both wicked and virtuous, and their differing cultures had existed for many millennia before the birth of those enlightened teachers. And the profound teachings that were offered since those times have only had a mixed or limited sense of absorption. Few Catholics understand Aquinas but they understand charity and the ten commandments; few Buddhists understand the theory of interdependent co-origination but they probably remember the eightfold path. Few Catholics practice austerity, few Buddhists practice meditation. On the whole, speaking for myself, I only teach what is called 'the path of the middle way'. That doctrine is probably most suitable for sentient beings in this inescapable world of relativity."

"So, who can be a Buddhist religious teacher in America today, in modern times, when that ancient spiritual Dharma only arrived to our country less than a century ago?"

"It is difficult to answer that. We are living in a Dharma-ending age, after all. Many so-called teachers are ignorant, or dishonest, or are egotistical and vain, seeking fame and followers, or are sexually abusive, or cheat, or take what is not theirs. They are only frail human beings."

"What advice can you give me?"

"Believe it or not, you are already more learned than most Buddhists in Asia. You like to talk about philosophy. They lack your curiosity, your thirst for understanding. Once you know the truth of suffering, know it deeply, you will accomplish a great deal. The way to gain that comprehension, that realization, is said to 'know thyself'. That simple teaching is the basis of all the world's wisdom traditions. But what is the self that it can be known? Is it just a body? What is that? Just levels of atoms, molecules, cells, tissues, organs, bones which somehow produce feelings and memories. Where then is that mind thirsting for truth? Where is the mind that observes the mind?"

"But that's my question to you."

"Yet the answer becomes a question itself. Find the mind that observes the mind. Make experiments. You are a scientist. Observe trial and error in yourself. You are a laboratory. You are still young and unformed. Perhaps if you are very lucky you will find a professor, a teacher, to help you."

Reuel thought about this conversation on the flight to Boston. The aspiration to keep a Buddhist approach to his life felt exotically Asian and not well grounded in his thoughts. Yet he was committed to be patient and open-minded. More pressing was his financial outlook. At very least, an ascetic penny-pinched doctoral degree would probably lead to a decent paying job in the fast-moving computer industry. Buddhism could just be an undertone.

❦

At MIT, he faced three years of graduate courses before commencing a Ph.D dissertation. The first year was fulfilling, and affirmed his capabilities in mathematical logic and historical linguistics. He enjoyed a summer internship at a robotics laboratory. The following year was intellectually challenging, with courses in electrical engineering and emerging issues in hardware development and miniaturization. He could foresee a future when general purpose computers could be portable and use a standard basic programming language. Also, he was fortunate in gaining periodic relief from his labors by means of revivifying sexual intimacies shared with several female graduate students who also sought such soothing comforts.

Confident in his progress Reuel relaxed the following Summer. He took up a new fashion called "jogging" on the paths along the Charles River, joined a "health club" featuring a pool and a weight room, and commenced a lifetime of morning calisthenics focusing on his spine and abdomen, his "core". Boston Harbor Boat Rentals provided a day-sailer several times when the weather was perfect and a female companion was willing.

Thoroughly restored, Reuel began his final pre-doctoral year of course-work. MIT's Visiting Professor, Desmond Muircheartaigh, from Ireland's York University, was presiding at the initial day of a weekly two-hour seminar. He had switched off the fluorescent ceiling fixtures when he entered the room opining that such lights impaired clear thinking. Candle light was best, he offered, but that was too much to ask. Nine graduate students sat on uncomfortable chairs around a beat-up rectangular table. One of its four corner legs was off by an inch which put paper cups of tea or coffee at hazard. The room felt cramped and cold and faced a dark Northern sky.

The students were asked to introduce themselves. They went around the table. Two females, six males. The first to speak was the short, slightly heavyset attractive woman with blue eyes, dark hair cut-short, a foreign accent and a reddish scar along her jaw below the ear. Reuel couldn't take his eyes off her.

"My name is Esther Halevi. I'm a visiting Fulbright Scholar at Harvard Law School, next door, where I am enrolled for a Master's degree. I am a graduate of the law faculty at Ben Gurion University in Israel and a member of the Tel Aviv Bar. My specialty is intellectual property law, patents, copyright, trade secrets and things like that. My interest at MIT and this seminar is to become acquainted with emerging innovations in computer science. And, forgive me if I may be so bold, Professor, how do you pronounce your name? I've only seen it in the course catalogue."

"Moriarty. Like Sherlock Holmes' opponent. Next."

They went around the table. There was Irving Susskind, an overweight logician visiting from Harvard's philosophy department who was completing a dissertation on Ludwig Wittgenstein. Next was Taghi Farvar, a bearded naturalized mathematician immigrant from Iran, and PhD candidate at MIT. Next was grey-haired Bernard Wilkinson, clearly the oldest student, who merely said he was on leave from the government, without further comment. Everyone understood this to mean he was from one of the intelligence agencies. There was Mei-Mei Szeto, a skinny Chinese American girl, with an undergraduate degree from Yale, and like Reuel among the youngest of the group. Next was athletic looking Herman Allione, an electrical engineer on leave from Raytheon Corporation to MIT to survey cutting edge technologies, and finally, the short and skinny and intense looking Walter Dowfeld, who described himself as a computer games hobbyist, and was seeking a Master of Science degree. And there was Reuel who disposed of himself in a sentence or two.

At the seminar's outset Professor Muircheartaigh acknowledged there was a lengthy tradition in philosophy, religion, psychology, and cognitive science about what constitutes a mind and what were its distinguishing properties. That was not to be a matter for this seminar. The name of the Seminar was "Machine versus Natural Language" and Professor Muircheartaigh said the task of this first day of the seminar was to discuss and by a majority vote put MIT's defining imprimatur on the well-known acrostic "NLP". There was one faction "out there" which insisted it stood for neuro-linguistic-programming; and there was another which claimed it referred to natural-language-processing. The final vote at day's end was 6-2. Reuel and Esther Halevi were the two for neuro-linguistics, the others carried the day. A few days later there was a half-humorous item in MIT's student newspaper "The Tech" which informed the readership that according to a graduate seminar on the question, *ipse dixit,* the acrostic NLP should henceforth be understood as referring to Natural Language Processing. And so, it became the touchstone.

At the end of the second week Reuel and Esther joined one another for coffee. They enjoyed a wide-ranging discussion wherein Reuel described his background, his interest in language and the human brain, in psycho-linguistics, his decision to reject medical school in favor of neuroscience at the Karolinska, his year at IBM, and his taking an academic gamble at MIT. He described frustration with the field of artificial intelligence and so-called thinking-machines. His real interest was in wet machines that could feel and originate thoughts and which socialized by signaling other "wet" machines with discrete sounds, which were called "words".

Esther told him of her family, her mother, a violinist, who was killed in a terrorist bombing. Her father, an immigrant from Russia, started as an electrician who became a computer hobbyist. Now he had a business that sold, constructed, and repaired computers which had then shaped her interest in technology. He was now a captain in the military reserves and had played a role in the Israeli army's early transition to solid-state computing innovations in cryptology after the development of integrated circuits. She learned LISP, the list-programming language, from him. Code-breaking was one of her high- school hobbies and in her required military service she was assigned to combat intelligence. She did an extra year of service and was discharged as a reserve lieutenant. Her experiences in military secrecy had led her to commercial issues in law school relating to eavesdropping, software piracy, copyright infringement, plagiarism of intellectual property, and so on, to becoming a lawyer.

They decided to go on and eat for an early pizza and found a place also serving red wine. After two glasses each, they found a joint track for amusement. In fact, they agreed that "amusement" was a sensed faculty of non-artificial intelligence, and thus possibly of mind. They concurred on the absence of good definitions of "intelligence" and "thinking" that were precise and general enough to apply to machines. Empathy and aesthetic sensitivity were obvious components of human intelligence, but not machine or artificial intelligence. This was even more so with a sense of humor. Then they began to laugh at examples of human folly that were actually unintelligent, and to the curious question of whether a machine could lie. Matters got even sillier when they got to the question of whether a machine could have a "mind". They were off to making competing registers evidencing the existence of a non-object called "mind". There was consciousness, imagination, perception, thought, reason, judgement, language, memory, ideas, emotion, contemplation, meditation, wit, brooding, pondering, surmising, laughing, introspection, deduction, supposing, conjecturing, anticipating, reckoning, concluding, reflecting, opining, deeming, judging, considering, concentrating, cogitation, studying, recalling, visualizing, instinct, wisdom, fantasizing, reconsidering, pretending, hoping, dreaming, day-dreaming, assuming, conceiving, inventing, understanding, intending, attention, sanity, joking, wishing, caring, annoying, approving, disliking, boring, disapproving, forgetting, when their list finally began thinning out. There was a side discussion over whether "mindless" would qualify and a deadlock on whether "brainstorming" should be admitted, except as a metaphor. He was an empiricist he insisted, and under the scientific physicalist interpretation, the so-called "mind" was produced by the brain. There was no other realm. Dualism was not permitted. She was not so sure, what about information?

They walked, maintaining their jollity, back towards her Harvard campus and as they passed Memorial Hall, which housed the psychology department, they saw a crowd of students waiting to enter. A glass framed announcement-board revealed the matter. In vertical white plastic letters, it read: "Tonight at 7:30 pm. -Assistant Professor Dr. Robert Adler -Title of his talk: PSYCHEDELICS or Mind-Manifesting Chemicals." After what they had just been discussing a mention of "mind-manifestation" was irresistible.

The audience filled the large room and was composed largely of undergraduates. Professor Adler's entrance was greeted by loud applause and a few cheers. One gained an immediate impression that "psychedelics" were a fact of first-hand experience for many of the youthful attendees. Adler was clearly appreciative of his reception and laughed and waved as he waited for the room to quiet down.

He was a young and pleasant looking man of medium height, with wire-rimmed glasses and a head of curly hair. He arrived onstage by dragging a small folding chair to the front of the platform and took a moment to push the lectern far to the rear. Eschewing any sign of academic costume, de rigueur in those days, he was in khaki slacks and a crimson sweatshirt emblazoned with the word HARVARD. Laughing softly all the time.

"Before I begin - you know I used to take cello lessons when I was a kid - I learned about tuning the instrument. So, before anything more let's all get on the same wavelength and chant the sound of the universe for a bit. OM, pronounced A U M, which is said to be it. And I'm sure you've all heard the expression 'Om is Where the Art is.' Right?"

He held up a finger as if he was the conductor of an orchestra and on the downbeat, he began in a melodic baritone: "aaahhuuuooommm." The room filled with the sound, and the volume grew palpably and increasingly resonant as the combined asynchronous individual voices were merged. Reuel and Esther joined in heartily.

It ended naturally on his signal, and he continued. "I'll bet they never heard that sound in Memorial Hall previously, in this hallowed birthplace of

American psychology. You know, William James used to speak here and talked about getting high on the newly discovered gas nitrous oxide. He actually said it was a variety of religious experience. Well, have times changed? Probably, and I have a special announcement to tell you about in a minute or two, but first, I'd like to tell you how I come to be here."

The audience settled down and the hall became noticeably quiet. Adler allowed a long moment of silence to ensue as his eyes appeared to look at every face.

"I was born in Rochester, New York, where my father, too old for the army, was the top lawyer for the electrical utility company. My mother worked for the Red Cross during the war and afterwards tried helping wounded veterans who had something that was then called 'shell shock.' She was the one who told me I should be a psychologist. So that's what I did. I got a PhD and instead of becoming some kind of therapist, I got my first job as a psychology instructor at Cornell. I published a few papers and then got hired with a tenure-track faculty position here at Harvard. And I had a colleague named Tommy O'Reilly, now in Mexico, whom many of you may have heard of. Well, he was interested in plants and fungi that screw around with your mind, like peyote, ayahuasca, maybe marijuana, and some kinds of mushrooms. When I say 'screw around' I mean only those plant compounds which actually appear to allow you to observe your own brain. Those are the compounds which we now call 'psychedelic'. And definitely do not refer to those plants which prevent you from looking at yourself, like opium. And after all, we knew that these kinds of psychoactive plants had been around for thousands of years, but weren't being studied scientifically. Getting a handle on dosage, for instance. So, some of us began to think there had to be chemical and molecular analogues which might provide interesting discoveries for psychologists, and even psychotherapists, to explore. That's when we realized that research chemists could provide us with pharmaceutical grade compounds like mescaline, psilocybin, and lysergic acid, among others. Of course, after experimenting on ourselves we made the discovery that we had blown our own minds. And there was no coming back." The audience broke up in laughter, and Adler started laughing more loudly than anyone.

"Well, I can't tell you how much we wanted to share these epic discoveries with the entire world. We felt like missionaries. As if, with a bit of courage about hallucinating, and transcending the weird unfamiliarity, it was a method to experience love and compassion and understanding of the entire universe just by swallowing a pill. Wild! We needed some kind of data on social consequences. So, we arranged a few experiments, on convicts in a prison, on priests in a church, and on undergraduates in a university. It made the newspapers, as all of you know, and we were suddenly treated as dangerous madmen. And so, this morning, Dean Howard, of Arts and Sciences, informed Tommy and myself that we were terminated from our faculty positions at Harvard. Fired. Told to clean out and vacate our offices by December 31."

A chorus of boos greeted this announcement, but Adler continued to laugh softly. Reuel and Esther looked at one another with raised eyebrows. Adler continued to talk, promising the audience that he would not be silenced in the future on the subject of mind-manifesting chemicals and that he would be speaking around the country throughout the following year, having been invited by numerous student organizations who were eager to hear what he had to say. Continuing to speak to the audience at Memorial Hall he related several jokes describing humorous stories about being under the influence of Lysergic Acid. Such as the tale of the hippie babysitter who put the infant in the oven and a turkey in the bassinet, or the man who did so many trips his couch had seatbelts, or the woman who lost weight because a dragon was guarding the refrigerator, or the fellow who thought the garden hose was a snake, and so forth.

Turning serious, Adler tried to describe what people called a "mystical experience", saying it might be a case of recreational mysticism. He stopped laughing and took a long pause.

"What is mysticism anyway? They say it's an absorbed union with the absolute. A self-surrender into a region inaccessible to the intellect. A transcendence of time and space into a profoundly positive feeling of understanding everything. A religious ecstasy. An ineffable feeling of the sacredness of reality and its paradoxical transience." He paused here for a moment. "You get the picture, but I'm not really sure what these beautiful fancy words mean. I hear those words in my head. I actually hear them when I'm thinking. I can hear the molecules talking to me."

It was Adler's anecdotes concerning auditory hallucinations that brought Reuel to the edge of his seat. Adler spoke convincingly about hearing grass grow, of having a voice coming out of a particular cumulus cloud talking clearly to him saying that he was wasting his life by just sunning himself in the back yard. And attempting to meditate while hearing his own voice shouting at him. He tried to explain these mental phenomena by postulating that the auditory cortex of his brain had actually taken over his mind. "What were thoughts anyway?" he asked. "Coded noises. I was having them in English, and I certainly couldn't have them in Chinese because I don't know a word of Chinese. I tried having thoughts in French which I studied in high school, but it was hopeless trying to think in French. I only have English speaking thoughts. Go figure."

This brought Reuel to close attention. He turned to Esther saying "I've got to go see that guy."

At the end, as they walked to Esther's apartment, they shared a feeling that they were missing something bold underway in America's youth culture. Discussion on this matter continued until her front door, where after a pregnant moment's pause, she asked if he would like to come in for a cup of tea. Half an hour later he moved from a chair to sit next to her on a small sofa and in moments leaned close to kiss her softly on the ear. Thereafter the autonomous evolutionary force of sexual arousal began its work, and before very long the mutual intimate and naked excitation of the flesh and its unique physical pleasure was underway.

When it was lovingly over, both of them relaxing in the afterglow, he ran his fingers over a serrated ridge of pink scar tissue which ran from elbow to shoulder on her right arm, and to above her breast where he touched a shallow puckered groove of rough skin.

"What happened?" he asked.

"Shrapnel. A single mortar round hit the lorry outside our unit's tent. My boyfriend was killed. I happened to be sleeping with my arm up. A few more inches and...." she left the phrase unfinished.

"Who did it?"

"Whoever it was. Someplace across the line in Gaza. Just a single round in the middle of the night. During a long truce. No combat. Just one round in peace time. Very normal."

"Hard to believe such a thing."

"Are you a pacifist?"

"Definitely not. Why do you ask?"

"You talked about Buddhism a lot."

"It's just an intellectual interest. About its theory of mind."

"Do you do drugs?"

"Vodka. Aquavit when I was in Sweden. Pot once in a while when someone passes me a smoke. How about you?"

"Also, once in a while. Hashish from Lebanon. *Shisha* from hookah, the water pipe. Also, alcohol sometimes, *slivovitsa*, plum brandy when among the orthodox."

"Psychedelics?"

"Not yet, but who knows? So far, the whole thing sounds like recreational mysticism to me. And you?

"Haven't tried it yet. But I'm curious."

The following day, academically sober, he sent a note addressed to Adler explaining that he was a doctoral candidate at MIT working in the area of psycholinguistics and would like to meet Dr. Adler before he departed from Harvard. He received a courteous reply offering regret at being out of town imminently, but would be happy to meet with Reuel following his return from Mexico in several months. He provided a mail address so they could stay in touch and added that Reuel's psycholinguistic research interests might indeed benefit from insights offered by the psychedelic experience. He looked forward to their meeting. Reuel wrote back expressing his appreciation.

At the next weekly meeting of MIT's "Machine versus Natural Language" seminar, Muircheartaigh asked each of the participants to describe their academic interest in greater detail. It was Reuel's turn. He sat tilting his chair back on its rear legs and rocked slightly as he spoke, animating his description with facial expressions and occasional hand gestures.

"Whatever is likely to happen in the future, decades from now, when you will probably be able to talk to a computer. But when you examine today's machine challenges in processing natural language you see numerous problems. Like machine recognition of human speech rather than just noise, having a machine process speech segments, recognizing sentence breaks, morphemes, words, parts of speech like verbs and nouns, subject and object, as well as the induction of grammar, summarizing and chunking phrases, understanding lexical semantics, inflections, synonyms, processing word-sense and disambiguation, extracting meanings, slangs, generating translations, even processing optical characters from a text, and that crude but important analytic tool we call "parsing", in order to test the conformability of words to a logical grammar. So, at this moment I'm interested in parsing technology applied to computer programming languages. While the simplest kind of parsing focuses on relationships between words in a sentence, at a higher processing level parsing will likely focus on constructing a tree-like structure using a probabilistic context free grammar, a stochastic grammar. You follow? This leads us to parsing recursive hierarchies for machine programming languages. One can imagine a source code made of linked lists forming major data structures, which programmers can manipulate for new kinds of syntax, or a new domain-specific language. For example, it should be fairly easy to compile a class of so-called autoclitics such as "when", "not", "if", "unless", "until" and so forth. Right now, for example, we have several new programming languages, kinds of baby-talk, allowing us to have a written conversation with a computer. And allowing it to control another device, for example, to move small objects in different directions, up, down, sideways, and put them in a box, and even attach names to small collections.

This was recently done on a DEC PDP-6 with a graphics terminal. I know IBM is working hard at this. So, anyway, while I find this all fairly interesting, it's still a far cry as an analogue of thought, what's going on in the human brain, which is really my main interest. I'll leave things there for the moment."

Sitting next to Reuel, it was Esther's turn. She leaned forward, her elbows on the table, with a yellow pencil in her hand, which was used to emphasize a point or two.

"Well, it's very interesting for me to follow Reuel's presentation because it raises some important issues in what is called intellectual-property. Let us ask in the simplest language about having a legal right to an invention. Just the way you have a legal right to your pencil or your shoe. Intellectual property is a time-limited right to prevent copying in exchange for making a full-disclosure. Do you know that president Thomas Jefferson wrote the first patent law? Well, by now we have a fairly well-established body of law about these matters, and yet because of technology at places like MIT and IBM, we can see that we are entering uncharted legal territory. Recently, in England, a patent was granted entitled "A Computer Arrangement for the Automatic Solution of Linear Programming Problems". This invention concerned the improved use of hardware memory management for a method used to solve an optimization problem in linear programming. In other words, a solution which could be implemented purely by software means. This is probably an early software patent. It is a proprietorship in something purely intellectual. It is not just a manufactured thing, like Mr. Edison's light-bulb. What is needed to claim such a new form of intellectual property? Traditionally, the following: novelty, usefulness or utility, the realistic possibility of the idea being brought into actual practice, and its non-obviousness to a practitioner skilled in the relevant art, such as someone in the computer industry. And by the way, that right can even extend to novel and living compositions of matter, like an antibiotic or a genetic invention. Now, patenting is different from another form of intellectual-property called "copyright". Copyright protection exists the moment you fix an expression in some tangible medium. This means the moment you save your words on paper, or sound to a recording, or your source code to a memory disk, or if you sketch out artwork for your computer game character, you automatically have copyright protection without doing anything further. In other words, patents should be thought of as protecting ideas, whereas copyright only protects a particular expression of an idea. There is a third form of intellectual-property which is mostly of interest to lawyers, not scientists, and that is the area of trademarks and trade-secrets. So, I'll stop here. Technological innovation is very important in the Israeli economy so you can understand my interest."

The others took their turns. Susskind was interested in Turing's "imitation test". Farvar was interested in algebraic formulations. Szeto was interested in the history of science. Wilkinson described government requirements at the Social Security Administration and the Post Office Department. Allione's interest was in designing graphic cathode-ray tube displays rather than using printers. And finally, Walter Dowfeld, expressing himself with intense seriousness, explained that he was interested in machine-intelligence for entertainment purposes, specifically in the design of games.

As the seminar broke Dowfeld made straight for Esther and Reuel and asked if he could have a word with them. They adjourned to the graduate student's common room at the end of the corridor.

He explained to them that he had recently incorporated a small company in Massachusetts, called "Lingo Inc." with a little money from his family. He was the only employee but had been working on the commercial idea of word-games for nearly a year. Some of the games were well-known, some of the others he had invented, and still others remained to be designed but to which he had made-up names, which might yet be trademarked. He looked at a card from his pocket and recited the appellations: *Spellits, Logopogo, Dabble, Makeone, Scrabble, Slangit, Semantix, Bananagram, Crossword, Hangman, Adlibs, Decrypton, Anomiamatix, Rimes4times, Anagramistix, Funpuns, Homonymix, Toponymix, Grammarbammer, Multilingua, Codebrake, Palindromix, Neologo, Vocabulo, and Riddlepiddle.*

He explained that it should be possible to play these vocabulary development and language games with a keyboard and a graphical display and that he was working on a variety of revenue models. Reuel and Esther thought this was rather cute and the three of them took a few minutes finding entertaining examples and playing with the concept. They agreed that in the future it might even be possible to play some such games aloud involving synthetic spoken words, or computer-generated language sounds.

Dowfeld continued. He was convinced that Reuel's parsing of recursive hierarchical file schemas, might have great possibilities in future source-codes for computer programming-languages, but would be immediately valuable in designing and crafting word games for his company, Lingo Inc. And furthermore, that trademark and copyright issues were incredibly important to his business concept. He lacked cash but would it be possible to employ them in an ongoing relationship in different capacities for shares in his company? They scratched their heads and asked for a week to consider the matter.

That evening, for several reasons, Esther suggested writing up a patent application, even if it was likely to be denied. First of all, the mere act of filing such an application would establish "prior art" and defensively prevent anyone else from alleging "novelty". Second of all, it would usually take several years before the Patent Office would even make a preliminary determination. Third of all, even if the patent claim was eventually denied, the very appearance of a patent application over several years was a psychological asset which could have aspirational financial value to Dowfeld's enterprise. Therefore, if there was to be an ongoing relationship with Lingo, Reuel should negotiate with Dowfeld for shares of stock in his company. As for herself, returning to Israel in a few months, she would merely send Lingo Inc. a modest bill for assisting Reuel and for her advice on the matter of trademarks and copyright.

Early in the following week Reuel and Dowfeld met at a coffee shop and before long shook hands on a contractual arrangement. Reuel would be named Vice-President and Director of Research for Lingo Inc. He would receive 40,000 of the new company's initial common stock shares, theoretically valued at one dollar per share, and Dowfeld, who would remain President and CEO, would hold 60,000 shares. Reuel assigned all rights to his work on machine languages over to Lingo Inc. and over ensuing months he provided the company with advice and assistance on a pay-per-diem basis to develop a *source code* and a compiled machine language for its software game products. Then, in mid-December of that year, a monomaniacal fund-raising effort by Dowfeld resulted in the Boston based Cabot Adventurers Fund purchasing 30,000 shares of the common stock of Lingo Inc. for $450,000. Reuel logically concluded that his shares should theoretically, or nominally, be worth $600,000 although there were no buyers. Capitalism was amazing. Finally, Esther had sent Lingo a bill of $10,000 for her legal services, which was paid promptly. They celebrated toward year's end with a champagne and oyster dinner at Lockober's.

The social seasons of those days displayed growing signs of protests against the Vietnam War. President Johnson was visiting the troops. There was a new Pacem-in-Terris Pope, John XXIII. Dr. King and Robert Kennedy had been assassinated. There were student riots everywhere. Seven undergraduates were shot at Kent State University. Street drugs became commonplace. The Chicago seven trial introduced America to "beatniks". Songsters and poets were becoming political. Hippies were engaging in cultural subversion, and LSD was easily available.

And there was a letter from Adler to Reuel.

> Dear Reuel,
> Thank you so much for reaching out to me. I meant to write you again. And apologies for the length of time it took your letter to reach me. I've been moving around Mexico and a few of its glorious beaches while attempting to keep a journal of my experiences. It's a real pleasure these days to hear from a fellow academic, and particularly one with your unique research background and interests. As I've been effectively blackballed by the institutional establishment. Most of my fellow explorers of the psychedelic realm are typically non-intellectual but are usually intelligent lay persons, including artists, poets, and musicians, as well as several psychotherapists who practice "the talking cure". The few academic psychologists around who are interested in what I am exploring come from theoretical schools like social science and behaviorism, with little hands-on empirical experience in either neuroscience or its machine analogues. I feel confident your first-hand acquaintance with this new class of "mind-manifesting" molecules will be fruitful, both on a personal

and professional level. I am certain that Dr. Albert Hoffman of Sandoz, our Christopher Columbus, would agree.

Anyway, I'll be coming to my parents in Rochester via California sometime in May for a family visit. We own a sweet lakeside summer cottage not far away, and perhaps the two of us could get together there over the Memorial Day weekend and together undertake some joint exploration into outer-space. So, by all means, please write to me again at this same address and share your thoughts about consciousness and mind.

Stay happy,

Robert

Reuel writes back to Adler.

Dear Robert,

It's been a busy while since I wrote. Thanks for your very kind letter and invitation. Forgive me for the length of what follows. It should give you a picture of where I'm coming from and why I'm interested in the emerging opportunity to experience a psychedelic "session" with Dr. Hoffman's Sandoz product. I certainly look forward to seeing you and appreciate the opportunity for us to share a "trip" together over Memorial Day Weekend. I'm hopeful from what I have heard that this might generate some innovative views on the subject of consciousness. Today's academic approach to the conception of a disembodied "mind" is terribly superficial, from the physiological as well as machine analogue approaches. Subjectivity remains as elusive as ever. Moreover, in my opinion, we need to understand the relation of language to thought, before we can get a better handle on consciousness. I'll be doing lots of psycholinguistics with Chomsky so that might help me a bit as I'm thinking of how to frame my PhD dissertation with the correct intellectual jargon.

Given our limited current understanding, when we speak of "mind" we are only hinting at a state of awareness which is hierarchically above mere feelings. Some of my theoretical work is on hierarchies, so, "mind" is probably only like an epiphenomenon, more like a secondary incident of underlying neural networks. As if it's an upper-level emergent feature, occurring simultaneously with a base-level physiological condition, but not directly related to it. It may emerge from, but can't influence the underlying process. In general, we treat our mental states as byproducts of brain activity, so no kind of dualism gets involved. Furthermore, the emergence of the natural-language of our thought-stream simply evolves as an adaptive hominid heuristic, probably amplified in a burst by the evolutionary tool-kit assembly of our paleolithic ancestors. Natural language should be considered as an evolved element of a culture, or a group system of behavior. And one which grows and passes from one individual to another by non-genetic means, especially by sound imitation. You can understand how remote this is from machine language. I really look forward to a psychedelic look at these propositions. Natural-language looks like a game from which we are destined to try to find meaning.

Anyway, this just off the top of my head.

Stay sane,

Reuel

That winter ended with a Christmas card from Luca Baca. He was in Seville studying Pope Alexander VI's *Patronato Real* in the Spanish archives relating to missionaries in the new pagan world of the Americas, based on the Church's earlier experiences in Asia. He wrote: "First Franciscans, then Jesuits, then Dominicans, but the Capuchins finally get Tibet! Feliz y Próspero Año." In closing he mentioned the likelihood of his coming to Cambridge in September for a colloquium at Harvard Divinity School.

Reuel's last academic year was underway. He could see his future on the horizon. Likely a faculty teaching position someplace. Handsome grants for research. Publication in prestige journals. A tenured junior appointment at a great university. Ultimately a full professorship with an endowed chair. It was intoxicating, in fact a poisonous lure. At MIT Reuel had earned mental muscle from experiencing the practice of working at fever pitch. He had increased his pre-doctoral course load and was determined to be at the top of the grading curve. Rewarding praise from the faculty only caused him to redouble his efforts. He cut back on sleep and was growing a sparse and scraggly see-through beard. Intimacy with Esther was reduced to once every few weeks. She had her own imperatives at Harvard Law School. Lingo Inc. was elaborating Reuel's contribution to its programming code and hiring employees who required hand-holding from him. Its corporate charter was expanding beyond word-games. Its growing ambitions became demanding and rewarding. Dowfeld had him focused on proprietary "apprentice-friendly" styles of source-code for machine-language programming. Kang Laboratories on Route 128 was investigating the company and making inquiries. There was talk of a possible merger. Dowfeld told him of the possible value of the company's shares. It defied belief.

There was a brief note from Adler in San Francisco.

> Dear Reuel,
>
> Enjoyed your thoughtful letter. All's well. Life is fascinating. Mexico was productive, beautiful. Mystery of human consciousness, and feeling unhappy for example, is bewildering and seems unapproachable by science. Trust we're still on for Memorial Day weekend. Best way to get to my family place on Lake Minneka is by car. Attached is my hand-drawn map with my Rochester phone number for anything last minute. There's no phone at the cabin. Can you manage a rental? Otherwise you can take a bus to Ithaca and I'll drive us from there. Looking forward.
>
> In haste,
>
> Bob

More from Reuel.

> Bob,
>
> Thanks for writing. I was wondering if we were still on. While human language is a different subject, why shouldn't human consciousness also be approached by science? I'll admit that neuroscientists have only tackled the 'easy' part of the phenomenon of consciousness, namely "where in the brain does it arise?" Broca's and Wernicke's areas on the brain's left hemisphere for example. That is, we only asked which brain processes correlate with consciousness, not how they cause it. The hard part of the problem is how and why do these physiological processes produce a conscious state of mind? Because it's obvious that physiological processes don't produce consciousness the way a pancreas produces insulin. Consciousness isn't a thing but rather an experience, so we perceive it subjectively. While the "C" word arises from the existence of a brain, the question is really of the nature of brains, not of pancreases, or rocks. I point out that you can easily see and read and understand these very words on this piece of paper automatically without the experience of being "conscious". You don't experience being conscious when your brain causes you to stop at a red light. Consciousness is about awareness of the subjectivity of meaning, like unhappiness, not about being aware that the weather is good. So, I'm hoping to get an insight or two from our psychedelic experience together. I can't wait

to getting into discussing this stuff with you. MIT is full of mechanics studying mechanisms yet still can't explain why the experience of redness is "red". My only academic chore over the summer is to brush up on my German for the doctoral duo. I've got Italian in the bag.

Hope your lake isn't ice-cold,

Reuel

As summer approached Reuel began to feel he was being afflicted by brain-overuse-injury. Academic life was taking a toll on his athletic body as well. His physical strength diminished, as if from a body-underuse-injury. Ironically, he began to wonder if the intellectual fatigue was actually all worth it, when Dowfeld called to tell him that Kang Labs would be acquiring Lingo in an exchange of shares. While they would be barred from selling their shares for two years, the theoretical market value appeared surrealistic. Restored by such financial consequences, Reuel indulged himself and bought a second-hand white convertible Porsche roadster, advertised on a campus bulletin board. And with that, planned to drive to the lake-side rendezvous with Robert Adler in his trophy vehicle.

Not long thereafter, on a lovely weekday afternoon toward the middle of May, Reuel and Esther sat on their particular bench facing the Charles River. They had agreed to meet at that familiar seat, midway between the Harvard and MIT campuses to make a farewell. Esther was to fly out of Boston to Tel Aviv the following morning. And as there was no telling when they would meet again, they felt the weight of the occasion but avoided talking about it. What was there to say, though much to feel? They let the silence flow like the calm river before them. A few sculling crews were out, preparing for a distant collegiate regatta. They sat holding hands, quietly, contemplating the unrushed and poignant beauty in which they were momentarily suspended. As their moment of separation arrived, Esther turned to him with a wistful expression on her face.

"Reuel, my dear friend, I may be pregnant."

"Are you serious? That's incredible!"

"I think so. I've missed my period."

"Oh my God! What to do?"

"Don't worry, I'll take care of it."

"What do you mean?"

"I mean I'll take care of it. Don't worry."

"Where?"

She smiled, "In Zanzibar. They have good doctors there."

"Are you crazy?"

"I'm joking. Israel is famous for good doctors."

"It's you I'm worried about."

"Don't worry about me. I'll be fine."

"We're so young."

"We are not so young any longer."

"What to say?"

"Say *Mazel Tov.*"

It went on this way for several touching minutes, irreversibly, until they stood and tightly embraced, holding one another, their cheeks pressed together. As they turned to go their separate directions, she blew him a kiss with her fingers and said "I'll write to you." His pained eyes stared at her to fix an image in his memory, onto his brain, consciously, intentionally. He never heard from her again. But their son appeared years later.

On the morning before leaving for Lake Minneka, Reuel went food shopping and bought six lamb chops on the assumption there would be a barbecue grill, two cans of baked beans, a box of dried spaghetti, a large can of tomato sauce, a foot-long Italian salami, a large tin of sardines, a circle of Brie cheese, four Danish pastries, three chocolate bars, a jar of peanut butter, a jar of grape jelly, four poppy-seed bagels, a whole wheat loaf, one bottle of Aquavit and two bottles of Chianti. All was bagged tightly behind the passenger seat.

A grey sky threatened and he put the convertible top down before starting the 340 miles west out of Boston. At the top of his thoughts was a slight concern that LSD might affect his performance on the two-upcoming doctoral language proficiency examinations. He was certain to cruise through the Italian test, the house language of his parents, but his German needed attention. There was only his undergraduate year at Columbia and some clumsy Deutsche conversations on occasions at IBM Europe. Irregular verbs and the charming triad of *"der" "die"* and *"das"*. He had rehearsed samples from German philosophers, trying out a number of short texts pertaining to *"verstand"* and *"gedanke"* and *"vorschlage"*, into his Englished brain of thoughts and propositions. There was a pile of German vocabulary cards on the passenger seat, successfully memorized. He determined to inoculate himself with the seven top-level lemmas of Wittgenstein's *Abhandlung Logisch-Philosophische*, inscribing them in large letters on a paper fastened to the upside of the car's sun-visor. *Die Welt ist alles, was der Fall ist. // Was der Fall ist, die Tatsache, ist das Bestehen von Sachverhalten. // Das logische Bild der Tatsachen ist der Gedanke. // Der Gedanke ist der sinnvolle Satz. // Der Satz ist eine Wahrheitsfunktion der Elementarsätze. // Die allgemeine Form der Wahrheitsfunktion ist die allgemeine Form des Satzes. // Wovon man nicht sprechen kann, darüber mus man schweigen.* This, in addition to stopping at roadside coffee and rest-stops to scan his Xeroxed specimen paragraphs from a variety of German language writers on mental operations: Frege, Cassirer, Alzheimer, Freud, Popper, Kant, Jaspers, and Wernicke. He intended to knock the examiners dead.

Some seven hours later, exactly as drawn on Adler's diagram, an unmarked dirt driveway led the Porsche a quarter of a mile off the paved and narrow county road to a cabin at a granite cliff edge, eight feet above Lake Minneka. While the glacier-scoured "finger lakes" of New York State range in length between 10 and 40 miles, scattered to their South are several small lakes, scarcely more than fingernail clippings in comparison. Lake Minneka, nearly a curved mile long, rested in a State-owned forest preserve containing a few legacy private in-holdings.

That was on a late Thursday afternoon and Adler was waiting for him on the porch of a small rectangular bungalow. Adler had apparently arrived earlier on a motorcycle, parked on the grass. They shook hands warmly, described their drives, unloaded Reuel's groceries, inspected the pantries, described their travels, surveyed the view of the lake, and compared food rations. There was some duplication, but nothing mattered. As dusk arrived, they sat outside on wicker chairs sharing Reuel's Aquavit and Bob Adler's marijuana, getting to know one another.

They each liked the other in an instant. They were physically of the same size and Adler was but four months older than Reuel. Each had whizzed through early school days. They swapped childhood experiences, parental biographies, adventure stories, great teachers, interests in science, favorite foods, board games, comparing Mexico and Sweden, Cornell and Columbia, tennis and sailing. And when getting to the realm of sexual history, Adler obliquely said something to the effect that his amatory experience was theoretically gender-neutral but usually seemed to have a homosexual tilt.

"Any problem with that?" he asked.

"God, no. Definitely not. My best friend is gay. It's like blue eyes or brown eyes as far as I'm concerned. Just part of our humanity. Not a culture without it."

"Who was your friend?"

"Luke? Luca Baca. I do love him, but not erotically. My parents loved him. You would too. He's doing a doctorate on the missionary history of the Catholic Church in Buddhist countries."

"I'd like that. What about religion? Ever had a religious experience?"

"Never. But non-theistic Buddhism seems very sensible to me."

"Nothing spiritual, transcendent?"

"Maybe love of nature. At times while sailing. Nothing really mystical about that. I don't think my body has a soul, if that's what you're asking. We could talk about that."

"Let's save it for tomorrow."

They ended the evening with a snack of Oreo cookies, milk, and called it a night. Adler smoked a cigarette. Everything was on a single floor, two small bedrooms on either side of the living and kitchen area, all the windows facing the lake. This was to be the setting of a neurological adventure.

Reuel had a restless night, with broken sleep tinged with a mixture of anticipation and anxiety. Then, quietly, early before breakfasting, as the sun rose over the forested opposite shore, they both descended a weathered wooden ladder to a small tethered raft and had a brief, verbally enlivening, swim in the icy water.

Then, swathed in large bath towels, dried, face-to-face, steaming coffee mugs in hand they began the day.

"So, Reuel..."

"Call me Roo, everyone does."

"I'm Bob, the same. We're going to know one another much better by tomorrow. How did you sleep?"

"A bit restless. Slightly nervous probably. But looking forward."

"Understood. Let me share with you what I know about Acid, Lysergic acid. Including what I don't know about it. I don't know how it works, or how it acts on the brain. Maybe you'll be able to tell me. Over the last couple of years, I've used various psychedelics probably over forty times. Sometimes high doses, some low. It's changed my personality for the better, but that's another story. Anyway, looking ahead to our trip together I can tell you just a few things. I think we should start our session inside the cabin after dark. Probably best if we skip dinner. We can put some relaxing music on. I'm figuring we'll use a dose of 250 micrograms. This is from our last stash of Sandoz ampoules, so its pharmaceutical grade. We each get a treated sugar cube."

"What's a fatal dose?"

"Nobody knows exactly. From studies on mice, we might conclude a couple of thousand mikes, but I've had doses over 500 and I'm still here. A lot of kids play with low doses, 20 to 50, which is like a social party buzz, not very deep. Slightly altered sense of reality. Lots of laughing. Also, there are some guys with chemistry degrees who are now making the stuff. I'm told it's not that complicated. Seems to have the same effect as Sandoz. They soak a sheet of blotter paper and cut it up into little squares. And I've got some LSD pills called "orange sunshine", roughly 200 micrograms. Technically it's still legal, but Nixon's putting an end to that pretty soon. It'll always be available, I think. Like pot. Like booze under prohibition. Psychiatrists get a medical permit. I think of it as a trans-substantiating sacrament. Spiritual juice. The genie's out of the bottle. More effective than blood into wine."

"How long will it last?"

"Only a lifetime. Right now, I'd say the strongest part is about two or three hours, tapering off altogether in about eight to ten hours. Dawn tomorrow could be pretty spectacular."

"Will we be able to talk? I'm into neurolinguistics."

There was a long pause as Adler appeared to be considering how to answer.

"Well, I suppose we could talk, but I don't think we would want to. Speech can seem pretty shallow. I know this might sound weird but communicating might make you believe in mental telepathy."

"Can we walk around?"

"Sure, but I don't think we'd want to. Stumbling about in the woods after dark might be ridiculously distracting. Actually, it's a good idea that we both agree to stay in and around the cabin until it gets light tomorrow. No jumping in the lake or driving a car."

"That's easy. In other advice?"

"No. Not really. Keep a good attitude. Avoid trying to control anything. Surrender to the flow. Enjoy the visual effects. We'll both be together."

"When should we start?"

"After dark. Maybe around nine. It's pretty peaceful. The sky looks promising. Stars always put on a cosmic show. Maybe take a nap this afternoon. By the way, anything you'd like? I'm going to make a run to town. The front tire on the bike needs some pressure. Might have a slow leak. Thought I'd buy some flowers too. Great looking at them tonight."

"Can't wait."

"Tell me, do you think feelings are different than thoughts? There's got to be some overlap, but when I feel sad or excited or feel the beauty of music I'm not really thinking. I'm just feeling. And when I'm writing an article or figuring out a grocery list or trying to plan something next month, I'm not aware of any particular feeling. What do you think? I'm not asking what you feel, but what you think."

Reuel took a moment. "Yeah. Good questions. Feeling's an affect, it's not a brain language issue, like when you think to yourself. It's more in the brainstem, not in the cortex. It's the difference between sentience, having feelings, and sapience, having thoughts. Dogs have feelings, hardly any thoughts. But maybe we're just playing with words, when we start talking about consciousness. You know, you can recognize a face unconsciously. And are you actually being conscious that you are hearing my words as I speak, or just understanding them unconsciously? Feelings are drivers, that have causal consequences. If you don't feel hungry, your digestive energy metabolism still goes on autonomously. But if you do feel hungry you get motivated to look for food and to eat. The same applies to other feeling or affects. If you're objectively in danger you don't run and hide unless you become aware of the danger, and feel scared."

"What about being scared of something that isn't there?" asked Adler.

"The brain stem can't tell the difference. Like I said, understanding's in the cortex. That's millions of years of an evolutionary adaptation, for self-defense, self-preservation."

"And is there a self?"

"Absolutely not. Only a strong illusion of one. That's the problem."

"Well, fasten your seat belt."

Adler took off on his afternoon errand. Reuel worked on his German verbs and successfully managed a nap. At tea-time, they made melted cheese sandwiches and shared a chocolate bar. They straightened out the room. They explored and found reading materials on the bookshelves and pulled out a few titles on art and photography. They placed two upholstered chairs to face one another. They listened to a jazz vocalist. They arranged the flowers. They sat meditatively on the porch and watched the night arrive. Adler smoked a cigarette.

At nine o'clock they each ingested a dosed sugar cube.

"Here we go" says Adler.

"Anything else?"

"Tell you what. Ask yourself a good question about something. Keep it to yourself. I think you'll find it answered."

Reuel nodded, vaguely wondering of what to inquire. His glance alighted on the stack of folio-sized books on the coffee table between them. The topmost volume was titled "Buddhist Sculptures", and a large black and white photograph of a carved stone figure, seated calmly on a small chair, filled the dust-jacket. It portrayed a man, unclothed and unadorned, save for a loose diaphanous cloth about his lower body. He wore a small cap close-fitted to his head, and had his right leg laid across the left knee, which had its foot on the ground. His left hand holds a small urn, resting on the ankle of the crossed foot. He is leaning forward, the elbow of his right arm barely resting on the knee of the crossed leg. The hand is raised, and the relaxed fingers seem about to touch his lips. He appears to be engaged in deep thought, eyes half-closed. His mouth reveals a faint smile. The fine-printed legend below the photo reads "The Bodhisattva Maitreya, the Buddha of the Future."

Why was he smiling? That would be his question.

Half an hour later, the first odd thing Reuel noticed were the tiny hairs on his forearm. He could clearly see every individual one. Each fine hair appeared to be glowing within a rainbow sheath of violet, indigo, blue, green, yellow, orange, red. It was unbelievable. He had never seen anything that amazing, the idea that they were always that way had never occurred to him. He wanted to mention it to Adler who was leaning back with his eyes closed, but Adler's body seemed to have been compressed into something flat and oddly two-dimensional. Moreover, the body appeared to be strangely liquid, its material visual edges skirting back and forth. And further, the upholstered chair on which Adler sat appeared to be defying gravity, he could see it floating a millimeter above the floor, merely creating an illusion it was attached. And the rug seemed to be crawling. Then, in quick realization he recalled the sugar cube and the word "acid", which for a moment gave a reassuring explanation, and he closed his eyes, surrendering to a colorful kaleidoscopic light-show, moving dancelike on his optic nerve back and forth between his retina and the brain's visual cortex. Suddenly, there was no such thing as time. No thought. Only a deep feeling of immediate unity, awe and interconnection with every atom in the universe. An unfamiliar kind of mental activity beyond neurology and beyond description, disembodied and inexpressible, far beyond words, indefinable, unimaginable, beyond meaning, beyond a beyond.

He felt no panic, just a sadness that all things being born were dying at every moment. He knew he would die. His parents were dead. David and Eliana, sweet poor dear Italian refugees to America, escapees from fascism, always doleful and withdrawn, with reticent joyless and worried lives listening to the radio news. He barely knew them. So regretful. They scarcely knew him, almost always leaving him alone with his encyclopedias. All dead. No family. And the dead unborn, dear Astrid Galen, was it he that caused her death? His failure of love with Ulla and his own unintended dear children, the little twins, guiltily unacknowledged, and now Esther Halevi pregnant. Life seemed out of control. He felt so ashamed and started to sob. Adler came over and clumsily tried to embrace him in a brotherly reassurance, in the soup of life together.

Adler went to a record player. Music suddenly filled the air. Every note caused shapes to change. Reuel felt a sudden elevation. He had never heard anything so beautiful, so instantly redeeming. A woman's sweet soprano voice over a carpet of supporting sound. The throat, the most ancient instrument from ancestral aeons. *Vox humana.* He could see Adler smiling, turning from the phonograph, approaching with the cardboard sleeve. He took it automatically and studied the cover. "Renata Tebaldi Sings Baroque Arias." Angelic geniuses. Handel, Bach, Vivaldi, Frescobaldi, Pachelbel, Purcell. He saw the greatness of humankind. How miraculous everything was.

Adler was just standing and staring at him. They looked into each other's eyes and Reuel wanted to look away but couldn't, and he could see himself inside Adler. It was a freaky experience and he found it unbelievable. Adler nodded, as if in agreement. Reuel could feel their consciousness' merging into a single non-verbal awareness. Now it seemed that there was really telepathy. Clearly it seemed. Massive and complex thoughts were passing between them, mind-to-mind. The size and clarity of the thoughts appeared inverse to time. And yes, music could definitely be the key to the universe. They agreed perfectly. Reuel saw and removed a flower, a small daisy, from a vase on a side table and offered it to Adler. It was received as if priceless. Every gesture was symbolic and signifying. There was no avoiding the now obvious fact that everything on earth had meaning, which was ordinarily hidden. He was looking inward to his pure being. Something indescribable. He was no longer a "me", but was a watcher, someone wiser and more powerful than the socially-conditioned puppet that he was, and was now observing.

Around midnight Reuel stood for the first time and walked around the room, examining its contours and contents as though seeing them for the first time. It was all a miracle that things could exist, could be made, and could be seen. The grandeur was overwhelming. He spoke for the first time in hours.

"I'm going to sit on the porch."

Adler nodded seriously, quietly, appreciatively.

There was a beautiful and still night, as was forecast. A crescent moon had disappeared below the horizon hours earlier and the transparent darkness of the starry heaven's vastness was fully revealed to every sentient being. He had no sense of time's passage or even the meaning of time. The known size and age of

what he was seeing defied comprehension. He was merely an infinitesimal parti-
cle in an expanding universe. He experienced a cognitive shift of the perceptual
vastness, reframing his reality and his place within it. The fact that there was
human knowledge nearly defied belief. The whole thing billions and billions of
years old, the size incomprehensible, kiloparsecs, megaparsecs, gigaparsecs. He
dredged up his college memory of Hubble's Constant, something like a cosmic
expansion of a hundred kilometers a second per megaparsec. He searched the
sky towards the northeast, found the inverted W of Cassiopeia and followed
the guide stars down to the faint dot of the Andromeda galaxy. He knew two
things. It was the most distant object you could see with the naked eye alone,
over 750 kiloparsecs distant from Earth. Since one parsec was approximately
equal to 3.25 light-years it meant that Andromeda was about 2.5 million light-
years away from where he was sitting. And that was merely our very nearest
galactic neighbor. A gigaparsec of light-years expansion was unfathomable. He
felt his head imploding from the infinitesimally miniscule quality of his hominid ignorance.

And he, poor Reuel little Antenor had the feeling of himself sitting on a
chair in space between those mathematical laws of relativity at the big end, and
of the quantum theory at the small end, where the pure and real physical properties beneath the skin of his own sentient body lay at the scale of atoms and
subatomic particles. A realm incredibly distant from his consciousness, where
there were six hundred thousand, million, million, million atoms in a gram of
hydrogen and the standard Angstrom unit of measurement was a hundred-mil-
lionth of a centimeter. Who was he? A tiny short-lived vibrating envelope of
stuff, at a time when physicists were saying that reality didn't actually exist until
it was observed. Was that why the Buddha was smiling? Was there a cosmic joke?

Was he just a fool? Was he an intellectual or not? Much more so than
Adler. Yet what possible meaning could that have? He could feel a change at the
apex of his mind's parabola, a reminder of mundane gravity, regaining a touch of
weight, descending, returning to earth. A sense of time. Re-entering the physical
and moral plane. It seemed clear to him that his normal waking consciousness
was only one type of consciousness. That there had to be other types that were

probably inaccessible. He felt he had been at the edge of something unknown, his mind somersaulting like a trapeze artist high in the air without a net, playing with his sanity over an abyss of absolute madness. Bewildered by an epistemological impasse of knowing about knowing to demonstrate that he really knew nothing about anything. His existence was a whim, time a hallucination, and meaning a majority consensus of the blind. The act of making sense between one-another had, in itself, no more sense than the gurgle of a stream. Like the death of an ego and the birth of an insight.

The mystery of his education. So many people thought he was an intellectual, but he could see the shallowness of human intellect. The mystery of thinking about thoughts. Why were his thoughts in English? How, when distracting thoughts came up and he tried to stop them, he got caught up in stopping them which created a duality between the one who is doing the stopping and that which is being stopped. If he tried to stop thought with thought, there would never be an end to it. If he got involved with thoughts and went on developing them, he wouldn't be able to stop. To practice awareness, he had to let go of thinking. Mind was a wonderful servant but a terrible master. There was a deeper being. Deeper than one he had ever considered. He no longer felt he had the brainpower.

He decided to go inside and listen to the soprano and found Adler was attempting to stand on his head and losing his balance. It made both of them laugh, hysterically, standing there looking at one another. They became like two madmen who were sharing an unspoken joke. In laughter's midst Reuel twigged that computers didn't laugh. Did dogs laugh? Did cavemen laugh? When did laughter begin? What did the ancients know of laughter? And the ancients themselves were not really very ancient, merely yesterday's ghosts. Yes, the Delphic Sybil said "know thyself"! That was funny. What a joke. There was no self. Just a stream with streams in and out and puddles, and calms and ripples, rapids, deep and shallow. The old philosophers, the blessed ancients whose shoulders we stand on. What did those Greeks think? Were we just prisoners observing shadow's in Plato's cave? What had just happened to him? Instantly, Aristotle's ghost emerged to his mind. Of course! The *peripeteia*! He could almost see Greek letters on his retina, περιπέτεια. It was the perfect word diagnosing his condition, the abrupt turning point, the sudden reversal of circumstance, the change by which action veers round to its opposite, the most powerful moment in a plot. *"Eureka!* he thought, "I have found it." The quantity of old thought displaced by the overflowing new mind, equal to the volume of insight he had just obtained, like Archimedes' bathtub spilling over.

He grew overjoyed. What a relief, what a blessed relief. He understood everything. Like standing on his head. He couldn't stop the pleasure. He once had it signaled before, totally unappreciated, ages ago, reading in old Max Muller's sacred and ancient Buddhist books of the East. And now he saw it plain and true. The mathematical logic of it all. It was just the logical four parts of Nagarjuna's "tetralemma", a suite of four discrete functions, of affirmation, negation, both and neither, an indivisible quaternity happening all at once. Freedom! Free at last! He grasped that his mind had just been teased completely out of thought by a chemical, and reorganized. He conjured the recall of that powerful Sanskrit word of Muller's that had once detained him, *paravritti,* something resembling Greek *peripeteia*, where the mind flips completely over at the root of consciousness through the realization of one's actual and eventual nothingness. Emptiness! *Sunyat*a. Being. Non-being. Both being and non-being. Neither being nor non-being. Emptiness. The sudden enlightenment! It had been revealed to him by a molecule. Fantastic! The simple conditioned relativity of our existence. When both Aristotle and Nagarjuna together had explained the humane default very clearly: The Middle Way, between here and there, the *Madhyamika*. Hooray!

Adler said "What are you thinking? You suddenly just stopped laughing."

"I did? When?"

"Just a second or two ago. We were laughing and the expression on your face suddenly changed completely."

"God, I thought it was more like an hour."

"No, it was just a second ago. Your face suddenly grew very serious."

"Ha!" And they started laughing again.

"So, what do you think?" asked Adler

"I'm like a chick trying to scratch out of an eggshell. It's still a little hard to think clearly. Hard to communicate what just happened. Still happening actually. The thoughts are so large and flowing so fast. Like expanded consciousness getting funneled down through the reducing valve of my brain, my nervous system."

"We're calling it re-entry. Descending back to the mundane."

"What time is it?"

"Around five. You'll enjoy the dawn soon. I'll make us some coffee."

"How do you keep doing this?

"Every time it's different, and yet the same."

"Think it causes brain damage?"

"Obviously."

"What if this becomes widespread?"

They started laughing uproariously, and could barely stop. Then they spent half an hour as Adler guided Reuel into successfully doing a headstand.

Later, with the arrival of dawn's glow, they grew serious, sat on the porch in a near ecstatic silence, as the light, the awesome light, the transfiguring light as it seemed, lighted upon them and made them think of a surmise which is called enlightenment.

"So, what do you think?" asked Adler, while smoking a cigarette.

Reuel turned to face him. "It's really about experience. Not thinking. I find it hard to communicate what just happened to me. You know, it's like trying to remember a dream. We don't really know why there is such a kind of weak memory. Probably the brain doing some kind of rewiring beyond my understanding. Actually, I'm at loss to describe what happened, leave alone explain it. Where are words when my mind is trying to search for a word?"

"Isn't that getting spiritual?" asked Adler. "Looking for something immaterial, otherworldly, ethereal, transcendent?"

"I know what you mean, but no. I'm a materialist, an empiricist. I don't believe in property dualism. That's for sissies who can't deal with hard problems."

"Ouch."

"No. It's something about how information gets organized in the brain into knowledge. Like the realization that information is something else other than matter or energy. It's like a code that's being deciphered. That's what's happening to us right now, as we try to talk about what just happened. Our heads are being reorganized."

"I think that after an acid trip you're never the same person again."

"No, that's too easy. We're never the same person even moment to moment. We're a different person every day just between breakfast and dinner. Taking an LSD trip is just another inflection point. There's nothing to life but change. All moments are impermanent. There is really no same static person."

There was a long pause. Adler stood up and stretched his arms out in greeting the first taste of the rising sun's light.

"I'm a psychologist" he said. "Ego-dissolution seems to be the key to understanding this. It's the characteristic component of transcendent, or mystical experiences. Psychedelics apparently catalyze a loss of subjective self-identity. It's like a simulated death and rebirth experience. There's a blurring of boundaries between the self and everything outside of it."

"You think it really change someone's world-view?"

"I think so. It's like dying before dying, so-to-speak. That changes the quality of life, and even our basic strategy of existence. I think it reduces our irrational middle-class drives, and maybe increases the ability to live in the present, and to enjoy simple life activities. For me there's been a radical opening to spirituality. Like Yoga and in meditation. I've been dreaming of making a journey to the East, to India."

"Self-improvement is one thing. Self-deception is another" said Reuel.

"Well, what's it all about? Where did it all come from? How did the universe originate? How did consciousness begin? What is it? Is it cosmic? Is there meaning to our existence?"

"Bob, those are the ancient questions. Don't lose sight of how gradually human consciousness and language came about in evolutionary terms. And not all questions have answers. We're just primitives of an unknown culture. I don't mean to be thick. Something profound happened to me last night. I see my old self as a puppet. A kid groping for academic credentials. A wanderer without a compass. A sucker for sexual pleasures and entertainments. A seeker of pointless information. I suddenly don't know why I should care about what I'm doing. But yet being alive is definitely miraculous. The world seems very new to me today. That's all. I feel lucky. And I don't know why that's the case."

"Well, let me know how things go. What's your program? I'll be in Cambridge the last week in September. I'll call you. Let's do something together. Take a journey to the East, maybe?"

"Ha! I've got two language proficiency exams and a dissertation to write."

"Just a thought. Got a title?"

"Recursive Syntactical Hierarchies."

"Jesus."

ॐ

Early in the morning on the following day, a holiday Monday, Reucl returned to Boston. He carried six "orange sunshine" pills in a folded white envelope and drove slowly, just at the speed limit. Driving was one of life's familiar employments, calculated to produce hours of uninterrupted mind-wandering. Though somewhat calmed by the purr of the Porsche's motor, he had an uneasy feeling that the LSD session might have damaged his memory. His score on the German vocabulary cards on the passenger seat was appallingly bad. How did the brain store memory? So many things in his life completely forgotten.

Whatever he had done or would do in the future would also ultimately be forgotten. And he himself would also be forgotten one day. No memory of him would exist. Why, then, do anything? How can anyone fail to see this? It seemed possible to live well only as long as dumbed-down life intoxicated us. Once we got sober, we can't help but see that it's all a delusion, a stupid delusion. To be intelligent was to see life in a way that seemed meaningless. We live, we work, we die, and everything we ever did crumbles to planetary dust. What was the point? Did LSD poison his mind? It was as if all at once, the familiar world had become strange, as if he was waking up in the middle of a bizarre dream. Like a monkey driving a machine down a road. Why am I doing this? he asked. What's the point? This wasn't about academic philosophy or examinations. It was about his existence. He disliked the direction of his thought wandering. But it wasn't hopeless. He determined to introduce a veto component and turn his thoughts. The memory of Phra Luang came into his head, with Buddhism's idea of the awakened mind, and its awareness. And a sudden recollection of that tantalizing word, *tathata*, that very first lovely Sanskrit word he discovered in Sammler's bookstore long ago, *tathata*, translated into English as "suchness". The Buddha's message perhaps, thusness. What a suggestive term. Almost indefinable. What else? Nothing else. Sleepers awake. Just being here and now. Feeling the positive reversal of thought, the *paravritti*. The turning around. Perhaps he could study Sanskrit and go to India one day. That could be interesting, something utterly new. He began to relax again. Actually, nothing was at stake. Perhaps German vocabulary was at stake. But absolutely, nothing really mattered. Yet, relatively, everything mattered. What a pleasant relief! His breathing slowed. It was not so bad being alive. Enjoy the drive. A beautiful morning. Put on sunglasses. Find some music on the radio.

A few weeks later he sat for his language proficiency qualification. No MIT doctorate without it. Pass or fail. Italian was easy. German a bone-breaker, his memory seemed damaged and he panicked by mysterious vocabulary losses, but finally graced by a lenient examiner into a marginal pass. One step closer. Only now to finish the dissertation.

There was a message from Lingo Inc.'s lawyers informing Reuel that his Lingo shares of common stock had been exchanged for shares of Kang Laboratories and were being held in escrow pending his instructions. Within days Reuel arranged to move the shares to an account in his name at the trust department of Cambridge Federal National Bank. Shortly thereafter he got a phone call from Walter Dowfeld inviting him to lunch.

"Roo, I need to see you. Let me give you an update on what's been happening. We completed our merger with Kang Labs and I've just been named Vice-President for program development. Word games are no longer that interesting to me. Turns out that the source-code interpretation you compiled into machine language and the patent application are a lot more valuable than we had realized. Kang is on a roll and believe it or not your share equity holding is easily in seven figures just now. Isn't that incredible! No public market yet, but there are private buyers if you like. But I think you ought to hold them for a long term. Computer industry growth is going exponential. Everybody's reaching for personnel capability. There's a real race on to build market-share for small general-purpose computers. Software development is going to be the key."

"Nice going!" said Reuel. "What do you need from me?"

"I need your ass for a couple of months. Put your dissertation on hold. Here's the situation. We got a production assembly factory going up near Waltham. Billy Kang just did a $20 million mortgage financing deal with First Boston for the property. The engineers say our first devices ought to be rolling out of production and up for sale by the end of the year."

"Wow. That's ambitious."

"Well, here's the thing. We've got to have the software package ready for disk installation not later than October and there's a problem. The source-code machine-language is really fine, and it's even juiced up. It's just that every buyer has their own special application requirement, whether it's a science lab, a grocery wholesaler, an accounting firm, a government department, an engineering shop, and I can go on. You get the picture. What we're desperate for right now is designing our standard interface for unique third-party application interface programs, their APIs, to operate off our operating system. You're the guy. I need you. Can you come for lunch tomorrow and talk about it with me?"

"Where?"

"Out near Waltham, just off Route 128. It's our new building, just finished, next to the future manufacturing plant. They're pouring the slab for it at the end of the week. Just take Exit 17 East and look for the signs 'Glendower Industrial Park'. You can't miss it. It's 63 acres for a new hi-tech architectural development. Go just past the huge white trailer which the architects are using, and look for the first building with the Kang name out front. Can't miss it."

"What time?"

"Say around noon. We love you."

It was understandable that the thought of acquiring considerable wealth drove thoughts of neurolinguistics, Buddhism, metaphysics, the significance of being, the phenomenon of consciousness, and the meaning of meaning out of his mind. Reuel had really never considered the possibility of becoming rich. His financial horizon had never stretched beyond the concept of a junior fellowship and faculty income at worst, or a high salary position with an enterprise such as IBM at best. The role of an intellectual entrepreneur had never really occurred to him. What would it be like to have a great deal of money?

His LSD experience was almost entirely forgotten. He was back on planet Earth. The following day, Reuel and Dowfeld lunched on tuna salad sandwiches and cans of Coca-Cola, as the software proposition was discussed. It was a feasible undertaking but the timing constraint made it a challenge. MIT and the dissertation would have to wait a few months. The financial consideration was definitely attractive.

"Here's the deal" said Dowfeld, handing him a one-page letter proposal. "It's pretty simple. You supervise and put a team of our people together and contract to deliver and integrate the API's by October 1. Forty thousand dollars as a fee plus expenses. You get half today, I've got the check in my drawer. The balance on completion. And here's the good part. If the integration is flawless and the disk installation is on time, Kang Labs will give you a bonus. A stock option for 10,000 shares."

"How does that work?"

"Jesus, you're a mathematician. This is just high school arithmetic. You get a right, for ten years, to buy the shares at the price they're valued at today. Once you exercise the right, and hold them for two years, you're free to sell them. Your profit would be a tax-favored capital gain."

"What if you go broke? You don't even really have any sales."

"Are you an idiot? First of all, you don't have to exercise the options, so there's no downside. Second of all, we'll have revenue next year, and be solidly in the black the year after that. Then the market price of the shares would be a fat multiple of our projected future earnings, which will go skyward. It's the new computer industry, dummy. We'll be one of the first companies out of the gate. Those option shares will be worth a fortune, trust me. And that's on top of the shares that you already own which are also worth a fortune and there are more buyers than you would believe."

"Sounds good."

"Believe it. Just sign here." He handed him the letter and a check made out for twenty thousand dollars.

Reuel studied the letter for less than a minute and signed it. Then they spent over an hour in technical discussions. When finished, Dowfeld accompanied him to the parking lot, and as they passed the white architectural trailer, a tall gangly woman came out a door carrying a briefcase and a roll of drawings in her hand.

"Hello, Walt" she said.

"Roz! Come meet Roo Antenor. He'll be coming here a lot."

"An engineer? He's wearing white socks."

"Please, I'm a metaphysician" said Reuel. "And I can work while standing on my head."

"He's invaluable, that means expensive" said Dowfeld. "And Roo, this is Roz Flaherty. She's our architect. Does great work on plumbing and sewer systems."

They continued the wisecracking, the jesting jocularity, as they reached Reuel's Porsche, when Dowfeld suddenly stopped and raised his hand.

"Hey, Roo, just had a good idea. Roz takes a cab here from Boston every morning and we usually get one to take her back. Why don't you give her a lift today?"

"Where to?"

"Beacon Hill" she said.

"No problem, that's just across the Charles. My pleasure. Mind if the top is down?"

"I love it. Improves my hair."

He looked her over. A red-head with curls. A cute freckled face. Small nose. Prominent teeth. Nearly his height. Athletic looking. Extraverted. Pugnacious. Self-confident.

"Jump in."

En route they exchanged biographical summaries. She grew up in Irish South Boston, a "Southie". Went to Tufts for a BA in architectural studies and then for a Master of Architecture from Harvard's Graduate School. Now she was a junior partner after five years at Dorsey Associates in Architectural Design, 'DAAD', the firm in charge of Glendower Industrial Park. A red-sox fan. A runner, twice in the Boston Marathon. Single. They had just started to have a conversation about the French philosopher Jean-Paul Sartre when they reached her address.

"To be continued?" he asked.

"Sure. I'm up there on Mondays. Want to pick me up?"

"Love to. What's your phone number?"

So it goes, he thought, on the brief drive back to his flat. Random collisions. They make the world go round.

On Monday there was a grey drizzle and the Porsche headed out with its top closed down.

"What were you saying about Sartre, the other day" Reuel asked.

"I like his theory of the absurd, but all that existential philosophy stuff is just a load of crap. All those navel-gazing philosophers just need to get an honest job."

"You don't think exploring the problem of human existence is interesting?"

"What exactly is the problem? Personally, I think baseball is a lot more interesting. And spending one's time being outwardly useful or creative is a hell of a lot more valuable to humanity. Give me an engineer over a philosopher every day of the week."

"Well, what about human suffering? Mental suffering."

"It just comes with the territory of being alive. We all suffer more or less."

"What does it mean?"

"What do you mean 'what does it mean'?"

"Just do you think we live in a meaningless universe?"

"Who the hell knows? You want to tie yourself in knots about something like that? That's nuts and a waste of time. Questions like that are too abstract and remote from concrete human experience."

"Unhappiness is a concrete human experience."

"Yeah, and what are you going to do about it? Look at your navel, or go to the movies. Moan and groan? Sartre ain't no help. Grow up. You just like to talk a lot."

"Are you Catholic?"

"I'm Irish. I love the rituals, but there's nobody upstairs. What are you?"

"Italian Jewish once upon a time. Now I'm becoming a Buddhist, and that's probably because there's nobody upstairs."

"Gimme a break. You think too much. Clever people are like wholesale grocers, they always weigh everything. Like that Sartre crap about existence preceding essence, and the chicken or the egg, just mind games."

"You said you liked the theory of the absurd. Doesn't that contain the idea that there's no meaning in the world?"

"Only whatever we monkeys give it. That's not real meaning. That's just monkey meaning."

"Well, what's life good for?"

"That's the wrong question. What's the good life? That's the question."

"Is there virtue?"

"Of course, don't be an idiot."

"How do we know it?"

"We just know it. Philosophizing won't ever give you a clear answer."

"Having an answer isn't enough. You have to do the math" he said.

"Like how many angels on the head of a pin?"

"Thinking there's a benevolent nihilism isn't an answer."

"There is no answer. Only experience. You're chasing your own shadow. And watch out, the 17 East turnout is up ahead."

"You up for dinner?"

"You up for a jog?"

"Sure. Where? When?"

"10K. Around the park's perimeter. I designed the trail myself. Today, instead of eating lunch. Ten loops."

"How about five? And tomorrow. I'll bring my shoes. Gimme a break."

"Deal."

And so began a non-physical relationship. She had an easy long-limbed stride, and seemed to lead her pace with her pointed chin held high. Watching her run was a rhythmic thing of beauty. There was no way he was her equal in cardiopulmonary stamina, but in the course of a few weeks he managed to reach the 10k mark without a pause, at a somewhat slower pace. Though they started at the same time, they rarely ran together. The game was for her to loop him by one additional kilometer so they might finish nearly together. On their drives back to Boston they spoke about physical fitness, the design of parcourse stations, breathing techniques, the utility of open-form office space, the changing ethnic patterns in Boston, Bauhaus design, the villas of Palladio, the drawings of Piranesi, magic ratios, Socrates' elucidation of the hypotenuse, why 1.618 was the "golden ratio", the Vietnam war, the physics of fore and aft sailing, the history of her firm, his sojourn in Sweden, and frequently their conversations turned to her scorn for philosophers. A dialectical center of gravity oscillated through the discourse in the wide space between intelligence and wisdom. She had endless anecdotes on the stupidity of intellectuals.

He quizzed her about what her mind did when she ran. Was it simply awareness without thought? If he attempted to allude indirectly to the Buddhist concept of emptiness and non-self, she would fix him with a look suggesting he was being preposterous, and could not be serious, and that if a person pursued such a philosophy, they would surely become suicidal, or at least dead to the world. The harsh reality of many human situations was beside the point. Unhappiness could not be destroyed by means of a philosophical theory. She accused him of straying into moral nihilism, and devaluing the idea of love. Not erotic or emotional love, but the universal love which was the foundation of humane goodness and ethics. The idea that human values were baseless, that life was meaningless, that knowledge was an illusion, that some set of entities did not exist, was utterly laughable. A philosophy for crackpots.

Each time he ventured to ask her for dinner she parried with a reasonable mention of a conflicting obligation. He chose not to press the point, confident that sooner or later it would happen. When it did it was at her initiative. She phoned him on a Saturday morning.

"You up for a double header at Fenway? The Sox have a shot at the pennant and are playing the Yankees today. Mantle's now playing first base and passing 500 homers. We could share some hot-dogs afterwards and sit in the Victory Gardens. Let's meet at the gate. We can walk there."

"You're on."

He bought two expensive seats from a scalper working the parking lot. The first row in the lower stands just below first base. She rewarded him with an approving nod. They were in virgin territory, no longer in a Porsche, no longer at Glendower Park's running track, the only venues they had ever shared. Today they were exceptionally cheerful and when the big Fenway organ blasted out the tune of "Take Me Out to the Ballgame" they joined the crowd at the top of their lungs.

The score at the bottom of the ninth inning of the first game was zero – zero.

"Nothing to nothing" he said. "There's nihilism!" She provided him an arch look. "There's only extra innings in baseball my boy, life doesn't provide them."

The Red Sox won the first game in the tenth inning, 1 – 0. Reuel and Rosalind walked under the stands, found the toilets, and bought peanuts and crackerjacks in the interim before the double header. The crowd was buzzing with excitement. If the Sox took the second game the pennant was in sight.

After an hour or more later, the stadium lights were turned on, just before the 7th inning stretch. And with the score 8-2, the Red Sox had momentum, as the Yankees had used two relief pitchers, Mantle struck out once, a pop-up foul tip was caught by the catcher, and at his third time up a grounder to the short-stop had him thrown out before nearing the plate. And the side was retired. Rosalind was jubilant. The next batting order favored Boston. There was a real chance for the league pennant.

"Let's get out of here" she said. "It's in the bag. There's no way New York's coming back. They started the eighth with their best half of the batting order and Boston holds the inning bottoms. Let's beat the crowd out. There's a deli on Boylston Street on the way to the Gardens. We can get takeout."

The hot-dogs were actually large Polish sausages, the potato fries some-what greasy, and all was washed down by large bottles of brown ale. They sat on a bench off to the side near the garden entrance. The combination of moonlight and the suffusing glow of city lights made it easy to see one another.

"Well, we finally had dinner together" he said. "But not very romantic."

"Oh, that's not in the cards for us."

"Ouch. Disappointing for me."

"Be serious. I already have two boyfriends, and as a matter of fact my tastes run to older men. You and I are friendly colleagues who just work and trot in the industrial park. What did you think?"

"Wasn't really thinking. Just feeling erotic attraction."

"Very flattering, but not in the cards my boy. You'll get over it. You won't even remember me a year from now. You're near the end of your contract, and in two weeks I'm off to redesign a new terminal building at Manchester airport in New Hampshire. I'm not into quick rolls in the hay."

"Do I have a problem?"

"I'm guessing, but I think your problem is self-intoxication."

"You mean because I've been saying there is no self?"

"Precisely. Who do you think is talking to me just now? Your head seems to be full of juvenile philosophy. Don't you think it's time for you to grow up? I mean you're a nice guy and all that, but I don't think you're serious. You just talk a lot."

He felt deflated. They stood to leave the gardens, found a trash receptacle for their dinner debris, and noticed a swell of happy fans emerging from the stadium gates to the accompaniment of a victory roar resonating from within. The league pennant was apparently in sight. But no kiss of farewell. They were both within a fair walking distance of homes.

"See you Monday on the track?" she asked.

"Maybe."

She gave him a small wave as they separated. Reuel walked home rather slowly, tasting a faint disappointment combined with mild amusement at himself. Was it just a game of monkeys exchanging signals? Well, he had work to do. There was a wrap-up meeting with Dowfeld and Billy Kang on Monday morning.

They met at ten o'clock in the CEO's office. Billy Kang was a short elderly man of Chinese extraction whose body showed an unmistakable fusion of muscularity and obesity. He was in shirt sleeves and dark tie with his jacket draped on the chair-back. A wisp of comb-over hair seemed pasted to his bare skull and he chewed on the stub of an unlit cigar, which he waved when he spoke.

"Antenor, everyone tells me that we ought to hire you. What the hell use is a Ph.D. two years from now going to do for you? The action is here and now. MIT doesn't have any sense of how fast things are moving in our industry. The entire country is getting wired up. Coding talent is still scarce. What's the point of being an academic?"

"I'm just more interested in philosophy than business" said Reuel.

"How does ten million sound to you?"

"What?"

"Look, you may not yet realize it but you're already worth a couple in the Kang stock you swapped from your Lingo shares, plus the options we gave you. Inside the two years it'll take to finish and defend a dissertation, that amount will more than double. And we're still a private company. There's going to be a public appetite for our shares, believe me. With the new stock options we'll offer you, your worth could likely be in eight figures. If you never sell any and just hang on, by the time you're my age it'll reach nine figures. You think I'm kidding? There are guys younger than you who are going to be billionaires yet."

"That's hard to believe."

"Well, I'll leave it to you. Think it over. Walt says your little team did a great job on the application interface."

"It's on time and hardly needs any tweaking" said Dowfeld, "but Roo's got an interesting revenue angle."

"What's that? Said Kang, turning to Reuel while biting on his wet cigar stub.

Reuel drew a deep breath and allowed a pause to linger for emphasis. "The client application problem wasn't that hard to fix. It's pretty much solved and the guys know how to build it out. Basically, we created an external schematic interface for buyers of Kang computers. It's designed to sit between a client's software application and our operating system. And here's my point, rather than keeping it in-house I think we should make it a public package. If we do that our clients will know how to write their software to our platform. Think of it as our partner interface which we contractually license to them. That way we can exercise real quality control by curating which external apps have access to our API. And here's a new financial angle: it could provide us with an additional revenue stream from licensing the partnered interface package separately from the hardware."

Kang tilted his chair and rolled his head back so that he seemed to be studying the ceiling. Then he swiveled with his back to them and looked out the window for several moments where he could see the rising steel frame of the factory under construction. Finally, he got out of his chair and came around to his visitors with his hand outstretched. They stood. He turned to Reuel.

"I've got an investor conference at the Ritz-Carlton on the fifteenth of October. The usual Wall Street crowd." He used his cigar stub to point at Reuel. "I'd like you to give them a little talk." He didn't wait for an answer as he held the office door open, and nodded as he gestured them out.

☙

On a Saturday morning, days later, Reuel was at Logan airport awaiting Luca Baca's arrival on a flight from Rome. He re-read his friend's letter received weeks earlier. It contained flight information, the name of the colloquium at Harvard Divinity School - "Syllabaries, Epigraphies and Abbreviations" - and the happy news of Luca's newly awarded the Pontifical Gregorian University's doctorate in "missiology", which Reuel's unabridged dictionary defined simply as the study of missionary activity. The letter had a warm post-script of thanks for putting him up during his stay. Reuel's affection for his closest and oldest friend filled his immediate mind.

Absent Luca's clerical collar, they had dinner that night at the Union Oyster House near Faneuil Hall. Their tongues loosened by an abundance of cold Pinot Grigio they spent most of the table talk describing the myriad events they had endured since their last meeting in Rome three years earlier, when Reuel had come down from Sweden. Something almost unconscious lay upon them. Something subtle, scarcely noticed, yet marking the fact they had commenced manhood, and were no longer youthful lads.

Luca had bedded down on the comfortable sofa in Reuel's tidy flat, where they shared the bathroom, and breakfasted together, slightly sleep-deprived, before going off to their institutional venues. For several days, aside from a few chess games, the pressure of dual academic obligations kept each of them from the leisurely open-ended and free-ranging style of personal conversations which had always been their particular pleasure. Luca's jet-lag hindered the task of completing the hand-out notes for his colloquium talk concerning Latin script abbreviations on Roman monuments. And Reuel's work at formalizing the structure of his dissertation outline for a scheduled meeting with his degree examiners kept him at his typewriter.

Finally, by Friday afternoon, their homework tasks completed, they breathed easily and saw little to distract them from the enjoyable intellectual and personal intimacies of their friendship. A relaxed weekend lay ahead. They went shopping for a takeout dinner and elected an oversized container of shrimp curry, some pears and a soft cheese, and a basket-bottomed half-gallon fiasco of Chianti.

Hours later, softened by wine and lounge pillows, their floating conversation reached the subject of psychedelics, the philosophical question of human consciousness, and the implications of Reuel's recent LSD experience on his state of mind, which opened the thread of their ensuing discussion.

"Luke, I've got to confess, all the MIT crap about machine intelligence bores the shit out of me. It's been the lure of computer industry money that keeps pulling me away from my fundamental interest in biology, language and the brain. And the nature of mind, or consciousness. And the philosophy that goes with all that. It's like I sold my soul to a soulless god of hardware robots."

"That's terrible! Tell me more."

"I think I first got sidetracked at the Karolinska in Sweden. I was like a woodpecker banging on a tree. Everybody was working on the easy problem of trying to understand consciousness by examining and tagging the functional dynamics and computational organization of the brain. Scientists just looking for explanations from physiology, biochemistry, and neuroanatomy, and arguing about neural correlates of consciousness being located in the posterior cortex, for example. You put a person's brain in an MRI scan, ask the subject to imagine itself, and bingo! Right there, right behind your forehead it lights up. That's where you claim to have your sense of self. Total bullshit. None of that remotely addresses the really hard problem. What is this thing we are clearly aware of and we call consciousness?"

"A gift of God, perhaps?"

"No, Luke, I'm still a reductionist. There's an evolved purpose behind our consciousness, and it's basically about survival and reproduction. I mean, if you think about something like daydreaming, what do you daydream about? Well, you usually daydream about your conditional existence first of all. Where's my next food or my job? How do I get sex? How do I impress people to advance my career? And you get emotional feelings. Evolution gave us emotions because they're useful for us."

"That seems obvious but hardly sounds very scientific."

"Right. It's as if there's something still missing. Something beneath science yet not superstition. Something more like history. I think it's something about the evolution of the hominids, way back. How brains get shaped by innate needs and the appearance of useful sounds we call "words", which lead to an entirely new kind of animal with self-awareness and the beginning of thoughts. *Cogito Ergo Sum* as that man said, but without the dualism."

Luca thought this over for a moment before replying. "Yes, it's true, that kind of Cartesian dualism is a bit old-fashioned. It's best we think more about a higher unity of the spirit and the flesh. Even the Church now re-emphasizes the unity of the Trinity. But listen. Roo, tell me more about your LSD experience. I'm really curious."

"It's nearly impossible to describe and hard to remember. I'm guessing that the brain is trying to do a couple of things at once. To segregate the immediate experience into component brain parts, the cortex, fissures, lobes, glands of the limbic system, the ganglia and brain stem and then simultaneously integrating and reassembling everything into a changed single state of some new and weird kind of meaning. Psychedelic chemicals seem to upset the entire evolutionary apple-cart. Almost like vanishing your mind into one of those food blenders. Mind altering molecules seem to generate the experience of observing your own ego-dissolution. And I know that sounds like a contradiction in terms. It's really bewildering, but almost miraculous."

"Well, buddy, I'm a priest, not a scientist, but I think our consciousness provides us with at least a couple of critical functions, to construct creative narratives about our lives and to feel our emotional response to them. Together, they give us the ability to imagine undreamed of possibilities, evaluate them, try to understand them, and plan future actions. And sooner or later, some of our kind, by an evolutionary act of grace, experience the sacred, the holy, the spiritual, the mysterious ineffability of Divine love, the presence of God in our own creation."

Reuel didn't want to argue this point with his old friend and swerved away from a discussion of spirituality. "My own logical thinking is that since consciousness involves self-awareness it leads one to the famous Russell paradox, about the set of all sets that aren't members of themselves. Know it?"

"The one that sounds like an old Jesuit exercise? Like can God be outside of the universe. And if I'm not mistaken, isn't it like Epimenides' paradox, about the Cretan who says that all Cretans are liars? How do we escape from paradox? And look, while it's true that consciousness involves self-awareness, and the ability to reflect deeply, even prayerfully, upon ourselves, it does seem to leave somethings out. Maybe there can't ever be a complete and consistent material theory of consciousness. Isn't it obvious that something non-material seems to be involved?"

"Well, remember, information is non-material. And under my Buddhist hat there is no static self to actually become the object of self-reference. In point of fact, mathematically speaking, consciousness of self-awareness resembles an incompleteness theorem."

"You've lost me. It sounds like you're saying that the absence of a soul is your evidence of incompleteness. Explain to me how we are different from robots without invoking what we call a soul. How conscious are robots? Can they have emotions?"

The question lingered in the air and Reuel continued in a desultory manner while refilling their glasses of Chianti. "Well, robots could be conscious at some level. You could say they have the intelligence of a cockroach or of reptiles."

"Hold on a minute Roo, you just switched a term, going from consciousness to intelligence. Let's drop intelligence from our discussion. How about emotions?"

"Okay. We don't say robots have emotion. We don't say that reptiles, wet robots if you like, have emotions. They can't laugh or know what they are. Let's just say that there are levels of consciousness. Take our consciousness of space, which is basically the back of the brain, the oldest part of our brain. That's a consciousness we share with reptiles. Now that I think of it, some animals even understand space better than us. Birds really live within space awareness centered on nests and food. Hawks can locate a mouse while flying, with an eyesight much better than ours. Like reptiles, and like us, they're conscious in the sense they understand their position in space with regard to prey, with regard to where they live. But the question is are they aware that they have that kind of consciousness. You see?"

"Let's play with this, Roo. Space awareness is one thing, but time awareness is completely different. We make plans, we pray, we strategize, scheme and make predictions about the future. Humans understand time in a way that lower animals don't. We can imagine the future in many dimensions — including dimensions of emotions, as well as space and time. And surely our human sense of time, knowing our mortality as we do, is a key to understanding our awareness of being conscious. What I call a soul, whether it's a troubled soul or not. And let's go further, do robots have a sense of social awareness? The consciousness of our relation to our brothers and sisters?"

This desultory discussion seemed to be producing a mental fatigue and a linguistic complexity, but they weren't ready to end it.

"Luke, I grant you that we're social animals. But we aren't alone that way. Lots of animals live in social packs, have hierarchies and emotions. Dogs for instance, leave alone chimpanzees. Supposedly the mid-part of our brain is the emotional and social brain. Obviously, robots lack social emotions. Etiquette, politeness, social hierarchy—all these things get encoded in the emotional brain, the monkey brain at the center of the brain which we share. It's the brain that understands our relationship to other members of our species. But the whole brain, the *homo sapiens* brain, which unifies space, time, and emotions simply operates to create a model of our place in space with our relationship to others and its relationship to time. Self-awareness is when you put yourself in this model of space, time, and relationship to others. Why is there any need for a soul in that? We have language and thought instead."

"It's not the mechanical need for a soul, Roo, rather it's the hunger for a soul. Once discovered it becomes a source of human richness by the grace of our creator. It is our redemption, indeed, our salvation." Here he stood up and went to the toilet for a pee.

Reuel thought about this while waiting for Luca's return. He sliced a pear in half and spread cheese on it. He wanted to avoid the arduous question of emptiness, of non-self. He decided to try another tack.

"But Luke, things like aesthetic appreciation, moral responsibility, loving kindness, aren't merely mechanical physical principles of some sort of pre-existing vitalism, they're simply higher constructs of human psychology and society. And many of these emotions that we have, that are instinctual, are basically hardwired into us because we have to make split-second decisions, which would take many, many minutes for the prefrontal cortex to rationally evaluate. We don't have time for that. If you see a tiger, you feel fear. That's because it's dangerous and you have to run away."

"If you see a saint, you feel love" said Luca. "Like the love of our creator. That's because it's healing, and you want to come near it. But it seems like you're just insisting we're biological robots. But what does that mean? What does that mean for people's feelings about the universe and a sense of who they are? Aren't humans special in that sense from other animals? While friendly, dogs and cats surely have a degree of consciousness, even simple emotions, do they have spiritual aspirations? They may have friendships; do they have spiritual love?"

Reuel gnawed at this. "It seems to me that you're ultimately begging the question of whether your spirituality is factually only a higher degree in a continuum of consciousness."

"Isn't it?" said Luca.

"Frankly, I don't know. That may lie in the future,"

"And your Buddhism? Is it spiritual?"

"It's practical. And still an engaging mystery to me."

"And how about LSD? Kindly enlighten me."

"How could I?"

"We could try some together."

"Are you serious? I've actually got a few tabs."

"When could we?"

"We could do it now. We'd be up all night."

They cleaned up the takeout dinner debris. This led to the idea of personal ablutions and each of them solemnly showered, though it was nearing midnight. Reuel had searched through his long-playing record collection and decided against Jazz, Ella Fitzgerald, or Bob Dylan. Instead, he picked a suitable religion-entreating selection to stack on the phonograph: Bach's B Minor Mass, Pergolesi's "Stabat Mater", The Boston Philharmonic's version of Handel's "Messiah", Vivaldi's "Gloria", the Budapest chamber ensemble performing late Beethoven quartets, Mozart's Requiem, Ulla's gift recording of Jascha Heifetz on Bach's violin partitas. And so prepared, they began their "trip".

There is a moment when someone suddenly realizes that the course of their life has been recast. This happened to Reuel at approximately 3 a.m. on the ensuing morning. Hours earlier a single tablet of "Orange Sunshine" containing approximately 200 micrograms of LSD had been dissolved in a small glass of water and divided into a pair of cups. Luca was calm without any sign of nervousness as Reuel, in a preliminary, described his experience with Adler, emphasizing they would use a much lower dose, and confessed how little he understood or could accurately communicate about the experience. He hid his nervousness at a confrontation with the Church of Rome in the event he was responsible for destroying the faith and career of one of its devoted adherents.

Luca lay back, propped up by cushions of the sofa, half reclining, calmly staring at the ceiling. Reuel on an easy chair, his feet on the cleared coffee table. The hallucinatory effects seemed much milder than his previous encounter with LSD. In fact, he was not sure of any precise moment when its effects actually began, only a shift in tone.

It was odd. His eyes were closed. For an inexplicable moment he spontaneously found himself trying to remember the name of Ulla's mother, Hedda. It led to mentally testing his vocabulary of Swedish words, and to the total disappearance of the Scandinavian nautical terms for boat winches, cleats and furlers. His attention found a worry that LSD might be affecting his memory and intelligence. Why were there such strange exudations? Wasn't there something about Vikings and mushrooms? Berserkers? Why was he thinking of them at all? He tried to recall the names of long-ago ball-players for the Chicago Cubs and couldn't. While some words and things were totally lost to memory, others seemed within near reach of search and retrieval, while still others merely hovered remaining annoyingly out of reach. What were names from the Vienna Circle's members? What was Raskolnikov's first name? Bloom's first name in "Ulysses"? Where was this river of hankering questions coming from? Where was the womb of questioning? And so forth, until his thought-stream branched to another level and contemplated the problematic question of by what mechanism the brain was evidently trying to search itself. How odd it seemed. The old term "engram" was no better than the ancient word phlogiston, and his mind abruptly popped up the term of "Hebbian" circuits, and then, distressingly, he totally forgot what he was thinking about at all, and his flow of thoughts utterly vanished at the bottom of a confusing and dislocating vortex. Was he losing his mind? Where was he? The room seemed like a cabin on a swaying ship. A sense of panic came, was reduced to fear, and then subsided to anxiety. He finally opened his eyes, sat up straight, and saw his friend looking heavenward and smiling radiantly, shaking his head slightly in amazement at what appeared to be ecstatic disbelief.

Handel's oratorio had just come to an end. Luca's facial expression of rapture as he lay on the sofa produced a swell of envy and admiration in Reuel and he felt mechanical, deprived of joy by his unrelenting intellectually critical mind, sinking, and unable to rise. And then, as they looked momentarily into one another's eyes, Reuel wanted to avert his gaze and found he could not. He wanted to find himself rescued by Luca's buoyant feelings and watched Luca open and raise his hands skyward, breathing deeply, speaking softly.

"Oh Reuel" he said. "the beauty, the incredible beauty, the vision of it, the richness of the music, the words, think of them ... 'comfort ye' ... 'I tell you a mystery' ... 'make straight in the desert a highway' ... 'we shall all be changed in the twinkling of an eye' ... 'they that walk in darkness will see a great light' ... 'rejoice greatly' ... 'hear tidings of great joy' .... 'the yoke is easy, the burden light'

... 'hallelujah' ... 'halleluja' ... how elevated, Reuel, how elevated, the beauty of it all. The glory."

Reuel was suddenly left like a heavy stone, speechless. His unforeseen emotions were exactly the opposite of what he had been expecting. Luca's rapture made him feel like an existential human failure. He searched but couldn't find his life-raft of Buddhism on a frightening sea of feeling. The precipitous unhappiness of his chemically altered mind was weighted by the idea of both personal and universal impermanence, and its implied emptiness, with an unnatural burden of philosophical meaninglessness and unfathomability. What was he to make of his unrequited yearning for fulfillment in the void? Was it not paradoxical? Even stupid? If craving was the source of suffering why should one crave for enlightenment? Did an end to unhappiness necessarily provide a clue to the attainment of rapturous joy? Did the Buddha enjoy himself, feel ecstasy, like Luca?

Reuel stood up, keeping his hand on the back of the armchair for balance. "Luke, give me a moment. I need to lie down for a bit. I'll be in the bedroom. It's okay. Don't mind me."

He went to the other room, lay on his back on the unmade bed, and attempted to review his actual life to date, and the prospect of its uncertain future. Was he suffering? Not apparently. Was he unhappy? Not really. What was he then? Here he paused, searching for a term. Yes, he decided, he was lucky. That was it. Thus far life had been good to him. Of course, there had been small disappointments. Of course, he had small pleasures. But on the whole he had lived within a sober unimposing range between excessive pleasure or pain. He was usually level-headed. His reach had not exceeded his grasp. Then why was he sinking, growing doleful, even morbid by the instant, like at this very moment? He decided it was because he couldn't control the perception of the feeling, like an unprogrammed emotional robot. Why should a wet robot executing a program even have feelings? He felt himself sinking further into darkness, into painful ignorance about his impermanent self and a sudden sense of the incredible confining shallowness of his life. He wished to be free. Did he really desire a PhD? To spend unexciting years writing about recursive semantic hierarchies? That seemed insane. It was the opposite of freedom. Was he losing his mind? Or was he coming to some kind of realization? What was he suddenly so unhappy about? What was making him painfully sad? A chemical or a liberated awareness of his loneliness? What exactly was the hurt?

From the other room he heard the recording of Jascha Heifetz playing the violin. He recognized the passage immediately, unmistakably. It was the chaconne from Bach's second partita, the piece he had heard Ulla perform a hundred times. He instantly recalled the transcendent night she played it under a full moon on the beach of Fire Island and told him she was pregnant with the twins, the little girls he had abandoned. That self-indulgent awareness now pained him deeply. He experienced a hurtful sense of guilt. He was no robot. He suddenly broke into tears and couldn't stop crying, somewhat out of control, and trying to muffle the vocal spasms so that Luca wouldn't hear him. He decided he needed to change his life.

He lay on the bed for more than an hour, alone in the world, struggling to compose himself. With feelings of emotional exhaustion, he surrendered to a fading pressure of thought. On seeing the faintest light of dawn through the bedroom window, and with a sudden anxious concern about Luca's welfare, he roused himself.

Luca was discovered sitting calmly on the sofa perusing back issues of Yachting World magazine and looked up with an expression of relief.

"Are you alright?" he asked. "I wasn't sure if I should come in. Sounded a bit like you were having some kind of existential crisis. I'd never heard you crying before. Was it the LSD?"

"It was a bummer" said Reuel. "Not exactly what I was expecting."

"Want to talk about it?"

"Not so easy to frame with words. Just a huge let-down. Like I've been kidding myself for years, and being back at square one."

"How so?"

"It was like everything I was doing was incredibly shallow. Like it was a game that didn't really mean very much. Like I was in a prison that was closing in on me. How about you?"

"For me it was fantastic and very beautiful. A real affirmation of inward grace, but not something I'd ever want to do again. Too much of a let-down coming back to earth. There's so much human unhappiness everywhere. I could see how much we need to feel sorry for one another, to share brotherly love. Christ's message."

"I was actually having trouble with my Buddhism."

"Oh? Tell me more."

"The bit about impermanence and the cause of suffering seems obvious to me. But the idea of emptiness and non-self really strains my imagination. I mean the idea that there's no permanent underlying unconditioned substance seems like some weird metaphysical case. I'm beginning to think it's just a doctrinal position which doesn't play any part in everyday reality, maybe except for monks and nuns in some state of hyper-absorption. Definitely not for us ordinary people in the laity."

"You're beginning to sound like a Jesuit!"

"Look, the fact is that our illusion of self-hood is ineradicable. It can't be explained and it's just only theoretically understood because everything appears conditioned and dependent on something else. But it seems sophomoric to argue that therefore there's no meaningful self. There's an experienced self, obviously, even if it's impermanent."

"Ah yes, your impermanence again. *Memento, homo, quia pulvis es, et in pulverem reverteris*" sayeth Pope Gregory. 'Remember, O human, that thou art dust, and to dust thou shalt return.' When you ask 'what does that impermanence mean?' you just can't help finding that each of us is an isolated being, born into the universe, and totally barred from knowing why. It's the mystery that we must solve. But it doesn't mean that life is meaningless. That is pure nihilism, 'nothingism'. And if you believe that nothing in the world has a real existence, then all's a fiction. But like someone pointed out, there are supreme fictions.

Like Tolstoy said, it's possible to live meaningfully only as long as life inebriates us; once we're merely sober, we can't help feeling that it's all a delusion, a stupid delusion, with nothing funny about it; it's only cruel and stupid. So then what? Where is there a supreme fictional veracity that can save us? I think the important thing is not to stop asking, not to stop until a truth behind the mystery gets revealed. The more you know the more there is to know. And then, perhaps, redemptive authenticity merely depends upon taking a walk around a lake."

"Nice work if you can get it. But suddenly, the world just stopped making sense. All at once, everything familiar became strange. Without warning, and I'm surrounded by hollow questions: 'Why am I doing this?' 'Where is it all heading?' 'Is this going anywhere?' 'What's the point?' It's like I woke up in the middle of a weird dream. Everything seems rather absurd. Maybe I should see it all as a harmless comedy. Just laugh and enjoy as much of life as I can."

"Well, my boy it all depends on your perspective, doesn't it? Laugh if you can, but existential crises bring up important questions worth exploring, like faith. An experience of meaninglessness can be painful, but trying to treat it like an illness, like a virus or tuberculosis is missing the point."

"Oh yeah, what is the point?"

"It's not to pathologize a person's healthy, intelligent and inquiring behavior. Keep searching, Roo. Deliverance is possible, believe me. And come on, let's eat breakfast."

Three days later Luca, now wearing his clerical collar, was bound for Rome. He and Reuel pensively embraced one another outside the Logan Airport departure lounge and promised to stay in touch. It had been a memorable visit. Reuel returned to his apartment and spent the rest of the day restoring it to perfection. He laundered the linens in the basement communal washing machine and dryer. He vacuumed every nook of the floor. Positioned table lamps and shades to perfection. He restored a variety of books to their shelves. Shook out his small antique Persian rug from a window. Purged the refrigerator of food remnants. Sponged and polished every surface of the kitchen and toilet. Plates and glasses were made spotless and aligned in rows. He straightened his wardrobe, moving garments from hooks to proper clothes-hangers, folding shirts geometrically into drawers, aligning his neckties and shoes. He took out the garbage to the downstairs bin and finally closed out his clean-up agenda by slowly examining and ordering papers and folders distributed about. And then, sitting down at last, he occupied nearly quarter of an hour staring at the idle IBM Selectric typewriter centered on his writing table. Thereafter, somewhat mended if not quite restored, he felt prepared for what lay ahead.

First was the chore of informing MIT and his three doctoral advisor-examiners that he was requesting – or taking - a leave of absence as a degree matriculant. He left identical addressed copies to that effect with the departmental secretary and recited his understanding that his fellowship and teaching-assistant stipends would terminate as of this notice. Without adding any explanation for his decision, he gathered a few personal items from his miniscule office and psychologically closed the erstwhile gate of the Massachusetts Institute of Technology behind him. No longer a PhD candidate, he was, in the conventional self-deprecating waggish parlance, merely an AbD. "All But Dissertation." And as for that, he recalled that the great Wittgenstein hadn't even completed a lowly undergraduate degree.

Next, still dressed as a disheveled graduate student, was his visit to the trust department of the Cambridge National Bank on Concord Avenue. Following Reuel's uncertain inquiry at a cashier's window he was ushered through some glass doors into the carpeted suite of offices referred to as Executive Banking. There he was politely greeted by Beverly Thesiger, Vice-President. She seemed like a young grandmother, slim, grey-haired, with rimless glasses perched on a thin nose. She briefly consulted his account record.

"Nice to see you again, Mr. Antenor. It's been a few months since we met to execute the trust agreement confirming our receipt of your shares of Kang Laboratories. We are at your disposal. I trust all is well?"

"I'm very well indeed, but I think I need a tutorial and some assistance on a matter. I hope you can help me."

"It will be my pleasure."

"Great, let me tell you what I know and what I'd like to do. First of all, am I correct that I'm not permitted to sell my Kang shares for two years since I got them in exchange for my Lingo shares, pursuant to the merger agreement between the two companies?"

"You are correct. And furthermore, in any case, attempting a sale would be problematic as there is no public market for those shares inasmuch as they represent your common stock equity in a private corporation. If you did wish to sell them you would have to negotiate a price with a buyer and then request approval from Kang. While there's currently no market price on the value of those shares, which are not publicly traded, I think I'm safe in saying that they would probably be worth several million dollars if there was a public market for them today. Let me point out that there's a fairly high likelihood to be a public offering of those shares in the next year or two. Or even the possibility of a publicly traded company like IBM making an acquisition of Kang. It's why I believe it would be inadvisable to sell them at this time. Given what seems to lie ahead for the computer industry, I would strongly advise you to hold those shares for at least another few years, since their value could easily grow to several multiples of their current worth. The concept of discounting a probable future growth into a present value is what continues to favor your holdings long term. Do you follow?"

"I think I do."

"Are you in need of cash?"

"Not really, not very much."

"Not going hungry or anything like that?"

"God no, just some books I don't indulge in buying, a tweed sport coat I've been eyeing, and a few restaurants I'd like to impress a date with. My folks left me a bit. I still have five figures in my checking account with you. No debt. Actually, the thing is, I'd like to give some of my shares away, as a gift. To my daughters."

"I see. Are they in need of cash?"

"No, they're over three years old, maybe more. Twins. Living in Stockholm with their mother. Comfortable Swedish middle-class family."

"Mr. Antenor, may I ask, do you have a will?"

"No."

"Do you have a lawyer? An accountant? Someone who does your taxes?"

"No. No. And no."

"Mr. Antenor, Reuel, if I may. It is time for you to grow up. You are a man of means. You are in need of estate-planning. You need a will. You do not want to die without one. Furthermore, once you have a lawyer, we can easily create the appropriate legal instruments to benefit others, like your daughters. A second trust account with you as trustee would probably be fairly simple to arrange. You just need someone to represent you and provide you with legal language and financial advice and protection. Do you follow?"

"I think I do."

"We are in no rush. Why don't you obtain legal counsel and we can go from there. And by the way, I should have mentioned this earlier, let me bring your attention to the fact that since our trust department is the custodian of your Kang shares it would be extremely simple for us to use them as collateral for a line-of-credit to your checking account. There's adequate coverage in our opinion so I think we'd be comfortable lending you up to a million. There's really no need to think of selling them at present. A secured line of credit is nearly the equivalent."

Reuel walked slowly out onto Concord Avenue with something that felt like a glow behind his eyes. He hadn't expected Ms. Thesiger's clarifying view of things. A line of credit up to a million dollars? His Kang shares had always seemed theoretical, hypothetical, and barely-half real. Kang scarcely had meaningful revenues, leave alone profit. Could the computer and software industry have that great a future potential? It seemed amazing. Apparently, there were banks and financiers who thought it was quite real indeed.

She said he needed a lawyer. He could only think immediately of the cocktail party he had attended with Esther Halevi. A small reputable Cambridge firm of three Jewish women partners, all Harvard law alumnae, who were celebrating a move to their new offices on Mt. Auburn street. As he recalled, they specialized in civil rights, domestic relations, estate planning and constitutional law with an emphasis in something called 'appellate practice'. They were found in the telephone directory: "Ottolenghi, Minzi & Cordoza."

The next day, wearing his best coat and tie he presented himself to their offices and was assigned a rather bookish second-year associate, Luisa Sanchez, who enrolled him as a client and explained the firm's billing procedures. With her help, in three weeks he had completed the satisfactory creation of a charitable trust called the Gemini Fund, executed the bank's line-of-credit facility, had drafts of his will, and had located an accountant who would also handle his tax obligations. Finally, to supplement the use of traveler's checks, he had obtained an amazing American Express credit card, one of the new tributes of digital technology. It could produce cash out of electricity. Unexpectedly, he felt well-to-do. It was his undeserved good luck to be at the birth of the machine-language game, an ironic version of Wittgenstein's *sprachspiel*, if nothing else. It felt like freedom from wage slavery! Was that simply a matter of money? It seemed that feeling of economic independence, the sense of liberty, could not fail to lead him to imaginative future possibilities.

And while in this frothy mental realm, as if to underscore the point, within a few days he received the expected call from Bob Adler, updating news of his forthcoming arrival in Cambridge. Could he crash at Reuel's? He was eager to catch up.

And so, they did. Adler described a social revolution unfolding in California in a neighborhood called Haight-Ashbury, as if it was an analogue of Vatican City. It was all because of psychedelics. There were new bookstores with new kinds of literary inventory. There were street communes. There were "acid tests" where hundreds of kids gathered to party and imbibe from open bowls of LSD-loaded punch to dance wildly to new forms of popular music that were being born. There were new kinds of folk singers with unbelievable lyrics, and poets and novelists who were creating a new métier. And further, a new form of politics was being created. It seemed a social revolution was underway. The anti-Vietnam war movement was gaining strength. Even academic philosophers like Herbert Marcuse could see what was happening. Norman Brown's "Life Against Death" was selling out in bookstores. Social psychologists were explaining how we were being emancipated from 'repressive desublimation' - what a concept! And that we were merely victims of a false tolerance that in reality was oppressive. And finally, always with the aid of psychedelics, we could see that our one-dimensional bourgeois character was destined for the trash bin of history. Here he drew a breath. "Maybe I'm dropping too much of the stuff. Actually, I'm afraid there's a lot of political resistance to what's happening."

But then, having reached his peroration he pointed a finger at Reuel and said: "And as for the academic examination of the subject of consciousness, which so fascinates you, U of C at Santa Cruz started a History of Consciousness program, leading to doctoral degrees. California's on to something, showing the way. It's a new world. And best of all, something spiritual is also starting up out there. The teachers are coming. Hindu meditation gurus, Sufi guides, Tibetan Lamas, Zen priests, Kundalini Yoga masters, you name it. All over the place. It's LSD man!"

"Nothing's forever" said Reuel, listening patiently. "Some of us live East of the Mississippi. Skepticism can also be mind-opening, like a different kind of psychedelic."

Days later, at Adler's entreaty, they highlighted the visit with a shared tab of "Orange Sunshine". Unlike Reuel's prior mournful experience of brain altering chemistry, on this occasion he felt joyful, relieved of all submerged academic and financial concerns. Sex was more interesting. Now he saw his future as an illuminated realm of possibility, where the cerebral weight of machine language, cognitive science and philosophy seemed as light and flimsy as air itself. The thought of his long-standing preoccupation with recursive syntactical hierarchies now appeared to him as a human comedy. A folly emblazoned and made emblematic by the limitless depth of anthropoid ignorance in the ocean of the eternal hereafter. The simplicity of it all seemed breathtaking and Reuel's several loud bursts of laughing to himself with delight apparently affected his companion with gloom.

Adler was sinking in the opposite direction, as if he had seen too much. Going from morose to despondent he finally became coherently confessional. He was unable to halt the flowing verbosity of his painful introspection. Floods of emotion lay beneath his words. Every sentence seemed to rise and fall, from hurt to indifference, from clarity to chaos, with an invisible hand of self-organization forming an architecture out of his thoughts and their naked truths.

"I'm telling you Roo, honestly, I feel sick of most of the people around me. I feel like I'm caught by the blades of a scissor. On the one hand I go around the country making speeches to college kids. Not even sure I know what I'm talking about and actually becoming a bagman for money they give me to buy acid. We're out of Orange Sunshine, by the way. The new stuff is called 'White Lightning'. More bang for the buck by our bootleg alchemists in California. I just feel that if I keep doing this, Nixon's FBI is going to bust me, sooner or later. On the other hand, I'm being pitched by a bunch of millionaire rich kids to head up a newly invented foundation to do research in Mexico, with a gigantic villa near Cuernavaca. To do research, whatever the hell they think that is. All they mean is people would come there to get turned on and we make notes about what they experience. It sounds tempting for rest and relaxation so I'll probably go. I really don't know if it's a joke or its serious. Lots of anecdotes to collect and pretend it's real data."

"What's the alternative?"

"I could just go quiet for a while. Stay with some friends in Colorado. Learn to ski. Try to write something. Cut back on using anything. Ever heard of dimethyl tryptamine? DMT? Or dimethoxymethyl-amphetamine? STP?"

"Never."

"There's a zoo of these chemicals out there. They sure fuck around with your neurotransmitters. Change how you see yourself. I think I've temporarily lost 20 IQ points, so help me. I'm turning into a spiritual junkie, in search of the miraculous."

"What does that mean?"

"It's just that I'm convinced there's something mysterious out there in the universe, that inhabits us. Something immaterial, something psychic and profound, transcendent, which allows the mind to consciously see itself."

"Bob, that's bullshit mystical dualism. There is no ghost in the machine. Your mind and your body aren't distinct and separate from one another. That kind of thinking went out the window with Descartes. The world is composed of just one kind of substance, the physical kind, there is no other kind. You're suffering from a category mistake. Like the guy who knows the basketball squad but can't locate the team-spirit."

"What about information?"

"It's just signals encoded into stuff. No stuff, no information."

"And what about the conscious mind? I'm not talking at the moment about the soul, but what about the mind?"

"That's an abstraction, not a thing. It makes no difference whether the world we see around us is the real world itself or only an internal perceptual copy of that world generated by neural processes in our brain. It's the same thing. Our brains contain some 85 billion neurons, each linked to thousands of others throughout our bodies. That's what we call embodied cognition."

"No Roo, no. Consciousness is something different. I feel sure of it. It's different than physical matter, and furthermore, if consciousness exists here it exists in the entire universe. I grant you that some intellectual functions like reasoning and memory, and emotions like love, hate, fear and joy are in the brain. But that's primitive and low-level subjective stuff, different than the conscious mind as such."

"Jesus, Bob. What on earth could that mean? The key attribute of what you, or we, are calling the conscious mind is that it's a private subjective turf to which no one but the brain's owner has access. Just because it's private doesn't mean it's also 'out there' even if we can talk with one another about it and try to study it. The problem remains that it's impossible to understand the phenomenon of consciousness because we can't get outside of our minds to discuss it."

"Roo, my friend, that's why science can't help us. We need a new way to look at this. So help me, that's why I really want to go to India. There are whole cultures over there, in thousands of years, with thousands of intellectual and philosophical geniuses, profound and analytical meditators. They keep insisting that mind and consciousness are real, not abstractions. That we can access the spiritual and immaterial character of the universe. It's the non-physical part of life. It's what makes us different from robots. It can't just be a laboratory subject. It has to be a first-person subject, not a third person subject. We can develop ourselves into a higher level of being. Understanding mind and consciousness can't be derived by looking into or at somebody else's brain or behavior. Using a first-person approach is logically necessary. Your own personal subjectivity demonstratively shows that consciousness has to be conceptualized as something distinct from the brain. That seems elementary to me."

"You really want to go to India?"

"Don't you?"

"Well, I'd like to travel. See the world."

"Where to?"

"Lots of places. I've got to go to Sweden again. Check out my kids."

"Yeah, I remember. When will you go?"

"In a few weeks. My lease here is up at the end of next month."

"What for? It's a nice pad."

"I'm leaving Cambridge."

"What?"

"I'm giving up the Ph.D."

"You're shitting me."

"No, it's serious. I scored some good money from a computer gig. Turned out bigger than anyone expected. I don't need to find a job these days. Want to see the world. Have some adventures. Find a girlfriend."

"Let's go to India together."

"When?"

"In a few months? When I'm finished with Cuernavaca."

"How?"

"We'll figure it out. Think about it. Meet me in Mexico."

"I might. India, wow! I'll let you know. That'll be a trip."

A week passed. The experience of financial freedom, hitherto unknown and unexpected, had a pronounced and far-reaching effect on Reuel, as it would on most people. It scattered the daily or weekly arrangement of his thoughts. It felt odd to give attention to the quotidian matters such as grocery shopping, laundry, stationary resupply, going to the movies, or even reading the local newspaper. Cambridge, Massachusetts seemed like a tiny provincial suburb of planet Earth, and MIT scarcely more than a local shoemaker's shop. Though freedom to travel was an intoxicating feeling, the only azimuth on his radar was a conjectured trip to Stockholm.

He located a city-block of storage lockers in nearby Somerville and signed a two-year lease on the space. It took half a day to fill it with the contents of his emptied apartment. Using his birthdate as the code to the heavy combination lock on the steel frame, he spent several minutes staring at the locker number to fix it in his memory. Then he drove his Porsche to a car dealer in Brookline and sold it within an hour. The minor financial loss seemed trivial. Finally, he informed the bank and law firm of his impending travel plans, and signed two memoranda of instruction concerning his forthcoming dispositions.

With scarcely a day remaining on his apartment lease, which now lacked bedding and linens, he terminated his telephone service, washed all the dishes, sponge-cleaned the empty refrigerator and packed a duffel bag and a back-pack with an assortment of clothes, toiletries, several books, and checked himself into the Ritz-Carlton for several nights of leisure to meditate on his prospective venture.

The following morning, refreshed by a chilly jog around Boston Common and a coffee at the Frog Pond Café, he made his first rough plan. He would stop for his very first visit to Britain for a week or more before flying on to Sweden, where he was not yet expected. That could involve another week or two. Thereafter, he thought of trying to visit Luca in Rome again with the hope of convincing him to visit Athens, all expenses paid. Beyond that, who could say? India sounded rather interesting, with Bob Adler as a companion, but that would be months off.

Nearer at hand, the psychological and geographical magnetism of the great British home island seemed irresistible. It was the mother tongue of his thoughts, the home of his familiar philosophers and authors, the very navel of the enlightenment and its old empire. There would be the chance for a taste of Shakespeare at the theatre, and a day or two at the British Museum, the National Gallery, the Victoria and Albert. Perhaps even side trips to Oxford and Cambridge, just to taste the air and browse the booksellers. This was what his intoxicating freedom was about, was it not? He could fly in first-class. And so, it developed and went, eclipsing much thought about mind or consciousness or the meaning of it all.

ẽ

The American sounding name of the London Hilton was reassuring. He took a large room overlooking Hyde Park and endured his first day of jet-lag by napping and studying a glossy bedside magazine called London for Tourists. The weather was cold and wet, and at the advice of the concierge he took a cab to Harrods on the Brompton Road and bought himself a hooded thigh-length insulated waterproof jacket. He assured himself that this new, if uncertain, emotional state, alone and untried, without an agenda, in a land far from home, was entirely normal.

He spent the next several days in serious visits to the famous museums. To see the Rosetta Stone, the Parthenon Marbles, the Egyptian mummies, the Sutton Hoo mask, the Etruscan mosaics, the East Asian collections, the world's greatest renaissance paintings, and the like. Saturating with the past. And he walked for miles, armed with a street map, tasting neighborhoods of inner London. Then there were cherished bookstores, which he had saved till the jet-lag was entirely over. Browsing at booksellers was surely one of the world's great pleasures which could be done entirely alone while standing upright. Hatchards and Waterstones on Piccadilly, were both immense but too upscale with trade books for his evolved polymathic taste. Foyle's on Charing Cross was entirely another matter, occupying a full day. It was like the Amazon.

London tourism finally accomplished, Reuel took the bus to Oxford, checked in to the descriptive Old Bank hotel, and began a rigorous tour of college yards which made Harvard University pathetically shabby by comparison. To his relief, the diversions of the Ashmolean and Pitt Rivers museums were of human scale, with individually absorbing exhibits, unlike the thronged mammoths of London.

It was the college-town bookstores which absorbed him in a universal browser's trance. Blackwell's and the Bodleian Library bookshop occupied an entire day. In the section on metaphysics, he examined a copy of The Concept of Mind by the British philosopher Gilbert Ryle. His own underlined copy was in a storage locker in Massachusetts. The dust-jacket made mention that Ryle was the Waynflete Professor of Metaphysical Philosophy and Fellow of Magdalen College, which lay a few blocks down the way, on the bank of the River Cherwell. Did he dare call on him? After all, the concept of mind preoccupied him these days.

Like Wittgenstein, Ryle was a keen observer of philosophical nonsense. He would ask what was wrong with saying there were three things in a field, i.e. two cows and one pair of cows, or whether the bunghole of an ale barrel is part of the barrel or not. Or most aptly, the imaginary specimen of a category mistake by a tourist, visiting Oxford and inspecting the colleges and the Bodleian and innocently asking a passerby "but where is the university?" The mistake being the presumption that the term "university" belonged to a category consisting of physical buildings rather than a type of an institution of learning. He decided to call on Ryle.

He walked down the High Street and, passing for a student, entered the college past the porter's lodge, and upon entering the great lawn of the Cloister totally lost his courage regarding his idea of visiting Ryle. I am insane, he thought, I have lost my mind, the mind which I do not have; only a bent brain. He retreated and walked across the High Street to have a look at the city botanical garden.

On the morning of the following day, Reuel took a bus to Cambridge and located himself at the University Arms hotel, immediately next to Emmanuel College. A glossy brochure at his bedside informed the reader that a famous alumnus of "Emma" was a student named John Harvard, who became an ordained minister in the Massachusetts Bay Colony, who upon his death of tuberculosis left a bequest of a few hundred pounds and some 400 books to support the creation of a college near Boston. How could Harvard possibly compare with Cambridge University entire and its 121 Nobel Prizes?

Reuel spent the next day at the Fitzwilliam Museum where much of his attention lay in the Egyptian galleries, and following a lunch of cheese and ale, spent the remainder of the afternoon studying the oil paintings and the several hundred watercolors of William Blake, as well as the poet's manuscript papers. Reuel's head was swimming with monuments of his own ignorance and insignificance. The evening found him at a chamber music recital of Beethoven quartets at the city's West Road concert hall.

On walking back to the hotel through a chilling drizzle he felt an unusual touch of melancholy descend on him. He realized that in more than a week he had scarcely spoken to anyone other than sales clerks, flight attendants, receptionists, guides, waiters, bartenders, taxi drivers, and the occasional pedestrian of whom he asked directions. The absence of personal relations, even if they were superficial, was a relatively new experience. In fact, he felt lonely. A lucky man, in good health, well-educated, of newly independent means who felt alone in the world. Alone. It seemed odd. Was it the absence of female companionship? No, it was deeper than that. It seemed to him that he was living in a riddle without an answer. Why should that produce the slight melancholy? Was that in his mind or in his brain? The form of the question intrigued him once again.

He lay in bed, unable to sleep. He found himself envious of Beethoven, indeed of all forms of musical creativity. Sounds minus words could easily be beautiful or harsh. And the Caravaggios at the Fitzwilliam were created, produced and viewed without words. It was words that troubled. Words that became questions that had no answers. When Polonius inquires of Hamlet what he is reading what does Hamlet say? "Words, words, words."

And what to make of words questioning feelings. Feelings weren't exactly cognitive stuff. He took the word "love", for example. The philosophers and brain scientists were quite a bit dodgy about this. Their words about such feelings seemed oblique, hollow, secondary. In fact, it was the poets, the playwrights, the story tellers, who did better in using words about feelings, holding up the mirror to nature as someone said. Empiricists, the Cambridge analytic philosophers, were merely playing with words about emotions. Was there a scientific answer about the nature of emotional feelings? Of affective consciousness? Just to be dismissed as something down in the lower brain of the vertebrates? He hadn't ever really thought very hard about this. The philosophers seemed out of court. Shakespeare had more to say than Noam Chomsky. What exactly was the neurobiology of sadness? Just in the subcortical realm of inarticulate feelings produced in the brain stem that he shared with most mammals?

These questions weighed on him. He didn't want to exaggerate and call it suffering. But the feeling of loneliness was not rescued by thinking, or some cognitive exercise ginned up in the brain's cortex. What was he supposed to do? Sit on his bed and meditate on his non-self? There was the thinking thing, and there was the feeling thing. Descartes' "I think therefore I am" would have had a lot more philosophical weight if he had merely said "I feel therefore I am."

He had a restless night of poor sleep. The weight of ignorance stayed with the next morning as he toured several colleges on the walk to Trinity. The awesome chapel of King's, the 14th century intimacy of Clare with its back and bridge on the River Cam, and then on to Gonville & Caius with its life-science stars from William Harvey to Watson and Crick. That would be the logical college for an aspiring brain scientist.

And then, last, he came to Trinity. The Vatican, the Pentagon. He imagined what it might be like to have been a callow aspiring geometer hoping for admission to Plato's Academy in Athens, with Socrates' ghost overlooking the matriculation of Aristotle. Reuel now stood in the shade under the massive gate opening onto the Great Court. He felt so inferior, of small intelligence, with a worthless career path, of low ambition, of pedestrian employment history, of a damaged IQ from the use of LSD, of chasing girls rather than hard study, and so on. Alone. He felt near to tears on what he might have been. Here in these buildings were the vibrations of Newton, and Maxwell, and Rutherford, and Bohr, and Babbage, and Whitehead, and Moore, Hardy, Ramanujan, Ramsey, Russell and Wittgenstein. Reuel Antenor with his petty B.A. from Columbia and an MIT dropout was just a worthless tourist with a scant bare-bones background in philosophy, neurobiology, computer science, and an abandoned boy's love of mathematics.

He fled back to the streets, found a pub, ate a shepherd's pie, drank a pint and decided he would try to reach Stockholm the next day. In theory, he had family there. He walked back to the Old Bank hotel and asked the concierge to engage a car and driver to drive him to London that evening. And specifically, to the hotel nearest Heathrow Airport. It cheered him up a touch to realize he was relatively unconcerned at the expense of these modest luxuries. He now had means.

That left the remainder of the day. Time for a bookstore. The choice was narrowed to Waterstones, Plurabelle Books, Heffers, and the Cambridge Press bookshop. At the concierge's recommendation, it was Heffers, where he quickly browsed the trade books on the ground floor and headed up the stairs to the academic and university press multitudes. The arrangements were meticulous: an immense section labeled "Science" where one could navigate through the ocean of "Evolution", to the continent of "Biology", down the river of "Physiology" to the cerebral estuary of the "Encephalon" where a brainy classicist wit had inked the guide card "from the Greek *en* 'inside' + *kephalē* 'head'. Reuel was happily lost for a while from the mundane world into the special heaven of bibliomania.

As if pulled by magnetism or gravity, within another hour he had gone on through the "Technology" galaxy and resisted the seductive orbits of "Electrical Engineering" and "Machine Language" alongside the immense neighboring planetary section labeled "Linguistics". By then he had the near- satiated feeling of a decamper from a banquet who was still in search of desert. Which he found. There was a wing labeled "Philosophy" past a wall named "Logic" to a corridor called "Metaphysics" which had a window at its end providing a welcome touch of bright illumination at a cul-de-sac with the unframed card "Analytics". And he could sit on the floor there with a small pile extracted from a row on a shelf following the letter W.

They were all there for sale, though not in chronological order. "*The Blue & Brown Books*", "*On Certainty*", "*Tractatus Logico-Philosophicus*", "*The Ontology of Mathematics*", and "*Philosophical Investigations*". He spent a cramped half-hour under the window examining the Ontology title, which was new to him. It contained student notes summarizing a free-wheeling discussion in 1939 between two celestial geniuses, Ludwig Wittgenstein and Alan Turing. It was beyond his understanding. He felt somewhat feeble-minded. It seemed the book was less about philosophy than it was about the psychology of mathematics, the mathematics of logic which was sadly far over his head. It seemed to be about understanding the difference, if there was one, between mathematical invention and mathematical discovery. He put the book aside. The *Blue & Brown* title was merely student notes concerning Wittgenstein's studies pertaining to the great summa of the Investigations and did not detain him. With a smile he picked up the *Tractatus* and re-examined the famous propositions. The last time he had been with the book had been in the stacks of Low Library at

Columbia University when he was a callow undergraduate philosophy major. He now thumbed the pages as if dealing with hand-written vellum sheets of a first known edition of The Holy Bible.

A clerk emerged from the shadows and informed him with a friendly nod that the store would be closing shortly. Reuel's thumb was at Proposition 6.5. *"When the answer cannot be put into words, neither can the question be put into words. The riddle does not exist. If a question can be framed at all, it is also possible to answer it."* The italic emphasis was in the original.

He stood up, preparing to leave, and turned to the page again. Now it was at proposition 6.52: *"We feel that even when all possible scientific questions have been answered, the problems of life remain completely untouched. Of course, there are then no questions left, and this is itself the answer."* Reuel sighed in anticipation, recalling what he would see following, in Proposition 6.522: *"There are, indeed, things that cannot be put into words. They make themselves manifest. They are what is mystical."* Which led finally to one of the best known of Ludwig's messages in Proposition 7: *"What can be said at all can be said clearly, and what we cannot talk about we must pass over in silence."* He remembered memorizing the words in German, practicing for his language proficiency examination in the Porsche, after his first LSD session with Bob Adler. *"Wovon man nicht sprechen kann, darüber mus man schweigen."* And then, as he closed the book, to the great philosopher's summing up: "The world is represented by thought, which is a proposition with sense, since they all—world, thought, and proposition— share the same logical form."

It made him mentally breathless to think of this all. He was, as they say in chess, a mere 'patzer' by comparison. Intending to buy something he went downstairs to the clerk carrying Blackwell's second edition of Philosophical Investigations with its English translation by Gertrude Anscombe, one of Wittgenstein's favorite students, chosen by him to be his translator. Ph.D Cambridge University, she was a Fellow of Sommerville College and Professor of Philosophy. The book cost £23 Sterling. He charged it to his American Express card.

Reuel emerged to the street and consulted the map folded in his pocket. It was a cool day in the late afternoon as he walked slowly and thoughtfully up the Huntingdon Road toward All Souls Lane. Exactly as depicted, there lay the cemetery, the Ascension Parish Burial Ground. After a bit of wandering within, he found it. A flat limestone slab in the grass. The bare legend read: 'Ludwig Wittgenstein 1889 – 1951'. The poor man, he thought. A well-known lifetime of tortured unhappiness and suffering. He wondered if anything might have been different if Ludwig had known of Buddhism. Reuel stood there for a while with a bowed head, regretting he didn't have a flower.

The hotel had a car and driver ready for him. It took barely a few minutes to pack his bag and check out. The drive in the early winter darkness was uneventful and he reached the Heathrow Airport Marriot in time for dinner in the hotel, where he read the International Herald Tribune over his food. Afterwards, up in his room he made three telephone calls. The first to SAS, booking a business class seat on the 10:30 a.m. flight to Stockholm's Arlanda airport on the following day. The second to The Grand Hotel in Stockholm, reserving a room with a view for a week. The third to the Bergstroms. He spoke to Hedda, the twins' grandmother, who was baby-sitting as Lennart and Ulla were at the cinema. She was excited, and assured him how happy they would all be to see him after all this time. Just a dozen phone calls over the years. What a wonderful surprise! She sounded sincere and Reuel promised to call after he was checked into The Grand.

There was a message waiting for him at the front desk when he arrived. Ulla's handwritten note, cheerfully inviting him to dinner. The twins would be excited to meet Uncle Roo from America. It was signed "From Ulla and Lennart." Armed with a bottle of champagne from the hotel, Reuel had the taxi stop at *Ahlens Varuhus*, where he bought two large fuzzy teddy bears and arrived to the Bergstroms punctually at six o'clock.

His first impressions: Ulla was apple-cheeked and had gained ten kilos. She embraced him heartily and kissed both of his cheeks. Smiling Lennart Bjork had also swelled in his mid-section, had lost a great deal of his curly hair, and held Reuel's hand warmly at length with both of his. The wide-eyed twins, now nearly four years old, bobbed in an obviously rehearsed gesture, and allowed themselves to be kissed with happy giggles as he presented his gifts. Grandmother Hedda cradled a solemn looking one-year-old boy in her arms and she blew Reuel a kiss.

They sat around on a sofa and soft armchairs sharing the champagne and exchanging profiled highlights of the past few years. The girls, officially known as Karen and Kristina Bjork Bergstrom, fidgeted quietly and politely whispered to one another. Reuel was unable to tell them apart and believed they were surely destined to be great beauties one day. The little boy, Lennart's son, was called Nils, and Ulla was presently three months pregnant with an unnamed child in utero. Ulla had her arms full with homemaking and motherhood and volunteering at the neighborhood nursery. Lennart was now assistant concert-master at the Stockholm Symphony and was likely to have the senior position in a year or two. Ulla had expanded her repertoire and with Lennart had formed the violin section of an informal string quartet of friends on Sunday afternoons at home. Hedda had her arms full looking after them all. As the time arrived for dinner, she gathered Nils and the twins to bed and sleep. Her own room was in the remodeled attic and she bowed out with a firm decision to have the entire family to a festive dinner three days later.

Finally, alone at table with Ulla and Lennart, over meatballs and potatoes and a carafe of red wine, Reuel explained the motive of his visit to Stockholm. Related how graduate school at MIT had led to extra-curricular work in the emerging computer industry, and then how his small stock ownership had surprisingly grown to have considerable value and was likely to become even greater in the future. As he felt a moral responsibility to support his children, he had created a separate charitable trust out of his shares, called the Gemini Fund, to benefit the girls. He now wished to transfer its administration to Sweden. At the moment he was the sole trustee but hoped Ulla and Lennart would join him in the managing the Fund. While there was a restriction on the sale of the shares, that restriction would be removed once the shares were publicly traded. He was told that was likely in a year or two. Did they have any questions?

They did. Why was it called the Gemini Fund? Was the fund restricted to the twins? Would it not be unsettling to their siblings? Were Nils and the forthcoming child in Ulla's womb excluded from the benefits?

"To tell you the truth" said Reuel, "I hadn't really given much thought about that. I do understand what you are saying."

"What is to be done?" asked Lennart. "We are just middle-class people Roo. We must not allow money to divide our family."

"I tell you what. Actually, there is no problem. The Fund doesn't have named beneficiaries. If you, Ulla and I are the three trustees we can disburse the funds to all the children, as we like. Even to immigrant children if we want. I have no problem with that. And you are the only family I know or have. I have no brothers or sisters or aunts and uncles or cousins. Only two daughters and the big family that loves them. There is no problem. The Bjork, Bergstrom, and Antenor families are joined."

"You are a good person" said Ulla. "I have always thought that. Kristina and Karen do not know you are their father. They call Lennart "Papa". And we are always wondering how and if, and when should we tell them. Only in the last few days did they learn they had an Uncle Roo. What do you think?"

"I leave it entirely to you. I will always love them, of course. I know you will do the right thing. Some day they will have to know, when they are older. But exactly when, is yours to say. Send them to college in America maybe. You two will decide."

Linnea called him at the hotel early the next morning.

"You could have told me you were coming" her first words when he answered the phone, half awake.

"Linnea?"

"Yes, yes. Me. Remember me?"

"Of course, I do."

"What are you doing today?"

"I have to meet Ulla and Lennart at the *Svenska Handelsbank. We want to set up some accounts. For the children.*"

"*And then? You can have dinner?*"

"*Okay.*"

"*Meet us at the restaurant. It's called De Akvarius.* You can walk there easily from the hotel. Only a few blocks."

"Who's us?

"My boyfriend Freddy. He made me call you. He wants to meet you. He has a radio news show. *Sverige Radio.* He's going to run for parliament. You'll like him. Seven o'clock, okay?"

That evening they greeted Reuel warmly. An American visitor was just what Freddy wanted. There was mostly a single subject: Vietnam, and Nixon's bombing of Cambodia. Whatever Reuel said would be on Sverige Radio tomorrow. "So, what do you think?" Freddy asked.

"It's horrible. I'm lucky I wasn't drafted. I had deferred status as a graduate student and a low classification as the father of two children. I might have gone to Canada had they called me. The whole thing has to be a colossal mistake. They call it the 'Red Menace' because of the Soviets, and Vietnam is supposed to be a falling domino. Australia could be next they say. It's crazy. The time of colonial empires is finished. French Indo-China is finished. Ho Chi Minh is just an anti-colonial liberation fighter, like those guys in Algeria. It's not about the Russians. It's about colonialism. Washington is just making a category error. It's tragic. I'm not interested in politics anyway. Too many crazy egomaniacs."

"Perfect" said Freddy. "You've given me tomorrow's radio program. I'll not mention your name."

The next day was relatively open. There was only a morning meeting in Kungsholm with a lawyer who had drafted a Memorandum of Understanding concerning the Gemini Trust in both Swedish and English. It was exact with instructions to the point. Reuel signed both notarized copies and cover letters to the Cambridge National Bank and his lawyers. His good deed in Stockholm was done.

He tried calling some old laboratory acquaintances at the Karolinska. Nobody had heard of them. He called IBM out in Kistagangen to say hello to Lars Soderberg. But he was now relocated to Brussels. That left the afternoon and evening free. Reuel gave thought of calling on Phra Luang but decided to postpone the idea until he was finished with the Bergstroms and ready to leave Sweden. That left only the thought of bookstores. He remembered two with a section of English titles. *Litterat Bokhandlare* on Rittgarten Gata, a cab ride away, and *De Boksäljare* near the Hotel, within walking distance. On the way he stopped at a newsvendor and bought a Herald Tribune to read over dinner. The Boksäljare had a balcony for foreign titles, French, German, and English. A hand-lettered card with an arrow pointed at some narrow tables *Engelska Facklitteratur*, English Non-Fiction. On the dust cover he recognized the head and shoulders photo of a sad looking man without a necktie looking off to the side, its title in large letters *"Filosofiska Utredningar, En ny översättning."* Immediately he saw it was "Philosophical Investigations, A new translation." He experienced a spasm of misery and regret and felt worthless. What was the meaning of the shallow life he was leading?

Reuel walked very slowly to the hotel in an unfamiliar feeling of melancholy. Everything seemed dull. He was alone in the world. If only something could change his mood. He wondered if there was a chance of picking up a woman at the hotel bar. Or perhaps he should call Luca in Rome and arrange a visit. Not quite at wit's end he gave serious thought to returning to MIT and resuming work on Recursive Syntactical Hierarchies.

The desk clerk handed him his keys and informed him that there was a message for him at his room. It was handwritten on hotel stationary.

Dear Reuel,

I drove down from Sundvall today to attend Hedda's family celebration for you tomorrow night and learned you were staying here at the Grand. If this reaches you in time and you have no other plans, I invite you to dinner in the very good restaurant here below deck. It would be a pleasure to catch up with you, father of my granddaughters.

Eric (Anderson) Room 431

Reuel was delighted and called him immediately to confirm. They met at the bar and shared several Akvavits diluted with cranberry juice and tonic water before coming to their table. Reuel described his intervening years, Anderson did the same, mostly about boat building, now smaller models, and the near loss of his finger while using an electric saw on a sheet of fiberglass.

"The chock came loose. And I must learn to use my goggles more often."

"Where's the Saga these days?"

"She's in the South. A French banker, an experienced sailor, bought her over three years ago and he took two months sailing her out the Baltic, down the coasts all the way to Cadiz, and then into the Med to a berth at Cannes. He took her to Lebanon and Turkey a few times. Now she charters back and forth to Mallorca every summer under a contract couple he uses as her crew. Doesn't trust bareboating. No way to compete with the big yachts for clients but very nice for a small family holiday with kids learning about boats. That Frenchie now has family medical issues. We keep in touch. He always has questions. Called me a few weeks ago saying she was for sale. Listed with a yacht broker."

"How much?" Reuel was immediately curious.

"I don't know. Could be a bargain. Don't tell me you're interested. You have that much money?"

"Depends. It's a thought. I loved working on her and taking her out. One of my life's high points under sail. Tell me more."

"Well, first of all, though I was against it, the man did a dual conversion from just a tiller to adding a wheel and he upgraded the self-steering. He put in a console forward in the cockpit, hinged the tiller so it folds up, and allows the self-steering to be adjusted from the pedestal. Overkill, in my opinion. There's now three ways to manage the helm. Crazy. I love the feeling of a tiller. It's no bother for me coming about."

"Awkward for guests on the bunks."

"Plus, he created a small crew cabin in the locker under the lazarette. That's it. Just wear and tear otherwise."

"Who's the Frenchman?"

"Name is Bernard Dufoy. Lives in Paris. In his late sixties, maybe. Used to be high-up in Société Générale. Now runs a private bank with some Arabs. Banque Zarqa, it's called. Wife has breast cancer. He's had hip surgery. Then something with a bad tremor in his hands. Saga's still tied up in Cannes. Crew lives on board caretaking her."

"Who are they?"

"Man holds a skipper's license from Trinidad. Ran a fishing boat down there. Decided to make some money doing luxury charters, came to work the Riviera. Young couple from French Antilles, Guadeloupe, mixed-race."

"The Caribbean."

"Ah."

After a few rounds of alcohol and much handshaking Hedda's big dinner took place as scheduled. A festive table laid out with flowers, candles, linens, silver utensils, old family porcelain, five carafes of red wine, and individual place settings. They were twelve. Grandparents Hedda and Eric at opposite ends of a rectangular table. The others: Ulla and Lennart; Lennart's brother Torval, a piano tuner and wife Lizbet, an elementary school teacher; the senior Bergstrom daughter Marta and her man Alex, like her in the Karolinska administration; youngest daughter Alice, a librarian, and her new husband Edvard, an architect; and finally, Linnea, a fashion designer and Reuel, unemployed. Freddy missing, out campaigning for parliament. The twins and little Nils were confined to the spacious attic room with a baby-sitter who reads them fairy tales by Hans Christian Anderson. Three hired servants and a cook in the kitchen.

Hedda rings a little bell, reminds them she has four sons-in-law at the table, Alex, Edvard, Lennart, and Reuel. She raises a welcoming glass to the one from America. Ulla tells a story of how she met Reuel. Lennart praises the intelligence and good looks of the twins and thanks Reuel for his help in creating them. Marta says he will always be welcome at the Karolinska. Eric says Reuel would be a first-class shipmate. Linnea stands and hopes he will come to Sweden many times, and says "skal och honnor" - Cheers and honor. The table rises and all say *"skal och honnor"*. All the time Reuel is thinking about possibly owning the Saga.

He shares a taxi with Eric back to the hotel.

"Could you tell me how to reach that French banker in Paris?" he asks. "I'd like to visit him. I've never been to Paris. It would be a good excuse. See the Louvre. The booksellers along the Seine. I would like to give him a call."

Within the next two days Reuel had completed his obligatory courtesies in Sweden. Had shared an exceptionally empathetic afternoon with Ulla and Lennart, spent a giggling avuncular half-hour alone with Karen and Kristina, still unable to tell them apart, and gave Hedda a comradely embrace of *au revoir*. Warmed with Eric's information he spoke with Bernard Dufoy in Paris and arranged to meet him in the following week at his house. Dufoy, in a thin voice filled with sighs, described it as a small mansion, "un petit manoir", on the Rue Caffarelli near the Parc du Temple Elie Wiesel. He recommended staying at a nearby hotel, La Chambre du Marais, on the Rue des Archives. He would be happy to discuss the Saga. He suggested arriving at 4:00 for tea.

Reuel made the appropriate hotel reservation, booked a seat on the Air France flight the following day, and decided to chance a possible visit with Phra Luang on his last afternoon in Stockholm. The *Sveriges Buddhistiska Samarbetsråd* was within walking distance of the hotel and when he arrived, unannounced, he found Phra Luang sitting alongside the receptionist examining an account ledger. The old man recognized him instantly and arranged for them to sit in the small room exactly where they had years earlier, with tea and cookies.

After an exchange of informative pleasantries, the former monk and sewing- machine manufacturer, came to their shared interest.

"So, have you discovered the meaning of life since we last met?" asked Phra Luang."

"Actually, I'm trying to discover the meaning of meaning" Reuel replied. "I seem these days to have a great deal more time to devote to this. Buddhism is endlessly fascinating. On the one hand it's extremely simple. On the other hand, it seems endlessly complex and deep. Meditation is a universe in my brain. And there are so many paths to choose from, so many schools. I'm thinking of visiting Asia. What do you think?"

"I recall your interest in meditation. It certainly provides a space for examining what is meant by meaning. I think many people, as they approach the middle years of their lives, become interested in this question about the meaning of life. And so interesting that few young people do so. I'm not sure I fully understand why that should be so, but it is quite evident. Perhaps people experience more suffering, less enjoyment as they age. Many religions deal with this question, not only Buddhism. And as in Buddhism, many religions also have a multitude of paths."

"What is one to do?"

"Perhaps it is simple. Fortunate if you find your teacher. To some extent you can even teach yourself. Only find and adhere to a path that appeals to you. Or even the few paths which seem more attractive than others. Do you know the *mångasmaker* chain of shops?"

"The ice-cream parlors?"

"Yes. They have over fifty flavors. How to choose? Most people have one or two favorites and try the others from time to time, depending on their mood. By choosing your own method of self-discovery, a path, or several paths, to meaning, will probably emerge if you keep searching. Mind and heart will have to lead you. Of course, much depends on your native level of understanding. The Buddha said that the most fortunate of his followers were like the lotus blossoms poised just near the surface of a pond."

"Let me ask you. How can emptiness be meaningful?

"That is the question, isn't it? If there were to be some thing that was not empty, there would then have to be some other thing called empty. However, if there is nothing that is non-empty. How could there be something empty? Playing with words is a good subject for meditation, isn't it? I think we discussed this a little bit a few years ago. I think so. And by the way, is the search for meaning actually unpleasant? In every form of Buddhism, dissatisfaction is usually regarded as a matter of a certain kind of ignorance. The relief which is present is traditionally linked to your intuition's insight into the oneness of all things. That is a condition beyond the meaning of meaning. That usually takes practice. Although I believe some can achieve it in a single instance. Do you wish to become a monk?"

"No, not at all. Just to become better educated. I'm not unhappy, just hungry for more knowledge."

"That is good, but knowledge is not the same as experience. It could well be that life, at least at it is usually lived by many people, actually is absurd when seen from a certain perspective. It could well be that a person's crisis of meaning doesn't come from seeing too little of reality; it may come from imagining more to reality than really exists. The hard part is to see the world as reality itself, not more or less."

"Well, look, that sounds rather difficult."

"Perhaps it depends on your approach. Consider experiencing meaning-lessness in different ways: First a belief that your life is meaningless, just an illusion. Or else, a belief that your life is meaningful, but for some reason you just can't see why. That's a kind of ignorance. Next take an opposite belief, say your life is meaningful but you understand that too is an illusion. Some individuals are sensitive and perceptive enough to actually see that rather interesting point of view. Then there's a view that life is a combination of being both meaningful and meaningless. It's meaningless in some ways, and meaningful in other ways, and it just depends on the state of your views on the matter. Actually, that particular view may not be so difficult."

"That's a very strange logic. I'm not sure I follow it. What if I ask you what you think is the meaning of life?"

"I don't think about such a question, which plays on words. There are many other questions that are more important. Like how to be kind, or helpful. Words that make up philosophical thoughts are actually experienced as learned sounds in your mind, part of what is called 'the mind stream'. Becoming aware and perceiving the subjective flow of mental events in your brain is a practical and simple way to cultivate self-knowledge and understanding. Beyond explanation or what you call meaning. Some people call it mystical. We call it *tathata*. You translate that as 'suchness' in English. We say that it is the essential nature of phenomenal existence. It is the basis of transcendental wisdom, which has nothing to do with the meaning of life. It has to do with experiencing unhappiness, which has no absolute meaning."

"Phra Luang, is reality knowable? What about philosophy? Buddhist philosophy. There are centuries of it."

"My young friend, most people, busy people, don't have time for philosophy. People work, put bread on the table, caring for others, struggling to survive, each one busy in their own way. Even busy while they seek pleasures. Busy, busy. Philosophy is for philosophers, and in all times, there are only few such people, and they too are struggling to survive. And many of them are unhappy."

"This what you teach?"

"I do not teach. I conduct ceremonies for Theravadin dharma followers at births, marriages and funerals. I am a Buddhist but no longer a monk. I manage a sewing machine company. And I share my thoughts with you. You will probably learn more if you go to Asia. Like an ice-cream shop, you will find other flavors. My own *Vipassana* tradition emphasizes the quiet meditative development of mindfulness and concentration by focusing your attention on the rising and falling breath. There is no philosophy."

Reuel flew to Paris the next day.

Three weeks later and Reuel was found sitting on the deck of the Saga, docked in Algeciras, Spain, waiting for his companions to return with final additions to the boat's food lockers. They were preparing to sail across the Atlantic Ocean to the Americas.

This situation came about in the following way. In Paris, Bernard Dufoy and his wife, experienced sailors, becoming afflicted with the maladies of aging, decided to give up boat ownership. Attractively priced, especially in terms of the disparity between the French franc and the American dollar, the Saga presented a seductive allure to Reuel's new solvency. This was underscored, following a phone call to Beverly Thesiger of the Cambridge National Bank, when she informed him that the prospective value of his shares in Kang Laboratories had markedly increased owing to credible rumors that a large publicly owned company was in discussion to acquire Kang.

Adding to his useful meeting with Monsieur Dufoy, Reuel's first visit to Paris led to a form of a satiating auto-intoxication and self-satisfaction which should have given pause to any philosophically minded Buddhist probationer. While, like all things, his feelings were impermanent they still lacked any mark of suffering. The pleasurable enthusiasm he derived from his good fortune had not only been inflamed by absorbing visits to the Louvre and the Musee de l'Homme, but also by the splendid company of a beautiful English-speaking and cheerfully self-described sex-worker. Ever attentive to the slightest sexual vibration Reuel made her acquaintance at the bar of his hotel early in the evening of his arrival in Paris. It led to a high-priced three-day liaison with "Michelle" as his chaperone, translator and daily companion. It made him buoyant and feeling somewhat indestructible. He had the highest regard for her professionalism and intelligence. She appeared to enjoy sexual activity as much as he. Perhaps it was insincere, he could not tell, but he provided her a sweet gratuity at the end. And also, his waterproof jacket as a gift to her boyfriend, an Air France co-pilot working the Pacific routes. It amazed him that a few months earlier he had been an impecunious graduate student who knew nothing of this particular side of life.

Having considered an attractive asking price of the Saga with Dufoy, in high five figures, Reuel was necessarily obliged to make a first-hand inspection in Cannes and to examine the real-world consequences of legally consummating such a speculative purchase. Not only did this require trialing her out on the Mediterranean, it also included such troubling questions of where she would be harbored, if she would be crewed and chartered out, how she would be maintained, insured, and how legally transferred to Reuel's ownership. Leave alone conflicting questions such as travelling to India with Bob Adler.

Putting aside these matters on the overnight train to Cannes, Reuel had visions of cruising the Aegean, visiting Greek islands and the Ionian coast of Turkey, possibly accompanied by an idealized woman, a "Michelle" plus-plus. However, reality began when he met Pierre and Gabrielle Ferrand, a physically attractive couple, and the Saga's crew. It emerged that these were two amiable youths who were coming to the end of their one-year engagement and awaiting instructions from Dufoy and a contractual termination stipend on assisting in the sale.

Many unresolved and lingering issues in Reuel's daydreams were met during a friendly and serious getting-acquainted dinner with the Ferrands at *La Harpy*, a waterfront sea-food restaurant in Cannes, fueled by an abundance of vin ordinaire. They were all three of the same age. The Ferrands, childhood friends of two mixed-race Creole ocean fishing families of the French Antilles, were both born in Guadeloupe, had married somewhat over a year earlier and had taken their honeymoon in a footloose journey to travel around the world. Having made their way to Panama, they waited at the Canal for a likely Westbound yacht. They found one, happy to have an addition to its experienced but understaffed crew. The *Fidele*, trophy of a Greek shipping magnate, was on her way to Tahiti where she would rendezvous with the owner and his guests for a sailing tour of French Polynesia. From Tahiti the Ferrands volunteered to cook and manage the galley on a tramp steamer to Noumea, in New Caledonia, the French dependency which contained nearly 25% of the world's nickel resources. They worked there in a restaurant for several weeks, accumulating wages, until they found an ore-carrying vessel destined for Marseille. The ship's captain was happy to give them passage as far as Singapore in exchange for cooking services. From Singapore they were able to buy air-fares to Phnom Penh, in French-speaking Cambodia, where they went to see the fabled Khmer Buddhist temple ruins of Angkor Wat. There they met a monk called Saon Nath who introduced them to the *Vipassana* form of Buddhist meditation. They seriously practiced this for a few weeks while living in a forest monastery. Naturally, this particular part of their narrative created an instant bond with Reuel.

Thereafter they traveled by bus through Thailand to Burma, and arrived to India by a ferry to Calcutta. Traveling Westward through India by train they stopped for several days at Bodh Gaya to pay homage at the legendary fig tree under which the Buddha experienced his enlightenment. Reuel was transfixed to hear their tale. Then, after reaching New Delhi, the Ferrands found a budget flight to Beirut via Dubai. In French speaking Lebanon they spent some days around the Arab boat club until they were able to join the crew of an Egyptian motor yacht headed for Monte Carlo on the Cote D'Azur. It was there that a broker found them work on the Saga. Dufoy paid them handsomely for their caretaking, and allowed them to profit from chartering Saga on cruises to Mallorca in the Balearics. With the arrival of winter, they remained shore-bound in Cannes and had agreed to stay caretaking until the boat was sold. Thereafter they had planned to take the first Air France non-stop homeward to either Martinique or Guadeloupe.

Those plans changed with the arrival of Reuel. First, they arranged a sea trial for him, as the potential buyer, from Cannes to the coast of Corsica. This revealed a number of things. First and foremost was the obvious fact that they were more experienced sailors than Reuel. On the other hand, he was more knowledgeable of the boat's construction and hull design having had the experience of working under Eric Anderson in Sundvall. The rigging, halyards, lines, sheets and shrouds were used but still solid. Sails had some stains but were in good condition with spares in a locker. The galley and cabins were immaculate. The upgraded self-steering mechanism was easily explained. The diesel engine, tested repeatedly, was smooth and in perfect condition, with spare batteries and a full fuel tank. The latest generation of radio electronics were easy to understand and performed reliably whenever tested. There was considerable discussion of the dual helm conversion, and repeated testing of the option of choosing the wheel versus a tiller. It could be advantageous in a heavy sea. Reuel overnighted in the comfortable master's cabin and stayed awake wondering if he was doing the right thing.

Sailing back to Cannes in a light breeze with Reuel at the helm, they came to the heart of the situation. It was Gabrielle who surfaced matters. She called him "Rool".

"Rool, we see you still not sure you buy this boat. Where you keep her? Saga is like a home. You travelling man. Who keep Saga when you away?"

"Gabby, I can find help. No?"

"Not so easy. It cost you money. Then, two, three years more, and is more than cost of whole boat. We know how big Dufoy pay, even before us. He tres riche."

"You know, but I helped build Saga in Sweden. It would be nice to buy her."

"We have idea" said Pierre. He took a short pause to look at Gabrielle. "You can buy boat. Then, you sell half of boat to us. We pay you over five years. Meanwhile you can use anytime."

"Now that is interesting. But how will you make money? Chartering the Med in July and August?"

"Rool, this boat not right for Mediterranean. Competition is from big yachts. This boat best for short charters for small family, rich couple, maybe with child or two, who want sailing experience with crew that teaches boat handling. In Med, is small market, short season. And without crew, bareboat charter to experienced sailors, very rare, complicated, big insurance, you understand?"

"I do. But how can this work?"

Pierre and Gabrielle again exchanged a meaningful look. She spoke up.

"Rool, Pierre and me, we can sail Saga to Caribbean. Ideal boat for there. Easy chartering to small parties. Long season. Many clients. American,

British, Canadian, Brazilian, French people naturellement, *C'est les tropiques*. *Les Caraïbes*, different kind sea from Mediterranean. Every night we anchoring off islands with calm shores, lee side, nice beaches. Day sailing with ocean experience. Fishing. Swimming. Many French people come to French Antilles. Martinique, Guadeloupe, St. Barthelemy, St. Martin, Marie-Galante, Les Saintes, La Desirade, all these our islands, where we live, our home waters, our Départments et Collectivités d'Outre Mer. We know, we fish, every island from Trinidad up to Haiti, leeward, windward, Grenadines, St. Vincent, US and British Virgins. *Nos eaux domestiques*. We can make good money. Pay you back easy in five years. You can have boat anytime you like. You are part owner. What you think?"

"You two want to sail the Saga across the Atlantic Ocean?"

"Is not problem" said Pierre. "Maybe one month to cross, maximum. Sailing West this time of year is easy, safe. *Naviguez vers le sud jusqu'à ce que le beurre fonde, puis tournez à droite*. You follow? Sail South till the butter melts, then turn right. Like Columbus. Very easy. Now is good time of year. No Summer calms, no big storms, toujours reliable trade winds astern from Africa, blow us across."

"How do you navigate?" asked Reuel.

"Easy. Dead-reckoning, only with ship's compass. We be sailing toward the giant North-South arc of Caribbean islands. A thousand kilometers long from Haiti all way down to Trinidad. Impossible to miss our sea. Exact like Columbus. Finding latitude easy. We measure azimuth of Polaris above horizon every night. No need to shoot sun. Radio contact begins once we near our islands."

"Just the two of you?"

"It work, trust us. Sloop-rigged single mainsail easy to manage. Plus Genoa jib. We have years experience. Saga easy boat, like home to us. We do short sleeps. Listen to music. Fish for tuna. Use self-steering set-up. Mostly hands-on tiller. Use wheel if in a squall. Tropical Atlantic is our home ocean."

"Well, what if I come too?"

"*Mon Dieu.* You? That is fantastic. Then we make three watches, four on eight off. You will become expert ocean sailor. Saga is your boat. Then we buy our half from you. Okay? You really sail with us to Guadeloupe? We give you party you never forget."

"I might go to Mexico."

"That so easy. Fly to Miami. Then, non-stop Mexico City."

"Jesus, this is unbelievable! Okay. I say let's do it! Count me in."

It took the three of them a week to complete the arrangements. A contract of sale was created. Reuel had Cambridge wire-transfer the funds to Dufoy's French bank. The three had their handwritten agreement on ownership shares and terms executed on a single sheet of paper, notarized, with copies made. Reuel sent one to his law firm. Then wrote air-mail, "special delivery" to Adler, apprising him of his plan to arrive and join him in Cuernavaca sometime in late March. Gabrielle and Pierre shopped for every imaginable supply with special attention to foodstuffs.

The voyage from Cannes to Algeciras, in the shadow of Gibraltar, was slow with grey skied calms requiring motoring much of the time. At this last Iberian port, they shopped for every conceivable contingency. They filled the fuel tank and made a reserve drum. They purchased 400 liters of fresh water in plastic containers. Much was lashed on deck with netting. The Saga sat comfortably low in the water, ready to go. On the seventh day of February, they sailed past the international light-house at Tangier and entered the Atlantic Ocean. Gabrielle took the 4 to 8 dog-watch, Reuel had the 8 to 12, and Pierre the 12 to 4. They first sailed South-Southwest towards the Canary Islands under shifting winds and established their daily rhythms. Proceeding onwards in this way until the latitude of Africa's Cape Verde where the constant and fairly dependable 'trade winds' began their kinetics. It was *vers l'ouest*, due West, and Polaris now fixed steadily with a hand's-breadth at arm's length above the Northern horizon.

They sailed. They were a compatible threesome. Their instinctive courtesy at the outset of their relationship evolved into an easygoing friendship. They discussed family histories, life stories, dreams, their time in India, Catholicism, the politics of France, the definition of "sexy", the value of meditation, wine and food preferences, cinema favorites, the future of Buddhism, calypso music, cannabis, voodoo, and the unique lure of the sea. Gabrielle ran the galley. Pierre, the manhandling of heavy materials, anything to do with the mast, and the boat's toilets. Reuel, the keeping of the boat's logs. They averaged 8 knots a day.

Under continuous favorable sea and wind conditions their confidence in the self-steering apparatus grew with each trial. There were minor squalls which revealed the merit of a wheel over the tiller. There were calms where they lay on deck with minimal clothing. Gabrielle went topless, indifferent to the beauty of her body, and then they agreed that nudity was the best policy in daytime calms. Reuel could not take his eyes off her. He kept sexual thoughts of her. The Ferrands were physically beautiful. Pierre some inches above six feet with a chiseled torso and a face that might have sailed back from Troy with Odysseus. Gabrielle, five feet seven, like a Thetis by Praxiteles, or like Brigitte Bardot but with dark hair cut short. Reuel, usually quite happy with his physique, began to think of himself as rather soft and substandard.

One day, near mid-ocean, in a near dead-calm, they lowered the sails, started the diesel to maneuver, and took individual turns swimming. First was naked Gabrielle, who jumped from the bowsprit, swam two turns around the Saga and came up the rope ladder. Then Pierre, wearing a face mask and snorkel tube who repeatedly submerged to inspect the hull, keel, and the propeller blades before breast-stroking about with loud whoops of joy. They motored close to him and threw a life-ring for him to hold effortlessly for a long float at his leisure. After coming aboard it was Reuel's turn.

"Are their sharks?" he asked, as he prepared a headlong dive over the side.

"Not here" said Gabrielle, "middle ocean is like Sahara Desert. Bottom so deep, sea life scarce, not many fish. Maybe flying fish, dolphins, some Tuna. That's all. No sharks."

Reuel swam away with a lazy backstroke and stopped to float on the salty sea when he was 60 or 70 yards out from the boat. There he had two consecutive experiences which he would never forget in all his life. He was floating so easily on his back, looking at the empty sky, and contemplating himself as a mere tiny speck on the surface of a vast ocean of the globe. Almost invisible in the scheme of things. Against the fabric of space and time in the universe as a whole, where and what was he, this little human? An atom. Nothing, nothing at all. What did it mean? That same question again of meaning. It seemed miraculous just to be. Wasn't that enough? Just to be? What a privilege! A sheer delight to be floating like this, surrounded by the vastness of infinity. This would never be forgotten so long as he lived. It was happiness itself, a reverie almost forgetting who he was. This mind stream lasted perhaps five minutes when he kindled awake with a start.

Where was he? With a burst of fear, he saw that the Saga was actually several hundred yards away! How could they possibly see him? He was a tiny dot in the waves. And the smooth sound of the motor was missing. Saga had simply drifted away! His amygdala caused a powerful surge of adrenaline to take over his entire brain. His survival was at stake. Panic! He had never been so frightened in his entire life. He could die. He would tire and drown. He started swimming with heart bursting speed towards the boat. How could they do this to him? The fiends, the bastards, they were stealing the boat and leaving him to die! Evil people. Nobody would ever know what had happened to him. How could they do this to him? How could they? His heart was pounding like mad from the effort of his strokes and he became seriously out of breath when he was forced to stop for an instant. He then heard the coughing sound of the diesel starting and could see Saga's prow turn towards him.

They came alongside, reverse gear bringing the boat to a halt. Pierre at the helm. Gabrielle sitting on the cabin roof with the boat's big binoculars strapped beneath her neck. "Nice swim?" she shouted out in a friendly and innocent voice. Reuel's flood of molecular relief was a surge so powerful that it immediately extinguished a feeling of volcanic anger. Guilty thoughts. Of course, he was a complete fool. Gabrielle had him in sight the entire time. Pierre had shut the engine and gone below to check the oil level and add a liter. Reuel came alongside. "Did you enjoy yourself?" asked Gabrielle, without the slightest appreciation of his panic. Reuel took a deep breath and came up the little rope ladder.

"It was fantastic" he said. "One of the greatest experiences of my life. I will never forget it. For a moment I thought you had forgotten about me."

"Are you crazy?" she said.

But he thought he had learned one useful lesson. Survival was certainly one meaning of life.

Reuel had the easiest watch, the eight till twelve shifts. Pierre had the noon and midnight to four shifts. Gabrielle had the dog-watch. This meant Reuel had quiet afternoons for reading from a cushioned nook he had arranged at the foot of the bowsprit. He had taken three books aboard. In addition to Wittgenstein's *"Philosophical Investigations"*, acquired in Cambridge, there were two other titles he had purchased in Paris. While browsing the open-air book stalls on the Quai des Grands Augustins along the Seine looking for something to read in English, he took a chance on a pair of second-hand books. One was called *"Portnoy's Complaint"*, which he recalled as having made a stir, by an author named Roth. The other was called *"Endurance"*, the story of Shackleton's expedition to Antarctica, by a writer named Lansing. These three, other than a few manuals, were the literary totality of the boat's library.

Sex, necessarily being more seductive than Antarctic hardship or modern philosophy, he first began reading the comic fiction of a 19-year-old male protagonist named Alexander Portnoy. This distressed individual clearly had a pitiful sex life, which dominated his need to masturbate. Goodness, thought Reuel, at the same age of 19 he had not only had the pleasure of various intimacies with girls during his undergraduate days at Columbia, but he had even fathered twins with the beautiful Ulla Bergstrom. And of course, he himself masturbated at times. As recently as a few days ago imagining Gabrielle. Almost everybody masturbated. What would the Buddha or Ludwig Wittgenstein think of Portnoy's evolutionary cravings and performances? Was it not a normal and healthy part of sexual enjoyment?

He turned down the corner of the book's page and let his thoughts roam freely. Apart from the Buddha and Wittgenstein, did Moses, Jesus, Immanuel Kant, Aristotle, Earnest Shackleton, Harry Truman, Albert Einstein, Charles

Darwin, Jonas Salk — one could go on — were they all wankers, jerking themselves off holding their penises with a loose fist and moving their hand up and down the shaft to reach orgasm and ejaculation, as he himself had done the night before last thinking of his crew mate. And poor Portnoy made the subject of such cruel comedy. This Roth author was really unfair and unkind. Picking on poor Portnoy for the imaginative use of a piece of meat?

Reuel recalled his first sexual experience with the opposite sex. It was called "heavy petting". He was 14 years old. She was an older classmate at New Trier High School in Winnetka. Maddy O'Brian. Roman Catholic. Wore a little cross around her neck. There were games of spin-the-bottle at a few birthday parties. Elsewhere, they took chances to put their tongues in one another's mouths. She let him touch her breasts but nothing below the waist. While she would not touch his penis through his pants, they agreed to masturbate themselves at the same time. A non-touching and mutually timed masturbation. She liked that just as much as he, but needed to preserve her virginity and avoid the frightening risk of pregnancy. Kid stuff.

And of course, he knew this for a fact, women rubbed their vulvas, especially the clitoris, with their index or middle fingers, or both. Or shpritzed bath faucet water there, or straddled cushions, or even used the arm of a chair, and some could even stimulate themselves sexually by crossing their legs tightly and clenching their muscles. He had even been told they could do this in public without anyone noticing. Even a girl named Sylvia he had once known in Greenwich Village confessed she could orgasm by force of will alone, although this might not strictly qualify as masturbation as no physical touching was involved.

And what about Marie Curie, Helen Keller, Indira Gandhi, Maria Callas, Rosa Luxemburg, Betsy Ross, Golda Meir, Jane Austen, Queen Elizabeth, Annie Oakley, Susan P. Anthony, Florence Nightingale, Emily Dickinson, Aspasia of Miletus, Cleopatra, had they all never been frigging themselves? Why pick on poor Portnoy? This Roth fellow should have had a visit with Dr Freud, who was certainly a wanker too.

At this moment Gabrielle put her head around the cabin bulkhead, wagged her fingers at Reuel and shouted "Rool, I made a salade nicoise. It will spoil if you don't eat it now." Pierre was at the helm and hollered "it's delicious, Rool, it's the last of the tomatoes". Reuel left the book face down and came aft. Food was more important than thinking of sex.

There was a heavy squall with large irregular waves, becoming severe towards the end of Reuel's watch. Saga's 19-meter length faced wave troughs of equal size. In the darkness the wind was growing stronger and choppy and coming from different directions as it rained on and off. They had lowered the mainsail and turned on the diesel trying to keep the heading. At the outset the tiller required continuous effort until Reuel gave up and changed over to the wheel pedestal. It was a relief. He could recommend it to Anderson back in Sundvall. Pierre stood alongside him as they discussed the outlook and foresaw these conditions would likely continue through the night. Sleep would be impossible and Pierre decided two persons should share the helm in such conditions. The watch below could make cheese with crackers, and thermoses of hot tea. Pierre was stalwart and reassuring. Reuel was glad for his friendship and company. They were becoming brotherly.

Near dawn the sea started calming and they could feel the center of turbulence moving off to the South. Reuel could not help but think of the mariners on Endurance, the Pequod, even the Nina, Pinta and Santa Maria. By noon they had the mainsail up and the worst was behind them. They had made a dent in the diesel fuel supply.

"Baby storm" said Gabrielle. "You like?"

"So so."

"Saga good boat. Like strong woman. Keeps going."

Reuel had finished reading Lansing's epic story of the "Endurance" and the extraordinary leadership of Shackleton, truly a saga. It made him feel like a cheap and petty adventurer. How could he ever compare himself with men of such fortitude, such perseverance, such indefatigability. It made him serious and reflective about his current life, which his brain mixed in together with the manifest physical feeling of his living human body on a vast sea.

There was a bracing wind astern driving them forward at more than 10 knots, the main to starboard, the genoa jib to port, wing by wing on following swells. Pierre was in heaven, as most yachtsmen would so be in those conditions. Reuel stood next to him, sharing in the rolling pleasure.

"Is this the meaning of life?" he asked.

"*Bien sur*. Exactly!"

"And tomorrow we die."

"Tomorrow is far away. We must live in the moment."

"Even when thinking of the future? Just as simple as that?"

"Naturallement. Ze meaning is just what you are experiencing. There is no other meaning. We survive until we die. You want to spend time looking for philosophy, for abstraction? What for? You will not find it. The happy man is fortunate because he is born that way. Becoming wise does not make you happy. The unhappy man, he can say '*je suis un malheureux et ce n'est ni ma faute ni celle de la vie*', it is not his fault or fault of his life. It is just what is, what happened. There is no meaning."

They remained standing for a long time in silence, next to one another, on the rolling sea, each alone with his thoughts.

Years later, when Reuel looked back on this oceanic voyage, there were several incidents that were permanently etched in his memory. Pierre's view of "meaning" was one. Another was of his panicked swim far from the boat. A third was of an occasion when he had crawled out on the bowsprit and a school of big-brained dolphins came racing alongside, the one closest, at two or three yards, surfing on the Saga's bow wave. Time and time again, for some seconds, at each passing one another, the dolphin's large eye scanned and looked directly at him, his eyes, sharing their minds, eye-to-eye. And lastly, the most unforgettable remembrance of all was his memory of making love with Gabrielle.

That had happened in the following manner. Gabrielle had the dog-watch, from four till eight. This meant that she had the helm at dusk and dawn. On those occasions when the Saga was not heeling over severely, the three of them would sit out in the cockpit sharing cloudy glasses of Pernod, conversing easily, and enjoying the sunsets. The Ferrands were talking about their time in Tahiti and Moorea. Reuel mentioned his Paris visit to the Louvre and his fondness for the paintings of Paul Gauguin. It was as if he had dropped a match on dry tinder.

'Ahh, Gauguin!" Pierre and Gabrielle exclaimed at once, together. She continued by explaining to Reuel that people in Guadeloupe and Martinique were very proud that Gauguin had spent many months there and had produced a dozen paintings in that French colony which had been warmly received in Paris. In fact, there were copies of his paintings on the walls of their elementary school in Basse-Terre. This was Gauguin's first taste of the tropics, she said, which ultimately led to his years in French Polynesia.

"He so love women" said Pierre. "Young girls, *vahine*, all his life. *Menage a trois, quatre, cinq, formidable!* He love sex. Tahiti girls love sex too."

"Are you sure?" Gabrielle asked coyly. Pierre grinned at her and winked.

"*Bien sur*" said Pierre, turning to Reuel. "Gaugin is painting nudes from morning till night. *Vahine* are his philosophy, meaning of life, like you ask of me. He make one painting of so many women. No men. He write in corner, *D'où venons-nous? Que sommes-nous? Où allons-nous?* Where do we come from? What are we? Where are we going?"

"I know it, I know it!" exclaimed Reuel. It's in the Museum of Fine Arts in Boston!"

"Tahiti" said Gabrielle, pointing her glass at Pierre. "He make *amour* with two girls and me in Tahiti. He owe me."

Pierre turned to Reuel. "*Soyez amoureuses vous serez heureuses.* 'Be in love, you will be happy'. That is name of Gauguin sculpture for his *vahine*."

"You owe me" she said to Pierre, with a cocked eyebrow.

At eight o'clock, it became Reuel's watch and he took the helm. Pierre and Gabrielle went forward and retired to their cabin, leaving Reuel alone at the tiller. Night's darkness came on and it produced a beautiful clarity with a near full moon rising above the horizon behind them and reflecting a path of light upon the smooth still ocean. A gentle steady breeze kept them moving. It was the perfect situation for invoking the self-steering apparatus, and Reuel reclined hands free and regarded the starlit heavens above.

An hour passed. He lay thinking of the "Philosophical Investigations" and the challenging difficulty of reading it slowly and losing the chain of thought. Of what use was it, he wondered. What if Wittgenstein had cruised a sea and contemplated the stars? Instead, he had been a miserable Austrian prisoner of the Italian army near the end of the Great War. Wasn't it "the case" that such things made a difference to one's philosophy?

At this point Pierre emerged from the cabin. He was stark naked in the bright moonlight. He smiled at Reuel.

"Rool, good you have self-steering on. Now you come with me. We go make Gabrielle happy. She excited. *Tres chaud.* Hot! Would like you make sex *a trois* with us. You like? I owe her from time in Tahiti. Is okay?"

"Definitely okay!"

Ever after, years later, Reuel would never forget that singular arousing sexual event. Poor Portnoy. And any time he saw a copy of any Gauguin painting he thought of them.

Then, one morning in their fourth week at sea they saw several Frigate Birds high above. A hint of islands ahead. They stayed keen. Gabrielle turned the boat's radio on at high volume and scanned the frequencies in hopes of hearing a signaling sound. Later that day, coming in and out within scratchy patches of static, they heard fragments of a human voice, its language unclear. Hours later there was the first hint of clear signal. An English voice, faint and breaking, saying something about a cricket match. They stayed tuned to the frequency when it finally became clear that they were listening to Radio Barbados. They had arrived to the New World.

Later, they tied in at Bridgetown Harbour, refueled, and after shopping to refill the larder with groceries, fresh water, wine and amenities, they found a nearby cafe and banqueted off a mouth-watering menu and two bottles of Bordeaux. It was journey's end. Future arrangements were understood. The Ferrands would send periodic remittances to Reuel's account at the Cambridge Bank. They would deduct for repairs and improvements, and the Saga would be insured against loss. Reuel would give notice if he wanted to use her. They exchanged contacts and addresses and walked around town to find a hotel for Reuel. There they kissed and embraced with some tears in their eyes, and then separated.

He spent two days in Bridgetown at the Hotel Stanley. He called Luisa Sanchez at the Cambridge law firm. There was no personal mail being held. His affairs were in order. He called Beverly Thesiger at the bank. She informed him that a publicly traded company, Digital Resources Corporation, had acquired Kang Laboratories with an exchange of stock. His stock options had vested and the new value of Reuel's now tradeable shares had nearly doubled. It was hard to believe. He renewed instructions to continue paying for all charges on his American Express card.

Reuel wrote a letter to Luca Baca describing his adventures, and sent a telegram to Bob Adler, advising him of his imminent arrival to Cuernavaca. He was ready and willing to go India together if that was still in Adler's thoughts. The novel freedom from other commitments in his life, open for adventures, produced an expanding sense of native curiosity about all phenomena, philosophies and facts. And the something lurking in his mind about Buddhist insights.

He took the semi-weekly Pan American Airways flight to Miami. There he stayed at a beach hotel for a few days of luxurious self-indulgence. They were punctuated by pensive excursions into "Philosophical Investigations" while reclining on a lounge chair beside an upmarket swimming pool. Satiated before long he booked a seat on the weekly Aeromexico flight to Mexico City. From there he hired a limousine to drive him the 50 odd miles to Cuernavaca where he was to find the Villa Dolores off the Calle Escondida in the Acapantzingo district. The palette of colors in sight so palpably different from the monotonous greys of England and Sweden and the bare Atlantic.

ॐ

On the following morning in Cuernavaca: "I'm ready to split" said Adler. "This place is getting to me. I started smoking dope again. My friend Betsy Wilcox and her sister rented this joint for six months as a center to study internal freedom. To support my flight from the university. But it's only like a zoo. I was supposed to write something. Instead, it's been visitor after visitor who just want to get turned on. Indian shamans with Ayahuasca. Mexican psychiatrists. Hippies wanting to get high with me. Yoga teachers. And even real materialists, self-help people against religion. So, with a little psychedelic assistance, I've had lots of time to reflect on life. Here's the thing. I'm totally cast out of classical academic conceptual disciplines. Behaviorism, and social psychology, therapeutics, schedules of reinforcement, statistics, cognitive style, aversive controls, cross-cultural differentials, motivational research, life-cycle development, personality studies, experimental methods, testing protocols, intelligence measuring. All bullshit. The whole crock of crap. I'm finished with it. The world's much bigger than that."

"Like what?"

"It's something that I'm beginning to understand. What interests me, just like James in Varieties of Religious Experience, is about all those things that science turns its nose up. What is intuition? Take mysticism for example. Why has it been there since the beginning of human history? There's something very real about hidden truths, a sense of an unseen order, about ultimate revelation, about divinity, about awe at the infinity of the cosmos, enlightenment, spirituality, liberation, union with the absolute, unearthly mysteries that defy expression. In other words, religious experience."

"Lots of woo-woo too."

"Yeah, you can make fun of it, but it's there. It's the supernatural, the esoteric, an enchantment, the magical, the occult, gnosticism, the kabbalah, neo-platonism, movements like freemasonry, theosophy, kinds of higher knowledge, the awakened intellect, transcendental truth."

"Gimme a break."

"Oh yeah? What do you think you're doing with your interest in Buddhist enlightenment? *Bodhi, Satori, Kensho, Prajna, Moksha, Vedanta, Advaita,* the real Yoga. You think that Buddhist stuff is natural science? The idea of actually awakening to the meaning of meaning? '*Aufklarung*' if you remember your German. What's it all about, eh?"

"Okay, I dunno."

"That's the whole thing about our relation to psychedelics. That it makes one think about spiritual things, like enlightenment, doesn't it?"

They went on this way until it ended in silence. Adler lit up a cigarette. This friendly discussion took place in the morning after Reuel's arrival as they sat in the shade of a large mango tree in the immense courtyard of the Villa Dolores. Adler had introduced him earlier to more than a dozen people who were passing through the villa.

"Look at them. They all come here in the name of what they call 'internal freedom'. Males, females, young, old, American and European, all of them separate from the Mayan staff. Check out that group over there at that far corner of the courtyard."

Adler gestured with his chin. At that moment, in a group of a dozen or more of the villa's residents, each one was carrying a large and heavy rock which they were forming into a circle.

"What are they doing?" asked Reuel.

"That's a story and a half. Today they are making a circle. Yesterday they made a triangle. Tomorrow they will make a square. That heavy work is supposed to make them aware of the idea of difficulty. Hard effort. They're working on themselves learning about making strenuous effort. Confronting what's tough."

"I don't get it."

"That's a perfect example. 'You don't get it.' You're not working at it hard enough. They're developing a theory of practice. Betsy invited them. They're here for a week, it's a workshop. Not my thing."

"Where'd they get that idea?"

"It's something called the 'Fourth Way'. The Gurdjieff people. Ouspensky, "Searching for the Miraculous". Madam Blavatsky. Theosophy. You name it. They all just have a theory that most of us don't possess a unified consciousness, that we just live our lives in a hypnotic state of 'waking sleep', but that with hard work and effort it's possible to be awakened to a higher state of consciousness and achieve full human potential."

"Same old, same old. Higher consciousness. Big deal."

"Yeah, sounds dull, but they call it a method of self-mastery, termed 'working-on-oneself' to raise your consciousness."

"Without even going to India."

"Exactly. Their theory is that traditional roads to spiritual enlightenment merely involved controlling your body, your emotions, and your mind. But those old approaches are only surviving forms which persist throughout history unchanged, and are unbalanced because they're based on religion. Their technique is to teach a fourth way that combines and integrates the traditional three ways of body, emotion and mind. That supposedly produces a well-balanced, and sane human being capable of dealing with all challenges that life presents. And get this, there's nothing spiritual about it. No religion involved. That re-invented 'fourth way' is different than the old perennial-wisdom ideas in that it isn't a permanent method. It gets invented as it goes. No specific institutions or forms, but moves by some particular laws of its own."

"Like what?"

"Like scientology today. Like EST. Like 'Arica'. Not spiritual. Just teaching how to increase and focus your attention and energy, so as to minimize day-dreaming and absent-mindedness. Always remembering the idea of working on yourself to begin a process of inner development which transforms you into what it should be, fully awake and enlightened."

"And that's why they're carrying heavy rocks over there?"

"You got it. And that's because their method is special because it isn't hidden in secrecy. It's just to keep arousing yourself, since they say most people live in a state of semi-hypnotic 'waking-sleep', and lack any interest or capability to understand their condition. People think they're conscious but they really aren't. They say the ordinary waking consciousness of human beings isn't consciousness at all but just a form of sleep. Humans are born asleep, live in sleep, and die in sleep, only imagining that they're awake with few exceptions. Of course, there's no explanation of what they mean by consciousness."

"Brilliant! Lift rocks!"

"Called working on yourself. Nothing mystical about it. Call for Dr. Freud."

"How'd they get here?"

"Beats me. Betsy invited them."

"Jesus, let's do it. Get to India and have some weird fun. I'm on vacation."

"Don't you believe in internal freedom?"

"I'm an empiricist, a scientific materialist. I just think continued research on the detailed mechanisms of the brain will make the so-called problem of consciousness fade away into irrelevancy and abstraction. And there's no contradiction about being spiritual, to use a word that needs clarification. You know, for me, spirituality means being open to things larger than myself, like appreciating beauty, like commitment to rules of moral behavior, my spirituality doesn't require belief in miracles. Maybe, unlike you these days, I'm still a believer in science."

"You'll have to tell me how you define science."

"Okay. I believe the central doctrine of science is that all events and properties in the universe are governed by laws. Laws which hold true at all times and places. You might argue that laws of nature are just our description of things, but science treats these as necessary rules that nature has to obey without exception, even if there were no humans around to make descriptions. Maybe it leaves us wondering why the universe is so admirably law-abiding, but it definitely is."

"But what do you think it means?"

"That question again. Maybe asking what it all means is just a persistent part of the human apparatus, up there with the need for food and shelter. We must differentiate those things we can and cannot understand through neuroscience. What's really interesting is why the question of meaning usually kicks in at the beginning of middle-age. That us, don't you think?"

"What about suffering?"

"You mean like a toothache?"

"No, come on. Why does depression feel bad?"

"Brain science isn't there yet. The self is dominated by affective feelings. I feel therefore I am. Consciousness is the system that encodes brain and body states essential for survival. It has crude and elementary perceptions about the world and the homeostatic states of the body. Obviously, there's a deep neuro-biological reality to emotional feelings. All we know is that affective processes come out of deep subcortical regions and networks of the brain. What you call 'feeling' is an interoceptive process, like feeling you're hungry, so we eat. Depression feels bad because it's metaphorically like hunger. How do you feed it to relieve it? Money, sex, pharmaceuticals, street drugs, achievement, fame, friendship, psychoanalysis, electro-shock-therapy, whatever. There is no why. It's something the genetically evolved brain is doing in particular states."

"So, what do you mean by meaning? Nothing at all? And what about uncertainty, intuition, and indeterminacy? What about beauty and ethics? You have scientific laws about consciousness?"

"Ignorance doesn't mean that there aren't laws."

"You just like talking about philosophy. Let's go to India."

"It's a deal."

ॐ

Their voyage to India had life changing consequences for both of them. From the outset their motives were not aligned. Adler was in search of cosmic faith and a devotion to the miraculous, in one form or another. Reuel was in search of adventurous travel, novelty, and the idea of learning a little more of Sanskrit and Buddhist philosophy. What they would do, where they would go after arriving, how they would proceed was left to *ad hoc* improvisation. In this manner they contrived to fly continuously from Mexico to New Delhi via a connection in Frankfurt, in a journey lasting 27 hours. They agreed to limit their baggage each to a single duffel bag. Adler would pay for his ticket in economy class. Reuel defrayed their upgrades to first-class.

On arrival they checked into the Ashoka Hotel where they decamped for several days without exiting until getting over the jet lag. While even the first taste of India in the hotel itself felt slightly exotic, to their relief the use of English, the linguistic heritage of the British Empire, was extremely common. Their first excursions out used the pervasive tuk-tuks, the three wheeled auto-rickshaw taxis. They explored the city and Old Delhi, and began making plans. The first stop was to the American Express office at Connaught Circus to purchase traveler's checks and wads of high denomination Rupees. They learned they could receive mail there, and that telephoning the United States was extremely difficult. They would have to book such a call at government post-offices a day or two ahead. However, shops with fax-machines could be found here and there and might serve their purposes in an emergency.

There were two planning toe-holds. The first was Adler's desire to see a place called Kurukshetra, which was where the great poetic and philosophical dialogue in the *Bhagavad Gita* between Prince Arjuna and the God Krishna occurred. Adler had read the Gita several times and was spiritually moved. The second idea, which they both agreed to, was simply to see the Taj Mahal, the most visited tourist spot in the India, some sixty miles South on the Delhi-Agra highway. India was full of cars for hire with drivers, had an enormous rail network, and many air-conditioned buses, but Reuel's sudden idea of buying a car intrigued them.

"I mean if you were a first-time visitor to the States" he said, "and had a few months to see the country, the best thing would be to use a car. And almost everybody in India speaks English. There's got to be petrol everywhere. We can get some good maps, split the driving, and use the left side lane like in Britain. Let's do it! I've got the money."

They took a tuk-tuk to an auto dealer and Reuel bought an "Ambassador" a fairly small 4-door sedan manufactured by Hindustan Motors, far and away the most common car in India, ever-present. The dealer was enormously pleased to help them, provided with the most up-to-date and detailed automobile maps of the entire country, and couldn't believe how swiftly they had agreed to the asking price, with his huge profit. Reuel could scarcely believe how inexpensive it was to buy the thing.

The following day, with their belongings, they took their first ride in the new car down the great state highway to Agra. Enjoying tourist views of the Taj, the great mausoleum which the Moghul Shah, Jahan, built for his wife, Mumtaz. Having fulfilled that sightseer mandate they stayed at a local hotel. Lacking an onward destination, an inquiry was made about nearby sights. The hotel owner recommended that they see Fatehpur Sikri, an important historic site, which involved only a slight detour, on a return to Delhi.

They drove to the most mysterious and impressive town the next morning. An immense hill-top palace complex had been completely abandoned in the 16th century owing to a lack of water and the episodic drought. A royal ghost town of red sandstone architecture forsaken by the Mughal emperor Akbar the Great. The only signs of people were small groups of men sitting idly on the wide imperial steps. Reuel and Adler took their ease in a shaded nook and were considering where to spend the night.

They were approached by a handsome light-skinned older boy, who came over and asked them in Hindi, and then in stilted English, where they were from.

"America" said Adler.

"*Achha*. You have tobacco?"

"Only cigarettes."

"Give me one?"

Adler gave him one from his package of Wills, the main Indian brand. The boy thanked him and sat down. They watched him remove the paper from the cigarette tube and roll the tobacco into a loose ball in his palm. Then, from his shirt pocket he took out a coin-sized slab of hashish and a tiny box of paper matches. After heating a corner of the dry resin, he crumpled some of it mixed into the tobacco as they watched him closely. Then, smiling, he extracted a small clay cylinder from another pocket and filled its wide end with the mixture.

"You speak English?" asked Reuel.

"*Achaa*. You know Hindi?" They shook their heads. "Hindi easy" said the boy. "You learn quick. I teach." He held up the little piece of hashish and said "*Charass*". Then the cylinder, "*Chillum*. You say 'pipe'. Now we smoke, okay? I show."

They nodded in delighted agreement. Cannabis. Welcome to India.

The boy held the pipe to his forehead for an instant, then skyward, said "*Bom, bom, Mahadev!*", folding his fingers to form a tube around the mouth-piece, lit the pipe, inhaled deeply, and passed it to Adler, who breathed in enthusiastically, and passed it on to Reuel, who did the same, after gleefully repeating the invocation "*Bom, bom, Mahadev!*". Boom, boom, great God.

Then they all sat quietly for half a minute, smiling, and holding their breaths and feeling the molecules enter their brains. Finally, the boy spoke.

"You tourists?"

Adler said "No, we are seekers. Who are you?"

"I am Raj Das. Also, I am Hervé, Hervé Félicité. My father French, my mother from Andhra Pradesh. You call me Raj Das."

"How old are you?" asked Reuel.

"I am eighteen. I speak English, Hindi, Tamil and of course French. I am poet. I am actor. I am writer. I write Hindi sci-fi stories. Also, I can sing."

"Do you live here?"

"No. Nobody live here. I am traveling. I go to Vrindavan tonight. Take bus."

"We came to India five days ago. First time" said Reuel. "My name is Roo, his name is Bob. We have car over there" he gestured. "Tell us about you."

"My father old French army doctor. Foreign legionnaire in old Vietnam colony. *Compagnie Française des Indes Orientales.* My father see colonial war, *contre* France, start. Before Dien Bien Phu battle. He no like. Quit army. Become pacifist. He move to Pondicherry in Tamil Nadu. You know? Old French colony city. He become medical doctor of *ashram* from Sri Aurobindo. You know him? Integral yoga? My mother from Tamil Nadu is medical nurse. They marry. I am son."

"Where is Vrindavan?" asked Adler.

"Not far. Easy on way to Delhi. You can take me?"

"Yes. Where can we stay tonight?"

"You stay in *ashram*. So many *ashrams* in Vrindavan. Very easy. You know Lord Krishna?"

"Yes. Bhagavad Gita."

"Yes, very good! Krishna come from Vrindavan. Vrindavan is Krishna city. Very holy. One thousand temples. I find you *ashram* tonight. Eat food. You sing *bhajans* tonight. 'Haré Krishna, Haré Rama.' Make you very happy. I stay with you. I show you India. You like babies."

They stayed in Vrindavan over four days. Adler could not get enough of various melodic devotional *bhajans*, chanting *"Sri Ram, Jai Ram, Jai, Jai Ram"*, in the *ashrams*, the musical offerings to Vishnu and his avatars. There was *"Haré Krishna, Haré Rama, Haré Haré."* And Adler was found singing it softly, as if muttering to himself as they walked through the city, *"Sri Krishna Govinda Haré Muraré, Yey nathen nara yeneva sudheva"*, repeating the sweet refrain over and over again, and insisting he could hear it in his mind even when he was silent. It even appeared as if Adler was attempting to gain faith in a Hindu God. The fact that they were now routinely smoking *charass* several times a day was of little concern.

On his part Reuel was absorbed in understanding the multiple hierarchies and dualities in Hindu polytheism. The teen-age boy, Raj Das, became his tutor who fluidly described the Vedic traditions where Vishnu was the supreme being protecting the universe, with Lakshmi his feminine side. And their descended earthly forms, avatars, like Rama and Sita, like Krishna and Radha. Krishna, for example, being just the eighth avatar of Vishnu, and the deity of compassion, tenderness, and love.

"Roo, if you get Krishna consciousness, you see him like baby eating butter, like mischief boy, kid playing flute, sweetheart with girls, hero, become like man, drive chariot, teaching Prince Arjuna in the Gita. *Haré Krishna.*"

"Where is Buddha among those gods?" asked Reuel.

"Oh, Lord Buddha is also Krishna. Lord Buddha is ninth avatar of Vishnu. Everyone knows. Buddha is Indian God. Dharma wheel, symbol of Buddhism, is center on flag of India. Buddhism is child of Hinduism."

This portrayal made Reuel feel somewhat comfortable. As if Raj Das was his Hesiod describing the Olympians: Zeus, Poseidon, Hera, Hephaestus, Athena, Dionysus, Artemis, Apollo, Ares, Demeter, Aphrodite and Hermes. He had absorbed enough for another day and was pressing to move on. Adler seemed to act as if he could stay in Vrindavan the rest of his life singing *bhajan* hymns.

"Raj Das, can you travel with us?" asked Reuel. "We can pay you."

"No. No pay. I like go with you little. In one month, I go to Bombay. You give me ticket, okay? I find work by Hindi cinema. I have friend there. I am acting, singing, I write scripts. Bollywood. You know if Marlon Brando singing?"

They agreed to travel together. Adler wanted to visit Kurukshetra, where the mythical battle of the Bhagavad Gita had taken place and where Prince Arjuna was taught the meaning of life from Krishna.

"*Achaa*" said Raj Das. "We go to Jyotisar there. Very holy place. Roo, you interest. Bob, you like much. You like Gita. You are *bhakti* yogi. You make good devotions. There is Banyan tree, child of Banyan tree where Krishna teach Karma and Dharma to his friend Arjuna. Arjuna worried, unhappy he making war. After, from there we must go Haridwar and Rishikesh. Take bath in Ganga river, okay?"

Over the next few weeks, they did exactly that. Raj Das provided an intensive continuing seminar on Hindu polytheism, Indian morés, practices, habits, and attitudes. He instructed them in toilet care, urination and defecation modalities while squatting and the use of a water pot, a *lota*, instead of toilet paper. He explained religious tics, the history and presence of castes, how to buy *charass*, the meaning of the *bindu*, the red dot on the forehead, the respect due women, the cultural difference between left and right hands, taught them a core vocabulary of Hindi words, explained the omnipresence of *saddhus*, taught the musical forms of ragas heard on the car radio, explained food combinations and courtesies, how to chew pan with betel nuts and spit, and helped them buy bed-rolls on which to sleep on string cots. In exchange, on their first occurrence in India, they turned Raj Das on to LSD.

Afterwards, coming down from the chemical high, Adler said "Raj, tell us, what do you think?"

"I don't know. I felt body melting. Like knowing all things, but no words. I see ground I sit on moving. All things dancing, like fire, *udana*, in out, *shakti* moving, *prana*, my breath, universe, like we being spirits like smoke, with little skin around our body. Cannot describe. All one thing. I so small, world so big. I feel sorry for you. I feel my Guru stay here with me, Aurobindo Sri, my home,

Pondicherry teach me find invisible super-mind, *satchitananda*, you understand? *Sat* means real, *chit* means conscious, *ananda* means happy, joy. I, I experience. I feel sorry for you." The rest was a sustained silence.

Later on, when they reached Haridwar on the mother river, Raj Das brought them to the crowded bathing ghat, immersed them in the Ganges, the Ganga Ma, initiated them in the sunset Ganga *aarti* ceremony where they lit tiny candles in cupped leaves of flowers, and set them afloat on the great river to the chanting song of thousands of fellow congregants, with bells and cymbals clanging, and the smoke of sandalwood incense. With Raj Das' encouragement they practiced their self-taught meditations at his instigation, and believed they were having one of the great times in their lives.

Raj Das took them twenty miles on, driving into the foothills of the Himalaya, higher up the river, to Rishikesh, the traditional last place where water descended from the heaven of mountains to reach Haridwar, downstream in the plains, the first place on Earth touched by Ganga's waters. They learned about *saddhus*. There was no certification to become a *saddhu*, only to live with few or no possessions, to beg for donated food, to avoid staying in one place, to be *anagarika*, homeless, visiting temples, and always thinking of religion. Frequently with the help of *charass*, just like themselves, smoking every day.

He taught them to say *"bom mahadev"* before the first puff. They stayed high while at the Divine Life Society's Sivananda Ashram, where they were formally inaugurated to the five cores of Yoga: postures, breathing, relaxation, meditation and diet. Rishikesh was a pilgrim's town, particularly sacred to Siva, who owned the mountains and the sacred river, and who was the merciful Lord of destruction, the king of Yogins, and spouse of his consort the fearful Kali. And, to make it a point of pride, Raj Das bragged that Rishikesh was the home seat of the yoga teacher of the Beatles.

After a week in Rishikesh, Raj Das entreated them to drive some 500 miles Eastward down the Grand Trunk Highway, following the course of the Ganges, to Varanasi, the British "Benares". In this crowded urban and spiritual heart of India, he said, they would truly come to understand religion and it might change their lives. He would leave them there and hoped they might buy him an Air India ticket for a flight to Bombay. Otherwise, he would go by rail.

It took them three days on the Grand Trunk Road, the most ancient highway in Asia, with an overnight at Lucknow. On reaching Varanasi they left the car in the Civil Lines, and stayed at a cheap hotel beside the stepped Dasashvamed Ghat at the river in the old city. They explored its lanes, drank teas, conversed with ochre robed saddhus, learned to eat new foods, attended sitar recitals of classical ragas till dawn, until they began to feel at home in India. And then and thus it became time for Raj Das to depart for Bollywood, leaving them on their own. They paid for his air-ticket to Bombay and made him a cash gift.

One day, after their second LSD trip in India, Reuel decided he would refrain from the psychedelic chemical evermore, concluding that it was destroying his intelligence. Adler, on the other hand, insisted it improved his own imagination and the cultivation of emotions such as empathy and love. It was clear to both of them that an inexplicable biochemical interaction revealed the intimate mysterious connection between the physiological brain and its familiar intangible effect that was called "mind".

It was at about this time that the trajectory of their lives began to diverge and it seemed clear that their aspirations led in mismatched directions. As if knowledge and understanding led to different targets. Adler, intoxicated by frequent low-doses of his "white lightning", appeared to be willingly engaged in the suspension of disbelief in pursuit of a divine teacher who would have him. Reuel, adhering to his empiricist nature, was more simply in search of expanded rationality. Consequently, it was rational to give up on LSD as he was convinced it was making him stupid. From this point on, their adventures in India led to different outcomes.

Reuel decided to visit to Benares Hindu University, BHU, famed in the nation, and by asking around soon gained a meeting with the Provost. Reuel, an apparently educated American intellect, acquainted with such things as machine-language and neurolinguistics was a rare bird when he appeared on the campus and was rather quickly elevated to tea with the senior mandarin. When the term 'neurolinguistics' came up their conversational discourse was vectored quickly towards the unique superiority of the Sanskrit language in gaining insights to the semantics and understanding of the human mind.

Reuel and the Provost each felt they were standing on familiar ground, but were curious of the other fellow's turf. The Provost had heard of Roman Jakobson, Edward Sapir and Ludwig Wittgenstein. Reuel had heard of Nagarjuna, Chandrakirti and Buddhaghosa. They wondered aloud if they could hybridize their knowledge? Ultimately, given Reuel's interest in Sanskrit, the Provost suggested that he might benefit meeting his learned colleague, the Rector of nearby Sanskrit College, also in Varanasi. He asked his Secretary to arrange it.

The following day Reuel was ushered into a cramped paper-filled room for his meeting with Amartya Shankar. The college was nested in a single ancient building in a small run-down campus and the Rector seemed indifferent, if not annoyed, with a foreign visitor interested in Buddhism that had been thrust upon him. The Rector was an elfin elderly man, bearded, bespectacled, and seated cross legged on a cushion at floor level. When Reuel was introduced the Rector nodded wearily, and gestured for Reuel to take a seat on the floor. An assistant provided a cushion and brought in cups of sweet milk-tea on a tray between them.

The difficulty appeared instantly. Reuel knew little of the Devanagari script and writing system, which was composed of 47 primary characters, with 14 vowels and 33 consonants. Without it, there was clearly no hope of learning Sanskrit. The Rector was blunt in his formidable British English.

"Young man, Sanskrit is the most ancient and perfect among the all the languages of the world. It is a storehouse of psychological knowledge about the subjective mind. It was developed over centuries and is an unsurpassed and invaluable treasure of the world. This language symbolizes our peculiar Indian tradition of logic and thought. It has exhibited full intellectual freedom in the search of truth, and has shown complete tolerance towards spiritual and other like kinds in the experiences of mankind. Sanskrit demonstrates catholicity towards universal truth. It contains not only a rich fund of knowledge of India's people, but it is also an unparalleled way of acquiring knowledge of the mind and the spirit. It is therefore significant for the entire world. You can only have a superficial knowledge of Buddhist philosophy without it. I cannot say more. What is your pleasure?"

Reuel was stumped. He didn't want to be there. It had been thrust upon him by the Provost at BHU.

"Do you have any advice for philosophers who rely on translations? I'm thinking of translators like Max Muller, Rhys Davids, Monier Williams, and others."

"That is difficult. Words have different meanings in European languages. Even in English can we know what we are referring to when we use words like "meaning" or "understanding". If someone says in your own language "I understand" how do you know? How then can you successfully translate words, like *dharma*, like *atman*, like *moksa*, like *dukkha*, like *karma*? You would only be playing a language-game like that fellow said, what's his name?"

"Wittgenstein?"

"Yes, him. How can Sanskrit be a game? Just a serious game? In my opinion, as you say, that is a bridge too far. Can I be of any further service to you, young man? As you can see..." he said, waving his hand at a room full of loose papers.

At their hotel early that evening Reuel and Adler compared notes on their day. Reuel's tame visit to Sanskrit college was dramatically eclipsed by Adler's day. He had hired a boatman to take him out on the Ganga and had been rowed down beneath the Manikarnika Ghat, the holiest cremation ground in India. He had watched hot ashes of bodies and charred wood hoed off the ghat's stone edge to fall into the river with hissing sounds. He insisted they go immediately to visit the ghat from above, on the ground, that night.

It was well past midnight when they set out, hoping to get there at a quiet hour. At first, they lost their way among the lanes, which produced a mild panic in Adler who had taken a low dose of LSD. Finally, at the ghat they were astonished to find it crowded at that hour. Scores of frail elderly people, with their families, had come from across the country to spend their final days absorbing the charisma of the sacred crematory. Night and day, for centuries, the fires never go out, with funeral parties waiting their turn. As if this made death seem less significant, merely a gateway to another life based on their karma, each body transformed by 3 to 4 hours of flame. Families paid for hundreds of pounds of dry pyre wood, camphor, locust, bamboo, and mango tree on the average, sandalwood for the rich. There was a cost for the treatment of corpses, shrouded bodies with thumbs tied together and anointed with ghee, with priests to read over them, and barefoot men to rotate the bodies in the fire. The ashes at end pushed into the Ganga where any remaining fleshy parts would be consumed by the throng of river turtles assembled below.

On arriving Reuel and Adler found a place to sit on the ghat steps not more the sixty or seventy feet from the nearest flames. Five pyres in various states of consumption were ablaze on the stone platform encircled by several tiers on three sides. Adler seemed filled with horror at first and started to tremble, but Reuel became silently reflective. They sat respectfully this way for some hours, deciding to observe the course of a single pyre from start to finish. Once, a man emerged from a family group towards a pyre with a stick and cracked open the charring skull of the body, ostensibly to liberate its soul.

While this all was happening, for some time, on the far side of the ghat, a weird girlish figure, illuminated by the fires, was standing in her sandals and swaying. A lone maiden dressed in a simple short grey sari, who kept looking at them as she rocked from one leg to the other. She was exceptionally attractive, tall, with loose raven hair around her shoulders. The most striking thing about her was the amazing redness of her eyes, as if crimson had been painted around them. It was noticeable even in the semi-darkness from where they sat. She stood, rocking and swiveling for hours as she watched them. It seemed eerie and somewhat spine-chilling. They avoided looking back directly at her for fear she would approach them and make some kind of scene. Finally, after a few hours, Reuel decided to leave, having had enough of this singular meditative experience of corpses and burning bodies. Adler, speaking solemnly and calmly, insisted he would stay on a while, explaining that he was gaining a spiritual understanding in what he was observing.

When Reuel awoke late the following morning he was surprised and became anxious that his friend had not returned to their hotel. They had not been separated previously in their journey and this absence was definitely unusual. In the hours that followed Reuel grew distressed. Had Bob Adler come into harm's way? Should the police be informed? The American Consulate? His mood of anxious uncertainty swelled.

However, at length, in the late afternoon, Adler arrived at the hotel with an aspect of nervous but untroubled excitement and described what had happened.

"You know, after you left, I stayed on at the ghat, trying to imagine my corpse being burned. I was crying a little, but still sort of calm, slightly wiped out coming down from that hit of acid. Then, not long after you split, at the first bit of dawn in the sky was when that weird girl came over. Remember her, the one with those weird red eyes who had been looking at us all night? They use a red betel-nut ointment dying the skin around her eyes and intended to make them like bloodshot. Weird. Anyway, she comes over and sits down next to me. Speaks fluent English! Intelligent. Good looking. Wants to know what I'm doing there. Asks why am I crying? We start talking. She's a Bengali girl from Calcutta named Durga Ganguli. Has a B.A. in comparative religion from Shantiniketan Visva-Bharati University in West Bengal. Place founded by Tagore, Nobel Prize and all that. Anyway, she says she's a yoga disciple who was sent by her guru, a woman, to meditate at the burning ghat for a few days. As a method in her *sadhana*, her practice, of unlearning deeply internalized cultural models of death. And also, she says, to realize that all opposites like life and death are illusory. Mind blowing listening to this stuff grammatically, from a girl. Turns out she's a devotee of this teacher, called Amrita Devi, who has lots of followers, who call her "Mataji". Anyway, she takes me to see her. It seems there's a Shaivite temple called Sudha Mandir not far from the ghat, and we walk there through the old part of town. Maybe half-mile or something. So, there's a morning *puja* going on when we get there. Maybe fifteen or so people sitting around, chanting stuff. This Mataji, Amrita Devi, an old roly-poly lady is sitting up on a little platform and throwing pinches of rice at everybody. We sit down. Nobody pays attention to us but I see the old lady looking closely at me. The *puja* ends, half the people leave, a few stay, Durga goes to the old lady and says something, and they gesture for me to come over. I do what they want. I say *namaste* and bow. Durga says I should sit down just in front of her teacher. So, I sit down. The old lady puts her hands around the sides of my head, holding it. We sit this way quietly without moving for minutes. I have no idea what's going on. Then without letting go of my head the whole time, through all of this, she says something in Bengali to Durga, who puts it in English. Durga translates: 'You are homosexual, you are ruled by *shakti*; you want to become enlightened but don't know how; you smoking much *charras*; you have given up science as your path; you are sincere, and your path is of *bhakta*.' This of course blows me away, like she's mind reading. She's still holding onto my head and won't let go. She tells me, through Durga's translation, that I am unbalanced in the understanding of my senses. I ask in what way. She's still holding my head and says that my eyes are weak and I'll soon have to start wearing glasses. She says my sense of touch is very refined but that I don't use it very much. She says my hearing is good. She says my sense of taste is neutral, which is also good. My sense of smell is very bad. I would have no way of describing the smell of coffee or coconut to myself or anyone else. And then she says I am fairly undeveloped in my awareness of body sensations and very weak in my sense of what my mind is doing. It is important, she says, that all seven senses have to be brought to the same level and harmonized. I tell her I thought there were only five senses. No, she says, there are seven senses. She will teach me if I want. She lets go of my head. She and Durga have a long conversation and I'm just sitting there in front of the old lady. Durga explains to me that most Westerners believe there are only five senses. Amrita Devi, Mataji, is famous for teaching about the other two senses. The first, easier to teach, is the skilled awareness of my body sensations, like hot, cold, hungry, sleepy, itchy mosquito bite, breath shallow or deep, fast or slow, toothache, feel my pulse rate, and things like that. She tells me that when you develop that sense, you can be like a yogi, you can sit naked in snow. Hold your breath for long time. Endure pain. Not feel hungry. Fall sleep immediately. Wake up exactly when. That is all from sixth sense, she says. What about seventh sense I ask. Durga and Mataji have another back and forth. Durga tells me Mataji knows I do drugs. Drugs, she says, can shape or destroy our seventh sense. Mataji says seventh sense development is more difficult, but most important. She says it's the key to sanity, the way to enlightenment, the most important of the seven senses. It requires getting practice from a teacher. It is what Krishna is teaching Arjuna. Says it's about self-observation, which can be called consciousness, knowing about how to perceive the mind-stream, being able to observe dreams, growing the feeling of love, giving life to ethics, seeing anger and fear, wondering at beauty, understanding the forms of attention, calmness, regulating your emotions, deepening your meditation, strengthening your determination, increasing your awareness, your happiness, your patience, your relationships, your contentment, being in contact with the absolute, and to experience your mind expanding without drugs. Well, you got to believe me when I say I'm blown away by all of this, understand?"

"I can imagine" says Reuel.

"Anyway, Mataji, Amrita Devi, tells Durga to bring me to her main ashram. It's near a town called Ramnagar, about a hundred miles north from here, in the Shivalik foothills. You can see the Himalayas. They have a bus going tonight. I'm going to go with them."

"Are you serious?"

"Damn right, I'm really serious. Someone to take me on. I might never get another chance."

ॐ

Adler was gone by the following day, notwithstanding the fact that traveling to India jointly together had always been his idea. As a result, Reuel now faced the circumstance that he was alone, a foreign stranger in India. Uncertain of what to do next, and possibly out of old habit, he decided to find a bookstore. Several inquiries yielded a common answer. The best bookstore in Varanasi, indeed the best bookstore in all of India for that matter, was the establishment of Motilal Banarsidas. It was a veritable warehouse of titles old and new, mostly of languages using Devanagari script, but with a large Indology section in English. A half-day perusing books on the history of Buddhism led Reuel to the idea of visiting nearby Sarnath, where the founder of the faith first presented his teaching one night on the Four Noble Truths, the Middle Way, and the Eight-fold Path, just exactly what he had first read about once long ago in Sammler's bookstore. The original turning of the 'Wheel of the Law'. The wheel on the flag of India.

Sarnath lay barely ten kilometers beyond Varanasi, and without further thought Reuel checked out of the hotel, took a rickshaw with his gear to the broad Civil Lines part of town where the Ambassador had been parked, and drove himself to the great Buddhist pilgrimage setting. The smoothness of the short automobile journey restored Reuel's confidence in his ability to travel by himself. By dusk he had located Sarnath's *dharmsala*, one of India's wide-spread rest-houses for travelers, where he stayed, intending to circumambulate the great commemorative stupa the following day. This was the place, the very place, where in its deer park on a full moon night, Siddhartha Gautama first taught the Dharma of enlightenment, and where the Buddhist *Sangha* came into existence.

It made him think about the feeling Christians could have when visiting the Holy Sepulcher in Jerusalem or when walking around Mount Tabor where Christ's transfiguration was revealed. Or the Jews at their ancient temple's western wall, or their Masada, or Muslims circling the Kaaba. Places where such and such a supernatural event had happened. Of course, there were other famous places too: Gettysburg, Pompei, the Parthenon, the Pyramids, Chichen Itza. Actually, one could even include the Eiffel Tower, Times Square, and the Grand Canyon. Was it all just a form of tourism? What actually was the difference between a Buddhist pilgrim and a Buddhist tourist? One could get a headache.

He circumambulated the great stupa three times and then sat on a bench to watch other pilgrims do the same. Without thinking of what he would do the following day, he walked over to see the Sarnath Museum which housed findings from excavations at the archeological site. Thousands of sculptures and artefacts from thousands of years before, like the prize of the Ashoka Pillar crowned by the Lion Capital, of four lions standing back-to-back, and now the official emblem of India.

He emerged from the museum in midafternoon and took three turns around the stupa again. On the other side of an unpaved peripheral road, he noticed a few men standing in a shallow trench and shoveling soil onto a square elevated screen for sifting the matter. A woman in overalls was supervising them and paying close attention to the sifting process. Reuel wandered over. She is a thin dark-skinned woman, perhaps in her 50s, with close cropped grey hair, and a small beaked nose.

"Finding anything? he asked.

"An earring, yesterday. Made in Japan, I fear, with an imitation ruby of glass. Probably lost by a tourist, I'm guessing twenty years ago, top few inches, before this whole area was sodded over."

"Why dig here?"

"We recently found a very old map, showed there was a Mahakala temple around here. We're just fishing. Paleography. Are you British?"

"American. Were there Buddhist temples here?"

"No, of course not. This was a Vedic area, according to the map, Probably Mahakala worship. Maha-Kala meaning 'Great Time'. In the Upanishads he is the God of consciousness, the basis of reality and existence, according to the Vedas. You interested in these things?"

"Only metaphysically, without superstitions. You working for the museum?"

"Not exactly. I'm with the ASI. Archaeological Survey of India. Ministry of Culture. You a Buddhist?"

"Not officially. Just very interested in the founder and the basics."

"Very sensible. Founders should always be the key. Siddhartha, Jesus, Moses, Mohammed. What follows them are just lots of commentary and arguments. Founder legends are just oral at the outset, and are really most interesting. But they eventually get transformed by written exegeses. The Pali earlier than the Sanskrit. By then you have the conventional divisions of the *tripitaka*: sutra, *vinaya*, and *abhidharma*; sermons, monastic rules, and metaphysics. And then, later, come the universities: Taxila, Nalanda, and Vikramasila. And the philosophers, like Buddhaghosa, Chandrakirti, Nagarjuna, Naropa; and many different schools, after the big ones, Theravada, the Mahayana, Vajrayana, which themselves begin splitting apart, and breaking into different viewpoints. And smaller schools start coming and going, and smaller schools having even smaller schools. The founder gets lost in the aftermath. The first little story gets lost. What to do?"

"Retell the story."

She made a gesture of shrugging her shoulders. At this moment the workmen left the shallow trench and called out the her. It's the end of their day. She tells them to put a tarpaulin over the sifting frame and they hold a casual discussion in Hindi. Finally, the workmen leave and she turns to Reuel.

"Walk with me over to my hostel, that way" she gestures. "I will have some tea made for us. We can talk. I am interested in your interest. How did you come here?"

"I have a car. I'm driving through India."

"That's quite unusual. Where are you going from here?"

"I'm not sure. But you were going to tell a founder story."

"Ah yes, of course. Sarnath. Let us walk while I tell you the account about this place. There is this young boy. His name is Siddhartha. It means 'straight path', born not far from here, at Lumbini. He is a prince of the Gautama family in the Sakya clan, who was born, and raised and had always lived in a castle, a great palace, which is surrounded by beautiful grounds. His mother and

father love and admire him. He is handsome. Girls fall in love with him. He is
a marvelous archer, he can throw a javelin further than anyone, he is an athlete,
musician, wrestler, poet, singer, horseman, a wise and brilliant young student.
Everybody loves him. He marries a beautiful devoted girl. He has a beautiful
son. He is so happy. But he never leaves palace grounds. You follow?"

"I do. Go on."

"One day, for the first time, he disregards the old rule not to leave the
palace grounds. He dresses like a simple stranger and goes out to see the nearby
town for the first time. He sees four things he hadn't ever seen before. He sees a
sick leper, he sees a very old man, and he sees a corpse being carried to a burial
ground. And finally, he sees a *sannyasi*, a yogic renunciate standing with a begging bowl. Siddhartha returns to the palace. He cannot sleep. He cannot forget
these unfamiliar sights. Things he has never seen before. They fill his mind. He
now becomes unhappy."

"Why does this make him unhappy?"

"Because what he saw makes him want to find and understand the meaning of life. He had never thought of such matters as old age, sickness and death
before. Even though everyone he knows will die. He determines to go in search
of meaning. He abandons the palace and his family. He cuts his long hair and
climbs over the palace wall one night and goes in search of the yogi ascetics in
loin cloths who practice austerities and meditative self-examination. He finds
and joins them. They welcome him. Their practice is never to sleep in the same
place twice. They wander and practice silence by day and eat only a single meal
at noon. They go off singly each morning and practice hours and hours of solitary meditation. They only speak to each other at night, after dark, and then
only to discuss their meditation."

"Rather extreme, don't you think?"

"Precisely, rather extreme. But he stays with them for seven years, wandering. That is the story. One day the little group are close to a town near Gaya.
As usual, they go their separate solitary ways in the morning. Then, in the late
afternoon, Siddhartha is walking back to join the others of the group. Just at

that moment, a sixteen-year-old girl named Sugata, from the nearby town, is driving some cows home and she sees him. He is skeletally thin from his austerities. Sugata is well brought-up, and seeing this holy man she wants to make an offering to him. The only thing she has to offer is a small coconut bowl half-filled with Kir, a sweet rice-pudding. She approaches, bows and offers him the Kir. Now mind this moment." She paused.

"Okay. I will."

"Siddhartha looks at her. She is pure. He looks at the Kir. It is pure. Everything suddenly seems pure. He sees there can be no harm in eating the Kir. Something new has come over him. The entire meaning of self-denying austerity suddenly vanishes. There has to be another way. He thanks Sugata and slowly consumes the Kir as she leaves. Siddhartha stands there thinking to himself about his life. He knows he is the most accomplished of the yogis. His opinions and discourses are valued models. He has excelled in everything he has ever undertaken in his life. Yet in his heart he feels he is no closer to understanding the nature of reality than on the night he left the palace."

Reuel remarks "Ripeness is all, isn't it? Like Shakespeare's fool: 'Men must endure their coming hence, even as their going hither. Ripeness is all.' Sorry to interrupt."

"No matter. You are right. Ripeness is all. And ripe Siddhartha thinks that if he, with all of his exceptional gifts of intellect and experience, cannot after trying for seven years to obtain enlightenment, then hardly anyone could. Something must be wrong. And moreover, if he cannot gain enlightenment right at this time, then no one can. And he sees a solitary *ficus* tree nearby casting a patch of shade from the dwindling late afternoon sun and he determines to sit under it to gain enlightenment through the coming night, and he swears to accomplish this by the time he sees the morning star. And according to the story, the legend, for the first time in seven years, he doesn't sit on the hard naked ground, but he gathers and makes a cushion out of a bundle of *kusa* grass and sits on it beneath the *ficus* tree to accomplish his goal, to find the root of dissatisfaction and suffering. Are you with me?"

"He becomes enlightened. Right?"

"Wait. We are coming here, to Sarnath, remember. Because at that moment, unbeknownst to Siddhartha, his four fellow yogis had gathered and had observed him swallowing the kir and talking to the girl, both forbidden by their rule of silence and to not taking food after their single mid-day meal. They are appalled at his apparent misbehavior. They think he is untrustworthy and they flee from having anything to do with him. Night begins and Siddhartha commences his lonely effort."

"Now it gets interesting, doesn't it?"

"It's said that at first he recollects all the human lives that have ever been, all who have come and gone, and he acknowledges the inevitability of birth and death. And in his next so-called watch, recognizing that birth and death affect all sentient beings, he sees that the law of causality, or *karma*, must determine the experience of whatever is born, with its inevitable quality of suffering. *Dukkha.* Where attraction, confusion and aversion drive the cycle of birth, life, and death. Understanding this, then in the third part of that night he realizes the clarity of the middle-way, and its eightfold path as the means of mental liberation from this cycle of causality. It is a path requiring the use of mindfulness and insight applied to understanding the coming and going of craving, ignorance and revulsion,"

"And then?"

"And then, at the sight of the morning star, in the last watch, with the perception of four noble truths, and in lucid awareness, he recognizes his own awakening. According to one written tradition, he describes what had happened to him in his own words. It is like poetry. I've committed it to memory. He says: 'My heart, thus knowing, thus seeing, was released from the fermentation of sensuality, released from the fermentation of becoming, released from the fermentation of ignorance. With such release, there was full knowledge. The task was done. There is nothing further for this world.'"

"And that is called 'Nirvana'?"

"Exactly. Siddhartha is now the Buddha. Awakened. Now follow me my young American friend. Imagine the situation. He is concerned that no one will believe him. He wanders about for days. He joins some simple merchants walking on a road. They are ordinary people. He tells them of his awakening. They are gently persuaded by his insights and pledge to follow his ideas, which are easily understood. He wanders on for some weeks until he comes to this very place, Sarnath, where we are walking just now. It is a clear night with a full moon. He sees the four determined ascetic yogis who ran away from him, sitting around a fire. He begs them for a kindness, only to hear him. They agree. And then, here in Sarnath, for the first time, formally, he turns the wheel of the law, reveals the precious doctrine of the *dharma*, makes clear the inherent nature of reality, and proclaims the perfection of the middle way, and by so enlightening the four discerning ascetic yogis, begins the creation of the Buddhist *sangha*. So, what do you think?"

"You're a Buddhist?"

"I'll say a crypto-Buddhist."

"What's your name?"

"I am called Chitra Lal. What's yours?"

"Antenor."

"Well Antenor, at any rate, now that we have arrived here at my hostel, courtesy of the Archaeological Survey, I shall ask Priti to prepare some tea for us."

She left him to himself under a roofed patio, surrounded by flower pots, and went inside the small building to give instructions to her household staff. Chitra Lal was the first person who had conversationally befriended him since he moved on by himself. And it clearly appeared she could acquaint him with India at a plane somewhat higher than Raj Das. He wanted to talk further with her. She emerged to the shaded patio carrying a plate of sweet biscuits.

"You said you were a crypto-Buddhist" he continued. "Could you explain to me what that means?"

"Very well. I'll try. Let me tell you something of myself. I live in Hindustan but am not myself a Hindu. I joined the Archeological Survey fourteen years ago. I've been a widow for almost six years, and I am without children. Indeed, without much family. My father was a medical doctor, an orthopedic surgeon who trained in Scotland and practiced in New Delhi. He was a Parsi. Do you know about the Parsis?" Reuel shook his head.

"We Parsis are a very small sect. Educated. Very successful, quite well off. These days there are probably fewer than 50 thousand Parsis in India. They are not Vedic, they are Zoroastrians, a most ancient religion, sometimes called fire worshippers. My mother was born a Christian. You know what Christians are. There are more than 25 million Christians in India. Christ was introduced to India by Saint Thomas the Apostle, who came to the Malabar Coast in 52 Anno Domini. Think of that! So, you see, as I said, I am not a Hindu. The only way to be a Hindu is to be born that way of Hindu parents. You cannot convert to Hinduism, in the broad sense, the way you can convert to being a Christian or a Muslim. Likewise, you cannot really convert to Buddhism by giving up other faiths, but you can adhere to Buddhism. Buddhism is a religion of adhesion, not conversion. Most interestingly, while there are only about 8 million who call themselves Buddhists in the land of its birth, there are very many, like myself, who take Buddhist teaching seriously, even if privately, but do not engage in any ritual practice or outward expression. That's why I call myself a crypto-Buddhist."

"I guess that makes me a crypto-Buddhist too" said Reuel.

"And are you a hippie?"

"What?"

"A hippie. I hear about hippies. Like American *saddhus*. They take drugs and come to India to find enlightenment. Is that like you?"

"Not exactly. I just wanted to travel and see the world. I was interested in Buddhism since I was in college."

"And why do you say you are interested in Buddhism?"

"Not sure I can explain. I was a student of philosophy. Buddhism was a new approach to the subject of consciousness and the mind, which was not at all covered in what I was studying. It seemed fairly intelligent."

"Do you believe in God?"

"No, not really. That's one of the reasons Buddhism appealed to me. It seemed uninterested in the whole subject of God, or Gods. I mean you can be a faithful Christian and still believe Buddhist doctrines. Am I right?"

"I think you are. Of course, as you said, that could make you a crypto-Buddhist too."

"So, what to do?"

"Personally, I think you should go to Bodh Gaya, where Siddhartha's enlightenment took place. It is the most supreme historic place for all Buddhists. There you will find the *ficus religiosa*, the Bo Tree, a scion, a direct descendant of the original tree under which the Buddha sat. You can make a pilgrimage by driving there, it's only about 200 kilometers from here. If you leave in the morning you will surely be there before dark."

"Thank you very much for that advice. I am indebted."

It took an entire day for Reuel to reach Bodh Gaya. The 200 kilometers from Sarnath consisted of roads filled with ox-carts bearing sugar cane cuttings, elephants who were moving logs, road repair crews involving long waits, constabularies inspecting one's papers, a turned-over truck requiring a detour through wheat fields, small towns astride roads with thronged markets hampering vehicular passage, single lane bridges over dry water courses, a lengthy stop in a queue for refueling, and a slow-served lunch of paneer samosas and milk tea.

On reaching Bodh Gaya at the start of darkness, a need to urinate led him to stop at the first likely looking shelter, a building with a gravel parking area and a small illuminated sign at its entrance giving notice of "Hotel Lodi". He could see a dining room and several happy-looking women in saris at the front desk. English speaking, they were so helpful and obliging that he decided to book a room there with bath and take food. This last devolved into light comedy owing to his unfamiliarity with the cuisine and dishes of India's South and the absence of a written menu.

On emerging from the hotel the following morning, Reuel saw an odd-looking elderly man trimming a row of multi-colored gladioli lining the entrance lane. The fellow noticed him immediately, putting down his shears and picking up a cane. He approached Reuel with a prominent limp.

"This your car?"

"Yes."

"Be a good fellow and park over there." He gestured. "Prefer to keep the entrance garden unobstructed. You came last night. No way to see the flowers. What's your name? Antenor? That you?" From his accent he was obviously an American. Reuel judged his age to be close to seventy. The man was wrapped with a grey sarong around his waist and a white shirt with rolled-up sleeves above.

"That's me, Reuel Antenor."

"Saw your name in the register. American, huh. Don't get many. I'm Dorsit, Brian Dorsit. Call me Brian. You a tourist or a pilgrim?"

"A little of each, I guess. Wanted to see the Bodhi tree."

"By yourself with a car? That's rich. Not many like that. Where you from?"

"Massachusetts. Where're you from?"

"Arkansas. 'Bout forty years ago."

"You work here?"

"Sure do. I own the place."

"No kidding? How'd that happen?"

"That's another story. Some other time. You want the tree? See that spire sticking up over there?" He pointed. "That's the Maha Bodhi Temple. That's where the tree is."

"There an ashram?"

"No, not there. You wanna meditate? Go past on that way, you'll come to the Burmese Vihara. That's the place to practice. *Vipassana* practice. Unless you want to hang with the Tibetans. Great people, but a weird kind of Buddhism. And do yourself a favor, avoid the Japs."

"How come?"

"That's another story. Some other time."

"Well, thanks for the advice. I'll go move the car."

At the Maha Bodhi temple Reuel copied other arrivals and performed three half-prostrations at the entrance. Then, joining a small crowd of devotees, he lit a stick of incense and made an offering with clasped hands under a leafy canopy of the alleged vegetative scion of the original *ficus religiosa*, Afterwards, as Dorsit had suggested, he walked on a few hundred yards and came to the Burmese Vihara. An attendant told him he was welcome to come and sit in the meditation hall at any time. At six o'clock, outside on the grass, the Venerable Kyaw Thant usually gave a brief talk in English.

Until that time Reuel's experience with meditation had been haphazard and without the benefit of any formal instruction. His earliest attempts took place when still an undergraduate at Columbia while taking the subway downtown to Greenwich Village. He would take the first available seat and tried being motionless while simply concentrating on listening to the machine roar of the train. Over the ensuing years he would find moments, or minutes, even a single hour, to sit quietly and observe the clamor of his mind settle into quietness and calmness. He never failed to examine the experience in light of his academic studies in philosophy and biology on "mind" and "consciousness". He had a vivid recollection of sitting together with Ulla, silently for considerable lengths, on the beach of Fire Island. At other times, specifically while reading modern philosophers like Wittgenstein, he would stop and closely observe his thought-stream and the formation of words in his brain. His readings in Buddhism had underscored the value, or importance to him, of meditation. He recalled meditating in Sweden after his visits with Phra Luang. Then, after dosing with LSD, the predisposition to meditate came on more frequently and was easily accommodated. He recalled meditating on the Saga after taking down the sail in the middle of the Gulf of Bosnia. He had meditated almost daily on the Saga in the mid-Atlantic. He had meditated with Adler in Cuernavaca. He had meditated with Raj Das, joining dozens of others in their brief visits to various ashrams. And while the precise definition of meditation remained elusive, the act of doing it was unmistakable and familiar. But now, the challenge of meditating at the Burmese Vihara in Bodh Gaya seemed to belong to another category. It had both intensity and duration. And so, Reuel began meditating there for long sessions, twice a day, for seven consecutive weeks.

His only secular experience and social companion in Bodh Gaya was with Brian Dorsit, nearly forty years his senior. They exchanged personal stories and worldly views at dinners in the hotel dining room. Dorsit seemed eager to share thoughts with a fellow American.

"I can't remember the last time I had a Yankee here. Most of my trade comes from South Asia, Ceylon, Burma, Cambodia, Siam. Word of mouth. Travel agents there know the Lodi Hotel. Only once in a while a few Westerners. Germans give us good reviews. No Japs."

"You say Siam, Ceylon. Not Thailand, Sri Lanka?"

"Old habit. That's what we called them back then. Been out here forever. Never back in the States since the war, since 1942."

"How'd you come to own the hotel?"

"It's a story. Got shot down. Jap POW camp. Near to died. Catholic nuns rescued me, nearly two years flat on my back. Got a job in Calcutta with Christian Famine Relief. Then in Lucknow. One thing led to another. Heard this place was for sale. It's been good to me. Nearly twenty years now. Lovely people here. Never thought of going back to Arkansas. And I get my military pension here. Don't know a soul in the States. Don't know what I'd do. I'm more Buddhist than Baptist by now."

"Were you a pilot?"

"Are you kiddin? I can't even do long-division. Took me two years to make sergeant. I was one of those guys who enlisted before Pearl Harbor. Got stationed at Lackland air base near San Antonio. Texas. Trained on engine motor repair. Pratt-Whitneys. Got sent to the Burma war against the Japs. Air Transport Command flying C-46s, C-47s, over "the hump", the Himalayas. Ferrying supplies to Kunming, Chiang-Kai-Shek's stronghold in Southwest China. Dangerous as hell. We lost over 600 planes, half of them to weather, or poor guys unable to get enough altitude and crashing into a mountain. 1943. We had a Curtis-Commando sitting in Kunming with a bum engine. They sent me over. Jap fighters strafed us. Wrecked the left wing. I bailed out. First time in my life. Scared shitless. Saw the Co go out seconds later. Plane went into a crazy spin. Pilot never got out. Nice guy. Casey, from Oklahoma. I landed real hard. Broke my hip to pieces. I was...."

A woman on the staff came over, interrupted, and whispered something to Dorsit.

"Oh Jesus" he said to Reuel. "Sorry. My chef's just quit. Gone to Patna. Learned his wife suddenly died. Another time."

Meditation. The mind observing itself. Reuel was now determined to intensify his experience. A first thing was to sit with an erect spine. He was unable to answer why this was more beneficial, than a slight slouch, but determined to practice it. Next, was sustained sitting cross-legged on doubled cushions. This was marginally painful and would lead to a distracting numbness. His adaptation was to fold his legs rather loosely and to cover his lower body with a large shawl skirted over his limbs. Within a week he had found a certain steady groove.

The next challenge was breath, at the heart of *Vipassana* practice. First was counting breaths from one to ten, over and over. While simple in principle it was, at first, difficult in practice. A number, like "ten" was just a word, a sound in his head. He observed that while counting occluded having thoughts, but that he would unintentionally stop enumerating the breaths and stray thoughts came to his mind. At length this became boring and he abandoned the practice of counting in favor of focusing on simply observing the act of breathing, in and out. This led to experimentation. At first, he tried slowing his breathing rate and taking deeper breaths. Then he experimented with slowing his exhalations. He tried counting within the breaths, and finally found a ratio which suited him, mentally enumerating from one to seven on inhalations, and then counting from one to eleven on exhalations. This ratio seemed to be his sweet spot and became so familiar that he could maintain it without counting by simply observing the ratio. He estimated he was taking six whole breaths a minute. It was comfortable but the instant he ceased to be watchful a river of thoughts commenced flowing and he was no longer mindful of breath. The teaching was the cessation of thought. Was it possible?

His thought-stream had a logic of its own which he could not decipher: A letter he intended to write to Luca. The view of Chicago from out on Lake Michigan. The naked body of Gabrielle and Pierre's ratification. The difficulty of discriminating his daughters, Karen from Kristina. How to resell the Ambassador. The defection of Adler to Shaktism. Dorsit's limp. The shares being held at Cambridge Trust. Wittgenstein's grave. The parents he barely knew, at their radio in Winnetka. Phra Luang telling him to focus on feeling his index finger touching his thumb. The fact that he was no longer observing his breath. The nature of thought. The rise and fall of words in his mind. Silent sounds in his brain. Recursive semantic hierarchies. *Rekursive semantische Hierarchien.* Immanuel Kant. *Ding an sich.* What is non-self? Death is non-self. The thing in itself, independent of observation? Was it a noumenon or phenomenon? It was hopeless. The thought-stream was relentless. Back to counting breaths from one to ten. What was the lesson?

This was typical, as he thought about it in his hotel room while going to bed, preparing to sleep. He had attended one of Thant's talks this day. The old teacher spoke softly with a distinct pause between sentences. What had he said? That through the control of breath the mind would become quiescent; but will be quiescent only so long as the breath remains controlled, and when the breath resumes of its own the mind also will again start moving and will wander as impelled by residual impressions. The source of this however was the same, for both mind and breath. The cessation of thought was difficult. Thought was the nature of the mind. The thought of "I" is the first thought of the mind; and that was selfhood. From where a self originates breath also originates. If he cannot stop breathing, he cannot stop self-recognition. He could slow breath, not stop it, by self-control. Self-control was the product of self-realization. And while mentally rehearsing Thant's lecture Reuel fell to sleep easily and lost himself to self-recognition.

There was another evening at table with Dorsit which haunted his thoughts of Buddhism for many years thereafter. It was about pain and the question of wickedness. Even more, it was a question of whether Buddhist teachers and devoted disciples could be evil just as well as being good. Or were these both merely a matter of illusion?

Reuel said "Brian, tell me about being a prisoner of war."

"Well, I can't say it was like death. Death was all around us, every day. For two years I thought I was just going to die in a few days. You can't imagine that, can you? Nothing's really like death because when you're dead you're nothing. Like in those Nazi death camps I heard about at the end of the war. Imagine it if you can, a death camp. I was in a Jap death camp. Only reason I'm alive is I had a protector. Angus Wentworth, god bless his soul. He kept me alive. You know, when I bailed out of that C-47 I didn't have time to think. All I could see under the chute was this jungle canopy coming up at me. I crashed so hard it broke my hip bones. Just knocked me out. Unconscious. Don't know how long I lay there. Some tribespeople found me. Nagas. City people called them headhunters. They saved me. One of them was holding me when I came to. Guy was trying to put some squashed-up mango in my mouth. Whenever I taste a mango I think of it. They carried me to a road where there was a small Jap truck with some half-dead British troops in back. Burma War. Try to imagine some wounded guys who can hardly talk, with cracked skulls, wet bullet wounds, and sick with Malaria and dysentery. You can't imagine it. I couldn't move. Japs just threw me in the back. I passed out again from the pain. Truck drove for a whole day. No water, no food. Finally came to some kind of holding place. Shoved us out of the truck. Two of the Brits were dead. I hit the ground on my butt and passed out from the pain. When I came to there's someone putting a canteen to my mouth. That was Angus Wentworth. You ever heard of Pearl Buck?"

"Sure. Nobel Prize for literature. I once saw a movie based on her book. 'The Good Earth'. She grew up in China. Her parents were missionaries. Right?"

"Right. Angus's parents were missionaries too. Like Buck, he grew up in China. His folks were Methodists, medical missionaries. Both of them doctors. Chinese women those days couldn't be touched by men. Angus had gone back to the States, got ordained as a Minister, and came back to China. Theology was his thing, not medicine. Got into Chinese Buddhism. Traveled all over studying it. A year in Korea. Two years studying in Japan. He was down in Malaya and Siam when Singapore fell. Escaped capture and worked his way North up through Burma heading for the Brits in India up in Assam, where our "Hump" ATC base was. Never got there. A Jap infantry squad spotted him, wearing his clerical collar and all. Brought him to the same holding pen where I got dumped. There for a few weeks. He nursed me. After that, for two years I was never more than twenty feet away from him."

"How'd you survive?"

"Like I said, he protected me. Fed me rice gruel. Made a crutch for me. Held me up. Made me walk with it. Finally, the Japs...." Dorsit stopped and nearly sobbed at this point. "Reuel" he said, "I gotta stop. I'll tell you another time. I don't like to think about it."

"Sure, I understand."

In the next days, Reuel's meditation steadied around slow breathing. He observed his thoughts. His thoughts weren't in Burmese or Swedish. His thoughts were in English. Did thoughts require language? He could imagine mathematical thoughts without language. He could imagine chess thoughts in pictures of board positions. He could imagine manually preparing food or reassembling a lab instrument without language. But when he thought of himself doing these various things, when he thought about meaning, he was in some way using language in his brain to think about what he was imagining. Certainly, most of the thoughts, the 'mind-stream' in his brain were in English. And what was English? Just sounds. Thoughts were just remembered sounds in his brain that signified. He tried experimenting by focusing on the sound of the meditation hall. His mind stayed quiet as he concentrated on listening. Auditory nerves were doing their job, but what or who was hearing it? This worked for a while until he commented to himself on what he was doing and observed he was commenting to himself using English sounds in his head about listening to the hall. And without any intent or apparent reason, with a dynamic of its own, he found himself thinking of Brian Dorsit's agony while wondering to himself if he could withstand that kind of punishing experience and he observed the mind-stream of himself thinking of that using English mental sounds. It was tiring. He was calm. It was boring. He observed being bored. What was the point? Was there a point? Dorsit could not stop feeling pain. What of pleasure? Why stop the feeling of pleasure? It brought up sexual fantasies. They were sweet. It brought up Shakespeare. *'When to the sessions of sweet silent thought I summon up remembrance of things...'* Why be indifferent to sweet mental pleasures, without craving them? Sweet was better than bitter, wasn't it? Should one get rid of both feelings and simply rest in the boredom? What was the point of meditating? To become better acquainted with his mind? To become the member of some clergy? To lose his mind in emptiness? To realize non-self by knowing the cause? What did it mean? What was the meaning of meaning? Mere recursive semantic hierarchies? It went on this way for days.

Dorsit had Reuel over to his small one room house, a stone's throw from the hotel, for samosas and two bottles of Kingfisher beer.

"How's your meditation going?" he asked.

"Well, it's interesting when it isn't boring. Seems self-indulgent sometimes. I think too much of it could dull the mind, like anything obsessive. But I'm just a *patzer*, as we say in chess. Provides me a taste of what it's like to be a monk."

"Do you think you can be a good Buddhist without meditating a lot?"

"Outwardly, yes; inwardly I'm not so sure. How about you? Ever put in the time?"

"Oh, hell yeah. Only reason I'm still alive, actually. 1943. Japs let me meditate with Angus. He really had their number. First thing he said to me when we got to the labor camp – 'POW bridge camp kilometer 91' - was to never forget that we were dealing with really crazy people, crazy Buddhists. Criminally insane Buddhists, he said. If we wanted to live, we had to play along with their heads, otherwise they'd kill us. Trick was to be that he's playing a Zen master and I'm gonna be his disciple. First day there, they lined us up. *Tenko*, they called it. This son-of-a-bitch camp commander, war criminal, Colonel Sanjuro Tanaka, walks the line-up, mostly Aussies, inspecting near a hundred of us, coming along toward Angus and me with a samurai sword in one of his hands. He tells his staffers to pull a really sick weak guy out a yard or two. Walks around to the side of him and suddenly, without warning, swings hard, half-cutting the guy's head off with the fucking sword. Just one big whack. Blood spurts two feet in the air. Guy goes down dead. Tanaka walks on, coming our way. He keeps eyeing the prisoners, looking for guys too sick to work. I know I'm done for, standing shakily on my crutch. As Tanaka comes in front of us Angus stands up straight and speaks to him in Japanese. Tanaka stops like he can't believe what he's hearing. His eyes grow wide in surprise. He puts the tip of the sword under Angus's chin and lifts his head an inch or two. Angus calmly returns the stare and says something for a bit and at the end puts his hand on my shoulder. Tanaka stands there looking at us silently for nearly a whole minute, says something to one of his staffers and continues down the line."

"Wild. What did Angus say?"

"Told him he should use his sword properly by holding it with two hands."

"What?"

"He told Tanaka that using one hand was a bad habit because the other held shields in the old days, while a real warrior, a samurai with true *bushido*, didn't need a shield and used two hands, like in kendo. And that furthermore he, Angus, was an ordained Zen priest in Japan and a disciple of Hakuun Yasutani

- made me memorize the name - and that he and I weren't soldiers who had been captured, only pilgrims, and I was his disciple."

"And that worked? That's really amazing."

"It worked. Tanaka made him camp translator, made him wash and clean and pray for Jap soldiers in sick bay, do funeral rites like a chaplain when one of them died from malaria or something. The rest of the time Angus and me just sat in front of our bamboo lean-to pretending to meditate. Just sitting. Japs call it *Shikantaza*. Just sitting. Funny thing is, there's really no difference between pretending to meditate and really meditating."

This remark stayed with Reuel. "Just sitting" was an interesting concept. It was somewhat different than observing or counting breaths, which were themselves slightly simplistic practices. Like trying to solve paradoxes. Of course, one could lose oneself in thoughts while at the same time aspiring to lose the self. How odd. Was a vacant mind the goal? Was there morality in emptiness? Was mere ecclesiastical stubbornness the goal? To prove to one's superiors how sincere or how virtuous one appeared? Just sitting as opposed to honest hard work to support a family or to create art? The point of meditation had to be more than the self-examination of one's non-selfhood. What if just sitting was merely a form of laziness in cultures which were used to sitting cross-legged on the ground? Could one be a good Buddhist if one rarely meditated? Could one be a good Christian if one rarely prayed? Such thoughts, such questions, went round and round in Reuel's mind as he sat in the Burmese vihara. What would Wittgenstein or Bertrand Russell think of what he was doing?

Reuel remembered his boyhood impressions of the Second World War. His parents were obsessed with the war in Europe. He recalled a side table with a map of Italy and red pins marking the allied campaign up the country's boot shape. The landing at Anzio. The bombing of Monte Casino. The capture of Mussolini by partisans and hanging his dead body upside-down by his heels. Could Buddhists have defeated Hitler? And more to the point was his memory of war in Asia seen through the movies. Guadalcanal. Tarawa. Okinawa. Strange names in the newspapers. And Hollywood portraying Japanese fanatics in the jungle, using Chinese actors, facing the courage of John Wayne on the big screen. And the bomb on Hiroshima killing tens of thousands of Buddhists. Where was Buddhist self-defense? He pursued this matter with Dorsit.

"Brian, what the hell were all those Japanese Buddhists think they were doing?"

"You really want to hear this?"

"I do."

"Christ. Long before I met him, Angus was in China with the American Methodist Church Mission, in Nanking in 1937. Over six weeks the invading Japs, actually, really, killed a few hundred thousand Chinese civilians. Now it's known as 'The Rape of Nanking'. Can you even imagine that number? Angus saw those atrocities with his own eyes. He gave it to me in detail. Couldn't get it out of his mind. Thousands of civilians led away in forced marches every day and mass-executed in a trench measuring about 300 yards long and 5 yards wide. Japs called it the 'Ten-Thousand-Corpse Ditch'. He couldn't imagine so much brutality. And rapes. Rape, rape, rape. Rape after rape. A thousand cases a night, and many by day. Any resistance or anything that seemed like disapproval, and you got a bayonet stab or a bullet. He told me people were hysterical. Women were carried off day and night. The whole fucking Japanese army was free to go and come and do whatever it pleased, whatever it wanted. Day after day Angus would see naked dead women in the street with sticks or bayonets in their cunts. Believe it or not, this was done by convinced Zen Buddhists, recruits, long-term meditators, and some of them priests. Tokyo newspapers reported a famous contest between two Jap officers, devoted Buddhists, competing to be the first to kill 100 people with a sword. I only wish Angus was here. He'd tell you lots more like this."

"Jesus. What was it like for you?"

"I was scared shitless. More than a year. Angus wouldn't let me die. He'd prop me up, use my crutch as a brace from behind, fold my hands on my lap, tell me to close my eyes and keep my mouth shut. Just look like I'm meditating. Labor units moving in front of us all day. Jap guards didn't understand

English. They were so brutal, so sadistic, and completely unpredictable. They looked down on the Aussie officers with contempt because they had surrendered instead of fighting to the last man. If one of them protested they'd put him in what they called 'ovens', small iron boxes sitting there in the fierce heat of day. Anyone attempting to escape was buried alive. Hard to imagine but you were forced to watch it. Everyone was sick. Malaria was common. We slept on mats on the ground. Men ate just enough to stay alive to work on the bridge. A watery diet of rice and a few vegetables, hardly a cup a day. We were just skin and bones with malnutrition. Living skeletons. Guys lost their vision, most everyone had unrelenting nerve pain. And dysentery, oh God, with people laying in their own shit hardly able to move. And tropical ulcers you'd get from bamboo scratches while working nearly naked in the jungle. Gruesome leg ulcers a foot long with rotting bone exposed. Japs wouldn't let Angus and me help any of our own. Only made us tend Jap soldiers in their sick bay. Made him chant a Buddhist prayer when one of them died."

"How on earth were you rescued?"

"Japs finally abandoned the camp. One day Tanaka and the high officers were gone. Just a few lieutenants with a captain in charge. We knew something was up. Japs were pulling out of Burma and Siam. Retreating to the Philippines to fight MacArthur. That was the worst time for us. There was no longer work on the bridge. There was no food brought in. We could hear air attacks on road supply lines. We were starving to death. Even the Japs guarding us. That's when the cannibalism began. When some of us prisoners died the Japs took their bodies to a hut for butchering of flesh from arms, legs, butts and they'd carry it off to their quarters to cut into small pieces and fried them. God's truth. Japs knew the end was coming. Remaining squads just disappeared into the jungle. Finally, there was just a non-com and five or six enlisted guys. They knew they were going to die. They even set-up a machine gun. It didn't help them. Every one of our guys who could move mobbed them in the middle of the night. Crushed their heads with stones. They were all gone. We didn't know what to do. Nobody strong enough to walk out. Four days. Angus led a few guys to find tropical tree fruit. Guanabana, Starfruit, Rambutan, Mango, Kiwis. Then a

Burmese tribal in a British uniform walked in with a small squad and a radio. A day later there was a truck with food and a doctor. We were evacuated. I passed out a few times. Angus was gone. I woke up in a hospital bed with needles in my arm and Bengali Catholic nuns looking after me. Flew me to Calcutta. Never saw Angus again. Had a letter from him a couple of years later. British intelligence seconded him to Mountbatten's staff. After the Jap surrender, he was in Tokyo for a year as a witness and working for the Japanese War Crimes Tribunal. Our camp commander, Sanjuro Tanaka, who'd been promoted to General in the last days, was tried, found guilty, and hanged. Angus died about ten years ago. Never had a pension. A civilian. Wasn't in the service. Didn't have a close family. Buried in a Methodist cemetery in Georgia. The Brits gave him a fancy medal of some kind. I owe him my life."

"Quite a story."

"You're lucky to be an American Buddhist in peace time. I still don't let any Japs in this hotel. I want to heave when I see Jap pilgrims approaching the Bo tree. Fucking Zen bastard mind-control fascists. I get nauseous when I hear them chant about emptiness in their temple."

Brian Dorsit's story perturbed Reuel's meditations in the Burmese vihara. Previously, on the whole, over some weeks, he had been able to attain a degree of one-pointedness, a calmness cradled in and on his breath. But now he had a mental upheaval into self-examination. He had been personally spared the horrors of insane wars which continued to take place all over the planet. Like Buddhist Vietnam. He had never killed or injured anyone. He had never gone hungry. He was in good health. He had enjoyed the love of women. He led an interesting life. He was studious. He was sincere. Were these just the marks of a self-indulgent man who had barely tasted real suffering, like that of Brian Dorsit? How could Buddhist teaching possibly have reduced Dorsit's suffering? There had been Buddhist armies engaged in killing since the time of the emperor Ashoka. There were presently cruel Buddhist armies in Burma and Sri Lanka. What possible excuse could there be for Buddhist killers? As for their victims, was there not a God-given right of violent self-defense? Truly, suffering was everywhere if not for everyone. Reuel thought back to the time of the founder, when life was short, nasty and brutal. Most everyone died young. To reach the age of 40 in those days made one an elder. There were no antibiotics. The Shakyamuni didn't know the mathematics of cannon trajectories, or the phenomenon of explosive artillery powders. Ancient Buddhism, the *Theravada*, was really mostly for retreatants, for an ascetic clergy, not for the lay masses of the *Mahayana*. Did either have a place in the modern world of industrial warfare, where Zen Buddhism had, in his lifetime, become a religion of will-power? Where the *dharma* was used as the spiritual backbone for national militaries? Who was entitled to ask such questions? He was sure he was entitled to ask such questions.

Yet, those questions shook him. He felt his meditation tenure at the Burmese vihara had become a counterfeit form of self-indulged virtue banking. Merely a dubious method of accumulating a so-called ecclesiastical merit. Was profound thought in an active mind like Wittgenstein's the enemy of enlightenment? Does a philosopher have to cure disease in himself before he can arrive at elementary notions of common sense and decency? Was it the reason intellectuals found it so difficult to have faith? If in our lives we were surrounded by death, it was as if health in our mind was surrounded by madness. His thoughts ran in circles as he tried getting out of a tortuous zigzagging thicket of questions to get straight out into the open. Could the path be in science? The human mind was obviously something produced by the history of organic life, not by a stone. *Homo sapiens* had a unique bundle of senses integrated by its evolved brain. He could see, hear, smell, touch, taste. He could sense gravity, direction, temperature, the position of his limbs while sitting on the floor of the vihara. And all of this together formed an electrochemically transduced sensorium in his own brain, which was clearly an organ which could even also sense or observe its own internal processes like thought, memory, logic, imagination and cognition. Was meditation a useful way to understand his sapience, his consciousness? Or was consciousness merely a case of the brain detecting itself in a virtual mirror which meant nothing at all? And yet, at the end of such self-reflection, he felt sure of one thing. He could detect nonsense, but he wanted more.

Several days later Reuel walked by an elderly nun, robed, with a shaved head, sitting on a small bench in the shade of a wall and obviously European. She smiled at him in a friendly way, which aroused his curiosity and they exchanged *Namaste* greetings. She gestured for him to sit next to her."

"Speak English" he asked.

"Necessarily" she replied "and I'm Swiss."

"Maroon robe. You're with the Tibetans?"

"Obviously. I'm a student of His Holiness."

"What are you studying?"

"The *Catuskoti*. I'm writing a book."

"What's that? That word."

"In Sanskrit it literally means 'the quadrilateral'. Fourfoldness, so to speak."

"Could you explain? I'm quite interested in numbers. I was once a math major."

"Consider for example, is the world finite? Or infinite? Or both finite and infinite? Or neither finite nor infinite? Do you see? Again, is the world eternal, not eternal, both eternal and not eternal, neither eternal nor not eternal? There are four positions. This originates when at the beginning of our teaching the Buddha refused to answer four questions regarding the beginning of the world. Namely, whether there was a beginning, or no beginning, or both, or neither. You understand?"

"Mmmm, sort of. Go on."

"For example, we say there are four kinds of persons found existing in the world. One who practices for their own welfare but not for the welfare of others; one who practices for the welfare of others but not for their own welfare; one who is practicing neither for their own welfare nor for the welfare of others; and one who is practicing both for their own welfare and for the welfare of others. Four situations. That is called the *Catuskoti*."

"Isn't that a confession of ignorance?"

"To the contrary. It is simply an affirmation, without an intention of denial. Everything is conventionally real, and is ultimately unreal. Everything has both characteristics. Nothing is ultimately real. Once again, everything is real, everything is not real, both real and not real, neither real nor not real. That is the Buddha's teaching."

"Ah ha! I see. And that of course explains Buddhist emptiness, *sunyata*!"

"You are very swift my young friend. And that understanding should lead you directly to the default and humane position which is called 'the middle way', the *Madhyamika*."

"Got it. Brilliant. What's your name?"

"Sister Khema."

"I'm very grateful. And somewhat fulfilled."

"Have a nice day."

ॐ

Reuel planned to leave Bodh Gaya a few days later. Dorsit wished him well, enjoining him to enjoy life and urged him not to drive through India after dark. As his plans were uncertain several possibilities were examined. It was too soon to return to America. The huge sub-continent of Asia continued to beckon. He examined his road map and considered driving South to the State of Tamil Nadu to see the holy mountain of Arunachala in Tiruvannamalai where the Hindu sage Ramana Maharshi had offered spiritual instruction on the Self. From there he would be close to the Pondicherry of his young friend Raj Das and the famous nearby Sri Aurobindo ashram. It was tempting, but had little to do with Buddhism. And while he was comfortable driving alone and all of India now seemed familiar and welcoming, the absence of a Buddhist destination was problematic. But this was soon resolved.

Recently he had discovered a small tea house on an unpaved lane. It was an unpretentious place where he could read quietly between morning and afternoon meditations. They offered a snack of roasted cashews with cardamon and sugar which he enjoyed with his milk tea. Having made his farewell to Kyaw Thant at the vihara that day before departing Bodh Gaya, Reuel had the afternoon free and decided to write a letter to Luca Baca. A table at the tea house seemed an ideal venue as it was usually quiet and unoccupied near mid-day. As he turned the corner in approach, he was pleasantly surprised to see the single customer at a square table, a young Tibetan Lama in maroon robes over a yellow tunic. Their eyes met, and with a nearly invisible gesture by the faintest motion of the Lama's chin Reuel sensed he was welcome to sit.

"*Namaste*" said Reuel.

"*Tashi delek*" said the young Lama.

"Do you speak English?" asked Reuel.

"I'm reading at Oxford University" replied the Lama.

"Good Lord! An intellectual! What concentration?"

"Comparative religion. MA."

"College?"

"Magdalen."

"Unbelievable! I was on the High some months ago, stood at the Cloister gate, wanted to call on Gilbert Ryle, but I didn't dare."

"Does that signify you are interested in metaphysical philosophy?"

"Well, I'm interested in Buddhism. I don't know if that helps. I'm mostly interested in understanding the mind. My name is Reuel, by the way" as he held out a hand and sat down at the table.

"My name is Sonam" said the Lama and extended a very soft hand, palm down.

Over tea, Reuel described his academic background, his experiences in India and his interest in Buddhism. He experienced an immediate friendly connection with the young Lama, who seemed to be of his own age. In the ensuing hours of back and forth they agreeably came to arrive at the idea of driving

Northwards to Darjeeling together, the beautiful "hill-station" in the Indian State of West Bengal. There, Reuel would be able to meet Sonam's teacher, Kunzang Namgyal Rinpoche, in his monastery, and be properly introduced to the path of Tibetan Buddhism, the Vajrayana. It would require two days on the road to drive there, some three hundred miles. Reuel's hitherto uncertain and indeterminant plans immediately crystallized and they decided to leave together the following morning at daybreak.

Under Reuel's questioning, shortly before the onset of their drive, Sonam briefly described his life. He had been born in Darjeeling where his family owned two hectares of a small hillside tea estate. Its early spring pickings, the "first flush" of a black oolong variety typically fetched the highest prices at the regular tea auctions, and his family lived in comfortable circumstances. They were descended from refugees who had escaped from Tibet after the Chinese invasion in 1959, along with the Dalai Lama, and many others. When Sonam was three years old a group of Lamas arrived at his household, allowed him to play with various objects, and then informed his parents that he was the reincarnation of an important Lama who had died in Tibet years earlier. His birth name was extinguished and he was renamed Sonam Rinchen Gyalwa Tulku. His parents were both honored and alarmed at this event and at the prospect of losing him into monastic life. A compromise was reached permitting a two-sided education, secular and religious. He then attended Cornwallis Boy's School in Darjeeling and spent weekends and holidays at Zangdo Palri Monastery where he was ordained. After completing the B.A. degree in philosophy at Shanti Niketan University he went on to Oxford. Unexpectedly, but during his second year, funeral ceremonies on the death of a senior Lama in his lineage, who had been living and teaching in the Tibetan Colony in Hyderabad, required his presence, and he had to leave Oxford for India in the midst of Hillary term. Having some months free before returning at Michaelmas he decided on a personal pilgrimage by bus to pay homage at Bodh Gaya, where he had never been. And thereafter intended to visit his family in Darjeeling. He smiled cheerfully and asked Reuel to consider that a great cosmic chain of causality led the two of them to meet in the place of the Buddha's enlightenment where they could share the good fortune of traveling to Darjeeling together in a private car.

At the end of this informative history Reuel asked if Sonam, a Tulku, could explain the plausibility of reincarnation to someone with a background in Western science and philosophy. Sonam promised he would do so in the course of their journey, and they departed Bodh Gaya the following morning at daybreak.

At the beginning of their drive, after discussing the weather, road conditions, where they could eat and spend the night, Reuel returned to the question of metempsychosis, the transmigration of a soul. Sonam spoke softly, at length, with his eyes on the road, as if talking to graduate fellows at Oxford. He explained that when the Buddha was asked if he existed after his death, he said he was not declaring such a thing. And when asked if he then did not exist after his death, he replied that he was not declaring such a thing. When inquired if he was then saying that he would both exist and not exist after his death, he answered that he had said no such thing. And finally, when asked if he was then saying that he would neither exist nor not exist after his death, the Buddha then made it absolutely clear that he had also declared that he had said no such thing.

"The *Catuskoti*!" said Reuel

"Precisely" said Sonam.

He went on. There was no such thing as a soul, he said, and the concept of reincarnation, he explained, was left over from pre-Vedic times. No doubt, as we are given the universal omnipresence of cycles of death and birth, the idea of transmigration began all over the world as an early stone-age superstition. On the whole, it appeared to be a global piece of folk mythology even before the time of the Buddha's birth, millennia ago. Etymologically, the Latinate word 'reincarnation' meant 'making-meat-again'. From the view of modern science, he said, it was preposterous, yet in Tibet, long cut off from the world, it became uniquely formalized as a sacred mystery. Functionally, it served as a method to handpick a hereditary custodian for a lineage of teachings. When an old Tulku died, a group of loyal elders convened to find the young successor of the

so-called rebirth whom they could mentor. The selected child was then empow-
ered and trained from a young age by followers of the deceased custodian of
the lineage. But of course, this did not mean that an old Tulku's meat was made
into meat once again. Although ideas could pass across generations, there was
no underlying meat anywhere, there is no soul, there was no entity, no capsule
to transmigrate across time. It was just a reified metaphor which illustrated the
term *karma*, in its sense of consequence. In order to understand the phenomenon, the *karma* of becoming a Tulku, one has to comprehend the Buddhist
spiritual principle of cause and effect. One could grasp how the intentions or
actions of an individual, or groups, cause and influence the future of others,
which are effects. The relationship between action and outcome, *karma* and
causality, was a central feature in all schools of Buddhism.

At this point Sonam stopped talking, and Reuel, while driving, wondered if his passenger had gone into a trance. They drove on in silence for many
miles before Sonam resumed speaking. Not once did he turn his head to look
at Reuel but fixed his gaze on the peopled road ahead as if he was teaching an
esoteric mathematical doctrine to intellects of a half-learned world.

Karma, he said, wasn't an external force, or a system of punishment or
reward for one's behavior dealt out by a judicial God who supervises reincar-
nations. It is the understanding that causes and effects humans generate by our
impermanent lives are not simply annihilated by our death, as if nothing else
results. To think that way encourages moral irresponsibility and material hedo-
nism. The concept of our *karma* should be understood as a complex natural law,
similar to gravity, where everything was connected to everything by a universal
system of causality. The causality principle meant that the existence of all real
events, like human behavioral individuality, necessarily have a cause, or causes.
This, of course, points to a necessary logical relationship, even if incalculable,
between events and the complex order between them. And while it is true that
causes always precede effects, matters naturally become more complicated by
the multiplicity of overlapping causes. But in all cases, all phenomena do arise
in dependence upon other phenomena, so we say that if this exists, then that
exists; and if this ceases to exist, then that also ceases to exist. The basic principle

is that all things, depend upon other things, and so all things are in some way connected. In this way his becoming a Tulku was an effect of a multiplicity of prior causes. Just as his presence in the same automobile as Reuel was merely the consequence of a multiplicity of prior or antecedent causes. As if life was made up of such random collisions and connections. What was one to make of this?

Once again, Sonam stopped talking, as if allowing dust to settle, as cloudy matter sinks in a fluid, resulting in a clarifying solution of thought. Reuel also kept his eyes on the road, with a pleasurable feeling of learned patience, and refrained from questioning. They drove on in silence.

At length, Sonam continued. This time he turned so as to look at Reuel who kept his eyes on the road. Sonam started by making a point about people's differences in their capacity to comprehend what was being expressed by the religious teaching on *karma*. Some individuals, of course, were of limited intelligence, whose minds were dull, but who were enraptured by the sounds of chanting, a belief in magic, the smell of incense, certain names or words, but lacked a genuine understanding of the mindful reality of human existence. However, most people were of average intelligence and were quite capable of understanding those particular truths which were unmistakably evident, as by ethics or kindness, for example. Everything that he had said so far about *karma* and causality was perceptible by such people because it referred to the materiality of their own experience. Indeed, it was also the basis of folk religion practiced by rather devoted lay people, who easily accepted some supernatural appearing elements of Buddhism, such as the so-called rebirth of a Tulku. But in truth, a Tulku was not reborn, a Tulku was manufactured. There is no afterlife of a person except for one that is imaginatively invented, and is claimed to be discovered. This is the reality of a fiction. Obviously, the absence of true reality is not exactly predictable. This truth should be quite clear to those endowed with still higher philosophical intelligence. And to comprehend the meaning of the chain of causality which exists below the surface world of physical phenomena, that even requires a very much higher level of intelligence. A much higher level. And he grew quiet again.

Reuel spoke for the first time. "I think you are really pointing to the conundrum of contingency. The numbers get very large, beyond calculation. The complexity of indeterminate causality, conditionality, approaches infinity, doesn't it?"

"Precisely correct" said Sonam. "And yet it's possible to deal with this by understanding that we humans are contingent and impermanent entities, who can only say: 'this appearing, that arising'. It's what is Buddhistically expressed in English as 'interdependent co-origination'. When this is, that is. When this is not, that is not. And of course, this involves an indirect and complex conditionality in outcomes, not Newton's scientific causality. So, this gets close to the very heart of the matter of which you ask. Because our philosophical Buddhism emphasizes the reality of the present moment, the here and now, rather than imagining what came before. We say '*Tenching drelwar jungwa*' for this. Our idea of dependence refers to conditions created by an incalculable plurality of causes, which necessarily co-originate phenomena within and across lifetimes. So yet again, all phenomena arise in dependence upon other phenomena. Tulkus are common in Tibet but are rare in Brazil, for example. It is the distribution of causality. What could be clearer than likelihood?"

They went on this way over two full days, accompanied with similar elucidations by Sonam over a variety of Tibetan Buddhist religious practices. His own Lama, Kunzang Namgyal Rinpoche, would surely provide better answers to Reuel's questions. In fact, he said, Reuel now had the fortunate *karma* in possibly being able to meet Kunzang Rinpoche in Darjeeling, who was known to only a few Westerners.

On the mid-afternoon of their arrival in Darjeeling, Sonam guided Reuel to a parking spot near the center of town. They walked the several blocks to the Planters Club, a musty 19th century building on Nehru Road above the Chauk Bazaar. Largely neglected by its tea planter membership, except at auctions, it was a curiosity of another time. Sonam had promised to collect him there the day after the morrow at noon. He would then attempt to introduce him to his own Lama, Kunzang Namgyal Rinpoche, his esteemed meditation master. As

Reuel climbed the irregular steps with his bag to the club entrance he had to pause at a dramatic sight, the unobstructed view of the third highest mountain in the world, Kanchenjunga, straddling India's border with Nepal and Tibet. It was the largest geographical feature he had ever seen, where its massive white irregular shape dominated the northern horizon.

The interior of the club was deserted and unstaffed, as if it had been abandoned intact, a century earlier. The rug in the broad reception lounge revealed worn areas where thousands of shoes and boots had once trod or loitered. The front desk was untended and not a soul in evidence. There was a hand-bell, but its clapper was missing. Reuel gave a loud shout, "Hello". No answer. At the far end of the broad lounge, he could see a glass paneled door to an unoccupied dining room. On his left was a wide-armed flight of stairs. To his right lay a billiard room which seemed diverting at the moment. He removed the cloth covering the game table, selected a cue from a rack on the wall, and spent most of an hour caroming balls on the green baize surface. After a while a small aged man in a white uniform appeared, and was horrified and apologetic that a potential guest had been kept waiting.

"Oh Sahib, a thousand pardons. We had no forewarning of your arrival. Our sincere apologies. I shall attend to you immediately. There was no record of your reservation. This is not the season. I am the only person on duty and was repairing a trellis in the garden. Be so good as to follow me to registration."

They went to the front desk where Reuel was asked to sign his details into a museum piece of a tall bound leather ledger. It was clear from earlier pages that entries went back into the 1930s. Yet, curiously, the entry above his own was dated on the previous day by an E. Horbein a U.S. passport number and an address in New Delhi.

"How long will you be staying with us, Sahib?"

"I'm not sure actually. But a few days at least."

"We are fortunate to have you. Many visitors nowadays prefer Darjeeling's modern hotels, with telephones in the rooms. But we have an atmosphere that others lack. We can offer you the Lipton suite. You are sure to find it spacious and comfortable. Do let the bath water run a while, as our roof tank is a trifle rusty. We shall have it nice and hot for you."

"Very nice. Do you serve food?"

"Oh yes, Sahib. Breakfast toast and egg at your pleasure. Dinner in the dining room is promptly at seven. Afternoon tea at your service. My name is Chandra and I shall show you to your room."

Reuel then spent a cool afternoon wandering the hilly town which felt not remotely similar to Bodh Gaya and was filled with people of mountain Asia, largely of Sherpa, Lepcha, and Tibetan ancestry. Before dinner he played at billiards again, masturbated, read an article on mathematical uncertainty from a learned journal in his bag, and had a bath in tinged warm water.

A few minutes before seven he descended to dinner. The large high ceilinged dining room had an electrified glass chandelier at its center. Scattered below were some two-dozen bare wooden tables of various sizes, except for two small ones set aside and separated, which were covered by starched cottons, crystal glasses, and polished silverware. A small uniformed waiter, a "bearer" in the local idiom, bowed and gestured for Reuel to be seated at one of them. Before he could choose, a tall and fit-looking woman entered the room behind him.

"Hello" he said.

"Hello."

"Should we sit at separate tables?"

"I think that would be rather silly. Should I tell our man here, Lakpa, to add a place setting, to this one?" She pointed at one of the tables and spoke to the bearer in a language Reuel couldn't recognize, asking him to change and consolidate the settings.

"Wow. What language is that?"

"Colloquial Tibetan. Shall we sit?"

"After you. Are you Hornbein? I saw the name in the registry before mine."

"Call me Elsie" she said as they sat down facing one another.

They regarded each other, face to face, for a few moments. For the first time in several months Reuel experienced a strong sensation of sexual attraction. She appeared older than he, perhaps by ten years or so, but quite attractive, blue-eyed, her light brown hair in a bun, with high cheekbones, a horsey lower jaw showing prominent teeth and full lips, plus well-endowed breasts with an inviting cleavage revealed by her low-cut shirt.

"My name is Reuel Antenor" said as he held out a hand across the table. She took it briefly with a surprisingly strong grip.

"What brings you to Darjeeling?" she asked. "Tourism? Mountaineering? Journalism?"

"No, not at all. I'm taking a year off from work. Bought a car in Delhi and am driving through India. Sort of interested in Buddhism. Met this young Lama in Bodh Gaya a few days ago and he convinced me to drive up here. Wants me to meet his teacher."

"That's interesting. Who's his teacher?"

"A Lama. His name's Kunzang Namgyal Rinpoche."

"That's quite surprising. I've always been told he doesn't see Westerners. But tell me about yourself if you don't mind. And wait just a moment." She beckoned the Tibetan attendant. "I'm going to have a whiskey. Would you like anything before we eat? The same? Good." She turned to the attendant and spoke to him in English. "Lakpa-la, two large McCallan's and some water on the side, no ice." Turning to Reuel she said "They know me here. Go on about yourself."

"I'm from Chicago. Winnetka actually. Went to Columbia in New York. Did a double major, math and philosophy. Analytics, theory of mind stuff. Got interested in languages, neurolinguistics. Worked at the Karolinska Institute in Stockholm for a year. Then for IBM. Software side. Went back to academics. Doctoral program at MIT, all but dissertation, 'AB.D'. My research topic, in case that means anything to you, was 'recursive semantic hierarchies'. Did some financially rewarding stuff in computer languages for a couple of tech companies. Took some LSD and decided to see India. How's that?"

The whiskeys arrived and they clinked glasses. He could not take his eyes off her.

"That's rather unique" she said. "Sounds like fairly high-level brainwork. What's your interest in Buddhism?"

"Started a long time ago. Got into some stuff from the Pali Text Society as an undergraduate. Mostly it's about the Buddhist point-of-view. I mean the business about the cause of suffering - not that I've suffered so much. It's the stuff about a certain insight which intrigues me. Sort of overlapped with academic interests in analytic philosophy. Wittgenstein in particular, if you follow. The conviction that there's something deep that lies beyond what's sayable, even beyond what's knowable. Leads to the insolubility of some of the problems of philosophy. The nature of consciousness. Meaning of meaning, that sort of thing. Stuff we feel but don't understand. But how about you? I have to say, you're quite attractive and don't exactly look like a tourist. What brings you to Darjeeling?"

"Business."

"You mean tea business? You work for Unilever, Nestle?"

"Nice try, but no. I work for Uncle Sam. Foreign service."

"You a diplomat?"

"I'm Cultural Attaché at our Embassy in Delhi."

"No kidding! Something going on out here in Darjeeling?"

"Next door actually. In Sikkim. King's married to an American gal. I just went to Gangtok to have a chat with her. Sikkim's about to be absorbed into India as a Federated State with a vague border on Tibet. Chinese neighbor makes people in India nervous. Like Ladakh in the Northwest, this a Buddhist corner of the country. The situation of Bhutan a bit less clear."

"You interested in Buddhism?" he asked, hoping she wouldn't be turned off.

"That's rather amusing. Well, I'm sort of an ex-Buddhist."

"What on earth does that mean?"

"I've a Ph.D in Tibetan studies from U.C. Berkeley."

"No shit!" he said, and her magnetic appeal grew in bounds. He tried to see if she was wearing a wedding ring, but her left hand was on her lap.

"Years ago, I was on a graduation holiday in India after finishing at Bryn Mawr. Tibetan refugee's situation in those days was heartbreaking. I ended up staying over a year. Started volunteering, picked up the language, practiced meditating with various Lamas, my spiritual insight got awakened, and I went back to the States on an academic track. Tibetan studies."

"What was your dissertation topic?"

"I did a translation and commentary of a 13th century meditation manual called 'The Unchanging Aspect of Mind'. Sort of boring actually. Esoteric mumbo-jumbo when I look back on it. But it got me a faculty job at University of Maryland, assistant prof. Only one year."

"How'd you get here?" he asked, feeling his growing hint of infatuation.

"Gave an evening lecture in Georgetown on the Tibetan refugees. Some hotshot dweeb from State in the audience convinced me to take the foreign service exam. Rest is history. Did tours in Japan, Thailand, Nepal. Ended up in Delhi. I'm America's Tibetan desk. You're looking at it."

"Why did you say you were 'an ex-Buddhist?'"

"I know too much."

"Are you married?" he asked. Still no sight of her left hand.

"Divorced. Twice. No kids." Then she signaled for Lakpa, ordered them another round of whiskies, and suggested they try the lamb curry. There was a Muslim cook.

Food came. They talked. His faint attempts at flirtation were ignored, as though unnoticed. They went on to exchange conversational pleasantries about academic life, sailing, the promise of computers, the new practice of jogging, Bob Dylan, cocaine, psychedelics, Vietnam, American politics, Indian roads, the Olympics, feminism, troubles in Kashmir, moon landings and space exploration. At length, as if aware they were hungry for something meatier and intellectually substantial, they starting talking about human language. Seeking for a lure to her, Reuel thought this could be his strong suit. He started aloud about Wittgenstein's dictum that what wasn't sayable wasn't knowable.

"I've frequently wondered if, when you talk about ideas in Sanskrit that you can't express in English, or German, about mental states. In other words, whether one could know more about consciousness and the mind by thinking and speaking in Sanskrit rather than English. You think Tibetan is like that?"

"Well," she answered, "that raises the great question of how Sanskrit Buddhism came to Tibet from India. You're talking about translations from Indo-European into Sino-Tibetan." He felt himself falling further in love.

She went on. "I think Tibetan is more allusive, more metaphoric, freer in the intuitive. But there's no question that a gigantic quantity of Sanskrit spiritual philosophy was translated and brought over. The older Pali to Sanskrit transmission was obviously many times easier."

He continued trying. "Sometimes I wonder if I could write code in Sanskrit. Machine language is so ridiculously indicative and idiotic. And it's infected how we talk. Everything has to be easy to use and understand. Ambiguity's the enemy, even though we consciously indulge in double meanings at times. English is lousy on subjunctive functions, with baby modal verbs like 'might', 'could', 'should'. Like right now, in a sense. At best you can get what's called 'negative capability', where you're able to be immersed in uncertainties, in mysteries, doubts, without any irritable reaching after fact and reason. I think this was too high a hurdle for old Ludwig. Logic, he wrote, threatened our capacity for wonder. Ultimately it sends one to sleep. I frequently regret I hadn't studied Sanskrit."

Elsie hesitated for a moment and observed "Well, you see, in Asia, when dealing with mental states concerning spiritual matters, and dealing with terms like 'enlightenment' or 'awakened', you are really dealing with feelings, not intellect."

He said "How do you know when you know something? Wittgenstein struggled with the problem of certainty. The question of whether it was just a feeling, a belief, or a fact."

She replied "Understandably. Most actions get based on what you feel to be true even without any conscious reasoning. You have an intuitive conviction about something without explanation. I think you know what I mean. And that's actually how the *Mahayana* evolved, by intuition. There was too much unsaid and unexplored in the early Sutras and the canonical philosophy of the *Abhidharma*. Do you follow?"

He sensed how much he wanted to follow her. "I'm trying" he said. "Most of my experience has been with the Southern schools, the *Theravada*. I just came from a few weeks in a Burmese meditation center in Bodh Gaya. The *Mahayana* seems enormous and complex by comparison. Probably that's why it's 'Maha'. I'm still not clear on how and why it happened."

She paused for a moment to help him. "You have to deal with the fact that Buddhism was an oral tradition for several hundred years before we get to the first writings, the *sutras*, the *vinaya*, the *abhidharma*. And it was just for clergy, for the benefit of monks and a few nuns. But the teachings are leaky. Lay people wanted a taste. Hundreds of years go by before common people actually see popular images of the Buddha. Before then it's just symbolic icons here and there, like a wheel, an umbrella, a pair of sandals. But finally, by the turn of a whole millennium, it starts to become a state religion. An empire for a while. All sorts of new philosophies about introspection, about unanswered questions, begin to surface. Buddhist universities like Nalanda get created."

"Where was that?" He would try to follow her wherever she was leading.

"Down by Rajgir, where the Buddha famously taught. Nalanda was probably one of the key places in the development of *Mahayana* thought. Sort of analogous to Oxbridge. By the 3rd century, Nagarjuna, probably one of the greatest thinkers in the history of Asian philosophy, was based there. He was sort of like a Columbus or Galileo in defining and defending a new way of looking at things. Specifically, by founding the *Madhyamika*, the 'middle-way' school of Buddhist philosophy and formalizing the concept of *sunyata*, emptiness. It's the great *Mahayana* theory of 'the perfection of wisdom', the *prajnaparamita*. The wisdom of the other shore. Nagarjuna's the man. You should study him. Basically, his philosophical works analyze all phenomena in order to show that nothing at all can exist independently. And yet, they are also not non-existent, since they exist conventionally, that is as empty dependent arisings."

"Oh, my travel chum from Bodh Gaya, Sonam Tulku, was going on about that, about causality" he said as his eyes kept returning to the slight cleavage revealed by her low-cut blouse.

"Its teaching on causality is the foundation of everything that followed" she said. "Nagarjuna's skepticism of our ability, in reason and language, to capture the nature of reality, is the key to the *Mahayana*. For our limited human minds, the teaching that impermanent reality is empty of true realized existence, is a great philosophical statement."

"I feel it myself. The echoes of old Ludwig. The problematic challenge of the unknowable."

"You have it. Nagarjuna sets up a tidal wave of philosophical thought. After a few hundred years you get the emergence of what's called the Yogachara tradition. A fellow named Vasubandhu, 5th century. He starts a school of philosophy more like psychology or epistemology. It focuses on the nature of cognition, perception, and consciousness. It reintroduces a main method which emphasizes meditation, as if it was an interior lens to study the mind. Nothing quite like that in the West."

"But how did they make those insights knowable to others? It must use language, or does it go mind-to-mind without speech?" In fact, he wondered if she could read his mind.

"Well, that's what kicks off the study for a theory of knowledge, especially with particular regard to its methods, its validity, and its scope. Dignaga's the man. 6th century. It's the beginning of Buddhist logic. Logic is logic, East or West. They start studying language itself, the experience of inferential reasoning and the question of perception. They come to the conclusion that there are two kinds of truth, absolute and conventional, and they try to focus on what distinguishes justified belief from mere opinion. Inevitably, this unleashes a whole bunch of 7th and 8th century metaphysicians. Chandrakirti, Aryadeva, Dharmakirti, Shantideva. All at Nalanda."

"My head's swimming" he muttered. Her brain and her breasts were involved.

"Yeah," she said, "but now, historically speaking, things get interesting. Buddhism begins to disappear from India, merely leaving its long shadow. Hindu and Vedic intellectual traditions strengthen and start to eclipse it. And Tibet gets pregnant so to speak. This is really interesting. Because Tibet presents a radically different linguistic, mental, social, physical, and geographical environment."

"How exactly did Tibet get pregnant?"

"You could say by writings and pilgrims from every direction and all mixed together. From Chinese Buddhists to the North and the East. Even Buddhists from Afghanistan in those pre-Islamic days. From Buddhists in Kashmir, Ladakh, Lahul and Spiti. And even right here, in Darjeeling, directly where we are sitting, great teachers from Nalanda would pass us by on their way to the Nathul-la, that big mountain pass, just up the road from us, that leads directly to Lhasa and Samye. By the 8th century the Kings of Tibet declare national allegiance to Buddhism."

"The *Vajrayana*?"

"Yes, *Vajrayana*, the Tibetan branch of the *Mahayana*, the 'great vehicle'. And the renaming of the *Mahayana* is revealing. You see, the Sanskrit word 'vajra', and the Tibetan word 'dorje', are like the supreme metaphor of Tibetan Buddhism. Physically and ritually, it's that oblong metallic ceremonial object you see in shops, frequently next to a bell. But philosophically it symbolizes the teaching, the *dharma*, imagined as the most powerful weapon in the universe. Indestructible like a diamond, with a sudden, instantaneous, and irresistible power, like a thunderbolt emerging from the void. For the Lamas, by means of ceremonial magic, the Vajra symbolizes Nagarjuna's nature of reality, emptiness, or *sunyata*. And by then, a thousand plus years past its historical origin, we're very far from the 'way of the elders', the Theravada. Lord only knows what an analytic philosopher like Wittgenstein would make of this."

"Too much more like sacramental poetry than Oxbridge logic."

"But nevertheless, it does open our minds to consider esoteric ways of thinking about the great mystery of being. And it's still a mystery, isn't it? And Tibet in those old days was a wild polytheistic and shamanic culture. Far more primitive and superstitious than the world around it. And moreover, the practice of Buddhism, you may have noticed, wherever it lands, has this funny way of taking on and incorporating the elements and habits of local cultures. Ritual magic, superstitions, do exist in the culture of most societies, even today. Take Christian baptism for instance, or even better, the universal superstition of prayer. Anyway, Buddhism comes to Tibet by means of a great linguistic translation."

Reuel wanted to move them away from where they sat. "This is absolutely fascinating to me. I want to hear more, but I think Lakpa wants to clean our table. How about continuing out on the parapet? We might see Kanchenjunga under moonlight." He said this wishfully imagining her naked for an instant, with her legs spread beneath him. Just a flash of mind, welcome but unsought.

They stood and made their way out onto the wide patio. An old-fashioned cushioned rocking divan faced the view toward the Himalaya. She declined his obvious attempt to maneuver seating them together, and she sat on a single lounge chair as he took the wide divan. It was apparent what he was trying to do.

"So much of this history is virgin ground for me" he said. "For a philosophically minded bookworm like myself I have to wonder if these far-out domains of thought are actually accessible. It's like going from explicit academic forms to more intuitive ones without knowing where they lead, or if they're truthful. It's not even clear to me where the impulse to philosophize comes from. Can it actually get usefully pushed to an edge? When I started as an undergraduate major, it was with a sense of wonder at philosophy's consistent, almost mathematical, reasoning capacity. But hearing you talk makes me think

I could go down a philosophical rabbit hole. My thoughts on age-old questions about time, space, infinity or identity, begin to seem beside the point."

She smiled rather tolerantly and pointed at him with a finger. "Suppose it's a matter of your motivation. What's the goal? What's your intention? Are you looking for a shared explanation in human language, or do you want something like experiencing a personal salvation called enlightenment? Buddhist enlightenment isn't about science, is it? Can music awaken us? Does Bach show us reality? Invention isn't the same as discovery. Christ and the Buddha are soteriological heroes so to speak, salvationists, saviors, where their faith heals. Newton and Einstein, even Shakespeare, are explainers, teleologists, if you like."

"Tell me again why you say you're an ex-Buddhist?"

"I became much more interested in anthropology and politics than religion."

"Where does *Vajrayana*, Tibetan studies, fit in your own scheme of things?"

"I put it in my evolutionary history department. The Chinese communists are about to deconstruct it all into irrelevance. As a fossil."

"And nothing left?"

"Well, there's always the tantric side of life."

"Oh, come on. What is that anyway?"

"It's a hobby, for weekends."

"Are you serious? Tantra? How about enlightening me?"

"Enlighten you or instruct you?"

"I assume they're the same. Why not initiate me?"

"That's clever. I can tell, you have sex on your mind."

"I'm all yours. I'm full of tantric lust."

"Mindless, I fear. It's too esoteric."

"Let me in on the secret."

"It's in front of you. It's what's slightly uncanny and weird. Where does it come from? Ever had that kind of queer feeling? Like what's unspoken between us at this very moment?"

"I'm not sure." He suddenly felt as if something eerie was taking place.

She said "What if I tell you I'm reading your mind? That you're having hidden fantasies of privately undressing me. How do I know that? Do I have occult powers, or not? Is it just shrewd guessing on my part? How does it make you feel when I tell you that? Where am I going with this? Does it unsettle you? Will you do exactly what I say?"

"Wow!"

"You see, it's not hard to play with people's heads. Imagine the precarious life in Tibet or India hundreds of years ago. Wild and uneducated people everywhere. Survival is uncertain, tribes, wars, plagues, ignorance, no Galileo, no television, no movies, no Darwin, few distractions, mere existence is unfathomable. Believe me, you would be ready to believe in the supernatural, the unearthly. That's the world inhabited by tantric ritual magic, the *Vajrayana*."

"But what's this thing called *tantra*?"

"Oh lord, simplistically it's a term representing a web, a cabbalistic weaving of connectiveness. It's a realm where hidden mysterious connections between the inner imaginative world of the person, and macrocosmic reality, can allow magical religious outcomes. In India, sometime in the 7th and 8th centuries, it's as if a group whom we might call 'bohemians' or 'hippies' today, started to gain social attention. What was believed to be culturally hidden, from a mystical world of spirits below ground, called *nagas*, start to surface. And from above, female sky deities start to descend. Sorcery appears, spooky practices like divination grow common, spells about sexuality materialize, with magical diagrams, bizarre incantations, retention of semen, freakish body postures, otherworldly visualizations, secret initiations, the presence of ghosts, and consumption of abnormal foods and liquids. All weird shamanistic tools of empowerment in the pre-Buddhist Tibet. Get the picture so far?"

"I rather think it would drive me away."

"But on the contrary, this breaking of natural taboos, these enigmatic transgressive visions, this experimental searching, create a strange and unprecedented kind of mystical and mental depth, almost as a kind of tribute to all that gets hidden in ordinary life. You can begin to see those practices unleashed following the classical Buddhist philosophical theory of emptiness. Radical yogic experimentation emerges from worshippers of the flexible 'middle way' articulated by Nagarjuna and his followers. And this strange avant-garde soup is what great teachers of that time bring to Tibet as they experimentally discriminate along various paths between sudden or gradual enlightenments."

"Look" said Reuel, "mediaeval Christianity had loads of hocus-pocus. King Arthur and Merlin. Transubstantiation. Papal indulgences. They were burning witches in Salem not so long ago. What did Buddhism bring to the world's crazy party of religious superstition?"

"It brought a unique theory of emptiness, which avoids nihilism. It sees our world as fluid, without a foundation or an inherent existence, but just as a weave of flowing constructions. So, in a universe where all events dissolve into the emptiness of form, experiencing emptiness in a religious ritual resembles a re-creation of the world in actuality. This is what two guys named Santaraksita and Kamalasila, both Nalanda alumni, bring to Tibet in the 8th century. Then, over the next few hundred years the new tantric cultural intervention, by transgressive men and women, comes on the scene. They seem to have or claim some unprecedented kind of perfectly awakened serenity. They're known as 'mad ones', taboo-breaking antinomians, libertarian ascetics with a bewildering self-confidence, who appear to possess magic powers. One might even say especially in that most mysterious matter of sexual behavior. The kind of thing that obviously interests you. Ever heard of Tilopa, the great poet renunciate?"

"I don't think so."

Tilopa, a so-called *mahasiddha*, was a meditation master who had supposedly attained perfect imperturbability, was paradoxically an ascetic who consorted among numerous wild ladies. He practiced a – let us say 'tantric' - set of magical sex behaviors intended to accelerate the process of attaining

Buddhahood. And he becomes a founder of a lineage possessing legendary powers of equanimity, powers of persuasion, of clairvoyance, virility, beautiful poetry, insight, happiness, sensory perfection, sexual excellence of course, and communion with divine forces. Not bad, eh?"

"Nice work if you can get it."

"Well, the historical influence of these *Mahasiddhas* was enormous, and eventually reached mythic proportions. Lots of this was embedded in their poetic songs of realization and their adulatory biographies, preserved in the Tibetan Buddhist canon. In my own opinion, it was the influence of these transgressive guys and gals who created the enchanting immediacy of the unique *Vajrayana* branch within the *Mahayana* tradition. You have to understand that all of these antinomian figures, all of these names, are today as familiar to Buddhist history as Luther, Hegel, Pascal or Kierkegaard are to Christians. Leave alone the utopian exponents of free love."

"But didn't orthodoxy have a tight grip? It's hard to imagine how they could get away with such radical behaviors against the traditional conservative and intellectual Buddhist philosophy of those days."

"They did it just by being fearless. They broke with the conventions of monastic life and abandoned the monastery to practice in caves, forests, and the country villages of Northern India and its mountain flanks on Tibet. As in our own *vajra*-place right here, our '*dorje-ling*'. And this, you understand, was in complete contrast to the settled monastic establishments of those middle-ages, when the Buddhist intelligentsia was concentrated in a few large celibate monastic universities like Nalanda. The *Mahasiddhas* adopted a life-style of itinerant heterosexual tramps. And Reuel, since it's fairly obvious you usually have sex on your mind, I should really tell you about Drukpa Kunley."

"Wait a minute, why is it obvious?"

"Takes one to know one."

"You speaking of yourself? You have sex on your mind?"

"Actually, I'm thinking of my boy-friend in New Delhi. I like hard-bodied older men, not, if you'll forgive me, graduate students with slight pot-bellies."

"Ouch! Just when I was falling in love."

"You know, you have to learn how to take intellectual teachings from a woman without having a hidden agenda. Our little seminar here isn't going to be a prelude to physical intimacy. That was on your mind. Confess it."

"True. I was finding it irresistible. But weren't you about to tell me about someone, since you saw I had sex on my mind?"

"Oh yes, about Drukpa Kunley. He was a Buddhist yogi known for his crazy methods of enlightening other beings, frequently women, who sought his blessing in the form of sexual intercourse. There's an open question as to whether he in turn sought their blessing to enhance his own enlightenment. But in either case it was his simple intention to show that it was entirely possible to be enlightened, to impart enlightenment, to gain enlightenment, and still lead a very healthy sex life. And also, to demonstrate that celibacy was not necessary for being enlightened. They say that Drukpa Kunley wouldn't bless anyone who came to seek his guidance unless they brought a beautiful woman and a bottle of wine. Such liberated women were called *khandros* in Tibetan, *dakinis* in Sanskrit, females who possess the power of transforming negative emotions into the luminous energy of enlightened awareness. They're also called 'sky-going mothers', pointing to the vast space denoting emptiness, and the insubstantiality of all perceived phenomena, which denotes pure potentiality for all possible human manifestations. It's also said that such ladies have a special power and responsibility to protect the integrity of oral transmissions. Know anyone like that? I should warn you, women like that can be wrathful in their protective functions."

"Like what you're doing right now?"

"Just be mindfully careful of your women, Reuel. The Tibetans say a *dakini* is an enlightened deity who can take the form of an ordinary woman so as to be accessible to the average person. But actually, she is a fierce immortal who can chew up the vital essence of ignorant men. Got it?"

This suddenly led to a prolonged silence, where they stared acutely at one another. Reuel experienced a trace of something uncanny, beyond description.

"Are there female Lamas?" he asked.

"Of course, there are. You should realize that in *Vajrayana* Buddhism, wisdom is personified as female. Energy is what is deemed to be masculine. It's the exact opposite of the Vedic tradition in India, where the feminine *shakti* is energy. The female line of *Vajrayana* insight-bearing teachers is an old tradition going back to one Yeshe Tsogyal, the 8th century semi-historical queen of Tibet, She's the wisdom-bearing mother of the *Vajrayana*. She's the celestial consort of Padmasambhava, the supreme missionary wizard, the guy who tames and masters the entire wild pantheon of pre-Buddhist Tibetan deities."

Reuel thought of Bob Adler, and said "You know, I came to India with a friend who ran off somewhere with a girl he found at the burning ghat in Varanasi to become a devotee of a *shakti* goddess. The whole thing sounds so mediaeval. Crazy. He was a psychology professor no less. Honestly, there's so much hocus-pocus nonsense going on compared to the original old-fashioned common-sense Buddhist *dharma* of India."

"Granted, but female and male are rather universal conditions, you know. We each have our possibilities and constraints. You are still hungry, but I've been fed, and am sated."

"Well then, why don't you just tell me what enlightenment means to you. There're all these weird doctrinal metaphorical fantasies pointing toward something without anyone really explaining what it is. Lots of attractive metaphors, like a finger pointing at the moon, like *bodhi* for being awakened, luminous, indicative, but absolutely nothing that's really sayable. It's my old philosopher's problem. The unspoken."

"But that's necessarily true" she said. "Of course, there's a real absence of clarity, beyond language, on understanding the meaning of enlightenment, the meaning of being awakened. And obviously, it begs the question of whether there are gradations in degree, and whether these states of mind can be fully experienced instantly, or whether they can only be achieved gradually. And once achieved, can they be lost in the flood of impermanence? The Tibetans seem to have developed a heuristic approach to such questions by dividing *dharma* listeners, followers, into three categories. There are the few who have been poorly educated since childhood or who have weak intellectual faculties; there the many who are of average intellect, whose understanding can be brought along incrementally, gradually, by practice and effort; and there are a small number of those who have the native gift of extremely high intelligence, who can make large mental leaps toward swift comprehension and insight. And as a result, there are three different types of teaching available. They call them outer teaching, inner teaching, and secret teaching, and they're only separated by the cognitive construct of words. I ask you, does that make sense?"

"I keep hearing about those three categories. But come on, I'm no dope. What do you think? Do you actually know secret teachings? Have you received them? You said you were an ex-Buddhist. What can you tell me? Have you taken an oath of some kind? Gimme a break!"

"Oh, even as an ex-Buddhist, I can give you a teaching but it might remain secret even if you hear it. Secret from you that is. As I just said, understanding is related to different levels of ability by different listeners. There's an inherent tension between methods which emphasize gradual practice and attainments, and methods which emphasize primordial liberation, simultaneous enlightenment, and non-activity."

"Sorry, but I can tell the difference between fiction and non-fiction. And it's not a matter of my IQ to realize that some people, even phonies and fraudsters, are pointing to something that's not really there, even if it's only called emptiness. The whole thing requiring suspension of disbelief. Remember, my Wittgenstein was absorbed by the difference between understanding and believing. I've been well over this ground. How would you know if I understand the secret teaching?"

"I won't know. The question is whether you will know."

"Why don't you try me out? We're fellow academics of reasonably high intelligence. Neither of us is a superstitious type. You're an ex-Buddhist and I'm just a pre-Buddhist. What could be simpler? Give it a try. And please, no slow strip-tease if you don't mind."

"Getting hungry, are we?"

"I've a mental erection, if that arouses you."

"Very well. As far as I know, the highest teaching on the Buddhist perfection of wisdom can almost be told while standing on one foot. The teaching is called perfect because it is an all-inclusive totality that leads to middle way realization, in avoiding extremes."

"That's just Aristotle."

"Aristotle got it from gymnosophists, but that's another story."

"Sorry to interrupt."

"Remember, we're in the cognitive construct of words. Understanding is allusive, not demonstrative. The teachers use the analogy of a mirror. The analogy is that one's true nature is like a mirror which reflects with complete openness, but is not affected by the reflections. The knowledge that ensues from recognizing this mirror-like clarity - which can't be found by searching - is a non-conceptual spiritual mystery, free from elaboration and is transcendent, beyond the intellect. Whatever we are aware of, think about, experience, or conceptualize, occurs to us from nowhere else than within consciousness. Therefore, when that consciousness is transformed into unmediated cognition – I'll say it again – 'unmediated cognition', that is called enlightenment or awakening. Large or small, temporary or durable, it is all the same."

"That's it?"

"That's it."

"Easy to say."

"Difficult to achieve."

"What's it good for?"

"The end of suffering. And now, I'm off to bed. There's a car coming for me early tomorrow."

"Share a bed?"

"Don't be ridiculous. Are you such a slow learner?"

In his bed that night Reuel had a restless sleep. He wondered if it was Darjeeling's altitude, at near 7,000 feet, that was keeping him awake and permitting unwanted questions to enter his mind. Doubtless there were tricks for keeping undesirable thoughts at bay, but knowing that they were tricks only augmented the problem. One could mentally recite a mantra over and over until exhaustion took over. One could count breaths, or count within breaths, solve logic problems, recall once memorized poems, reminisce physical love details, half-remembered movies, revision helming a boat, recall childhood chess games with his old friend Luca Baca, look back on electroencephalograph experiments, recall LSD with Adler, watch bodies burn at the ghat, but naught availed. Underlying it all, unexamined, uninvited but intrusive, was a single question. Why on earth was he interested in Buddhism? He wasn't exactly suffering in life. Why not return attention to computer science, to the evolution of human language, to career enhancement, to making more money, to adventure on the high sea? To finding a mate? Yet the unanswered question lingered.

In the dark he went to the window, opened the blinds, and looked out at the enormous shape of Kangchenjunga, a white fang in the dark blue sky. Why was he here in India? What would he do with the car? What was Elsie Hornbein telling him? Was there such a thing as magic? Was magic just something explainable by science? There was something so nonsensical about sky-going spirits. Was there actually such a thing as enlightenment? It was evidently such an intriguing question for philosophers. He went back to bed and lay with his thoughts. When did this Buddhist interest begin? In that Chinese laundry? At Sammler's bookstore in his first year at Columbia? The Pali Text Society. The four noble truths. The eightfold path. Very sensible. Very wise. Easily explained in simple language. Easily understood. Almost self-evident. A bit of adhesion, no conversion required. And in Stockholm, Phra Luang showed a few tricks for calming the mind. Then why was that historical crowd from Nagarjuna to Drukpa Kunley so important? Because millennia before, pre-literate people didn't understand forces like magnetic rocks and thunder-clapped lightning and the omnipresence of death? And sitting quietly alone in a cave would provide answers? Was there such a thing as too much introspection? It was tiresome. He gave up and fell asleep.

The following morning, when Reuel arrived to the dining room, Hornbein was finishing her coffee and near her time to leave. There was a car and driver waiting for her. Reuel sat down next to her and spoke with unaffected sincerity.

"Elsie, I want to thank you for that instructive seminar last night. It filled big gaps in my knowledge. But while the cultural evolution of ideas is understandable, it still begs the question of where the biological brain comes into the picture. My wizard Ludwig says that science threatens our human capacity for wonder. That science may be a way sending us to sleep again. What do you think? I mean wonder is something more than curiosity, isn't it? And I still don't know why you say you're an ex-Buddhist."

She regarded him with a half-smile. "If you keep asking questions about Buddhism you might just figure it out yourself. You could start by asking whether it's just another religion occupied with a thaumaturgic mumbo-jumbo of sacramental rites involving the suspension of disbelief. Or if it's not at all a superstitious religion but merely a secular philosophy with a unique half-explanatory world-view. Or possibly instead, if Buddhism isn't simply a collection of first person non-intellectual methods of introspection, like meditation, with various practices for social conduct. That seems to suggest three separate realms for Buddhist self-identification. Or must they all overlap? As an ex-Buddhist, my question, is whether you can go beyond them. Going beyond Buddhism, so to speak. 'Going beyond' is a well-known Buddhist trope, if I'm not mistaken. Right? Gone, gone, gone away, gone all the way beyond."

"Elsie, you do give me a lot to think about. The *mahayana* is still a bit new to me. I feel like I'm just scratching at the surface. All these people who've spent whole lifetimes at it."

"What are your plans after Darjeeling?"

"Heading back to the States, I guess. Probably a stop in Japan. I met this guy in Bodh Gaya who was in a Japanese prisoner of war camp in Burma. It was really odd. He loved Buddhism but hated Zen."

"Hated Zen Buddhism?"

"Yeah. Kept saying that its tolerance, indifference, to sadistic militarism revealed the flaw in Zen's view of unattached enlightenment. Its philosophical non-duality, worshipping emptiness, seeing life as an illusion, all that crap just excusing, rationalizing war and atrocities. That mother country, Japan, where Zen masters lead to the unbelievable murderous rape of Nanking and sadistic prison camps. This business of Zen and the sword going hand-in-hand, and concerns about right and wrong considered as a sickness of the mind. Seems like a pathological end-point, of the *mahayana* doesn't it? Zen turning into the religion of will-power, with a thousand years of samurai perfection. He said it was the ultimate perversion of Buddhism. Sounds pretty harsh. It might wreck my appetite for more Buddhist tourism. Think it's worth going there? Japan, I mean."

"It all depends of course, doesn't it? Practically speaking, it won't be as easy as India, where English is fairly common, and spiritual inquiry is open-heartedly universal and relatively undisciplined. You could hang around Japanese universities but they might be as dry as dust-bins and their monastery practice is very strict, some say rigid. Why not study Zen back in the States? It's the coming thing, I hear. Good books. Suzuki Daizets, Alan Watts. Meditation's becoming fashionable."

"What do you recommend?"

"Can't say. I worked at the Embassy in Tokyo for a year and a half. Still have friends there. Despite years of *mahayana* study, I felt rather uncomfortable there. They really don't take well to women in their *sangha*. The pattern of hereditary family temple ownership is mostly a commercial business for weddings and funerals, with little to do with meditative practice. Younger people think it's all passé. But Japan's Buddhism gets wrapped in a beautiful aesthetic sensibility; I think, expressed in poetry, in flower arrangement, scroll paintings, the sound of a *shakuhachi* flute. And a Taoist attitude gets mixed in rather peacefully, along with Shinto's self-inflated sense of superiority. I personally think Zen's over-emphasis on prolonged meditation is misplaced. It's militaristic and crushes spontaneity, if you follow. It's almost the very opposite of the instantaneous mind-to-mind transmission they claim as heritage. Of course, there are plenty of places where you can sit *zazen* peacefully. Useful if you could find someone to point you around."

"Know anyone?"

She paused for a moment, reflectively, removed a notebook from her handbag, searched and found a name which she wrote on a scrap, and handed it to him.

"As a matter of fact, I do. Her name is Hideko Sato. We were friendly for a long time. I just thought of her because of the war. She once wrote a screenplay for a movie about Japanese religious soldiers in Nanking. It was very daring of her to do such a thing. There were actually real threats against her life. Needless to say, nothing came of it. Your story about Zen and war-crimes made me think of her. She finally quit the film industry. Last I heard she works as a potter, in Nara. About your age. Probably unmarried. Not bad looking. Speaks English. Very sharp. Actually, an intellectual. You might like her. She's an ex-Buddhist too."

"Sounds tempting. Military Buddhism's really a sad story. Not a good precedent for getting enlightened."

"Well. That's the thing. Buddhism and nationalist war. Zen and the sword. The mentality of the soldier. All that stuff. *Bushido*, the way of the warrior, it was the main part of her movie script. A character who's the top brain of the officer class, on the mind-set, the neuro-cultural psychology of war-fighters."

"Christ, I'm just a pacifist."

"Could be interesting if you met her to talk about Zen and national security."

"I'm a bit weak on politics."

"Politics is thought in action, right? Your sense of curiosity might grow into a sense of wonder. Do you think consciousness is limitless?"

"No. I think we evolved from war-like apes who call ourselves humans. Science seems to be affirming that we're just apes. Our brains are limited by evolutionary definition."

"I think I smell an ex-Buddhist on the horizon. Skepticism trumps belief, doesn't it?"

"Experience trumps skepticism. That's the vanishing point."

"You mentioned that you were going to meet Kunzang Namgyal Rinpoche today?"

"Yeah. His nephew Sonam Tulku, who brought me here, is supposed to introduce me to him, this afternoon, I think."

"That's a special piece of luck. You know, Kunzang Rinpoche is a very famous Lama in these parts, but he does no teaching, rejects disciples, and sees very few people. I've never met anybody who has ever seen him."

"What's he famous for?"

"His meditation. They say he rarely ever talks. His only transmission is that he gives out roasted barley powder. He'll probably give you some. Supposedly did nine years of solitary meditation. Three times, each for three years, in a cave in Bhutan. In the interims he grew and harvested barley on a monastery property, which he roasts and grinds to *tsampa*, a flour. It gets thrown into the air during rituals. Otherwise mixed with salt-butter tea into a ball of paste and eaten. And now that I'm at it, let me give you a piece of advice since you're getting a rare opportunity to meet him."

"Okay."

"You can actually link into a great chain of meditators. Kunzang Lama holds a direct unbroken lineage to Naropa, who also did years of solitary meditation, in Ladakh. So, don't waste your time asking him questions about enlightenment. Just ask Kunzang Rinpoche to meditate with you. That's all. Nothing more. Do you know Naropa's yoga instructions?"

"No."

"Just pay attention to your consciousness. Let it settle. No aims, no ideas, no reflections, no analysis, no intentions. Let it settle itself. Don't recall, let go of what has passed. Forget about breath. Don't imagine. Let go of what may come. Don't think. Let go of what is happening now. Don't examine. Don't try to figure anything out. Don't control. No words in your mind. Don't try to make anything happen. Just rest. Let go. Relax, right now, rest."

For a few moments Reuel believed he grasped what she was disclosing. They sat there quietly for a minute. Then he said "I'll try. Nice work if you can get it."

"Listen, Reuel. In my view, for whatever it's worth, is that all other Buddhist methods are intellectual fabrications."

"That's awesome. I think you must be one of those *dakinis*. Thanks for all the instruction and advice."

"Anytime."

"Are you against Buddhism?"

"Of course not. But I'm skeptical of too much introspective passivity. And that's another story. Anyway, I've got a flight to catch at Siliguri. My driver keeps pointing to his watch. It was nice meeting you."

"Have a safe journey. It was my pleasure to meet you. I certainly enjoyed the mental intimacy." He winked.

Smiling broadly, she shook her head in a friendly reproach, pressed her palms together, bowed slightly, and took her leave.

ཅ

With a few hours before the expected arrival of Sonam Tulku, Reuel decided to have a stroll through the nearby market area, busy with shops and goods. To his pleasure he found a bookstore which obviously catered, to English language readers, presumably tourists. There were shelves of guide books to the area, on flora and fauna, on mountaineering expeditions, on British colonial history, and a variety of a dilettantish introductions to Tibetan Buddhism. A large folio-sized volume entitled The Art of Tibet caught his eye, and with the proprietor's nod of approval Reuel extracted the book and took a seat.

Over half an hour he studied the color plates depicting *Vajrayana* Buddhist deities on painted scrolls, thangkas, each with a descriptive text beneath. Preeminent was a scroll portraying the great shaman, Padmasambhava, the legendary transmitter of Buddhism to Tibet. Depicted seated, in his human form, feet relaxed in royal comfort, and a smiling face with his eyes wide open in a piercing wrathful gaze. He wears a five-petal lotus hat and in one of his hands holds a staff on which three heads are impaled, as if shish-kebab.

A textual inscription beneath the color plate are his words in quotation marks:

"My father is the wisdom of intrinsic awareness, my mother is the ultimate voidness of reality, I belong to the form of non-duality from the sphere of awareness. I am of no caste and no creed. I am from the unborn sphere of all phenomena. I consume concepts of duality as my diet. I am sustained by perplexity; and I am here to destroy lust, anger and sloth."

On reading this, for some moments, Reuel raised his eyes to the bookstore ceiling and tried to digest the meaning of such thoughts. He shook his head slightly as if in admiration, and went on to turn the pages. There were numerous deities portrayed in supernatural form.

There was a pictured scroll of a protector deity named Dorje Drolo which caused Reuel to stop and wonder about exactly what he was looking at. Could Hieronymus Bosch come up with this? The portrayed being had fangs, an overbite, and three eyes. His hair was bright red and curly, giving off sparks. He wore Tibetan boots, and a monk's robes, with two white conch shell earrings, and a garland of severed heads around his neck. Blazing red with wrathful power, he held weapons, and was dancing fearlessly on the back of a pregnant tigress surrounded by flames.

The legend below the plate informed Reuel that Dorje Drolo was the manifestation of the wrathful Buddha of the degenerate era. He embodies forces of insight and compassion beyond logic and convention. He invokes the fearlessness and spontaneity of an awakened state, intentionally transforming clinging and hesitancy into enlightened activity. An enlarged bold line of text printed in a different font declares: "Completely out of order he is the perfect expression of crazy wisdom." Reuel considered buying the folio-sized book but was deterred at the thought of adding to his lightweight baggage.

By way of contrast, several plates further on was a scroll depicting in human form an exceptionally beautiful goddess of healing named Tara. Her alluring face and playful smile seemed to rise off the page. Sitting cross-legged on an immense lotus throne, she is surrounded by an ocean of smaller blossoms, and a constellation of tiny ones filling the sky as if stars. Her right hand holds the stem of a full blue lotus, her left hand in a gesture of reassurance and protection from fear. There is a third eye in the middle of her forehead, and eyes on the upturned soles of her feet and the palms of her hands. The only other thing supernatural about her is her exceptional beauty. Also, that her entire skin is in the color of a green melon.

The text beneath the scroll states that Tara is a heavenly deity called the "Mother of Liberation", expressing the compassion and loving kindness which emerges in the void of emptiness. She is said to relieve ordinary minds which are rigidly serious or tightly gripped by dualistic distinctions. She hears the cries of beings experiencing misery in the suffering-laden cycle of life and death in all that exists, without beginning or end.

Reuel laid the folio on his lap and pondered the extraordinary experience of exposure to such a rich polytheism. Did Olympus entertain such elaborate conceptualization? Would Hesiod have known of such transfigurations? Could Aeschylus contemplate Gods and Goddesses acting for the positive welfare of all sentient beings? Was all this constructed mythology to be swallowed up by the tsunami of modernity? Or reduced to fairy-tales for children? He could feel a tremor in his sense of identity. As if the complex rind of his body had become porous, like a dry thing left to soak in a bucket. What could Sonam's *guru*, Kunzang Namgyal Rinpoche, know anything of him in just a few hours?

About to leave the bookstore he carelessly opened the volume to its centerfold for a last look at the contents. The painted scroll surprised him for an instant. It portrayed a naked man and woman seated on a large white lotus, in coital union. He is sitting cross-legged and upright. She is settled upon his lap, her spine to the viewer, her legs wrapped around his rear, in orgasm.

The back of her body is ivory-colored, her elbows are spread high and wide as her hands clutch the back of his neck pulling him close. With her head tilted, her face is seen in profile. It displays an expression of ecstasy.

The skin of her partner's naked body is sky blue. His low cupped hands clasp the base of her spine. His hair is a topknot. Above the obscured part of his face, his open eyes gaze exactly at us. It was something beyond pornography.

Reuel was transfixed and unhurried, immersed in the magnetic mystery of such imagery. He consciously delayed any desire to peruse the text below. But at length he lowered his eyes to the rows of little glyphs, pictures of sounds from an English alphabet that formed words and offered meanings. They relate that this was the pictured male and female gods *Kuntuzangpo* and *Kuntuzangmo*, - or *Samanthabhadra* and *Samanthabhadri* in Sanskrit. They are *yab* and *yum*. They are of the father as intrinsic awareness, and of the mother as the ultimate sphere of reality. They are the primordial union of skillful-means and wisdom, the ecstasy of non-duality, the bliss of emptiness. It seemed extremely unphilosophical yet highly poetic

Somehow this idea cleared his mind of thoughts. For a while he just sat there with the book on his lap, as if he was no longer in Darjeeling, as if he was in outer space. Finally, he returned the folio to its shelf, thanked the proprietor and made his way back to the Planters Club.

An hour later Sonam Tulku arrived. Without robes, he was dressed simply in secular dark slacks and a white shirt.

"So, out of uniform?" asked Reuel.

"It's a lot easier. I'm back to Oxford next week, Michaelmas term begins. I'm now just your average "Wog", your westernized oriental gentleman. Did you rest well?"

"I had an extremely interesting time with an American diplomat who had some business in Sikkim. She was rather learned on the *Vajrayana*. Spoke Tibetan."

"Elsie Hornbein?"

"You know her?"

"I met her once at a reception in Delhi. But we all know her by reputation. She's very devoted to His Holiness, the Dalai Lama, and she's been extremely protective of all the refugees in India. It was your good fortune to meet her. But shall we have some tea? Some momos? I thought we could go see Rinpoche later today, this afternoon. He's at his best then."

"Is it walking distance?"

"Hardly" he chuckled. "He's in Kalimpong. We can drive there in less than an hour. Hope you don't mind."

"Not at all. Tell me about him. Hornbein says he's very reclusive."

"To say the least. He's quite old. Rinpoche is now in his eighties, just lives in a small temple with a few attendants. Refuses to have disciples. Discourages visitors except for a few Lamas. I'm his nephew so I can just show up. It's been a couple of years."

"I'll be honored."

"We'll see. When do you go back to America?"

"Soon. Ever been to the States?"

"Never. Maybe one day."

At table in a small restaurant near the parking lot, their conversation strayed onto the subject of teaching methods and what were called 'preliminary practices' in Buddhism, or 'propaedeutics' at Oxford. Sonam was forthcoming.

"Of course, for us, much depends on subject matter which can have the character of outer, inner, and even secret teachings. And a great deal depends on the student. On their receptivity and eagerness, on their ignorance or half-knowledge, on their imagination and intellect. And teachings themselves can be elucidated in small or large logical steps, or demonstrated by evidence, or hinted at using metaphors, or even physical gestures. And of course, there were truths beyond the capability of ordinary language to convey."

"You say ordinary language. Is there another kind, for example like what I call machine language?"

"But we ourselves are machines with language" said Sonam. "Though it's true that many Lamas use what we call 'twilight language', that isn't ordinary. But types of codes are a language if I'm not mistaken. They could include visual, verbal and nonverbal communications which can be quite incomprehensible to the uninitiated."

"What about mind-to-mind transmission without language? Without signs or symbols?" asked Reuel.

"To transfer consciousness in that way depends on the relationship. It is like a flame being transferred from one candle to another."

"And the rest is silence?"

"And the rest is silence. Like your Mr. Wittgenstein, beyond language."

"What about brain science? Will we be able to explain religious experience and behavior in neuroscientific terms? There must be correlations of neural phenomena with subjective experiences of spirituality, and good hypotheses to explain those phenomena. It seems to me that your psychology of comparative religion examines theoretical mental states rather than neural ones. Surely, there has to be a neurological and evolutionary basis for subjective experiences which we categorize as spiritual or religious. I don't think Oxford would deny that."

"Look Reuel, the study of comparative religion might not deny that, but simply not be interested in that so-called scientific space. Perhaps it's the difference between seeking truth for the purpose of personal salvation or redemption, rather than for the purpose of intellectual explanation. Soteriology versus eschatology as we say. For me there's a legitimate field of study to understand human beliefs and practices regarding the sacred, the numinous, the spiritual and divine. And it's not just academic or institutional. Myth-making and story-telling began in paleolithic times, long before there were institutions. Humans consistently perceive something they regard as holy, sacred, spiritual, and divine. Mysticism is the perennial philosophy. All theisms are heuristic."

"What about psychedelic experiences? LSD, Mescaline, for example. They clearly relate mystical experiences empirically to brain events or neurological processes. I grant you that not everyone is interested in the science, but there's stuff going on in the brain-stem, the limbic system, the temporal lobe, the anterior insula, the cingulate cortex, that not only give us our sense of self, but also the feeling of what's inexpressible, beyond description, ineffable."

"Granted, but those very altered states of consciousness, ecstatic or subtle, spontaneous or gradual, point to hidden meanings, to mysteries, don't they? Liberating insight can plausibly be achieved by interior revelation, not by external knowledge or descriptive language. I'm only saying that science has a tendency to force widely differing mental phenomena into a kind of strait-jacket, which may well exclude ultimate or unknown truths."

"Sonam, one of those so-called unknown truths was the error that the sun revolved around the earth. I think the power of self-deception in matters concerning interior revelation is enormous. Coded ignorance about ultimate truths could be just proof of human folly. In Varanasi, a few months ago, a friend of mine, a brilliant university professor of psychology, ran off to join a *shakti* worshipping cult of a Hindu goddess. Does that deserve respect?"

"As in all matters, that depends. Myth may be preferred over historical reality. Sophia and Athena are feminine personifications of wisdom. Mary, Jesus and Siddhartha are not mere historical figures, but archetypal primordial beings. Subjectively they are guides to a great truth that heals."

"I don't think we're getting very far."

"Patience, my friend. Let's go see Rinpoche."

They retrieved the car and enjoyed a pleasant drive weaving up and down among soft hills, tea plantations, forests, Indian Army bases, and dramatic views of Kanchenjunga. On reaching Kalimpong in the late afternoon they stretched their legs by walking up to the top of Durpin Hill to the Zangdok-Palri monastery, where for a time they accumulated merit by repeatedly circumambulating its handsome Tibetan *chörten*, or *stupa* in Sanskrit.

Several hundred yards below the monastic buildings, lay the quadrangle of a small temple, approached through a crooked footpath in a grove of cedars. Within the surrounding high whitewashed walls lay the abode of the wordless Lama. The only sign of what lay within the square enclosure was the inconspicuous sight of a golden rooftop finial pointing to the sky. The sole entrance to the space was through a thick wooden door on which a large wooden mallet hung from a hook. To one side a simple stone slab served as a bench, from which they could remove their shoes. Preparing themselves, Sonam and Reuel sat there quietly for a time, listening to the breeze and the tattle of bird-calls in the cedars.

"Before we go in, let me describe the situation" said Sonam. "Rinpoche is my uncle, my mother's oldest brother. He's famous for his great meditation lineage but he never took disciples. Aside from one or two attendants he's always lived in silent solitude, and rarely receives visitors. Also, I don't think he's ever had a foreign visitor. The last time I saw him was about two years ago, just before I left for England. He doesn't know I'm here, leave alone that I'm bringing a Westerner. So, I'll try explaining. You might be the only one he's ever received if he agrees. He's a very keen listener and exceptionally intuitive but he rarely ever speaks. You're free to talk to him, but don't expect him to say anything. Okay?"

"Yes, of course. Okay."

"I'll go in first for a while and you wait out here. If he agrees to see you, I'll come and take you in."

"Sure. But I don't need to talk with him. I just want to sit with him."

"Of course, that's actually a very good idea. Give me some time. I'll be back."

Sonam rose from the bench, took the large mallet from its hook, and unhurriedly gave three emphatic knocks to the heavy door. More than a full minute passed before a young attendant clad in a dark woolen skirt and a sweater opened the door. There was a moment of pleasant mutual greeting in Tibetan, and Sonam gestured to Reuel before stepping inside.

Reuel estimated it was more than a half an hour before Sonam returned. The passage of time had been pleasant. Reuel had listened to the avian warbling, the breeze on the cedars, and let his mind drift to places in India, to thoughts of his lawyers and shares of stock, to Roz Flaherty and the Boston Red Sox, to Stockholm, to wondering about the Saga, to Blackwell's bookstore, to Bob Adler, to his morning's conversation with Hornbein, and was then thinking of how to sell or dispose of his automobile on leaving India when Sonam opened the door and gestured for Reuel to join him in the large courtyard.

To the left was a simple squat-roofed two-story building containing a kitchen, toilets, a storage area, and hinting at living quarters above. A covered portal over stone slabs formed a passageway to the separate building on the right, which was clearly a religious structure. In the near shape of a cube was the small temple which had revealed the golden finial on its high roof. Two small windows flanked a heavy door. The lintel above the entrance was artfully carved and painted of two recumbent deer, each facing a large wheel. The traditional emblem of the ancient Nalanda University, with its evocation of the deer-park at Sarnath where the newly enlightened Siddhartha performed his first turning of the wheel of the Buddhist Dharma.

Sonam said "Now, pay attention. I told Rinpoche a little about you and that you just wanted to sit with him, without talking. It's alright. Just the two of you. So, go in and take a seat on the floor. I'll come by for you, in about an hour. Okay?"

"Thank you, Sonam. Thank you very much."

Unescorted, Reuel entered the square interior of the little temple. There was a faint smell of incense within its unadorned white walls. The fading light from the small windows behind him revealed an aspect dramatic in its simplicity. A polished wooden floor. More than half-way back, a foot-high platform crossed from wall to wall, from left to right. The old Lama was sitting upright and cross-legged on a large woolen rug woven in the mimicry of a tiger skin. His hands were cupped on his lap. He had a brown robe skirting about his lower body and a faded yellow tunic on his nearly skeletal frame, with long grey hair flowing down his back.

The Lama's eyes remained closed on his impassive face and he made no sign of acknowledging his visitor's presence. Reuel experienced a moment of uncertainty before sitting on the solitary flat cushion centered before the platform. He and the Lama appeared separated by eight earthly feet, and in a sense as if by astrophysical light years. Reuel settled down and prepared to refresh his mind by summoning an echo of his meditations at the Burmese vihara in Bodh Gaya. Centering himself, he fixed a half-lidded gaze to the foreground wood floor and took three relaxing slow deep breaths to begin putting his mind at rest. A quarter of an hour passed, and then Reuel suddenly looked up.

The immobile Lama was staring directly at him with wide open unblinking eyes. Time seemed suspended as they regarded one another, mind to mind. And then Kunzang Rinpoche slowly raised his right hand to the level of his throat, with his forefinger pointing upward. In a deep and pleasant voice, he simply said "ahhhh", and then returned the hand to his lap and closed his eyes.

In the many years which followed this unusual moment, which he took as personal instruction, Reuel, with very little effort, found he could reconstruct the odd feeling of being consciously aware of what he could only describe as pure emptiness. As if by some miraculous paradox a wide-awake brain could contemplate itself while in deep sleep. But how was it possible to describe nothingness to a scientist? Neuroscience had come up with the term 'default mode network' to characterize the condition of his brain at wakeful meditative rest, unoccupied by tasks, de-activated, aimless, unfocussed and relaxed. And yet, at bottom, there had still been mind-wandering, ruminative trains of thought, restless streams of consciousness, soundless words forming spontaneously and shepherding his mind in so-called meditation. And this, of course, was still something, not nothing. Yet what Reuel believed he had experienced following the indicative "ahhhh" was a durable and formative taste of the absolute nature of emptiness. It persisted. It went beyond. It was not blackness. Not whiteness. Both blackness and whiteness. Neither blackness and whiteness together. Think of yes. Think of no. Think of both. Think of neither. Mathematics. A paraconsistent tetralemma. Self-knowledge was impossible. Silence.

Time rules. Nothing lasts. On realizing his insight's impermanence and its possibilities, Reuel was comforted by the realization. With a feeling of a wordless delight that sought expression, he sensed the selfishness of his pleasure. An awareness of universal unsatisfactoriness. The infinite forms of pain and desire. The virtue of kindness. The compassion for other minds, for all beings. The compassion for himself. Everything was destined for death. Bliss destroyed by time. It was all happening at once. Everything was connected in the silence of emptiness. Thought could cease.

With no sense of time having passed, Reuel felt a hand on his shoulder as Sonam leaned over and softly murmured in his ear, "I thought I'd come and get you. It's been well over an hour. We should head back before it gets dark."

He gave Reuel a hand in standing and they took a few steps moving backward towards the door. The Lama remained utterly still, eyes closed, as before. Reuel put his hands together and made a bow in his direction. Sonam did the same. Reuel turned and whispered to him.

"Sonam, I know Rinpoche rarely speaks and avoids conversations. But I do have a single question I would like to ask of him. Would it be possible?"

"You could try but it might not be worth the effort."

"He could answer me in a single word."

"A single word? What's the question?"

"Ask him if he could compress everything that he knows into just one word and to tell me of it."

Sonam gave him a wry look, hesitated a moment, shrugged his shoulder slightly and walked to the platform and sat down next to his uncle. The

Lama didn't move or open his eyes. Sonam leaned close, cupped his hand, and whispered Reuel's question to the famous Buddhist meditator. Some moments passed. Then the Lama smiled very faintly, remained motionless, and without opening his eyes whispered a word to his nephew. Sonam stood up quietly, bowed and came back to the door where Reuel was waiting.

"What did he say?" asked Reuel.

"*Emaho.*"

"That's a Tibetan word compressing everything that he knows?"

"Yes."

"What's the word mean in English?"

"Amazement."

Outside the small temple, they put on their shoes while sitting on the stone slab. Reuel began the thread of a conversation.

"Well, that was definitely enlightening."

"So, you are now enlightened?"

"Maybe I was briefly enlightened and that I retain a memory of it. It was really very odd. I felt that Rinpoche and I were consciously sharing an identical unified mental space. He had been looking at me and then raised his hand with his finger pointed up and said 'ahhhh' and it was like a switch was thrown. How could that be?"

"As they say, 'ripeness is all'. If you are ripe you can recognize it instantly. Others may be less fortunate. Some take years of practice just to lay a foundation for bringing body, speech and mind into harmony with the vast expanse we call perfection. That expanse, for mind-nature, for the blissful state of liberation, is the taste of reality. Some will never perceive it, some perceive it and then lose it. Others can remember it. A few can hold it."

"Nice work if you can get it. But what was the meaning of 'ahhhh'?"

"It signifies that compassion can be expressed. Perhaps it was just a sound that says Dharma can be shared. The sound originates at the position of the throat, between the head and the heart. The three realms of body, speech and mind. *Om, Ah, Hung.* The sound of speech can point to the formless realm of absolute truth and pure being. Sound can create understanding between sentient beings. Of that something which is always present but inaccessible. We observe the everyday desire realm, of names and forms and physical appearance, the *samsara*, which imprisons us between birth and death. But, through speech, we may find a revealing realm of shared enlightenment. Speech is a bridge between the formless and the material realms. That middle way, the *Madhyamika*, is the meaning of Rinpoche's 'ahhhh.'"

They stayed quiet for a while, sharing the idea, the mood, and observing the remains of the day. The clouds, the birds in the trees, observing everything that is begotten, born, and dies.

Reuel spoke up. "Sonam, I think I've had a long day between Elsie Hornbein this morning and Kunzang Rinpoche this afternoon."

"That's enough for a single day. You can feel science and religion begging at one another, don't you think? Naturalism versus internalism. If a meaning of life is happiness, the problem is surely how to achieve it."

"Sonam, they need you at Oxford."

"Speaking of which, I must go now to make my farewell to Rinpoche. I'm leaving India in a few days and I might not get to see him again in this life. He's quite old, as you saw. Please spare me some few minutes with him."

"Take your time. I'm comfortable sitting out here. It's very peaceful"

Near half an hour passed before Sonam emerged. He stood in front of Reuel and touched him on the shoulder. "Reuel, my friend, this is something remarkable. Rinpoche wishes to offer you the opportunity to formally take the traditional Buddhist refuges from him, and to bestow a Buddhist name on you. He's never done that for a Westerner. It's really most unusual. He wants me to bring you to him early tomorrow morning, at the beginning of the new day. What do you think?"

"Wow! I don't know what to say. It's really amazing."

"The word you were given pleased him. *Emaho*. Amazement. Look, we can stay in Kalimpong tonight and only drive back to Darjeeling tomorrow. What do you say?"

"It's a precious gesture. Of course, I would welcome it. I'm really humbled. I'm extremely grateful."

"Say no more."

That evening they stayed at a small hostel where they shared a room. They dined on lamb and cabbage momos at a table in the back of the kitchen area. Reuel was somewhat honored at having been offered a formal initiation to membership in the Buddhist *sangha* by Kunzang Rinpoche. Nevertheless, he experienced a slight loss of self-confidence concerning several matters and decided to broach them with his re-incarnated Tulku friend.

"Sonam, help me out. I know you understand my commitment to naturalism, to Western science, to the modern world. And so far, my fondness for Buddhism and its philosophy has been almost entirely secular, at least from my point of view. In a very real sense, my estimation of Buddhist doctrine was something like an approach to mental or psychological health. It made a great deal of common sense. It was even rather therapeutic in its methods for self-understanding, particularly by its approach to unhappiness."

"Go on."

"You know very well that I have an antipathy to mumbo-jumbo and the supernatural. For example, I certainly don't believe in the god of the Bible. So, you can understand that I have a certain reluctance to be initiated into a universe of Tibetan polytheism. Just yesterday I was in a shop, looking through an illustrated book on the gods of the *Vajrayana*: Padmasambhava, Tara, Samantabhadra, and so on. What am I to make of them? Am I to worship these strange deities? Is that what Kunzang Lama expects of me?"

"No. I don't think so. I actually told him you were an egghead so to speak, a boffin, intellectually developed. Also, that you had a strong academic background, although I don't think he has a clue of what that signifies. But I do rely on his superior judgement as my master, my root guide. So as for supernatural beings, with special powers, who supposedly interact with us in ways that carry us to new levels of consciousness, I personally abstain. But let me point out that belief in the existence of such beings, even if they are actually fictions, can have a generative effect on minds."

"For the simple-minded and the muddle-headed, I agree."

"But let us speak of imaginative metaphors for unknown forces beyond the grounded preoccupations of ordinary life. Deities are heuristic devices in cultures. The culture of deities has been among humans since the beginning of sapience in the paleolithic, no? There is no ancient culture on any part of the planet that has failed to imagine gods and goddesses. That is definitely true for Tibet. Millenia ago the inhabitants of that very harsh land, confronted with phenomena they could not comprehend, like thunderstorms, invented shamanistic deities. So did the Inca and the Aztec. So did the aboriginals of Australia. So did the tribes of the middle East and Greece. And so forth."

Reuel replied "But this is the twentieth century. You know that Hesiod's gods and goddesses on Olympus aren't worshipped any longer. If there are no deities why are there sacramental thangkas in actual use portraying them currently? I say that obviously there are no such deities, but according to the paintings there are deities. This is like saying that according to the Pope there's an immortal soul, but of course there is no immortal soul. Why should I take Padmasambhava more seriously? Does it matter if I am regularly chanting his mantra, '*Om Ah Hum Vajra Guru Padma Siddhi Hum*'? Is that to be part of my spiritual development?"

"You have to be a fictional realist. It's a different ontology. Don't make the category error. Grasp the idea of a supreme fiction where divinities are valuable symbolic idealizations of virtue. You have to go beyond pictures and language to grasp the essence of the Dharma's message, even as you discard the symbols and words with which it is formed. I say once again, belief and opinion are two very different matters."

"It's like genteel hypocrisy."

"So be it. It's a cultural ointment. And as for tomorrow's meeting with Rinpoche, let me say that the great teachers truly understand the presence of different levels of intellect. You know, conventionally there are those of lower levels who spin prayer wheels and mutter magic words, and those of middle or average intelligence who absorb the outer teachings while respecting the existence of something hidden; and there are those of high intellect who gain access to the esoteric, the inner teachings. In other words, there are those who treat deities faithfully as real, those who treat deities metaphorically as guides, and those who have gone beyond all deities. 'Gone, gone beyond, gone all the way beyond', isn't that right? Of course, realization, enlightenment, and awakening have nothing to do with deities. Just go to Rinpoche tomorrow with an open mind, that's all."

The following daybreak began as a beautiful and still morning under a cloudless blue sky. Reuel and Sonam abstained from taking food and limited themselves to glasses of salt-butter tea. Then it took a quarter of an hour to walk silently from the hostel to the temple. They sat on the stone slab for a few minutes to remove their shoes and collect their thoughts. Sonam spoke softly.

"Now, we prepare to go in. As this is a sacred ceremony, before sitting down on our cushions, we will perform three half prostrations. Start by standing facing Rinpoche with your palms together. Then we go down on our knees and touch our heads to the ground with our hands outstretched. Three times. Then we sit. Rinpoche will speak to you. I will translate. Okay?"

"Of course."

They entered the temple's shadowed interior. There was a smell of incense. Kunzang Rinpoche was sitting quietly on the embroidered tiger skin rug with his eyes closed at the center of the platform. Two cushions were on the floor close before him. Reuel and Sonam performed their three prostrations and then sat quietly for a few minutes, letting their minds settle.

The Lama, then opened his eyes and looked at Reuel as he averred softly, in a hoarse whisper, a series of brief pronouncements. Each utterance was followed by a pause, allowing it to be rendered in English by Sonam, as follows, with his first translation:

"Our living world is only a fraction of the universe. It does not pursue an end or have a purpose. There is no final causality. Our existence in time is not pre-ordained."

A pause.

"Our life consists of many random collisions where chance results in necessity. That is the meaning of causality. Everything existing in the universe is the fruit of coincidences and their unavoidable consequences."

A pause.

"Our confused wandering through earthly existence between our birth and death is called 'samsara'. Everywhere there is suffering, from which there is no immunity. One thing or another will kill you."

A pause.

"Everything is impermanent. A life has as little chance of enduring as a candle flame in a gust of wind. The land of death closes in on you day by day like the shadow of a mountain at sunset. Is there a truth that will calm anxiety at the inevitability of death?"

A pause.

"You were born into human existence. It is precious. You are fortunate to have human life. You have the gift of health. You have body, speech and a mind. You have senses. You have a right to be joyful. You have energy and are capable of effort."

A pause.

"You must not forget this situation. From this moment on, you must remember and understand how to remain in stillness. To have clear wakefulness. Within luminous emptiness."

A pause.

"You can rest in comfort and ease, in calmness. This is called suchness. *Tathata*. From now on you will be able to realize the essential nature of consciousness, which includes both appearance and emptiness. It is beyond description and transcends everything relative."

A pause.

"This is the ancient connection between human beings and the frozen universe of being alone. This you shall accept."

A long pause

"Now Reuel" said Sonam on his own, "you must say the refuge formula to Rinpoche, first in English and then after me in Tibetan."

"I'm ready." And Reuel repeated the following utterances.

"I take refuge in the Lama"

"*Lama -la kyab su chio*"

"I take refuge in the Buddha"

"*Sangye-la kyab su chio*"

"I take refuge in the Dharma"

"*Choe-la kyab su chio*"

"I take refuge in the Sangha"

"*Gedun-la kyab su chio*"

Then they sat quietly for a long while.

Finally, Kunzang Lama said something to Sonam, while looking closely at Reuel.

Sonam said "Rinpoche now gives you your Buddhist name: '*Yeshe Gyagspo*'."

"*Yeshe Gyagspo*" Reuel repeated cautiously.

"Yes. It means Swift Wisdom."

"Swift wisdom!" He felt a moment's pleasure and released it swiftly.

They stood and bowed to the Lama and walked facing backwards to the door, emerging into sunlight. Sonam turned to Reuel with an affectionate smile.

"Reuel, my friend, since you have taken the refuges you are now technically a confirmed Buddhist and a member of its *sangha*. Moreover, you must appreciate that Rinpoche, who is now your root guide, has actually transmitted to you the meditation without form. That is very important and extremely rare. You are very fortunate."

"The meditation without form?"

"Yes."

That night, having returned to Darjeeling, Reuel had a dream that he was at a bowling alley in Chicago. He watched his ball make a gentle curve as it rolled slowly down the lane to strike the fore pin. All went down. It half-woke him and a programmatic syllabus of the near future blossomed into his imagination. He would join with Sonam Tulku and fly to New Delhi with him. There he would collect all his mail. There he would attempt to call on Elsie Hornbein at the embassy to tell her of his experience. Then he would buy a ticket and fly to San Francisco after stopping briefly in Thailand, or possibly Japan. He would make a gift of the Ambassador sedan to Kunzang Rinpoche's temple. They could sell it for benefit. His life, facing an open door, continued to be interesting.

So, on the following day he joined Sonam on a bus ride to Siliguri, down in the plains, where a non-stop Air India flight in the evening would fly them to Delhi. During the drive, they became even warmer friends, and exchanged stories of their boyhoods and undergraduate life. In getting to know one another better it appeared that Sonam liked sex with girls as much as himself, intellectual academics and spiritual dedication notwithstanding.

While ticketing at the Siliguri airport Reuel paid to upgrade Sonam's fare to first class so they might sit together. Having more than an hour to wait before boarding they ended up on plastic chairs at a small rickety table in the passenger's lounge, drinking English tea from cardboard cups.

"So, Sonam, do tell me what you're reading at Magdalen. Comparative religion, you said. Isn't that really evolutionary anthropology? I'd call it naturalism. I assume that as our human brain evolved, it built incrementally on much earlier, more primitive brain structures. That seems obvious. And our modern brain, with all of its philosophical theories, has to deal with the fact that over time these old primitive structures are there, which can rise up and overpower higher functions. That explains our harmful impulses doesn't it? Will we learn the terrible lesson that our neocortex really is little more than a thin layer of tissue grafted onto the much larger limbic system, our emotion-driven primitive brain? Isn't the neocortex just a fair-weather accretion, useful only in times of abundance and ease? So, when real threats arrive is it inevitably pushed aside by the lizard brain with its desperate, frenzied attempts to achieve security at all costs? And doesn't that, the ancient brain anatomy, explain depression, anxiety, the lack of ethics, the inability to find durable reward or motivation in life's joys. *Dukkha*. Unsatisfactoriness. Hurt. The hunger for relief for something new when there are no more gods. Schopenhauer rather than Rousseau. Suffering everywhere, as the founder said. The old pre-modern, pre-literate brain, of the Buddha's time simply dealt with near universal life that was nasty, brutal and very short. Today's brain doesn't know what to do in a world of antibiotics, electricity and Hollywood."

"No, Reuel, that's not my cut at it. I'm looking at it with a philosophical lens. What I see, universally, is the attempt by all religions to deliver an escape from unhappiness, even if it's done by hocus-pocus. It's the old distinction between salvation and explanation. The superseding problem of mind is always to determine the nature of reality. I join Westernizers of Buddhism who present it as compatible with accepting the rigorous methods of science. A philosophical commitment to clarity and rigorous argumentation is what I find and value in analytic philosophy in the West. Your Wittgenstein for example. But I trust the Dharma teaching on non-self which merely tries to obtain a state of non-conceptual intuition, mostly through the practice of meditation. And let me add, also possibly available sometimes for everyone, during the extremely brief experience of sexual orgasm."

"Three cheers for that opportunity."

A boy came over with a kettle and refilled their tea cups. They both rested mentally quiet, without words in their minds, sharing a brief unintended non-conceptual meditation. An overhead fan turned slowly. A fly annoyed them.

Reuel broke the silence.

"Again, shouldn't we think of the brain as a wet machine? A contraption, a device, operating in accordance with laws of nature, determined by its own internal mechanisms, beyond survival or pleasure. Imagine a machine without a purpose, or its purpose is just self-adaptive emergence."

Sonam answered "Its purpose is to avoid suffering. And you have to think of the healing power of ideas, even if there could be unconscious ideas. Conscious mental states, after all, are only affects of your wet machine. And that machine has parts. There's a thinking machine, an expressing machine, a feeling machine. But on top of this, the machine seems to produce a mental realm which can experience the immanence of a nonmaterial spiritual reality."

"A 'ghost in the machine.'"

"Precisely, a ghost. But old master Ryle at Magdalen did us well by showing the error of analyzing a relation between 'mind' and 'body' as if they were terms of the same logical category. Just another lazy category mistake attempting to reduce mental reality to the same logical status as physical reality. We're just repeating ourselves. That's obvious by now, isn't it?"

"Obvious to us. But the unifying entity is still called 'the self', and what's that? If we Buddhists say that *anatta*, or non-self is the goal of self-knowledge we're just playing a semantic game, no?"

"Well, there's a blurring between self and soul. And a soul is not necessarily a ghost in the machine. Spinoza imagined a soul as a spiritual automaton, which attempts to be self-directed, determined by its own internal machinery, like a watch. For Spinoza, the soul refers to the self-causing activity of nature, which seeks enlightenment. This 'nature', Spinoza tells us, should be considered as a passive but omnipresent element of an infinite causal chain. Nature is just doing what nature does. The desire to avoid suffering always remains with us."

"But how does non-conceptual awareness deal with the pain of a broken toe? Given nature's absence of self-nature, its emptiness, there's still something that feels hurt."

"Look Reuel. Think of Nagarjuna's two realities, two ontological truths, absolute and conventional, the way things are empty and the way they are perceived. The ultimate truth and the relative or provisional truth. The phenomenal but indeterminate truth, neither real nor unreal. Out of that, comes our great teaching of a middle way, the *Madhyamika*. The two truths are resolved into non-duality as our own lived experience. When that's grasped intuitively or intellectually it's called 'realization'. Unfortunately, these subtle philosophical systems might be purposeful only for spiritual elites, not for the masses. They have hidden meanings and teachings. And that remains regrettable in this imperfect and ignorant world. That may be the political problem of our time."

"I'm not yet convinced" said Reuel. "I don't like metaphysical hierarchies like that. The logic of reality means that naturalism is different from metaphysics. You don't have to be an intellectual, but the soul's search for enlightenment must stay with the commitment to follow a logical argument wherever it leads. Buddhists metaphysics has to always run into opposition when its practices lead to results that outrun empirical verifiability."

"But Reuel, there being no actual thing as the ultimate nature of reality, the question of its logical structure simply doesn't arise. The Buddha had an implicit syllabus against speculative metaphysics. He opposed all attempts to use reason alone to prove the existence of things that are by nature imperceptible. The question of enlightenment remains beyond empirical verification."

"Why three realms? The number three is a big deal, isn't it?"

"In the Buddha's time, long before there was writing, sentient beings just used small numbers to improve their memory of the Dharma. One nirvana, two natures, three realms, four truths, five precepts, six perfections, seven factors of awakening, eightfold path, and so on. Rather common I would think in preliterate societies, preliterate metaphysics. Like ten commandments, or the imaginary magic of the unity of the Trinity."

Then, a woman's soft voice speaking in Hindi came on over the loud-speaker, announcing that their flight was ready for boarding. The late hour, the noise of the plane, and a certain mental fatigue had them dozing on the flight. It was close to midnight when they reached New Delhi and as they debarked the conversation turned to the mundane.

"Where are you staying?" asked Reuel.

"I'll overnight at Tibet House. There's a hostel. My flight to London leaves tomorrow afternoon. What about you?"

"I guess I'll go back to the Ashoka."

"A wonderful old hotel. What are your plans?"

"A few days to do laundry, catch up with mail, read newspapers, relax a bit, see if I can reach Hornbein at the Embassy, and book my flight back to the States. India's been quite a trip for me. Ever thought of coming to America?"

"You can never tell. Maybe one of these days. I've another year or so at Oxford. You can always reach me through the porter's lodge at Magdalen. And let me say once more it was extremely generous of you to give the car to Rinpoche."

"It was a bargain." Reuel tore a sheet from a small notepad in his bag and wrote out information concerning his lawyers as contacts in Cambridge.

"They'll know where I can be found. I don't have a home address yet. Sonam, I'd be very happy to see you again, whenever."

Luggage retrieved, they ambled to the taxi queue, turned a handshake into a warm and extended embrace, and made their farewells.

ॐ

Reuel stayed in India for three more days. In that time, he called at the American Embassy and learned to his disappointment that Elsie Hornbein was in Washington and would not return for two weeks. He went to the American Express office in Connaught Circus and collected several letters that were being held for him. He waited until he was back at the Ashoka Hotel before opening the envelopes. One was from his lawyers informing him that they had used their fiduciary discretion to approve an exchange of his Kang Laboratory shares for stock in Digital Resources Corporation on very favorable terms. As DRC was now a publicly traded company his shares could now be sold at any-time without restriction. They awaited his instructions.

There was a letter from Pierre Ferrand in Guadeloupe to the effect that the first season of chartering the Saga in the Caribbean had been profitable and that he and Gabrielle would like to buy out Reuel's partial ownership. There was also a letter on corporate stationary from Walter Dowfeld with a San Francisco return address. He had joined a hardware technology group called Silicon Systems Corporation in the Bay area, provided details, and urged Reuel to contact him if and when he was next in California.

And then there was a letter from Luca Baca in Rome.

Dearest Roo,

I'm back in Rome, having spent a month at Witwatersrand University, Johannesburg. Took an adventure into the "bush" and saw the world as it was before Adam & Eve, pure and without sin. (Though some predators.) What's with you? Did you go to India? Hope your lawyers forward mail. I'm off to Japan soon for some research on traces of St. Francis Xavier, our first church missionary out there 400+ yrs ago. We're hunting for references to his presence in Japanese archives of those days. The imperial court gave us permission. Rome's Vatican archives have a letter from StFX in Japan to Ignatius Loyola, (SJ co-founder). Admires Buddhist style of lengthy meditation. Challenges re metempsychosis and vegetarianism. Despair they have a first principle of absolute emptiness, of all that is. Deny existence of first mover. Their theodicy: any God who creates a world containing evil is inherently impious!!! I'll be staying with my former roommate from the Gregoriana, Father Felipe "Testsuko" Delgado who is originally from Philippines, now Pastor at the Holy Rosary parish church in the Kyoto diocese. I'm reachable there if you head out this way. (362 Shimomaruya-cho, Nakagyo-ku, Kyoto, Japan, 604-8006.) I'm to be adjunct faculty in theology at Kyoto's Doshisha University for the next two months. Thinking of you often. Hope, as always, you find a sweet taste of Holy Spirit.

Brotherly love,
Luke

Deciding immediately to forego Bangkok, and following a swift exchange of telegrams, it was agreed that Luca would meet Reuel at the airport upon the arrival of his non-stop flight from Delhi to Osaka. From there, a short train ride would take them to Kyoto. And so, in this way, Reuel ended his passage to and from India.

☙

The rectory of the Holy Rosary church in Kyoto was a semi-detached two-story wooden building with sleeping quarters on its upper floor. The two Catholic padres, Luca Baca and Felipe Delgado shared a small suite containing a pair of beds. They were in love with one another. Both Christian love, agape, as well as eros. Reuel, their visiting guest, was provided with a well-furnished room for himself across their corridor and welcome to stay as long as he liked before flying on to San Francisco.

While Luca was taller and thin, Felipe was short and stout, built like a muscular wrestler. They lavished affection on Reuel, introducing him to various sights, sounds, foods and entertainments of Japan. Felipe's clerical duties were light and Luca's modest academic research obligations afforded them the pleasures of hosting their visitor. Raw fish, rock gardens, Sumo wrestling, scroll paintings, Kabuki theatre, national museums, demonstrations of flower arrangements, and long walks filled many days.

Knowing of his interest in Buddhist meditation they guided Reuel to Minato-in, an always open traditional zendo in Kyoto's Shokoku-ji temple complex. It allowed him an opportunity to sit *zazen* with others on tatami mats in an incense filled hall, and to compare the experience with the Burmese vihara in Bodh Gaya. Using a sheet of English letters, he enjoyed chanting the Japanese translation of the Sanskrit short Prajnaparamita Sutra - the

"Perfection of Wisdom Sutra", the so-called "Heart Sutra" - with its rhythmic drum accompaniment.

Kan ji zai bo sa gyo- jin han-nya ha ra mi ta ji sho- ken go on kai ku- do is-sai ku yaku.

Sha ri shi shiki fu I ku- ku-fu I shiki shiki soku ze ku- ku- soku ze shiki.

Ju so- gyo- shiki yaku bu nyo ze.

Sha ri shi ze sho ho- ku- so-

Fu sho- fu metsu fu ku fu jo-fu zo- fu gen ze ko ku- chu-

Mu shiki mu ju so- gyo- shiki mu gen-ni bi zes-shin I mu shiki sho- ko-mi soku ho- mu gen kai nai shi mu I shiki kai mu mu myo- yaku mu mu myo-jin.

Nai shi mu ro- shi yaku mu ro- shi jin mu ku shu metsu do- mu chi yaku mu toku I mu sho tok'ko.

Bo dai sat-ta e han-nya ha ra mi ta ko shim-mu kei ge mu kei ge ko mu u ku fu on ri is-sai ten do- mu so- ku gyo- ne han.

San ze sho butsu e han-nya ha ra mi ta ko

Toku a noku ta ra sam-myaku sam-bo dai.

Ko chi han-nya ha ra mi ta ze dai shin shu ze dai myo- shu ze mu jo- shu ze mu to- to- shu no- jo is-sai ku shin jitsu fu ko.

Ko setsu han-mya ha ra mi ta shu soku setsu shu watsu

Gya tei gya tei ha ra gya tei hara so- gya tei.

Bodhi sva-ha- ka han-nya shin gyo.

On the reverse side he found someone's English translation.

Avalokiteshvara, while practicing deeply with the Insight that Brings Us to the Other Shore, suddenly discovered that all of the five *Skandhas* are equally empty, and with this realization he overcame all Ill-being.

"Listen Sariputra, this Body itself is Emptiness and Emptiness itself is this Body. This Body is not other than Emptiness and Emptiness is not other than this Body.

The same is true of Feelings, Perceptions, Mental Formations, and Consciousness.

"Listen Sariputra, all phenomena bear the mark of Emptiness; their true nature is the nature of no Birth no Death, no Being no Non-being, no Defilement no Purity, no Increasing no Decreasing.

"That is why in Emptiness, Body, Feelings, Perceptions,

Mental Formations and Consciousness are not separate self-entities.

The Eighteen Realms of Phenomena which are the six Sense Organs, the six Sense Objects, and the six Consciousnesses are also not separate self-entities.

The Twelve Links of Interdependent Arising and their Extinction are also not separate self-entities.

Ill-being, the Causes of Ill-being, the End of Ill-being, the Path, insight and attainment, are also not separate self-entities.

Whoever can see this no longer needs anything to attain.

Bodhisattvas who practice the Insight that Brings Us to the Other Shore see no more obstacles in their mind, and because there are no more obstacles in their mind, they can overcome all fear, destroy all wrong perceptions and realize Perfect Nirvana.

"All Buddhas in the past, present and future by practicing the Insight that Brings Us to the Other Shore are all capable of attaining

Authentic and Perfect Enlightenment.

"Therefore Sariputra, it should be known that the Insight that Brings Us to the Other Shore is a Great Mantra, the most illuminating mantra, the highest *mantra*, a *mantra* beyond compare, the True Wisdom that has the power to put an end to all kinds of suffering.

Therefore let us proclaim a *mantra* to praise the Insight that Brings Us to the Other Shore.

Gate, Gate, Paragate, Parasamgate, Bodhi Svaha!

Gate, Gate, Paragate, Parasamgate, Bodhi Svaha!

Gate, Gate, Paragate, Parasamgate, Bodhi Svaha!"

[Gone, gone, gone beyond, gone altogether beyond, awakened, all hail]

Other than the periodic rhythmic sutra chanting, meditation in the zendo was not very different from his experience in the Burmese vihara. Maintaining a neutral feeling he observed that holding his mind in purposeless awareness was relatively comfortable and at ease. He had learned the practice. Though sitting up very straight in the Zen manner required occasional thought.

Aimless recollections from his past life came and went through his mind with relative indifference. Moments of regret were tolerated and released. Possible futures were like clouds in the sky. Passing remembrances of LSD and Bob Adler evoked a thin smile. Reminiscences of sexual pleasures were slightly adhesive, lingering, but these too entered the mind-stream flow and vanished. He observed that it was simple to recenter on his breath beneath the perceptible transience of thoughts and images. In comfort and ease, as his meditation guide Kunzang Namgyal Rinpoche had conveyed to him in Kalimpong.

But at night, before falling asleep, lustful sexual thoughts frequently surfaced in his mind, materializing in a tumescent vascular erection. There were inventive favorite fantasies. These days his fresh unconsummated desire for Elsie Hornbein still remained at the top of his list. She had vanished in New Delhi but he could visualize her in his room at the Planters Club. He lingered on imaginary fragments of carnal conversation, venereal images of her nakedness, and sensual fantasies about what his fingertips were touching. Though Hornbein had actually said 'nothing-doing', yet still her 'no' was somehow erotic, as it begat his arousal by its shy possibility of a 'yes'. And this, inevitably, all vanished into the emptiness of impermanence and sleep.

One evening at a small restaurant, after several flasks of saké, Felipe the Catholic asked Reuel about Buddhism's views of human sexual behavior. Was celibacy important? Was sexuality sacramental?

Reuel replied thoughtfully. "I think it's about individual choice. Some priests and monks and nuns take vows of celibacy, avoiding desire. Others, even some great teachers, yogis, philosophers, artists, all celebrate sex. In the tantric traditions it's definitely sacramental. Some say it's the only method of getting a taste of the divine."

"That's understandable" said Luca, "but where do morality, ethics, fit in?"

Reuel replied, as if a lay tutor. "Well, curiously, Buddhist philosophy seems less interested in ethics than in existential issues. But my impression is that lay Buddhists, at least, are enjoined to adhere to the five precepts. And observe the third precept which concerns avoiding sexual misconduct. I guess that precept relates simply to avoid causing suffering by one's sexual behavior. Adultery, as in the ten commandments, is probably the main human breach of this precept. But sexual hunger is everywhere."

"But what of two consenting adults, without issues of fidelity?" asked Felipe.

"Well, I'm not aware of any canonical scriptures containing regulations or recommendations for lay people. Even with regards to masturbation, or contraceptives, or homosexuality, or particular sexual practices. I think it's just about keeping with the Buddhist ethical principle of doing no harm. Avoiding shame, guilt and remorse, and socially taboo forms of sexuality like involving children, or even animals. I guess obsessive sexual activities could also be seen as being included in the third precept. The Dharma is about mindfulness, that's all."

Felipe swallowed a cupful of saké and said "there's an old subculture in Japan. I've always been tempted to ask Fumiko about Japanese sexuality, but I don't dare. She's boldly straightforward. Probably would ask me about my own activities, heaven forbid. She was once a geisha, you know."

Such as it was, the rectory household was lightly managed by the handsome woman in her late fifties called "Sister Fumiko". Always in a navy-blue kimono, she briskly made their beds, swept the floors, and prepared vegetarian rice bowls for dinner, four nights a week. Three nights were out for Padre's favorite restaurants. Fumiko lived alone in a small wooden cabin attached by a roofed lane to the ground floor of the rectory. After dark, following her services, she invariably retired to her bedchamber and for an hour or two extemporized in the pentatonic scale of her *shamisen*. In her hands this plucked three-stringed traditional Japanese musical instrument produced a haunting poetic evocation of melancholy. Lifelong, she had learned to perform with it since early childhood as central to her training of becoming a geisha in those long-ago days before the war.

Felipe had related the story of Fumiko Kawabata which he had learned from his predecessor, Father Bonifacio Cortez, who had also come from the Philippines and who had had a lengthy tenure. Somehow, she had come to the Catholic faith and to becoming part of the Holy Rosary church during those years.

"Reuel, you understand, that of Japan's 125 million people only about 1% are Christians, out of which only a few hundred thousand are of our Catholic persuasion. Curiously, most Japanese seem to be simultaneous adherents of two entirely different faiths. One, imported, just like Christianity, is the religion of Buddhism from India and China, with its Nipponese sects of today, Tendai, Nichiren, Shingon, Amida, and Zen. The other faith is the ancient native Shinto religion. And Shinto has a unique culture unlike any other in the world. Specifically, in Fumiko's case, it produced the remarkable heritage of female performing artists who are called geisha. You should grasp that our Fumiko Kawabata was born to be a geisha."

Luca said "Hold on, that was a long time ago."

Reuel asked "Was she a prostitute?"

"No, no, no." said Felipe, "those girls, long ago before the war, were like trained actresses, with artistic skills, like dance or singing. It's true that some of them were willing courtesans with an upper-class client or two whom they liked or admired. I think Fumiko was brought up to be an entertainer, with clever conversation, and her skill at the shamisen. It was only after the war that American GI's gave the word geisha the meaning of a whore. At least that's what I was told by Father Bonifacio. I've never asked her about this myself, although I've taken her confession, which is quite pure."

"She's a real Catholic?" asked Reuel.

"Oh yes, for many years. I learned that before the war that her main inamorata was a high army officer, a general, who was later tried as one of the minor war criminals. Then, after the atom bombs, losing her mother's family in Hiroshima, and learning about the horrible war crimes, and gave up on both Buddhism and Shinto. Gave up everything in her past except the shamisen. She withdrew totally from men. She had few friends. I was told she worked as a clerk in a department store. Then in an art gallery. But she disliked her life, even her own country. Bonifacio said she was a very unhappy woman before converting.

But as you know, Jesus saves. I don't know the details of how she came to us, to Christianity, but she is faithful to the rosary. She has learned forgiveness. You can see how she is usually cheerful and outgoing, and she has a good sense of humor. We depend on her."

Later that night, while preparing for bed, Reuel glanced at the small bookcase in his room. He had perused most of the haphazardly arranged volumes since arriving at the rectory. The shelves contained a variety of uninteresting secular titles, many of which were clearly intended for tourists, while a few others bore captions relating to economics, cemeteries, foreign trade, and the second world war. Most were octavo sized, and some larger in quarto. There was little that interested him. But as he undressed this night his glance noticed a narrow volume that was easily overlooked. It was folio-sized and lay horizontally with its spine to the rear and its foredges half-shadowed by the vertical titles which rested upon it.

Half-naked, his curiosity aroused, Reuel extracted the volume and examined the black buckram spine. He found German words in faded gold letters "*Buch Band Eins – Geschichte – DIE SCHWEBENDE WELT von Heinrich Ernst*". Gratified at having passed MIT's language proficiency requirement, it took him only a few moments of vocabulary recollection to produce the translation: "Volume One – History – THE FLOATING WORLD by Heinrich Ernst."

Cradling the book, he sat on the edge of the bed and scanned the opening pages. It was clearly an academic product, printed in Leipzig a score of years earlier. The table of contents indicated there was a second volume: *Buch Band Zwei – Farbtafeln*, i.e. "Volume Two – Color Plates". He looked at the bookcase but there was no sign of an accompanying volume. It was clear that the main text was a history of some sort covering Japanese graphic arts. He made out the words *rollbilder, radierungen, holzschnitte*, i.e. scroll paintings, etchings, woodcuts.

At the bottom of the table of contents was the text: *KERNSTÜCK -"Der Traum der Fischerfrau". Ein shunga vom Architekten Katsushika Hokusai. Es stellt eine Frau dar, die sich in einer ekstatischen Umarmung mit zwei Oktopussen hingibt. – 1814*

He easily translated it: Centerpiece - "The Dream of the Fisherman's Wife". A *shunga* by the artist Katsushika Hokusai. It depicts a woman engaged in an ecstatic embrace with two octopuses.

He turned immediately to the colored centerpiece. Portrayed there was a glossy color print of a naked woman, seeming to lay back in passive pleasure. She is beautiful, long-haired, her eyes closed, and she rests horizontally on a bed of coral covered in green seaweed. Just below the haired mound of her vulva her legs are spread by an incredibly large octopus with bulging eyes who rests between her limbs and has its beak in her vagina, its eight arms of suction cups fondling her body. By the side of her head at her left shoulder a very small octopus loosely embraces her neck with its tentacles, its beak lightly touching her lips. Her facial expression is of contained ecstasy.

Reuel placed the book on the floor, doused the light, smiled to himself. He suddenly felt starved again for sexual contact and went to sleep imaginatively dreaming of Elsie Hornbein once more, not appreciating the fact that he would never see or hear from her ever again.

On the following evening, Reuel was by himself at the Rectory. Felipe had been called overnight to the Archdiocese in Tokyo and Luca was attending a formal event at Doshisha University. Reuel was alone at dinner and tried engaging Fumiko in conversation. It felt somewhat tentative owing to her uncertain English and the subject he had in mind concerning the particular German book he brought with him to the table.

"Fumiko-san, I was told you were geisha, long time ago, before war."

"No. I maiko, not full geisha."

"What is maiko?"

"Maiko is beginner geisha."

"Ah so. You know *shunga*?"

She drew her head back with her eyes suddenly wide-open in surprised amusement. She wagged a finger at him.

"*Shunga* for old men. You boy."

"You know Hokusai?"

"Everybody know. Fuji-san views. Great wave. Everybody know."

"Hokusai also make *shunga*. I show you picture."

Reuel opened the book to show her the centerpiece of the fisherman's wife and the octopuses. Fumiko's jaw dropped and she covered her mouth with her hand.

"Fumiko-san. You know where is second book? *Shunga* pictures?"

She looked incredulous, but nodded faintly.

"You show me?"

They went to her cabin, removing their footwear before entering. Its interior was elaborately furnished in a Japanese style that might have been common a century earlier. Bamboo tatami mats, the patterned fabrics, the smell of aloes incense, the lanterns, the tea bowl, its caddy and whisk, the cushions, a scroll painting of a man fishing with a long pole in a landscape in clouds, and another of a willow tree and three crows.

Fumiko made a cushion for him to sit on the floor and from a flat drawer of a closed chest, she extracted Volume Two and offered it to him. Reuel waited to learn if she would say anything, but she merely sat at the edge of a small brocaded chaise and took up her long-necked lute. She plucked a few test notes on its three strands and adjusted a peg reducing tension on the lowest string, so that it buzzed to create the weird twanging timbre of the *shamisen*.

"You play old man" she said. "I maiko. I play *shamisen*. You look pictures."

It began. For almost an hour of sustained absorption, it was as if they had been transported into a fictional fantasy realm, where time and identity were meaningless, as if magic and illusion had evaporated the exterior world and they were simply alone, in a chamber floating in an empty universe.

Reuel's captivation by scores of colored plates of erotic paintings and woodcuts was immersive. The representations of human anatomies engaged in sexual congress were beyond anything he had ever seen. The kaleidoscopic minutiae down to single hairs of an orifice, the facial expressions, the extraordinary variety of positions, the elaborate embroidered details of the kimonos which frequently half-wrapped the various participants, single, two, three, or four of them, on almost every plate, in the same genders or not, with enormous phalluses, moist female genitalia, the featured nipples of breasts, it was almost hallucinatory. Amorous couples reading poetry while fingering one another. Couples staring fascinated and wide eyed at their partner's genitals. Unions of old and young revealing intense ecstasy by the drawing of their curled toes. The visual force of pudenda partially penetrated. The pictured voyeurism of a man lifting a woman's kimono hem as she shows him her cunt. The voyeurism of a woman peeking at her lesbian friends in pleasure. A lazy union in a hammock viewed through the mesh. A wife and a male friend fucking while the adjacent husband sleeps. A curious smiling female lifts a man's loincloth so as to enjoy seeing his erection. Two lovers pretending they are sumo wrestlers while a third is the umpire. A male partner staring down at his cock at the moment it enters her orifice. A woman writing a poem as a man enters her from behind. One woman holding her lady friend on her lap while spreading her legs open as a prepared naked male is wetting his member with saliva from his mouth. A young girl with an aged man who can't get it up. A young man and an old widow. A bored man on his back as a courtesan is about to sit on his face. A variety of facial expressions at their moments of orgasm. A girl holding up the hem of her kimono in her teeth as she shows herself to an eager boy. The happy eroticism of a suggestive kiss on the lips of the couple who are in the act of disrobing. The languid abandonment of a lady who spreads her legs in the butterfly posture. A female ass high in the air as her partner approaches to lick it. A portrayal of a rape. A page-filling close-up of just a face with tongue extended toward a pair of thighs bracketing a vertical image from pink clitoris to tawny anus, every little hair carefully drawn, and the wet juices unmistakable from hints of a reflected light. And there it was, Hokusai's dream of a fisherman's wife embraced by the octopi. And the following page of a rugged fellow holding his lover's nipple in his teeth as she looks toward the sky. And an orgy of six having serious fun. The page entitled '*Nähert sich der matratze aus fleisch*' that is, 'approaching the mattress of flesh', showed a fully dressed couple, smiling at a commencement, their hands buried in one another's garments. Another page filled with a gigantic close-up of a coitus. A plate of two maidens in lesbian activity. One of mixed threesomes in imaginative combinations. Another with fantastic acrobatic anatomies. A naked female painter's model, legs spread wide, looks bored as a male artist dips his paintbrush in a bowl of water preparing to stroke her vagina with it. A couple in 69 each deeply absorbed in studying the other's genitals. A naked lady sitting backwards on her male partner penetrating her from behind as she sips tea from a bowl. A woman in coitus with her hand covering her partner's mouth as her face reveals anxiety that they will be heard by someone unseen nearby. A plate featuring a cat watching a couple go at it. Scores of such colorful portrayals. The last, at the very end, wistful and tender, where a solitary young beauty, with a languid expression of satisfaction on her face, is enclosed in a magnificent purple silk kimono, and sits on the floor, her knees pulled up, as she gazes down to regard her hidden hand at work in the cloaked region below, in her industry of self-gratification.

While a single *shunga* plate or two had the potential of arousal, experiencing scores of these images one after another, at one time, had a desensitizing effect on Reuel. They seemed like artistic drawings of mere half-clothed marionettes in action. Or as if watching animals in the zoo. It felt abstract as every unreal moment of that detached effect was sharpened and underscored by the atonal twang of Fumiko's *shamisen*.

When he finally looked up at her she was sitting upright, still at the edge of her chaise. Staring fixedly at his eyes as he closed the folio, she plucked the strings with a loud mechanical finish of terminal chords, as if to say 'so then? so then?' and they sat in a prolonged silence. Finally, she spoke in a soft voice, saying "life is mysterious".

Studying Fumiko, he visualized her decades earlier, as a young apprentice geisha, utterly beautiful and artistic. Now, still a handsome woman, much older than he, an ugly foreign gaijin, an outsider, with a robotic lust in his viscera, who felt an unwanted half-desire to open her kimono and spread her legs. Was this sinfully ugly, Reuel asked himself. What did Fumiko want?

But she stood up, placed the *shamisen* down on her bed, put her palms together and bowed slightly. "Good night, Reuel-san. Have pleasant dreams."

Arriving at breakfast the next morning Luca informed Reuel that he was invited to lunch with Professor Akira Miyamoto at the faculty club of Doshisha University. Miyamoto held a chair in both philosophy and theology departments and had expressed interest in meeting Luca's American intellectual friend who was interested in Buddhism. Concerning Doshisha, Luca explained to his friend how US Commodore Perry's arrival to Edo Bay gave rise to the Meiji Restoration, which led Japan to adopt Western ideas about higher learning. Doshisha University, originally established in 1875 by Christian educators, was today one of the most selective and prestigious universities in Japan. Reuel was delighted to accept the luncheon invitation, and borrowed a necktie and cardigan sweater for the occasion.

Professor Miyamoto was a handsome man in his sixties with a thick head of white hair, horn-rimmed eyeglasses, and was dressed in a grey business suit. Luca wore his clerical collar. Reuel apologized for lack of a proper jacket in the formal atmosphere of the faculty club. Miyamoto waved his hand, no matter.

After traditional cordialities and ordering their cold lunch Miyamoto said "I am very glad to have an American academic as a guest. For family reasons I am unable to travel. When our friend said that you were a mathematician and a philosophy concentrator who worked on machine language and was now studying Buddhism, I became eager to meet you. I meet so few Westerners with such a background, and trusting that metaphysics is of common interest, permit me to ask, to start us off, and in all sincerity, what do you imagine is the meaning of enlightenment? Luca speaks of salvation and grace. But he is Catholic. What do you think?"

Reuel thoughtfully fingered the tableware as he assembled an answer to this opening gambit. "To tell you the truth, I'm not sure it has a meaning. I think you probably know that the concept of being awakened, of enlightenment, has had a lot less weight in the Western philosophical tradition than in Asia. I think its nearest equivalent is the problem of meaning, or as we sometimes say, the meaning of meaning. And this, of course, begs the question of what is mind and consciousness. Which I believe must be understood as a condition precedent in the brain, before talking about enlightenment."

"Very well" said Miyamoto, "but in that case we must trust in logic and science to help us. Indeed, I am neither a Buddhist nor a Christian or of any other faith other than that of logic, rationality and knowledge. Epistemology, if you like. A faith in questioning. In my opinion there shouldn't be any incompatibility between natural science and the practice of Buddhist metaphysics. I don't like to use the word 'salvation'. But the concerns of what Buddhists describe as their 'deliverance-from-suffering-philosophy' is affected by how knowledge of their methodology is attained. How something like insight is learned is the question of Buddhist epistemology. And that is the investigation of what distinguishes logically justified belief from mere opinion. Yet, somehow, the concerns of the Buddhist 'deliverance-from-suffering-tradition' can lead us away from the modern philosopher's commitment to follow the argument wherever it leads. Otherwise. it's just stubborn stupidity or a convincing imagination, like science fiction."

"Then let me ask you Professor Miyamoto...."

"Call me Akira."

"What is meant by the word '*satori*' in Japan?"

"I would say that like the word 'awakening', it is an evasive term which traditionally describes seeing into one's true nature, without stating what is meant by 'true nature' or of even the meaning of one's own 'self' if you follow me. Zen Buddhism is presented to Westerners as a teaching on the 'deliverance-from-suffering-tradition' which Christian people term 'salvation.' I know that in English, some people use different words like 'realization' rather than the poetical 'enlightenment' to translate *satori*. For myself, I prefer, psychologically speaking, to call it an 'understanding'."

Reuel asked "As the experience is embedded in time, may I ask if *satori* is momentary or is it enduring? Is it ephemeral or is it life changing? And furthermore, is it causal?"

"Ah so. *Satori* does have this traditional sense of being sudden, as if within a metaphysical jurisdiction of the momentary. It even makes a fetish of the momentary! But we live in time, and how do we fit it into reality with our perspectival minds? How far does supreme knowledge extend? After all, we are just evolved apes. What can we really know about the universe and ourselves as knowers of the universe?"

"I'm asking you that question." said Reuel.

"Well, many people think there is a problem with how we can fit consciousness, or the mind, into a mindless universe. But there's an even deeper problem at the outset of such an inquiry, which is how can we know ourselves as knowers of our position in the universe? We don't know anything relevant about the universe *a priori,* by just thinking about it. It is basically impossible to know absolutely everything about physical reality. We can only know anything to the extent it is measurable, or at least observable. But can we observe our own mind, and do so without error, even as I change my own mental state by virtue of thinking about it?"

Luca interjected "It does sound like a paradox of self-consciousness. If I'm conscious of consciousness, consciously thinking about thinking, I change the state that I'm observing because my overall mental state is now different. Just as you said."

Miyamoto then picked this up. "This is where conventional logic does not apply. The Buddhist philosopher Nagarjuna, you recall? If there's no such thing as the ultimate nature of reality, then obviously, the question of logical structure isn't present. Technically speaking, the Heart Sutra on emptiness, teaches an uncommitted form of negation, which doesn't entail affirmation of any alternative. That's why '*satori*' is just brain activity which produces subjective understanding. It's like immersing and enjoying science-fiction, in my opinion. No? Do you follow?"

Reuel replied, "I'm just a novice in this area but I think that the Buddhist metaphysicians of ancient times would have a problem if their practices lead to modern standards of inquiry, which outrun verification in the natural sciences. Counterfeiting enlightenment must be an old problem. Is there any empirical evidence of what you call '*satori*', or sudden awakening? Is it just that some-body cleverly outwits a paradox in a koan, or engages in a private mind-to-mind meeting, Zen's *dokusan* interview with a teacher? There are surely lots of Zen students who illustrate their progress, like schoolchildren who cheat their teacher by copying answers out of a book without having worked the answer out for themselves. What I'm getting at is whether it isn't just another language game? When we, thinking animals, try to articulate our self-conception lin-guistically, by describing ourselves as 'conscious', or 'rational', our language itself doesn't guarantee that anything in physical or biological reality corresponds to this exact concept. How do we know that we're awakened without appreciating that the word '*satori*' picks out something in a reality that isn't made of words but of neurons?"

Luca joined the line of discourse. "Aren't we talking about self-knowl-edge? Saint Thomas says that while God the creator knows himself by default, we earthly humans need to exercise time and effort to know our own minds. And that is the old eternal struggle for self-knowledge, isn't it? And further-more, self-knowledge isn't only hard-won, but it's always subject to revision. It's a moving target. Finally, let me say that while knowing that you don't know, is good, but that belief belongs to a different category than knowledge."

Reuel picked it up. "I agree. The self, if it exists, is certainly fluid. But I think we all have to conclude, even though we don't entirely know how, that there's no consciousness of one's self without a neural correlate. Some part of the brain has to be there for me to exist, and to ask such questions. But you see, what exactly are we looking for? It's not as if the words 'consciousness' or '*satori*' have one meaning that we can look at, and find the correlate for that meaning in the nervous system. How should a specific meaning of the English word 'consciousness' or the Japanese word '*satori*' be represented in brains? That is my question."

Miyamoto said "Of course, there might be better and non-scientific ways of understanding the Buddhist teaching of non-self. Poetic ways, for example. The Zen approach tries to attain a state of non-conceptual intuition through a practice of meditation. Just by sitting still."

Reuel said "Then there's no reason why it couldn't also be achieved by a walking meditation. And yet we're entitled to ask who is really to judge what is achieved by this? How long must one sit, for example? Nine years?

"That's exactly why awakening is always subject to revision" said Luca.

Miyamoto continued. "Of course, '*satori*' isn't necessarily incompatible with scientific naturalism. While Zen has no interest in anything supernatural, yet at the same time, it's totally indifferent to the methods of the natural sciences as a way of finding out the physical nature of reality. I suppose that's why Zen has the reputation of being anti-intellectual, with its distaste for philosophical studies. A subjective mind-to-mind transmission in private practice seems to be its principal validation. And that inevitably gets us into the 'theory of mind' business, doesn't it?"

Luca came in again. "I might have some knowledge of my own mind that might seem straightforward, but isn't it similar to the mind-reading we do towards other people? Self-knowledge implies a theory of mind. It's the ability to keep track of what someone else thinks, or knows, even if it isn't immediately obvious from their behavior. And these are just our own mental representations, which might not even be true, and have to get revised. I might say something about myself which would mean different things to different people. Reading other minds isn't something we're born with. And so, I think reading my own mind isn't something I was born with. It comes from some kind of mental development. And we have to act on an understanding that other minds can hold different beliefs about the world to one's own. That's likely true about the three of us at this table."

"It might be the case that the mind is nowhere nearly as unified as we think" said Miyamoto, "just as the brain might not be as unified. If the mind is not unified, if there is a sense in which there is not a single self, but maybe many selves in one animal, why would the brain have to be unified as the underlying material-energetic reality?"

Reuel said "That's where natural science comes in. I do like Luca's idea of mind-reading applied to your own mind. The classical theory-of-mind is our ability to impute the mental states of others. But it is interesting to apply the theory to ourselves. It must involve having recursive understandings of descriptions. When I wonder if you know that it's raining outside and that our plans need to change, I'm supposing the state of your knowing about the weather. I can also think about my own mind just as well with a little effort. I can actually make judgements about my own cognitive processes. I can even be guilty of lying to myself, deceiving myself. Even about the experience of awakening, of *satori*. Isn't that so?"

Miyamoto went on. "If self-awareness is a privileged theory of mind directed at ourselves, just as we mind-read about others, then surely this is mostly a matter of how we make inferences. Just like taking a third-person perspective on ourselves. Frequently we make inferences which are erroneous, like you said, even about ourselves. That's why this leads to the necessary questioning of the genuineness of '*satori*', 'enlightenment', 'awakening', et cetera. That's what I'm trying to get at. Genuineness."

Reuel added "But obviously, at the same time, attributing awareness to ourselves and to others is itself direct evidence of consciousness, isn't it? Inference is an activity our brains are doing. And brains evolved long before the existence of language. There's nothing English or Japanese about brains. I'm pretty sure that the meaning of the word '*satori*', which is about subjective experience, doesn't have its precise equivalent in other natural languages, like German *aufklärung*, or 'awakening', or something else in English. Sometimes we even end up importing the foreign word to our native language. '*Satori*' for example, gets to be an imported word that's like a fresh seed sewn on the ground of an old discussion. The problem in language, before we speak about reality, is that we have to be aware of the vocabulary we use for expressing our knowledge. And that lands us right back to the paradox of self-consciousness. In fact, we experience the thought of our own awareness with silent words, silent meanings, silent sounds in our heads, without real syntax."

Miyamoto went on. "Having silent sounds, thoughts, in your head isn't the same as real silence. Luca told me mister Wittgenstein is one of your favorites. Do you think there are ideas we can know without language, knowledges of which we cannot speak? You know his famous sentence: 'What we cannot speak about we must pass over in silence.' What do you think that means for philosophy?"

Reuel replied "Logically it means you put up a language argument or shut up. Philosophers think about thinking. And we argue about the structure of arguments, which is why logic is required. But we won't know a great deal about the absolute nature of reality because in order to do so we have to rule out an infinite number of hypotheses, most of which can't even be tested. We can't even remotely demonstrate in principle that we can ever have a full account of what exists, a complete list of all the facts. There's no single overall theory for all the facts. It's impossible for me to imagine that we will ever have a grand unified theory about reality. I think we are permanently blind. The whole thing is just amazing. The existence of inferential thought in the mind seems miraculous."

Luca said "Bingo."

Miyamoto said "Take numbers. You are a mathematician. Numbers aren't real objects in space and time, are they? The number two isn't located in a specific place. It would be misguided to wonder where the number three is today. Is the number seven a fact even if it is a universal mental construct? If I think about noodles, they won't satisfy my hunger. Imagined noodles are not a kind of food. Do you think 'satori' is a fact?

Reuel answered "Our talking about it is a fact. We're just primitives of an unknown culture. Realms of wonder, like beauty, have nothing to do with abstractions like numbers or logic. Wittgenstein was clear on this. Just think of music for example, sunsets, Buddhist art."

"Well," said Miyamoto, "we're beginning to go in circles, trying to understand how phenomenal consciousness fits into mindless reality. There are illusions. That's the problem. And it's not enough to point out the presence of an illusion if we can't even explain how it arises. The problem is that some of our arguments about illusionism get used in order to undermine the value of rationality. If we can overcome the element of illusion into a legitimate knowledge claim, then we begin to know how things really are. Evolution has merely provided us with a mental tool structure that hides absolute reality from us. Possibly our whole conscious mental life is just a kind of lawful illusion. But enough about *satori* for today. After all, we can learn how to ride a bicycle without words, but Buddhist enlightenment still remains elusive. And speaking of beauty, you should see our main collection of Buddhist art in the National Museum in Nara. And the Todai-ji temple. You must go see them. Would you like some more coffee?"

"Yes," said Reuel, "it's very refreshing, even exciting for me, to have a discussion of *satori* at this level. I thank you for the invitation. A philosophy lunch seminar at a distinguished university. Makes me feel nostalgic."

"We must do it again. When are you leaving Japan?"

"Probably in the next week or so. I'm eager to get home. I've been away almost a year."

"Well, perhaps we can meet again before you leave. I would enjoy it. When someone confronts Zen, a beginner's mind can be useful."

Luca said "Not necessarily. When someone confronts Christianity, a beginner's mind can be a hindrance. Imagine an old person trying to learn Latin without difficulty. It's always hesitant, rarely self-assured."

"Perhaps that's only true for slow-learners" said Miyamoto. "At any rate, *sayonara*, until we meet again."

"*Sayonara*" said Reuel.

All three bowed slightly.

ॐ

The next day, deciding to see the National Museum, Reuel took an evening train for the brief trip to Nara, booked himself for two nights at the Mikasa hotel, and after showering and breakfast began the morning with a visit to the world's largest bronze statue of the Buddha, 50 feet high, in the Todai-ji temple complex which lay next to the National Museum. The gigantic metallic enormity of the historic sage's iconic representation seemed almost to signify an extra-planetary influence. The small temple park which surrounded it contained a number of tame grey deer, and provided Reuel with a small bench whereon he meditated for a while. And, thereafter, went on to the museum.

While many secular examples of Japan's artistic culture were everywhere abundant and impressive, the museum's Buddhist art collection left him rather cold and disappointed. The sculptures seemed rigid and understated in comparison to curvaceous sensuality of the workmanship he had seen in India, and the pale scroll paintings lacked the colored energetic flamboyance of Tibetan art. The most satisfying and absorbing works to his taste were the unsanctified ink and wash paintings of mother nature, her trees, ponds, hills, and clouds, where here and there was a small figure or two, and an occasional temple, all expressing the Japanese word "*yugen*", for things deep and mysterious.

Finished with viewing the exhibits, he found a cafeteria for a coffee, a bookstall with uninteresting titles, and a large giftshop with a cage of canaries at its entrance. Lured in by the thought of a souvenir, he examined various museum reproductions, and was nearly tempted to buy a miniature of the Todai-ji bronze Buddha, when he strolled over to a wall bearing contemporary crafts by local artists. There was a shelf of three tea bowls which caught his eye. The squarish hand-formed one in the middle was appealing and he considered buying it. It had a brown glaze, descending half-down in a ragged circle of tears, to the unaffected dull black surface of the circular lower portion. The prickly coarse clay texture of the glazed exterior provided a noticeable sensation to his touch. And the bowl's highly polished interior revealed a streak of autumnal red descending from a narrow and blistered part of the otherwise smooth rim. It was an object of beauty. He was tempted, but fearful it could be damaged before he reached Cambridge. A small white card in Japanese and English showed its price in Yen, equivalent to nearly six hundred dollars. The artist's name was Hideko Sato.

The memory stirred in his mind and was quickly verified within his wallet, wherein a torn crease of paper with that name and a telephone number lay in the billfold. Elsie Hornbein had given it to him when asked if she knew anyone in Japan. It was after they had talked of Dorsit's experience of atrocities in Burma by soldiers trained in Zen. There was something about her friend Hideko, a movie idea she was undertaking about Japanese religious soldiers in Nanking. Threats of some kind against her. What else did Elsie say? Yes! That Hideko was unmarried, spoke English, and was now a potter. Reuel determined on the spot to buy the tea bowl with his credit card and call her. The gift-shop clerk was amused, cushioned the bowl with wadding in a small wooden box, tied it up with a ribbon, and assisted Reuel with the phone call.

Hideko answered on the third ring. "*Moshi moshi.*"

"Hideko?"

"*Hai.*"

"I am friend of Elsie Hornbein. You speak English?"

"Pretty good. You know Elsie?"

"Yes, I do, she gave me your telephone number. I am in Nara, at the National Museum. I just bought a beautiful tea bowl you made. I would like to meet you. I just came down from Kyoto."

"Wow. What's your name?"

"My name is Reuel. Could I take you to dinner?"

"No. That's very nice, but I'm working. Maybe later this week?"

"I was heading back to Kyoto tomorrow."

"So sorry."

"Elsie told me about the movie you tried to make, about Buddhist soldiers. So, I wanted to meet you."

There was a very long pause. Reuel wondered if she was still there.

"Hello?" he said.

"Elsie maybe save my life" she answered.

"What? How?"

"Long story."

"Maybe we could have some tea? Not dinner."

"Okay. You come now to my workshop. I can tell you. I have kiln to manage. You know what is kiln?"

"Yes. Where do I go?"

"Take taxi to Naramachi district. Tell driver number 12 Shibbatsu-ji. You will see green metal garage with two chimneys. Ring bell."

"Wonderful. I'm on my way. Thank you."

The taxi dropped him at that address. It was on a narrow street filled with small houses, many decorated with flower pots and short bushes. Some boys were flying a kite. The green metal shed, an anomaly on the street, was attached to a white and narrow two-story building. He studied the neighborhood for a moment, unable to draw a conclusion, and rang the bell.

A moment later she opened the door and studied him for several seconds without saying a word. Reuel saw a tall woman, nearly his own height and age, her black hair streaked with grey, clad in overalls, wearing glasses, a lit cigarette in her lips, and an exceptionally beautiful face. Instantly he experienced an intense wish for her to love him. It had been a long time since he had experienced that feeling.

"I'm Reuel."

"Come in. I'm in the middle of firing."

He entered a large cement-floored and overcrowded shed. There were skylights. There was a potter's wheel. He saw mounds of clays of different shades half-wrapped with moist cloths on stands of various heights. There were short open-topped barrels. There were stained tables on saw-horses crowded with varieties of rasps and files, pincers, trowels, tongs and instruments with unclear meanings. There were shelves of labeled metal cans of colored dyes and glazes. There were racks of brushes in all sizes and shapes. There were chest high pedestals bearing other covered heaps of clay. There were two kilns each with its own chimney on either side of a window facing a back yard. There was a refrigerator. There was a large sink. There were buckets of muddy water. There was an office chair on wheels and several benches. There were cigarette packages and ashtrays. A half-full whiskey bottle and some unclean glasses. A four-burner cooking range with a single cast iron kettle emitting steam from its spout.

"I can only offer you tea bags" she said, unless you would prefer what I'm drinking, cold saké."

"Oh, saké, that would be very nice. Yes. Better to talk with, no?"

"So, yes definitely, for the two of us. You will have to forgive me if I interrupt. I have two new tea bowls cooking in that old fashioned wood-fired kiln, and I have to pay attention. But kindly tell me about yourself while I work. About Elsie. Find a place to sit, please."

She removed a bottle of saké from the refrigerator, found a fresh cylindrical glass which she wiped with a slightly used towel, and filled Reuel's half-way up. "*Kampai*" she said with a gesture, and took a long swallow. Reuel echoed the *kampai* and sat on a bench to watch her carefully attend a kiln, and then add wood to the fire.

"You see" she said while pointing, "I have a gas-fired kiln over there, but this wood-fired one is more delicate and challenging, and I have to pay close attention to the thermometer on this side."

"Are there electric kilns?" he asked, to keep the conversation going.

"Of course, but I don't like them. They're for factories. Tea bowls made for export. You realize, Japan's greatest bowls, national treasures, were made centuries ago, long before electricity or gas." She said this while turning from him to remove the lids of two short drum-like barrels which she rolled close to the kiln. "Don't mind me, you can talk. Tell me about yourself. I just have to pay attention for the next few minutes."

Reuel felt awkward, but provided a capsule of his circumstance and upbringing to her back while she was turned away. He described his academic interest in philosophy, his recent journey through India, his experience with Buddhist meditations, both Theravadin and Mahayanist, and while avoiding mention of his brief enlightenment initiation experience received from Kunzang Rinpoche, he ended by recounting his tutorial on *Vajrayana* history from Elsie Hornbein in Darjeeling.

"And now you want a taste of Zen? Anyway, I love Elsie" she said over her shoulder. "I owe her a lot. She may have saved my life. Give me a moment, just here. I have to move the bowls exactly. Right now!"

With a set of tongs, she grasped one glowing bowl, dropping it into a barrel, causing a large burst of smoke, and replaced the lid. She did this rapidly again with the second bowl, dropping it into the other barrel, which burst into flame for a moment before it was lidded. Then, finally, she turned to Reuel with a smile of satisfaction.

"Now we can talk" she said. "Do you want my view of Zen?"

"What's in the barrels?" he asked.

"I had the first one filled with sawdust. The second was filled with straw. That made a big flame for a moment. It changes how they cool, and the smoke adds a special quality."

"How does that work?"

"The short or the long version?"

"The long version. I have a science background." He saw a touch of pleasure on her face.

"All right. Once in a while I throw a bowl on the wheel when I have something very particular in mind. But mostly I like hand forming them spontaneously using my intuition. There are some special fireclays I use for the first firing which gives me a slightly porous hard form when it cools. The porosity is very important. Then I paint on different slips, some thick some thin. Some are waxy which melt off in the kiln. Other coats are from glazes that fix different color stains and textures, like smooth or with crackling. Sometimes matte, sometimes glossy. Then everything, absolutely everything, depends on temperatures and timings, both in the second firing, sometimes very hot, sometimes low, sometimes fast, sometimes slow, and all of this again during the cooling times, like now in those barrels. And almost always, unpredictable results. Frozen accidents. That's the beauty."

"And the barrels? Reducing chambers?"

"Ah, you know, exactly! You see, usually I do cooling in open air, but sometimes I use my barrels for charring to add special character. They slow the chemical reaction and help fix the colors. And the smoke is important because it stains the unglazed surface parts black. From the carbon."

"I see" he said, "Let me show you something" and went to his bag. He removed the small wood box from the museum gift shop, opened it, took out the bowl and showed it to her.

"Ohhhhhh" she exclaimed, with an expression of surprise and sincere delight on her face. "Ohhhhh" once again. And still once more as she held out two hands to take the bowl from him. She looked it over carefully, fondly, turning it over to look at the bottom. "Look" she said, while holding it out for him to see, "the imprint of my seal. I made this over a year ago. It's a good piece. How nice to see it again. How much did you pay?"

"Around six hundred dollars. I couldn't resist when I saw your name. It was my ticket to meet you."

"Expensive ticket" she said, somewhat coyly. She then refilled their saké glasses and sat down on the rolling office chair to face him, inspecting him again, more closely. "Now, why did you want to meet me so much?"

"It's something about Zen at war. About Buddhist violence."

"I see. Well, you know, it's possible that Zen is not really about Buddhism."

"Are you serious?"

"Well, we can talk about it. What were you doing in Kyoto?"

"I'm on my way home from India. I was visiting a friend who is on the faculty at Doshisha. We had lunch with a professor who insisted I go down to Nara to see the museum."

"Which professor?"

"Miyamoto."

"You had lunch with Professor Miyamoto? That's something. He's the national atheist. Miyamoto-san is very special in Japan."

"You know him?"

"I took a course from him."

"You were at Doshisha?"

"Yes. I've an honors degree in European history. Twelve years ago."

"Oh my, I didn't know that. Your English sounds pretty good."

"So, what did Elsie tell you about me?"

"Hardly anything. Just that you got in trouble trying to make a film about Zen and war. Nothing else really. I became interested in that subject because I met someone in India who had been a prisoner of war in a cruel Japanese army camp in Burma."

"Yes. Well, I can tell you about my story."

"She also said you were an ex-Buddhist."

"Ah."

"And unmarried."

"Ah ha."

"Tell me a little about yourself. Where did you grow up? How did you come to know Elsie?"

"It's a long story."

"I have the time" he insisted. "You are rather interesting I think."

She gave him several closer looks of examination and went to the refrigerator to refill their glasses again from the rest of the bottle. She sat down on the rolling chair again, growing slightly more friendly and curious of him.

"*Kampai*" she said, raising her glass.

"*Kampai.*"

"Tell me how old you are" she inquired.

"I'm nearly thirty-eight. How about you?"

"I am about one year less. I was born in Kyoto."

"Do you remember the war?"

"Of course. At first, when I was little, it was something far away, in Korea and China. We listened to the radio. Then, when we bombed Pearl Harbor everything changed. Food changed. Clothes changed. Men went far away. Necessities hard to find. My mother became a nurse. Father was away two years in the Philippines. Almost died from malaria. We collected scrap metal. Food was scarce."

"How is it that you speak English so well?"

"From my father, plus I spent about a year in California.

"You did?"

"Yes, and before that, I had English at college, Doshisha. From Shakespeare to H.G. Wells, believe it or not. At home, as a child before the war. Father was adoctor who had studied English. Before I was born, before he married, he was two years in Madison, Wisconsin, studying diseases, one of which almost killed him. He became an infectious disease officer with our army in the Philippines. After years away he came back to us in a hospital ship, nearly dead from Malaria. When war ended, American Sixth Army Occupation Corps headquarters was located in Kyoto. Father became the principal Japanese doctor for civilian medical needs, for infectious diseases. Very common. Before anti-biotics. American doctors came to our house many times. Bringing us food. English was like our second language. We were a non-religious household. Shinto was disgraced. Emperor worship was finished. Buddhism was just passive and useless, and Zen

Buddhism, especially, was badly stained. The whole pre-war Japanese culture was a heap of rubble and ashes. Kyoto, the cultural and intellectual center of old Japan, fortunately without factories, was mostly untouched. Do you know, at only the last minute, Americans picked Nagasaki for the second bomb, instead of Kyoto?"

"Yes, I heard that. That very terrible weapon. Radioactivity maybe worse than sudden death. I do feel for so many of you. My heart feels sad, and tender."

She gave him one more piercing look of examination, and continued rather freely. "Later, in college, at Doshisha, I was a communist, an atheist, a party girl. I fell in with a group of friends who were getting into the film business. People around Kurosawa. You know him?"

"Of course. 'Rashomon.'"

"This was around when he was making 'Ikiru'. We were a little wild. Young survivors. I started smoking cigarettes. Even hashish from India. Dancing to crazy music. Parties all the time. Love affairs. We thought we were revolutionaries. I wanted to make a movie about the war and Buddhism. Friends wanted to help. A well-known actor was going to play the leading part. We liked the Stanislavsky method. So I studied Zen a little to get inside my character's minds. I wrote a screenplay."

"What was the plot?"

"Hahh. Takes place long ago. In Nanking, China, 1937. Only six characters with speaking parts. Three men. A general, a lieutenant, and a sergeant. And the three women they rape. It was to begin at the first few days of the great massacre of civilians. Hundreds of thousands were killed, and intentionally so. Civilians. Thousands of children. I believe history made Hiroshima to be the payback."

"What happened to the idea? Elsie said you had trouble."

"Yes. Trouble. They might have killed me. You know, when preparing, first I studied a little Zen, just to get a taste. Hard for a woman. Zen temples, priests, many of them army veterans, rejected me. Then I found Hakura Roshi.

Old man. He laughed at me. Rengejo-in temple. Small village in North. Soto Zen meditation. Just sitting. Tells me to watch my mind. I sit every day for many weeks. Roshi tells me to let go of my thoughts 'like leaves flowing down a river'. Always says meditation about letting thoughts go. But I like watching my thoughts. What is use of boredom? I'm writing a movie script, not just day-dreaming. I try to let go. Maybe some way meditation helps me train my brain to be better at thinking, for creative writing. Okay. I am still curious. Why stop thinking? I like my thoughts. Work out problems. Thinking can be beneficial. Can even be relaxing. At university, so many of us, young, are comfortable thinking about our studies, chemistry, law, history, Marxism, whatever. Practice improving our skill at thinking, making us more creative. Yes, everything is impermanent. Obvious. So what? I think Zen students don't look like they are enjoying life. If they are lucky maybe self-reflection makes them enjoy present moment, just to be alive. But you know, there are people who like themselves, without vanity, without egoism. For me, the delight I take in my thoughts is delight in my own strange life. Maybe Zen is only for unsatisfied people. No?"

"Are you ever unhappy?"

"Don't be foolish."

"Hideko, you're obviously a thoughtful person. I hear what you're saying. I'm sort of interested in whether there is such a thing as having a scientific view about inner peace. Not just like psychoanalysis, only to cure people. But under-standing what the brain is doing when it searches for meaning. It's very difficult."

"It sounds like you're trying to solve a paradox."

"Maybe, but maybe not. Take the Buddhist teaching on emptiness. Few people are able to understand the depth of that doctrine. Where everything gets connected by chance. How you and I meet today. What does it mean?"

"Listen, oh, what is your name again?"

"Reuel"

"Listen Reuel, maybe you think too much. Some over-educated people are like goldsmiths, they weigh everything. Some people suffer from a disease of the intellect. This can happen, like when you just said that about all phenomena being empty. That famous doctrine, the Heart Sutra that gets chanted. Almost the only text they know. The famous void. But then comes nihilism, whether you like it or not. Like Zen at war. You know koans? You know the one about the monk who cuts a cat in two just to make a point? You say it's just a story to illustrate something. Non-attachment. But that's what happened in Nanking. Buddhism makes lots of very easy excuses for a spectator. I actually took a course on Zen history at Doshisha. It's just as bad as your Christian history. Wars everywhere. For me, I think Zen has no real view of society, of politics, of economics, no idea of human progress, material or spiritual. It is always about other things. About its selfish mind. It will support any government, militaristic, fascistic, communistic or so-called democratic. And Zen's own organization is unchangeably feudalistic. And quietistic, and retreatist, and self-assured about this non-self business, and it actually teaches indifference as a way of thought."

"Wow. Ouch. I'd better stop." He closed his eyes and took a breath. "Come back to Elsie. Tell me more."

More saké was poured before she answered.

"Maybe she saved my life. Many people connected to the film business hear about my project. I get many warnings. More than a year. Priests come to see me. Once they come and get on knees to beg me. Some people refuse to talk with me. One investor changes his mind. Some actors withdraw. Cameraman is frightened. I get anonymous letters. I start getting threats. One day I get call from this lady at American embassy. The cultural attaché. Elsie. Japanese movies are big cultural thing in America. She hears about me. I go to see her. We become friends. One day she tells me her people have learned that Yakuza have made contract to kill me. You heard of Yakuza?"

"Yeah. Japanese gangsters. Like American mafia."

"Yakuza stories get used in Japanese crime movies. Yakuza frighten everybody. Many Yakuza actually do morning Zen meditations. Some Yakuza even become Zen priests. This is really true. Elsie then tells me a Japanese veteran's group is sending warnings to stop my movie idea. I know this. It becomes gossip.

Many people know about it. I try to be brave. Elsie tells me she is Tibetan Buddhist and wants to protect me. American military police have informers from inside Yakuza. Old veterans. Yakuza are going to kill me they say, soon. Make it look like accident. For first time I am now very frightened. I am so young. American diplomats hear about this. A planned crime about historical events, politics. I cannot control. What to do? Elsie asks if I can afford to go to America. With visitor's visa or student visa. Disappear for a time. Forget about movie she says. Okay, I liked opportunity to go to America. Hollywood. So, I have enough money to buy a ticket. Mother's family, distant cousins, are Nisei, Japanese Americans in California. I can go see them. Elsie says to bring my passport. And I get visa. I leave home. Goodbye. End of film project. Elsie saved my life. Everybody happy. In my mind whole thing is just shriveled remains of my younger wasted self."

"You don't look so wasted."

"That was long ago. Now, I'm getting to be an old potter. See the wrinkles around my eyes? In Japan, for a woman, my age is considered old. When you're young you don't pay enough attention to shortness of life. You don't realize in spiritual teachings that there is a hidden physiology, like a clock in your body over time. History doesn't tell us what we need to learn about growing into our physical old age. Physical old age, not mental. Did Bodhidharma have rheumatism? Did Lao-Tze suffer from hemorrhoids? Was Confucius bothered by cold weather? All we have is lots of story-telling."

She poured the last of the saké.

"*Kampai*"

"*Kampai*"

"What about pleasure?" he asked. He could feel the alcohol. "The two of us can still have pleasure, can't we?"

"You're very clever."

"Are you reading my mind?"

"I think so. Do you know Ikkyu, that sex-loving Zen master?"

"No. Sounds pretty good."

"See that ink scroll of calligraphy over there" she pointed, "between those two small windows. It's a poem by Ikkyu Sojun. I will translate it for you."

She recited it with only a few hesitations

Evening rain on the lake, the moon amid the clouds
How wonderful to recite poems night after night
Studying Zen, one loses Original Mind
And such a river of love to sleep with a beautiful woman

"I can definitely relate to that" he said.

"Really?"

She went on. "According to the legend, five centuries ago, on a summer night, Ikkyu, a young monk, was meditating when he heard the cry of crows and had a deep realization, a *satori*, which came to him. He decided at once to be true to himself and began a crazy career as a poet and a brothel regular. He simply taught that sexual desire was a natural need, no different than the thirst for water. Denying sexual desire failed the purpose of Zen, he said, which was to help a person discover their true nature."

"I can't possibly disagree" said Reuel, sensing a faint shared murmur of arousal. And pondered why was she was telling him this. Maybe it was the saké.

"Sexual desire" she said while looking directly at him, "according to Ikkyu, was a part of a person's nature. Enlightenment could actually be deepened by partaking in sex, with lovers, prostitutes and even monastic homosexuality. Ikkyu says that sex is part of human nature, and is therefore purer than hypocritical monastic practice. Brothels offered him a better audience than temples for teaching the unity of opposites, the idea that light and dark were one, your non-duality. He used pleasure and poetry to get Zen meaning through to common people."

Reuel took a moment before he spoke. "Hideko, you know, this is quite amazing. There must be some kind of secret underground message I'm getting.

You see, Elsie told me almost the exact same story about another sex-pot, but that was about a Tibetan Buddhist yogi-poet named Drukpa Kunley. It's fantastic, both of these guys sound like Allen Ginsberg."

"Who?"

"An American Buddhist poet into free-love. Polymorphous pleasure. It's in the air. The magnetism of sex. I can feel it. You must feel it. It's a fearless thirst."

"What is it really?" she asked.

"A hunger for intimacy. The universe wants to reproduce itself. That feeling of attraction. Don't you feel it? We have to be honest."

"Let's slow down. It's better that way. I think those wild poets want us to do something which is simple in principle, but which we find difficult. Maybe because the modern age. Just to experience some kind of natural contentment with our modern feelings is difficult. Like doing things slowly. Our modern sense of rushed time becomes like a sickness. In the old days, before electricity, it was fairly common to be relaxed. To play with a cat. To pull weeds from a garden. To hear a neighbor tell a story. To listen to birds. Living in the moment, and for the moment. Feeling at home among life's natural variety. The attraction between man and woman coming slowly, in balance. Don't you think?"

For nearly a minute, they sat staring intensely at one another, almost like a contest. Then she began to laugh and tried to explain. "Look at what's going on right now. Really, we have to laugh at ourselves."

Reuel chuckled softly in a reflex, saying "we're laughing at ourselves that we're laughing."

"This must be enlightenment" she said with a grin. "You know, it's true. Honestly, I swear, once, long ago, while reading the Heart Sutra, I began to laugh without knowing why. Can you imagine if humor was a virtuous object of life? A solution to all paradoxes?"

"Nice work if you can get it" he said, "but there's too much pain and cruelty out there, and suffering is everywhere as I've heard. Think of Zen at war."

"No. Stop. Just don't think about that, in our here and now. Stop those thoughts. Sense our momentariness, where we are like puppets in a show. And we know the plot, don't we?"

"I think you are ahead of me."

She stood up and made a gesture toward the street. "I'm getting hungry. Let's go next door to my house. I'll cook us some ramen with crabmeat. Be patient. I'll heat up some more saké."

An hour later they were in bed together.

It happened as follows. Hideko's house, adjacent to her metal work-shed, was a compact two-story building of small rooms with low ceilings. Aside from a lavatory and entry foyer, the street level floor consisted of a single wooden planked-floor room combining an open modern kitchen with a wide and comfortably furnished living and dining area. One entire wall was filled with shelves of books. A door to the rear opened on a yard revealing a vegetable garden and a miniscule hut. The upper story of the house, reached by a narrow flight of stairs, led to a short corridor. On one side was a sleeping room with a broad bed resting on a floor of tatami mats. On the corridor's other side, a bathing room furnished with a slate floor, a closeted toilet, sink, shower stall, and a deep porcelain tub.

When he entered the house Reuel had a sensation of visceral pleasure. For the first time since leaving Cambridge over a year earlier he experienced the feeling of being in someone's personal space. There had been numerous hotel rooms, a ship's cabin, a commune house in Cuernavaca, roadside lodges in India, the Planters Club, and Kyoto's church rectory. This was a woman's lived-in home, imbued with her personality, her intimacies, and the patina of years.

At first, they stayed silent. As Reuel took his time quietly inspecting the bookshelves, at least two-thirds filled with Japanese titles, Hideko filled a metal pot with boiling water and immersed a fresh bottle of saké in it. While waiting for it to heat, she put a long-playing record of a solo *shakuhachi* flute on a phonograph, at a low volume. Then two thick glass tumblers taken from a cupboard were then half-filled with the warm fortified rice wine.

They sat at opposite ends of a sofa preparing to enjoy the taste of the drinks.

"*Kampai*" she said, "once again."

"*Kampai*".

They drained their glasses in a few long draughts. "If Japan's taste interests you" she remarked, "I explain that this is a special saké from Kubota, in Niigata prefecture. I serve it a little less than hot. Do you notice velvety texture, long-lasting taste? And strong *umami*. You know what is *umami*?"

"No."

"A fifth flavor. Not well-known in U.S., but important in Japan. Not sweet, not salty, not bitter, not sour. Umami. Maybe like meat. Maybe like Zen. Maybe like you, has a strange personality. Flavor hard to describe. But you are a scientist. What shall we talk about? Tell me, what is *umami*?"

Reuel sensed she was inviting him to something. He tried going along. "I would say there are vibrations in the brain, which we can recognize but are hard to put into words. Like my brain's hopeful thoughts about a new person I meet. For that matter, even the brain's thoughts about itself. Even when sitting still. So many things are hard to describe. Like what all that saké is doing to us right now."

"I can see you" she said, testing him, "but here are wavelengths we don't see and vibrations we don't hear, aroma molecules we can't smell or taste, there are objects so small that we do not feel. And so, we know there are invisible psychic forces at work on us which we are unable to clarify. Don't you agree?"

"Like right now" he remarked.

"Like right now" she said with an odd intonation, and stood up. "We're hungry. No? Time to eat?"

She went to the stove, lowered the flame, and stirred the noodles and the crabmeat. He rose and followed her, and brought his body to press himself gently against the contour of her back, timidly bringing his hands forward about her waist, his face softly in her hair. A long moment passed this way before she turned, wiping her hands on the sides of her overalls, and pulled him close, wet tongues began probing and dancing in their mouths as eyeglasses skewed on her nose.

They tottered to the sofa, enjoying the pleasure of their faces glued to one another. Fumbling with one hand he unbuckled the clasps holding the straps of her overalls and awkwardly began to pull them down. He reached up under her shirt and fondled her unsheathed breasts. He lowered his hand, discovering she was not wearing underpants. Her hand reached for the bulge of his erection and in an unintended climax of sudden sexual excitement which he could not forestall he ejaculated into his pants.

"Ohh" he groaned, "I didn't want that to happen so quick. It's been a long time since I've been with anybody."

"I know. I can tell" she said rather kindly. "But now there's no rush. Let's go upstairs. I'll bring us food."

Up in the bedroom Reuel undressed rapidly, slipped half under the coverlet, propped himself against the headboard with a pillow, and waited. He tried to watch his thoughts but they were out of control. He surrendered to a resigned patience. Cosmic forces were obviously in charge.

Minutes passed and he grew calm. Then Hideko arrived carrying a tray with two steaming bowls, chopsticks, and fresh glasses of saké. She was barefooted, overalls missing, and now clad only in her shirt which reached mid-thigh. Sitting cross-legged on top of the covers she offered Reuel a bowl and smiled shyly at him.

"How are you?" she asked.

"I'm restored, and very happy."

They ate their small portions of ramen in silence and finished the wine.

"How long since you were with a woman?" she asked.

"A great many months now. And once in Mexico. A houseful of people using drugs. In India I was very sexually hot for Elsie but she had no interest. How about you? How long has it been?"

"A few months. Desire comes and goes. I can content myself."

"No boyfriend?"

"No more boyfriends. No more Japanese boyfriends."

"I'm lucky then."

"You are lucky. The moment I saw you."

"I return to Kyoto tomorrow."

"That's okay. You are lucky today. I teach a pottery class every evening tomorrow and after."

"I love you."

"Very nice. Nothing lasts. I am going to bathe."

He watched her leave the room, a beautiful and sexually desirable body. He felt calm now, alone with his thoughts, unsure of trying to guess what she expected of him. He breathed slowly, listening to the water filling her bath. Without a touch of anxiety, he hoped the thread of his self-confidence wasn't misplaced. As if in a meditation practice, he let his thoughts dissolve into nothingness. Observing the ineffable touchstone of the absolute nothing which Kunzang Rinpoche had given him in Kalimpong.

Time passed and Hideko returned to the bedchamber clad only in an oversized silken kimono, embroidered densely with colorful dragon-flies and white lotus blossoms on a blue background. She sat cross-legged again on the coverlet next to him. The loose kimono robe with its wide sleeves covered her entire body, even her folded hands. A cocked eyebrow, a wanton look upon her face, and like *umami*, a faint odor on her of musk and flowers which defied description.

Reuel observed a surge of prurient recollection and said to her "We look exactly like a picture from a collection of *shunga* paintings I saw in Kyoto. As if we were live models about to fuck."

"What about their faces?" she asked. "Don't the geisha look bored to you?"

"I don't think so. They seem to be concentrating on their private sensations."

"Not sharing?"

"Good question."

"Who do you think enjoys sex more?" she asked. "Women or men?"

"I've never been a woman. Whom do you think?"

"Women." She provided him a dissolute smile.

"Do you have filthy thoughts?"

"Many."

He pushed the coverlet down, exposing himself, aroused. She looked at his parts with interest for a moment, then opened her kimono wide, revealing her naked self and came to him, stretched out, to kiss him lasciviously on the mouth. His fingers reached down for her.

"Now we go very, very, very slowly" she whispered, "let's keep looking at our faces."

"Yes" he said, "exactly. Let's share it, very slowly."

In over the half century which followed this single night with Hideko Sato, Reuel's memory had been stamped and sealed by the amazing excitation and the duration of its erotic intensity. It is well-known that one of the most excruciating forms of physical pain is found in the prolonged act of giving birth. Yet its memory remains entirely mental, and can even be recalled with a shrug. Similarly, it is well-known that one of the most intense forms of physical pleasure is found in the crescendo of sexual climax. Yet its memory also remains entirely mental, and may be recalled with a mere sigh or less. In general, such are the stoical joys of sorrows remembered, and the wistful sorrows of joys recalled. So it was.

So, following rounds of erotic sexual exertion, artfully practicing the skill of prolonging its pace, they found a quiet span to talk as intimates now, almost as if they were siblings of forgotten ancestors. Reuel told Hideko of Greenwich Village, of philosophy study, of Ulla and his daughters, of his friend

Bob Adler, of the boat he sailed across an ocean, of his experience at the birth of the computer industry with IBM, of the doctoral program at the Massachusetts Institute of Technology, of the meaning of machine language, and of the strange conjunction of LSD and spiritual thought along with his long-standing interest to hybridize neuroscience with Buddhism.

"And what about you?" he then asked. "What happened when you were in the States? How did you become a potter?"

"American culture was so different. That trip changed me a lot. I was on a three-month tourist visa so an idea of applying to UCLA in film studies was out. I didn't have much money, leave alone tuition, and there were no jobs of any kind in Hollywood for a foreigner. So, that's when I gave up on the whole idea of making movies. The only people I knew of in America were some third cousins, born in the U.S., whose parents came over from Japan in the 1920s. They had a raisin farm up in the big valley. I went to see them and ended up picking grapes with a friendly bunch of Mexicans. Then a grand-uncle died and the family went down for a funeral ceremony in Ventura, where there was a long-standing Nisei Soto sect Zen community. I was amazed to see that two of the priests were westerners in robes. Turns out that its meditation zendo also got used by rock climbers, and surfers, cyclists and kids coming from UC Santa Barbara. I had no idea Zen was getting popular in America. The Roshi, Daichi Wanaka, came over from Japan about eight years before, when the old Roshi died. After the funeral I ended up talking to one of the western priests, a very relaxed and friendly guy and so I decided to give up cutting grapes, to hang out and share rooms with these western Zen students. For some of them it was more like a social club than a religious institution. I ended up going rock-climbing in Yosemite with my new friends once every few weeks and occasionally practiced sitting by doing wall-facing when back in Ventura. Wanaka Roshi's talks were all about letting go. Thinking about thinking is wasted energy he says. Just practice the usual Zen stuff, open-mind, non-attachment, observe the emptiness, no picking and choosing, practice indifference. Blah blah. Heard it all before. But I'm not a serious student so I don't get *dokusan* interviews with him. Then, one day, I see the Roshi with one of the serious western students shopping in the

Ventura food market. He sees me and we speak courteously one or two minutes in Japanese. I don't think he knows my name. I ask about his transmission lineage, He says 'Oda Sakomoto Roshi'. I make polite little bow and move away. Oda Sakomoto was Japan's main apologist for military war crimes. And Oda Sakomoto was probably the single main person in the effort to stop my film project. I believe he asked the Yakuza to kill me."

"Wow, that must have been a shock. But Wanaka Roshi didn't know who you were?"

"No. I was just another polite Japanese face from the Nisei community. But I never wanted to go back to that Zendo afterwards."

"Was Sakomoto with the army in China?"

"No. He spent the war in Tokyo, at army headquarters. Always giving interviews in newspapers. 'Religion must preserve the existence of the State' was his philosophy. Zen was a religion of will-power. Always claiming that imperial-way Buddhism enables soldiers to die on the battlefield in a noble cause. Victory in a just war was a task of Buddhism. Zen would raise bushido, the iron-willed samurai moral code combined with the emptiness of self. That the ordinary world of life and death was identical with Nirvana. Can you imagine? To find calmness as you kill or are killed yourself? Sakomoto was one of the Buddhist leaders who encouraged the drafting of young boys to become kamikaze pilots on a one-way trip to non-existence. And even after the war, when there were trials for military crimes. Hundreds of senior officers were executed. Sakomoto was their main prison chaplain who accompanied them to the hanging platform. This was the imperial Zen master who gave his lineage transmission to little Wanaka Roshi of Ventura. And who was the Zen master who publicly wished that I would die."

"What then?" Reuel asked.

"I went rock-climbing. We had some cliffs, crags, where there were short routes. Some guys would come from Santa Barbara. One of them was Japanese, named Nanao Fukuda. Older than the others. Studying engineering. Good looking. Makes a direct move towards me. I am pretty unattached girl, fresh from Japan. He is homesick. We climb together. We go to motel. We make love. I go to Santa Barbara with him while he finishes degree. Live together. Overstay my visa. We are very happy. I get pregnant. We get married at county office in Oxnard. Nanao graduates with master's degree. I have miscarriage. We go back to Japan, to Okinawa, to Uruma prefecture. Fukuda family owns a textile factory. Makes sheets, towels, pillow cases, bedspreads, shirts and socks. Nanao is oldest son. Hard working at family business. Four years. We are happy together. But I cannot get pregnant."

"And Buddhism?"

"Just family events. We were not interested. Nanao used to say that Zen Buddhism was entirely based on a philosophy of indifference, that's all. And from what I've seen, I agree. Not just indifference, but a whole philosophy of indifference."

"You we're a housewife?"

"I was a housewife. Much free time. I became close friend of Nanao's older sister, Etsuko. She was an amateur potter. Had a little studio with a wheel. She teaches me about clay and how to throw pots. Enjoyable hobby. We play with glazes. We take our pots to be fired in Tsuboya district, famous for ceramic dishes and lion-dog figures. I start studying ceramics. I drive to Tsuboya some days every week. I become unpaid apprentice working with electric kilns. Then big tragedy. My husband, Nanao is killed in automobile crash. Head on collision from drunk driver coming round a curve at high speed at night with no headlights. Both drivers killed almost instantly. I am widow. Family in mourning. I am in Nanao's will. There is also large insurance. Family is kind to me. I am in big empty house. What to do? Tsuboya kiln master tells me there is small ceramic workshop for sale in Nara. Old proprietor died. Very low price. I fly to Osaka, rent a car, drive down here, meet with broker, inspect the workshop and house, so I buy everything, and begin my new life in Nara. That was almost five years ago. Now I am established for my tea bowls and am making hot love with an American visitor. Life is mysterious, isn't it?"

Following these biographical exchanges, they rested naked, holding hands, in a rather long and meditative silence, each wondering if they had unwittingly quenched their erotic fires. But then, finally, Reuel stirred up a few hot embers still around by probing Hideko on the subjects of masturbation and multiple partners.

Then they made love again, this time more as brother and sister, as intimate, honest, and sympathetic familiars, and after some epic climaxes, and after resting again, in one another's arms, they began to talk, now heart to heart.

"Do you think an orgasm gives us a taste of *nirvana*?" he asked.

"Maybe just the opposite" she replied. "Emptiness doesn't feel pleasurable, does it? And what's the point of enlightenment anyway? Is it just some kind of illusion to comfort us? Is craving the enjoyment of fucking sinful? It seems to me that if free sex is sin, and sin is only the illusion that sin is sin, then *satori* is also an illusion, and all this business about an end to suffering is also an illusion. And, forgive me, but all this constipated Zen sitting in a hard effort to be enlightened is just a lot of nonsense."

"But you never practiced that much. You're only a skeptical outsider."

"Oh yes? But what if I'm quick and practical? How about all those poor unenlightened people who have to work, feed children, put a roof over their heads, or all those who have died five minutes before they became enlightened? No, no I say, the universe itself must suffer in being what it is, and we must suffer with it. And the universe has joy, and we must be happy with it. So, I think, our universe is a paradox, and we have to laugh with it and at it. Like I said before when we were laughing in the studio."

"Are you saying that there's no such thing as realization?"

"No, just that it's momentary, and it doesn't last, and doesn't necessarily have to be life-changing. And doesn't necessarily require weird practices like self-denial. Suppose a person practices living in a cave for nine years and just the day before getting enlightened, that person dies! Was it all worth it? Does the effort to get enlightened require or assume that you have a fairly long life? And what's the point of struggling for enlightenment if the day before or after you get it, we die? Look, my dear Reuel, in other words, we must get it now, at this very instant, in a world in which every next moment may be our last. If not now, then when?"

"Those are strong views. Perhaps that's why Elsie told me you we're an ex-Buddhist. For myself, I don't think that being uninterested in a philosophical understanding of life is a helpful idea."

"You can be a Buddhist atheist, you know, but it still labels everything in a ritualistic way, and makes so many artificial categories, and creates a false consciousness which actually gets in the way of understanding reality. In my opinion almost everything ritualistic smacks of priests and rites which ultimately turn rotten. Religion is just a madness which jumps into the vacuum of the non-religious. I lived among Buddhists since childhood. But you come to it all grown up, like an old person trying to learn a new language without easy success. There's always insecurity in acquiring a new way of thinking. You never become fluent in it. A person is like an empty tire tube, inflated by the cultural mind in which they're born. The only question is the nature of the gas."

"You're beginning to sound like a Marxist."

"Marxists are just like Buddhists. I'm just a potter. I choose ugly truths over beautiful lies. One of my talents is making a virtue out of necessity. There's so much variety in life. So many interesting things around us just at home, where it's possible to be at ease and in balance. Why seek for something that isn't there?""

Reuel began experiencing the disadvantage one feels in a foreign country and felt weakened by the strength of her mind. In the cloud of contemplative silence that followed this tail-end conversation they both gradually fell asleep half-embracing under the coverlet.

The late daybreak was scarcely noticeable beyond the curtained windows. They finally stirred, opening their eyes simultaneously when a telephone was heard ringing, unanswered, from the floor below. She smiled at him.

"How are you?" she whispered.

"Very happy." They hugged for a bit, face-to-face, side-by-side. Reuel stroked her back down to the cleavage of her buttocks, then tentatively lower in slow slow motion, found moistness and touched an orifice. She exhaled deeply into his ear and brought her knee up over his hip. Her free arm drew his haunch close, pulling him in to enter her, two non-selves making quiet love. Two bodies, sharing the same mind. They lay on their sides this way, enjoying the slow and gentle sways for some minutes, abandoning any thirst for a climax, until at end, the slow sweet diminuendo of a final soft chord faded out into its own emptiness.

In the late morning they showered, dressed, went down, shared a breakfast of miso soup, pickled vegetable salad on steamed rice, and faced the day. Hideko suggested they take a walk to a nearby park where a group of ducklings had been hatched and could be seen testing themselves on a pond. She pointed out sights of the neighborhood, revealing how small things were actually quite interesting. The contents of a laundry line. The contrast of aged ceramic flower pots holding fresh flowers. The unique beard of the postman delivering mail. The dragon kite caught on the electric wires. Was it not all wonderful?

"When do you return to Kyoto? She asked.

"This afternoon, I suppose. There are frequent trains. Could we call a taxi to the station?"

"Of course. Bu let's walk back. I want to invite you to a tea ceremony, for the very first use of your bowl. In my little tea hut. Would you like that? To remember me."

"I will never forget you."

When they returned to the house Hideko asked Reuel to excuse her while she prepared herself. She changed out of her modern pants, pullover sweater and street shoes, in favor of a solid-colored grey kimono and a pair of thick slippers. Her hair was fixed up with a large comb above her neck. Asking Reuel for the bowl from the museum shop she placed it carefully into a hemp bag carried under her shoulder. Then she removed a large lacquered box from a closet, bowed slightly to him and said something softly in Japanese. Translating it to English, the formulaic words formally stated that she would have to prepare for his arrival and would return shortly to invite him. She urged him to feel at home, and exited to her back yard.

Alone in the house for a quarter of an hour Reuel wandered to the bookshelves and examined the titles. Almost all were in Japanese but there were nearly two dozen in English and he was amused to find, in addition to several books on pottery, technical manuals on the chemistry of glazes, an atlas of the United States, Volume One of Toynbee's "Study of History", H. G. Wells "The War of the Worlds", George Bernard Shaw's "Major Barbara", Margaret Mitchell's "Gone With the Wind", David Reisman's "The Lonely Crowd", and Oswald Spengler's "Decline of the West". This last holding his interest until Hideko rang a little bell, and stood waiting for him by the rear door to the yard.

"You are now my guest" she said. "Have you been to a tea ceremony before?"

"No. Never."

"It is said that tea ceremony should guide the guest to the reality of nothing special. Just an occasion to offer some aesthetic and intellectual enjoyment with peace-of-mind. So, nothing special, just tea. Just a few moments of harmony and tranquility taken in the middle of a day. Not very much talking. Guest enjoying the simplicity of the ritual in an atmosphere distinct from the fast pace of everyday life. Okay?"

"Thank you, Hideko, for inviting me."

She motioned for him to follow her into the yard. A dozen large flat stones embedded in the grass led to a small hut. There was a modest vegetable garden on its right. Hideko gestured to a sloped shelf on the ground near the entrance for him to leave his shoes. The lintel of the doorway was deliberately low and required him to stoop in order to enter the ceremonial room. A tatami mat floor measured barely eight-by-eight feet, and the ceiling lay closer to seven. There was a hanging scroll with three kanji characters in a shallow alcove. Two small cushions on the floor faced one another. Hers was yellow, his green. They sat facing each other, hardly more than a yard between them. On her left was a polished slab of tree trunk supporting a little bronze vase cast to imitate a cloth sack. A single fresh yellow flower emerged from the false tied-off neck. To her right, a cold electric hot-plate on which a cast-iron kettle rested alongside a low table holding utensils and a lacquered red cylinder. Reuel's empty tea bowl lay by itself on a bamboo mat at her knees.

They sat facing one another quietly for a few moments, looking into one another's eyes, Hideko the host, smiling benevolently, and Reuel reciprocating expectedly. Speaking softly to him in a near whisper, she explained that this would be a highly simplified and reduced ceremony, but was nevertheless able to reveal the absolute nature of things. She pointed at the few implements she would use, and with formal gestures opened the red cylinder, revealing the bright green powdered tea contents for an instant. With a measured and courtly voice, she now related to him the obvious order of the forthcoming events. That she would scoop some powdered tea into the bowl and use a whisk to mix it into a froth with hot water. Then she would place the bowl on the little bamboo mat before him. And that, she explained, was almost the entirety of the ceremony.

"That's it?" he asked. "Just me?"

"Yes, I am only the host. Traditionally, our conversation should be a bit limited. Perhaps concerning just only to what's in this room. So, I'll turn on the hot-plate and we will wait relaxed and at ease until the water is ready and I offer you the bowl. Okay?"

She flicked on the electrical switch.

They sat quietly, waiting for the water to heat, entirely relaxed. Following her instruction to constrain discourse to what was in the tea room, Reuel's gaze fixed on the hanging scroll. Indicating it with the motion of his chin he asked for a translation.

"Three characters" she replied. "From top to bottom. 'Worry'. 'Mind'. 'Enemy'. Meaning that worry is the enemy of the mind."

"Brilliant" he offered. "Anything more I should know? Do I drink it all at once?"

"No, a few sips. Actually, three and a half sips is best. Also, maybe, since this is your bowl, there's an etiquette that might interest. Very old fashioned. Your bowl has an interesting imperfection. There's an odd irregularity on the rim, from a blistering while in the kiln. That kind of flaw is prized, and then is considered the front of the bowl. So, I place the bowl on your mat with the imperfection facing you. You pick up the bowl with your right hand to put it on your left palm. And then you turn it clockwise so that the front now faces me, the host. You don't want to drink from that side, you see."

"I see."

The ensuing gestural choreography was like the ancient Buddhist instruction concerning a finger pointing at the moon. The tea ceremony was understood as a mere dumb show, conveying the meaning of an obvious mystery, a lunar reality called 'satori'.

Afterwards, the ceremony completed, utensils put away, hot-plate turned off, his bowl wiped clean with a small towel, they returned to the house, his goods repacked, and telephoned for a taxi. As they waited in the kitchen Hideko poured them each a small cup of saké.

"*Kampai*" she said, "one for the road."

"*Kampai*."

They hugged one another.

"This has been very beautiful for me, Hideko. I can't ever forget you."

"Reuel, may we say we were enlightened for a single day? We may never see one another again. Let's imagine we can hold a small jeweled box in our brains containing the memory of what happened between us. Every once in a while, perhaps years from now, perhaps forever, as long as we live, we can open the little box in our mind and remember the special day we had together. That's all."

That evening Reuel was back in Kyoto. Fumiko greeted him at the rectory and made him a ham sandwich with pickles. Luca and Felipe were out at a lecture and Reuel, sleep-deprived, retired early.

Late on the following morning he reserved a first-class ticket on a non-stop flight from Osaka and San Francisco, to depart on an evening two days later. When Luca and Felipe asked him about his overnight in Nara. He replied casually that he had met a girl and spent the night with her. Bashfully, they let the subject drop. They asked if he would he like to see Tokyo, but he demurred, saying he didn't want his final impression of Japan to be of a giant and crowded neon-lit traffic-filled urban metropole.

"Then perhaps we could make a farewell bon-voyage dinner here?" said Luca. "We saw Miyamoto yesterday. He remarked he would like to hear your impressions of the Buddhist art in Nara. We could ask him to join us."

"With Miyamoto? That would be very nice. I enjoyed the mental gymnastics at our lunch the other day."

"Specifically?" said Luca.

"Well, what, actually, is the meaning of Zen?"

Miyamoto, bearing a handful of chrysanthemums, arrived at the rectory for their farewell dinner on the following day. Fumiko had laid out a formal table setting to which she served them a series of small platters in spaced intervals. The four consumers lubricated themselves with intermediate rounds of saké. Felipe described the difficulties of locating centuries old imperial records concerning Christian missionaries. Miyamoto told a story concerning a misleading student translation of an American idiom. Luca talked of his impending journey to study Christian missionizing in South America. Reuel described a swim in mid-ocean. Then Miyamoto took a turn to lead them into the maze of academic philosophy.

"Luca reminds me you were a philosophy major in college. I confess my own excursions into Western thought have led to more questions than answers. Take Immanuel Kant, for example. His idea of the 'thing in itself', his *ding an sich*, necessarily includes the objectivity of the 'self', does it not? His idea of the transcendental noumenon would merely be another term for a kind of mistaken intellectual intuition, would it not?" Could he conceive of our fascinating Buddhist emptiness of the non-existent self?"

"Well," said Reuel, "Your point is well-taken, and though I'm a little rusty, as I recall, Schopenhauer's critique of Kant argues that he is making a category error, between the knower and the known. And Schopenhauer, by the way, has certain credentials as the first European Buddhist, or at least a proto-Buddhist. So, Kant's misleading error, for all his brilliance, is well recognized. Philosophy, from Plato to Nietzsche, is full of errors. I've no doubt that Buddhist philosophy is also full of errors. Would you agree?"

"One hundred percent. Art is less prone to error, I think. What were your impressions of Nara's museum by the way?

"I confess that I found most of the exhibits rather dull. Maybe it was just my mood. There was such a colorless portrayal of Buddhist peacefulness. Very skilled, but offering such a quiet and somber repetitiveness, which I found to be almost boring. Rarely were there any signs of turbulence or passion, no references to sickness, old age, and death, as if the Buddha was always in heaven, the emperor always on his throne, and all was right with the world. As if calmness, without much more, was the goal of life. I wondered if I was missing something."

"I think perhaps you were witnessing the undercurrent of Taoism in Japanese culture" said Miyamoto. "The social longing for calmness against a background of political upheavals, samurai wars, and other conflicts over the centuries. I personally believe the non-theistic meditation practice of the Zen sect was probably a haven for personal withdrawal, calmness and non-engagement."

"Someone said to me recently that Zen had merely become a cult of indifference" remarked Reuel. "And, even that, at least superficially, seems to be losing ground in today's manic industrial and technological Japan. As if the country got a message but never opened the envelope."

"It's the godless pathology of modernity" said Luca. "Zen is bound to become popular in the West. I'm only a visitor here. And while I see that there are deistic Buddhist sects built on salvational faith, Zen's atheism seems to be a hollow vessel. Lots of family-owned Zen temples here simply do a type of inherited business at births and funerals. And though there are some teaching-temples where there is a genuine practice, from what I've heard there's also a degree of false Zen, with hypocrites and lazy time-servers, like in all other religions. But from my Christian point of view, atheistic Zen itself, in its most radical forms, seems to be saying that everything that can be deconstructed will be so, and if nothing then remains, let it be so. In fact, Zen may just be a selfish side of the idea of non-self. Its attainment of a calmness in the experience of the moment seems to me as utterly empty of any social significance. Fortunately, it has a very weak missionary spirit, and so doesn't really interfere with other people's lives. It doesn't have, and doesn't want, an excuse to force people into heaven. I'll admit that, as for evidence of Buddhist apathy, we should remember that fervor can be of great danger to social harmony. Calmness is good but it's of minor value. And nothing I've said is really incompatible with Christian doctrine."

Felipe spoke up. "Of course, there is Christian meditation too, but meditation can mean so many different things, even if it's merely just sitting still. And I have the impression from watching television, from Manila as well as Tokyo, that many kinds of meditation teachers seem corrupted for commercial gain as self-help celebrities. I'm not picking on Buddhists, but I think the question remains whether obsessive meditation encourages unhealthy narcissistic and self-obsessed mindsets. And is Zen practice so perfect that it couldn't possibly be itself an obstacle to spirituality?"

"You are entirely correct" said Miyamoto. "Speaking as a kind of ex-Buddhist, I believe that lengthy sitting in *zazen*, without dualities, where neither good or evil has any significance is problematic, to say the least. The sadness is that such ideas are accepted, in my opinion, by people of modest intelligence as great truths which sound so pleasing to the ear. And people are attracted to them just as moths in the night are drawn to their burning death by the candle light. Ethics, morality, compassion are too easily abandoned through the liberating indifference of the void. As you know, at many times Zen has witnessed brutality with calm indifference."

"Look, please understand, we speak as Catholic followers of Francis Xavier" said Luca. "Most people have no interest in existential philosophy. But the moment we start asking 'what is the meaning of life', the lack of an immediate answer simply reveals the world as a darkness. A spontaneous spiritual life, up to that moment of questioning, gets extinguished. The moment the question is asked we realize our illness, ignorance and loss of faith. It's of no use recapitulating various laws of health, we need the medicine of salvation. Prayer works. Meditation in itself is of only minor help in my view."

"I don't entirely agree" said Miyamoto. "While there are so many schools of what is called meditation which all produce a degree of self-awareness, that is good on the whole. But that self-awareness is not a given. It is something that gets cultivated, which has the distinct possibility that it can fail in many peculiar ways. Just as we can be mistaken about what we perceive, so sometimes the model we have of ourselves in meditation can also be quite wrong. If you take the widespread Buddhist idea that our whole conscious mental life is a kind of lawful illusion, you can only conclude that evolution has provided us with a mental tool structure that hides reality from us. Philosophically, self-consciousness is then a logical paradox."

Reuel carelessly added "At the moment, my current difficulty with the values of Zen Buddhism is in learning of its record in military atrocities. The presence of evil in Buddhism. I just met someone in Nara who had collected an archive of Buddhist war-crimes not so long ago, and had even attempted, unsuccessfully, to make a movie about such a thing."

This statement quickly disconnected the abstract and light-spirited colloquies from the table. There was a lingering sober silence. Felipe knowing of the Japanese occupation of the Philippines, nodded gravely, muttering "We are all sinners". Luca felt embarrassed and turned his head to examine his fingernails. Miyamoto knotted his eyebrows and asked "Who was the person that you met in Nara?"

Reuel raised his shoulders and opened his hands. "Actually, a former student of yours, at Doshisha."

Miyamoto leaned forward, thrusting his head out the way a turtle does from its carapace and inquired softly "Hideko Sato?"

"Yes."

"Amazing. How on earth did you come to meet her?"

"Someone from the American Embassy years ago, mentioned her and gave me her phone number. And then, by chance, I bought a tea bowl she once made, at the gift shop of the museum. So, I called her."

"Absolutely amazing. She made quite a commotion in Japan. In the newspapers and everything, many years ago. The Zen sect was not ready for her."

"What did you think about her?"

"I didn't recall her as a student at first, but it came out later. The communist students claimed my lectures on European ideas of liberty and equality inspired their own revolutionary goals. The silenced memory of the war years had to be broken. Her film idea had nothing to do with me, but I thought she showed great courage. It was a national event for a few weeks, a long time ago. By now, almost totally forgotten. As if she had disappeared. Tell me about her. What is she doing?"

"She makes beautiful tea-bowls, that's all. A wonderful person. But I think she has great bitterness about Zen, and Buddhist war crimes."

"Still? Yet, you know, it's possible to conclude that Zen and Buddhism are not really one and the same. Zen was easily embodied into the physical religion of the sword, the religion of samurai warriors in the Kamakura period, in the 12th century. While Buddhism was just a feudal dream, a rather un-Japanese religion imported from India and China. And speaking of war, remember, it was not long after the life of the historical Buddha that merciless imperial armies of the Maurya emperor Ashoka made the founder's name into a pan-Asian religion. As you know, Christian armies have also used their founder's name to enable the slaughter of innocents. And let us not forget today's Buddhist military forces in the world of the *Theravada*, today's Buddhist armies in Siam and Burma and Ceylon, whose soldiers are paid to kill and will do so if ordered. So, you might see, Hideko Sato's politics was merely that of a passionate young person lacking the calmness of historical contextualization."

"You make it sound simple."

"It's the advantage of examining the coldness of Zen with a cold-eye itself. You might even conclude that meditation is neither necessary or desirable for someone seeking to enter a spiritual life, and to ask what was the use of *zazen*? Was it to cultivate imperial loyalty while being completely morally bankrupt?"

Reuel inquired, "Professor Miyamoto, in your opinion, can philosophy protect a culture from atrocities, from evil?"

"No. Absolutely not. Deep philosophy is a whore. She will sleep with anyone. Are you familiar with Martin Heidegger?"

"I've avoided him. I'm Jewish."

"Ah, so. Tell me what you do know of him."

"Not very much. I know he wrote that that Jewish people were agents of a liberty and equality which disfigured the ancient pagan world. That genocide was the logical result of the Jews accelerating technology and modernity, and he actually blamed the Holocaust on its victims themselves. I looked into 'Being and Time' but it felt like word-games with a lot of gibberish."

"And his concept of '*Dasein*', of 'being there', where did that come from?"

"I think he found it was a kind of existential prescientific understanding, beyond logic or even abstraction as ways of knowing."

"Exactly. And where did he get such ideas? I'll tell you. From Japanese Zen intellectuals with whom he had contact. They thought he was not only the Western Philosopher who best understood Taoism and Zen intellectually, but one who had intuitively experienced the essence of it as well. That is a fact of which they wrote. And Heidegger even plagiarized, almost verbatim, major concepts of Asian spirituality from German translations of Taoist and Zen Buddhist classics."

"I didn't know that."

"And furthermore, let me point out that Heidegger and his friends paid back his philosophical borrowing by reciprocating with the export of virulent anti-Semitism to Japan, which had its own endemic fear of liberalism. And this malignant doctrine was prominently approved by its leading Zen teachers. Did you know that? Imagine that, anti-Semitism in a country without any Jews."

"I had no idea."

"Let me point out that history provides us with plenty of Buddhist victims as well as criminals. The poor spiritually devoted Tibetans suffered painfully from the insatiable cruelty of an atheistic Chinese communist army which conquered their country. And relatively speaking, only yesterday, we witnessed the bloody slaughter of close to a million Vietnamese Buddhists who had the misfortune of objecting to the occupation of their country by an American army. You don't speak of that, do you?"

"Ouch" said Reuel.

"One day you may become an ex-Buddhist too" added Miyamoto.

Luca interceded. "You realize this is an old subject for the Church. It's the question of theodicy. Why does God permit the manifestation of evil in his world? Is an all-knowing, all-powerful, all-good God logically possible in the light of evil's obvious existence? Some theologians argue that God is not omnipotent, and so can't be responsible for evil. Others, like Saint Augustine reject the idea that evil exists in itself, regarding it instead as a corruption of goodness, caused by humanity's abuse of free will. The usual answer is that evil was the result of humanity's original sin, tasting the fruit of knowledge and learning of the combined existence of sex and death."

"And what is your view, dear Luca?" asked Miyamoto.

"My answer is somewhat Jesuitical. Perhaps God was merely the creator of the world, like the Brahma of the Hindus, who then totally retired from activity and left the burden of evil to his only begotten son, the God of Love, to save us."

"You know, by the way, many things are much easier to explain if there is a God than if there isn't" added Felipe.

"Is it essential to have a belief in Christian mythology that you guys are alleging?" asked Reuel, "or can it be just your routine conventional opinion?"

Luca thought for a moment. "No. It's an understanding acquired through intuition rather than faith, and which transcends intellectual discriminations."

"Nice work if you can get it" said Reuel. "Personally, I think that kindness, compassion, pleasure and morality are actually innate biological and social forms of happiness which don't require religion or philosophy. Likewise, evil seems to be just another name for biological and social forms of suffering. This remains true whatever the form which our animal brain detects. *Homo Sapiens* has merely added in a language layer."

"I do believe that someone said that suffering is everywhere," added Miyamoto.

"So is pleasure" said Reuel. "It comes with the territory of being. You can enjoy it without a desperate craving for it. Sometimes it's just offered to you. And desire could just as easily be a wish for the benefit of others. I'm beginning to think that Buddhism for beginners is not the same as Buddhism for adepts."

"And what about fear? Anxiety? Such primary emotions" remarked Luca.

"What about courage? What about Ikkyu and Drukpa Kunley? What exactly are they refuting?" answered Reuel. "They certainly had a lot of sex."

Abruptly, there was another awkward silence and Fumiko appeared to ask if they would like to open another bottle. The consensus was to refrain and shortly thereafter a taxi was called for Professor Miyamoto.

"Time contains horizons, so table-talk must end", Miyamoto remarked as they waited at the threshold. "We should enjoy the fullness of sharing ideas. How many people, persons like us, do you think can have an evening such as this? I once had a student, a social scientist, a demographer, who tried to answer that kind of question. He added up all the philosophy professors at the world's universities. He calculated the readership of intellectual and literary journals. He approximated the number of the world's religious scholars. He estimated the number of doctorates and so forth. His rough conjecture was that there were probably less than six hundred thousand people on the planet who could have an informed and intelligent discussion on the nature of the human mind. That comes to about one tenth of one percent of the world's population. Isn't that interesting?"

They laughed along with him. Miyamoto thanked them for the hospitality and wished Reuel a safe journey back to America.

ॐ

Two days later, near midnight and jet lagged, Reuel lay sleepless in bed at San Francisco's Fairmont Hotel. The long trans-Pacific flight on Pan American's new double-decker 747 was luxurious but disorienting. His nervous system deemed it afternoon in Kyoto and he was still wide-awake, a disordered embodied mind searching for a level of coherence. He was now in secular America, that was clear, and modernity's evolved gadgets had obviously enabled his planetary circuit.

Was it of any significance at all that the Buddha, circa 500 B.C.E. could not imagine such a thing? No one could read science-fiction in those times either. Hardly anyone could read. While the Buddha had always opposed all attempts to use logic or reason alone to determine the existence of things that were by nature then imperceptible, the increase in scientific knowledge by way of small increments had obviously changed what was knowable. Comparatively speaking, the Buddha was only a wise rustic bumpkin. Reuel's discomfort at his own out-of-focus identity and his place in the world felt acute. Had he just wasted a year of his life? The archaic idea of liberation from philosophical unease seemed timeworn and theoretical against the real power of what was unmistakably modern San Francisco. The Buddha's agenda against speculative metaphysics on the meaning of life seemed reduced to shopworn banality. The definition of reality obviously consisted in that which didn't go away when you wanted it to go away. He was now in late 20th century America, far from Bodh Gaya or Darjeeling, with no idea of what to do with himself. He had postponed thinking about it. What was clear was that he now needed to come up with a plan, an agenda. He turned on the television set in the cabinet, stared at its offerings with a feeling of disgust, and shut it off. He called room service, ordered an omelet, a carafe of hot chocolate, and the day's edition of the San Francisco Examiner. And so armed, eventually falling to sleep, he began his readjustment.

He woke up around noon, Pacific Standard Time, performed his canonic sit-ups, push-ups, squats and stretches, and ordered up a breakfast of toast and coffee. Then, after sending out his negligible garments to be laundered, he stationed himself with a telephone at a window overlooking the city. His first call was to Luisa Sanchez, the legal associate at Ottolenghi, Minzi & Cordoza. He was informed she was no longer at the firm and had moved to the legal department of Boston Capital Trust Company. His account was now managed by Rosalie Ginzburg who was momentarily out for lunch. The firm was holding all of his mail and looked forward to his return to Cambridge.

He turned to his next chore by writing a letter on hotel stationary to Pierre Ferrand in Guadeloupe, French West Indies. A brief message informing Pierre that he had just returned to America and was in fact agreeable to selling his partial ownership of the Saga. He suggested they discuss the terms over a long-distance telephone conversation after he returned to Massachusetts. His best regards to Gabrielle.

He thought of calling United Airlines to book a flight to Boston but wondered if he should stay in San Francisco for few days to get over his jet-lag and to enjoy exploring the city which was new to him. He wanted to stretch his legs and decided to take a stroll around Nob Hill. But unfortunately, it had started to rain. But to his pleasure he realized the hotel had a gymnasium. Did Nagarjuna understand the power of strenuous cardio-physical exercise to pacify the mind?

An hour and a half later, after a tiring workout on a stationary treadmill and a circuit of dumbbells before a large mirror, he told himself he had endured too much Asian brain work, and not enough body work. *Mens sana in corpore sano*, was a worthy modern goal. He recalled his displeasure when Elsie

Hornbein suggested he had a pot-belly. He swore to improve his sexual appeal and to make physical fitness a permanent endeavor. If nothing else, wasn't this an overdue and earned piece of wisdom?

Returning up to his room Reuel showered, shaved, and for want of a better idea decided to meditate for a spell. As he sat on the bed his attention turned easily to the familiar space of breaths and the on-and-off passing flow of thoughts. A half-hour passed this way when a transient recollection of Walter Dowfeld punctured into his mind and adhered. Scarcely aware that he was no longer meditating, he found himself recalling the letter from Dowfeld at the American Express office in Delhi. His attention lit up, as he realized Dowfeld was in San Francisco, and he actually had a friend in the city. Meditation ended abruptly as he got up and located the crumpled letter in his bag. There it was, on Silicon Systems Corporation stationary, and a telephone number, with a message for Reuel to contact him if, as, and when he was next in California. In such a way does reality steal a march on the paradox of empty mindfulness.

They shared a ten-minute phone call. Dowfeld suggested meeting for dinner at the City Club. Reuel demurred, he lacked a jacket and so much as a necktie, but they could dine less formally somewhere. Dowfeld recommended a Japanese restaurant called 'Sushi Bliss' near his apartment, which was barely a five-minute walk from the Fairmont. He reserved them a booth at seven o'clock.

Over Japanese whiskeys Reuel curated his narrative. No mention was made of LSD or hashish, nor of Bob Adler's conversion to the celestial empowerments of *shaktiism*, or to the studious practice of meditation, or the taking of Buddhist refuges. Instead, Dowfeld was treated to descriptions of Cambridge and Oxford, of Reuel's daughters in Stockholm, the Louvre, and a lengthy account of sailing the Atlantic, as well as house parties in Mexico, the art of driving on Indian roads, third-world poverty, burning ghats, Tibetan refugees, and Japanese industrial modernity.

"I'd love to see India" Dowfeld said. "Those Indian coding programmers are taking over the valley. Fucking software geniuses. Have any women?"

"A night in Kyoto."

"A geisha?"

"No, a potter. None of your business. What about you? Never thought I'd see you in California. What happened?"

"A head-hunter made an irresistible offer. Salary, stock options, a BMW, the works. Pioneering the future. You can't believe how much the industry's changed this last year. California's been pirating talent from Route 128. There's a migration going on. It's a new world out here."

"Tell me more."

"Remember, when you started with punch cards, tape drives, and mainframes in sealed rooms? That's now like the stone age, or the Wright Brothers. Digital Resources took over our models at Kang labs and came out with a plug-in minicomputer the size of a big valise, with an integrated monitor, unchained, 60 pounds, believe it or not. That was just the beginning. Mobile computing is ready to go wherever it's needed, and corporate time-sharing's becoming a commonplace standard. Check out what's going on with microprocessors. Intel's marketing a programmable chip a half-inch long. Basically, it's like a whole computer with 2300 mini-transistors in an integrated circuit carved onto a silicon slice. It's processing 4 bits of data per stroke, and at 750 kilohertz runs over 90,000 operations a second."

"That's awesome!"

"That's nothing. Remember Gordon Moore?"

"At Fairchild?"

"Moved to Intel. He's shown the fabricated density of integrated circuit components can keep doubling every year or two with almost no end in sight. They'll be smaller, faster, cheaper and need less power every year. Intel's predicting mother boards of integrated circuits, each with 30,000 transistors and 16-bit processing at a clock speed of more than 700,000 ops a second within ten years. Can you believe that? And if Moore is right in another ten that's going to be considered slow. So help me, one day people are going to have computers on desks running off a flashlight battery, if you can imagine that. Maybe even in their pockets and on their wrists. Dick Tracy stuff. Not only that, there's a group in Palo Alto working on spoken commands. They've got a tethered mechanical insect that can execute the words "go" and "stop" and "right" and "left". That's just a beginning. Whole sentences of two-way speech will be going to come one day. It's just a matter of getting the combinatorial syntax and the compositional semantics right. Even the coded meaning of a rising inflection."

"Quite a jump from our old days at Lingo" said Reuel. "I can imagine it. We'll probably have thinking machines playing chess with us before long. Even smarter than us in some weird ways. But we're still locked into von Neumann's processor and memory architecture, don't you think? But where do you fit into all this, Walt? What's the grunt work at Silicon Systems up to?"

"Come out and see our joint. We're designing graphical user interfaces, and pushing more processing cores per chip. High density raster-pixeled bit-mapped imaging has arrived. The days of green alphabets on black screens are completely over. There'll be color on your monitor before long, and refresh rates are going to be so fast you'll be able to see full motion imagery. And not only that. Think about the user end. Xerox is pushing the idea of cursor control with a tethered manual widget to point and click on displays with drop-down menus. That's going to totally change the command language game at the user level. At mid-level, C+ language running UNIX is definitely becoming the standard for a whole variety of devices with cross platform compilers. The entire idea of the instruction set and machine codes are evolving pretty fast. Syntax is the next game. It's a new world, Reuel. You ought to get aboard."

"I don't know. Office life. Kind of boring when I look back at where I've been, to think about desk work again."

"Why? Too many single-minded nerds around?"

"You said it, I didn't."

"Don't you want to make a fortune? Billy Kang just lateraled out of the business to go into investment banking."

"What's that?"

"Runs a pile of old New England money looking for opportunities in the industry. He started a firm called Omega Ventures a couple of months ago. Really big bucks. Put a shit load into Silicon Systems with us. You ought to get in touch with him back in Cambridge. He really liked you. Try hooking up with him. No desk work involved. You've got a good nose. Make some more money."

"I don't really know what's next. It's only a question of when enough money is enough. Anyway, I always keep getting more interested in biology than computers. I just keep coming back to the brain. Neurolinguistics, where I once started out. The wetware. That's where the action is. How do we understand ourselves? What's it all about?"

Dowfeld shrugged. "Come on. It's about having a good life. What else?"

"What's a good life?"

"How about lots of sex? That's biology isn't it?"

"Maybe a little shallow? I think I should have gone to medical school. Neurolinguistics. Wet-coding. The brain's just an enormous computer examining itself for bugs."

"Good luck!"

"Well, it is, isn't it? Take the hippocampus, for example, it's mostly a memory bank."

"You're talking about analogies, not essential duplications. And how will you give a computer hormones?"

"I'm talking about thoughts, not feelings" said Reuel.

"And never the 'twain shall meet? Look, mimicry of the brain is an engaging idea. And there has to be something like an 'artificial intelligence' in the future, put aside a counterfeit barrier to understanding the meaning of something. I mean, could a robot have a will to fuck? How are you going to simulate neuronal subjectivity?"

"I just want to get at the physiology of thought. That's more than just a matter of brain calculations. There's culture and evolution behind it. That's why I find neurolinguistics so attractive. Take something simple like left brain right brain. Like how does lateralization work in having thoughts. If language is mostly based in the left cerebrum, does that mean that philosophical thought is also lateralized? Structure-function issues? I sometimes wonder what would have happened if we stuck to Lingo and our language games. That's what Wittgenstein called what we're doing right now, playing high level language games. I don't know where I go from here. Maybe I could get Billy Kang's Omega Ventures to find investment opportunities in something like that. Or I could start a company, make a pitch. Computation is just computation, right?"

Reuel wondered what Kunzang Namgyal Rinpoche would make of what he was saying and then remembered the "ahhhh".

That night at the hotel, still sleepless, Reuel realized he was going to return to the secular materialistic world of Boston. There was no good choice. Perhaps he would meet an ideal woman there, a thoughtful sexually free crypto-Buddhist with antibodies. The idea of joining Billy Kang at his new venture-banking shop stayed in his mind. Money, money, money. The recent unexpected wealth and his wild year of travel had somehow ruined him for the academic world. Scouting for investment opportunities in the future of the computer industry did have a certain intellectual appeal. The future of the digital age might be a bit like science-fiction, but it would certainly require a thorough grasp of mathematical logic. He had the baseline skills. But the work-a-day problems ahead would be very dry. There wouldn't be much moisture in the laboratories.

What did the brain want? That was the question. Was it just to be free of suffering? To seek pleasure? To what end? Schopenhauer's 'will to live' seemed to be an irreducible preposterous accident of the universe. Subjectivity, consciousness, was irreducible. He couldn't find an explanation possible at lower levels. It was just too complex. It was as if the ladder of a solution demanded a belief in ghosts. Theologians would defer to politicians who would defer to social scientists. Social scientists deferred to psychologists and psychologists deferred to biologists. Biologists deferred to chemists who in their turn deferred to physicists. Physicists deferred to mathematicians, and mathematicians deferred to the Holy Ghost who deferred to emptiness. *Sunyata.* And out of this stew emerged the 'self' with a soul that didn't want to suffer. It was crazy. Like free will. You end up with weirdness. Water was just hydrogen and oxygen, but hydrogen just gets burned in a fire sustained by oxygen, and yet water puts out fire. Go figure.

He got out of bed and stood looking West out the window over San Francisco's lights. He had to find the rigor. He could examine himself thinking. Ruminating. His old question. Was thought possible without language? Or did language evolve in order to think? Its main use seemed to be to transfer thoughts from one mind to another mind. That meant thought had to come first and language was only its expression. And there were so many limitations. We couldn't express everything we think. He kept coming back to the sounds of thought. We definitely had memories of sounds, remembering tunes like the opening of Beethoven's fifth or of Christmas carols. Why did some few people have perfect pitch, where middle C at 256 Hertz gets remembered? And the frequencies of the human voice get reduced and embodied into grey matter. *Homo* is made sapient by our earliest use of words. The joining of words to make sentences. All the levels coming together to convey semantic ideas through phrasings in our heads. Words, words, words. Cognition depending on our culturally configured body in the world. Perhaps the sympathetic nervous system's architecture was increasingly analogous to a computer's, its word memory located down in the hippocampus and the exorbitant verbose processing taking place up in the sky of the neocortex. Like moist Turing machines without the halting-problem of dry silicon. Would humans realize their role as mere reproducing sexual performers essential to attend the hardware of a world dominated by the command languages of artificial intelligence?

Does orgasm provide a secret meaning to the quadrilateral emptiness of the universe?

And where then was conscious thought? There was such an immense complexity in the prolix higher brain, that thin layer of dense neuronal tissue grafted by evolution onto our limbic system, the ancient seat of emotions and feelings. Perhaps its huge surplus of linguistic processing power had accidentally created a fundamental imbalance, with far more operational functionality than was necessary for mere survival on the mundane earth. It was as if that garrulous and extra-large upper brain was primed for misbehavior, providing us humans with an amplified capacity for neurosis, fixations, derangements, infatuations, manias, technological delusions, and cognitive obsessions like Buddhist enlightenment.

In other words, it seemed entirely possible that a large brain could make one more stupid.

Reuel just wanted to understand the barrier of meaning.

So he packed his bag.

END OF PART ONE

❦

$A \wedge ((\neg B), (\neg A) \wedge B, (\neg A) \wedge (\neg B), A \wedge B$

The mathematical logic formulation of the tetralemma, the theorem of para-consistency, is also known as the *Catuskoti*. It can be expressed verbally as follows: *A* and (not-*B*), (not-*A*) and *B*, (not-*A*) and (not-*B*), both *A* and *B*.